Wizard Stone

WIZARD STONE
THE MAGIC OF LARLION BOOK 1

BY
DEE MALTBY

WIZARD STONE
Copyright © 2021 by Dee Maltby
Print Edition

Published by R&D Reflections

Cover design and map by McCarthy Arts & Letters
Edited by Angie Ramey

Paperback ISBN: 979-8-9851231-0-4
Ebook ISBN: 979-8-9851231-1-1

ALL RIGHTS RESERVED.

No part of this work may be used, reproduced, or transmitted in any form or by any means, electronic or mechanical, without prior permission in writing from the publisher, except in the case of brief quotations embodied in articles or reviews.

WIZARD STONE

The spell starts when the young wizard Beneban plunges off a mountain and into a whole lot of excitement. Danger, romance, swordfights, adventures and even ice dragons are on the horizon, as Beneban fights for his freedom.

Wizards don't have friends. Beneban believed this when he escaped from the clutches of Ztavin, the evil wizard with whom he'd apprenticed. But after freeing himself by making a bad bargain, his quest leads him to discover many wonders in the Kingdom of Larlion, including both enemies and allies. Much to his surprise, Beneban is befriended by strange and magical creatures… tiny Worfs, a giant horned feline, the mysterious and powerful Forest Lady, and a three-handed, fur-covered soldier in the Grand Lar's army.

With treachery and danger on every side, can Beneban use his great powers and magical sword to save himself from assassins and a life of indentured service and fulfill his mission without betraying his new friends?

Advance Praise for *Wizard Stone*

"Prepare to be enchanted! Best wizardry I've come across since Harry Potter. Dee Maltby is an up and coming fantasy writer to be watched."

—*Meara Platt,*
author of the DARK GARDENS fantasy series

Readers of EARTHSEA and SHANNARA will enjoy WIZARD STONE, the adventure of Beneban, a young wizard on the run from his oppressive master. Along the way Beneban runs into new friends, new enemies, and a great many new dangers in this exciting fantasy adventure."

—*Jonathan Moeller,*
author of THE GHOSTS and CLOAK MAGE series

DEDICATION

With heartfelt thanks to Holly and Angie, for making this dream come true, and most of all, to my dear husband and personal wizard, Bob, whose hard work, support, great love and patience magically made these books possible.

TABLE OF CONTENTS

About the Book	v
Dedication	vii
Chapter 1	1
Chapter 2	13
Chapter 3	17
Chapter 4	29
Chapter 5	39
Chapter 6	49
Chapter 7	59
Chapter 8	75
Chapter 9	91
Chapter 10	99
Chapter 11	113
Chapter 12	131
Chapter 13	143
Chapter 14	161
Chapter 15	173
Chapter 16	185
Chapter 17	201

Chapter 18	217
Chapter 19	233
Chapter 20	253
Chapter 21	277
Chapter 22	293
Chapter 23	313
Chapter 24	337
Chapter 25	367
Chapter 26	393
Chapter 27	419
Chapter 28	433
About Wizard Wind	439
Books by Dee Maltby	441
Acknowledgements	443
About the Author	445

Kingdom of Larlion
THE FARTHER LANDS
(Vartenland)
Ameling
NORTH PLAINS
Og-Dan
Og-Dan
Andeling
Boriling
Oreling
High Kalds
Little Kald
Desert
Great Shrine
and Sartenruhn
KALD MOUNTAINS
Black Keep
Oasis
HIGH KALD
DESERT
Bardling
Streeling
Terreling
Forest
Ariling
Torling
Dinling
Larling
Dawling
Settled Plains
Tor Bridge
Great
Swamp
Larlingarde
Mergoling
Dark
Fortress

CHAPTER 1

High on a wind-lashed path, one snowdrift shuddered and shifted. Something lived and moved within it as it clung to the sheer mountain wall. From the drift, a slender figure struggled to his knees. He seemed puny against the fanged peaks. The scarlet rags of a wizard's cloak whipped wildly in the wind as he scrabbled through the drifts, desperate to uncover some object torn from his hands by the storm.

Wind pounded him. Lightning slashed gray skies. A drumbeat of rock rumbled about him and was echoed by the thunder's roar.

Now the young wizard hurled a triumphant shout into the wind's howl as he staggered to his feet. He, Beneban, brandished a golden sword. It shimmered in the flicker of lightning. Redeemed from the drift, Heldenhaft threw back the lightning's glare with an edge that snarled with its own golden powers.

"At least you won't have this," Beneban bellowed into the storm. Intent on returning the sword to its sheath, his feet slipped on the ice.

A giant hand of wind slapped him. Balance lost, he cried out as he fell and cracked his head.

A great alviar, aloft on the wild wind, swooped on wings wider than a man is tall to consider the wizard as food. Warned by Beneban's cry that his prey still lived, the enormous raptor hesitated. The gale tore him away.

Relentless wind pushed the fallen wizard toward the chasm. His hands scrabbled for purchase as his fingernails tore on the icy path. Ice crystals blasted his face and stole his breath.

Evil laughter rode the wind. It mocked his feeble battle.

Again, lightning crashed, and the blast of ozone roused Beneban to full consciousness.

His feet now dangled over space. Still, he hurled defiance back into the hungry wind and shouted, "But with my life ends also your hope," as though to continue some manic argument.

The wind slowed.

For a moment, the shimmergreen gossamer of the wizard's hair floated gently about his tormented face. His head sank.

"Perhaps – that is best after all," he whispered. His body, long disciplined to obey his will, released its struggle. Slowly, he began to slip over the chasm's edge as blackness filled his mind...

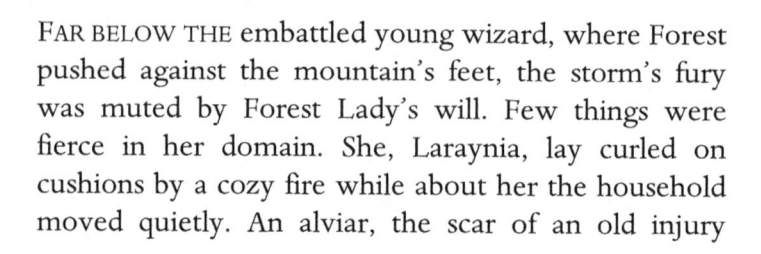

FAR BELOW THE embattled young wizard, where Forest pushed against the mountain's feet, the storm's fury was muted by Forest Lady's will. Few things were fierce in her domain. She, Laraynia, lay curled on cushions by a cozy fire while about her the household moved quietly. An alviar, the scar of an old injury marking its fierce head, perched on the mantel and preened metallic feathers. By the door, a large blue ursyn sprawled. Larger than ordinary bears, and rumored to be magical, he grumbled in peaceful sleep, dreaming of leaping high above the trees.

In one corner a white-haired woman wove scarlet fellan in and out of a loom. Old Saray, the Lady's companion since childhood, worked the fellan expertly despite her age-cramped hands.

At her feet, tiny Worf twins played an intricate pebble game, bickering and giggling in their piping voices. Their pointed ears barely came up to Saray's knees as they squatted on their short legs. Their long slender fingers, which made their kind such prized weavers, moved with a speed and accuracy that defied human sight.

Abruptly, Laraynia straightened as an unusually violent blast shook the cottage. Her inner calm trembled. A frown sketched tiny lines between her wide-set gray eyes.

Saray's loom stopped its clatter. The alviar mantled his wings and screamed. The ursyn rumbled halfway to his feet, and for a moment the Worfs' hands were still.

"Be silent!" Laraynia breathed. "Someone needs my help."

Forest Lady's tilted eyes widened. They gathered green sparks as she sought again for the touch which had cried out in fear. She found nothing other than that absence of thought that marks abandonment of the will to live.

This *must* be changed, she knew. Whoever was caught by the storm must be saved. Many futures, many lives depended on the one who hung in the balance.

Now her slender fingers touched and stroked the green stone fastened about her throat on a narrow silver band. She hummed a commanding three-note melody over and over.

The stone cleared and brightened as the room seemed to fade. Laraynia's spirit, high on the mountain, probed for that deserted will to live and determinedly, she sought a spark of strength within it. She searched, also, for help nearer to the threat...

As he slid, Beneban's hand tore through a toughneedled barbelbush. As the pain penetrated his emptied mind, his fist clenched involuntarily around the daggered stem. One foot kicked in reflex to the pain. It grazed an edge of rock. Sudden unwanted hope slipped into his mind.

His foot tested the rock and found it solid. Still he wavered. Despair urged him toward the easy path. If he let go, he could rest...

A whiplash of command crashed into his mind. It called him by his true name, a name that should have been known to him alone.

"Mygyn! You are needed. Fight! Reach to the left!"

For an instant longer, Beneban hung in indecision, between earth and sky, death and life. Then, prodded by this other's will, by their knowledge of his secret name, he forced his foot left. It found a narrow ledge, and above it was another handhold.

Later he wouldn't remember details of that bitter struggle, only in part directed by his own determination. But at length he lay once more, breathless and worn, on the glazed pathway. Exhaustion would have held him there to become a frozen boulder buried in snow, but his mental discipline, honed and trained over many years, rejected that option. It was a struggle to pull Heldenhaft loose from the rocks where she was jammed. Then he scrambled to put his back against the solid rock wall, huddled the feeble warmth of his tattered scarlet cloak close, and eyed his position.

There was little to encourage him. The black wind had died, but sheer rock climbed or fell on all sides. Blood dripped from his hand, and scratches on his face and arms added pain to his exhaustion.

Even if travel were possible, the cold was bitter. The only close shelter was the evil one he had just escaped.

Without other options, he asked with cynicism and a rare trace of humility, "What now?"

Rational thought had nearly convinced him that the voice in his mind had been a last, desperate flight of his will. To his surprise, an answer came at once.

"Wait, Mygyn!"

Curiosity and a trace of fear touched him. "Who are you? How do you hold my secret name?"

The only response was a breath of tranquility, a touch of warmth, and the repeated command, "Wait, Mygyn!"

Exhausted, no longer tempted by the rocky depths, he obeyed. He huddled into his rags and concentrated on banishing the cold. Through long discipline, his life force centered down to its essence until only his eyes seemed alive. For a time, their ambered gold scanned the path. Then they, too, closed. Snow feathered about him in little bursts of wind. Nothing else moved.

LARAYNIA CHECKED ONCE more that Beneban's will was firm.

"He'll do for a bit," Saray said. Her old hands steadily worked the loom.

Thus assured, Forest Lady sent her mind to search Beneban's area in widening circles. His wizard power was spent. He urgently needed shelter and warmth.

She soon encountered another consciousness, not human, but intelligent and aware. This was the fierce mind of a wild female kalting.

Not subject to coercion, the beast was reluctant to move from her kits and her warm cave. At first she snarled. She rubbed her great paw over her ears. The voice wouldn't leave her alone.

Finally she conceded mastery to Laraynia's insistence and pushed through the snow that blocked the mouth of her den. She picked her way through the bitter drifted landscape and, at length, paused on a boulder overlooking the huddled scarlet heap she had been asked to help.

IN HIS TRANCE, Beneban's memory had returned to the black tower room of Ztavin's hold. As he shivered against the rock wall, his mind repeated the spell that had freed him:

*Triple binding, loose me from this bondage; set
me free.
Mine, my will to my command, freed to act without
thy hand.
Gifting only thou may'st claim,
Nor for three years have my name.*

The room shimmered with anger, though Ztavin was held motionless by the spell the younger wizard had dredged from the depths of the dusty library.

"You put a potion in my wine at supper?" The black wizard's anger made the air dense and hard to breathe.

"Never trust a prisoner." Beneban's words were flat.

"Prisoner? I have fostered you, taught you, given you the freedom of a library unequalled anywhere. Too much freedom, obviously."

"Ten years gone you tricked me into bondage. Since then you've taught me only what would be useful to you! Despite your efforts, I am not convinced that evil should be used, even for good purpose. It is time for me to go."

"But – I need you," wheedled the old wizard. "Some things you don't yet understand. There is power you can't dream of, not without me. And you," Ztavin added slyly, "you want that power."

The young wizard fell silent for a moment, but his hand never left his Omera, the rough red wizard stone he had worn forever and without which he would fade away and die.

"I do want that power," he admitted finally. "Our joined strength could reach any goal. But our goals are different. Our paths cannot merge."

"Then go!" Ztavin's voice thundered. Flickers of red fury lit the corners of the room. "But first, the gift you owe me for ten years of care and teaching."

"Be grateful I don't pay in your own coin," Beneban said bitterly. "What 'gift' will you take for my freedom?"

"A... *small* thing." Now Ztavin's voice purred. "You have heard of the Larstone?"

"The hereditary stone of power of the lars, rulers of Larlion? Certainly," Beneban answered. "It gives them command of natural forces."

"The stone has many powers. Some are unknown—to anyone. It was lost many years gone by. Find it and give it to me." Now Ztavin's laugh was the silken slither of the scaly vischen. His hand moved slightly on the arm of his chair.

"And if I can't find it?" Beneban wondered.

"Then you join your will, your power to mine. Permanently."

"You mean I become your slave." His voice was toneless.

"Pah," spat Ztavin. "Slaves are easily come by. No, you become my ready coworker. You give me your true name, your will, unless you can convince me to take some other forfeit at that time." Again the older wizard's hand twitched.

This time Beneban saw the movement, and recognized the danger. He spoke quickly:

I bind myself to bring this gift,
the Larstone which you do decree,
or lose my forfeit, name and will
in years not more nor less than three.
Now loose these bonds and set me free.

Beneban saw Ztavin's hand grope stiffly toward his black Omera. It was just too late. As the last words of the spell reached him, the black wizard grasped the stone. The air gathered itself, a whirlwind that whipped Beneban's scarlet cloak like giant wings.

"Go then, ungrateful one," snarled Ztavin.

The casement slammed open on the gale. Beneban dove for the window. A gale blasted him as he escaped. He spun and tumbled like a feather. A howl of maniacal laughter echoed behind him.

"Go, fool," Ztavin roared. "Your first master but stirred your power. I could have given you the key to rouse it fully. You would have bargained more straightly if you knew what you truly are."

Whirled and twisted by the fierce wind of the sztaq, Beneban spun down, down to stillness and... the awareness that he was not alone.

THE WIND HAD eased where Beneban huddled against the rock. Now a persistent rumble penetrated his trance. Not Ztavin's curse and snarl, or the roar of wind, and surely not the silence of death. A cold whisper of snow touched his face, and then another touch, warm, rough, slightly damp.

Curious, he groped for consciousness.

His eyes of burnt amber stared into the slanted emerald eyes of the largest kalting he had ever seen. Its golden fur was dusted with snow. The middle two of its six feet, their pads suction-cupped for traction, were firmly planted on the ice before him. The broad feline face was crowned by the single, bow-shaped golden horn that marked a female. A steady rumble came from her powerful chest.

"Am I to be dinner then?" Beneban chuckled wryly. "Well, better to feed a beauty like you than that monster above."

The kalting examined him curiously. A large rough tongue sandpapered his face. Then, impatient, the blunt muzzle nudged him.

"You have another plan than dinner in mind," Beneban decided. Then he repeated an earlier question: "What now?" But the stranger's will within his mind had fled.

The kalting scanned him briefly, then turned her back and waited.

"I doubt I'll... improve with age," Beneban said. A laugh bubbled beneath the chatter of his teeth. The massive head swiveled on its long supple neck, her emerald eyes expectant.

"Yes, you want me to do something, but what?"

Again the kalting pushed him gently with her broad muzzle. Beneban began to slide. Her powerful jaws locked on his arm to drag him back from the cliff edge.

"That was w-wild," Beneban gasped. "But let's not do it again." He was suddenly very glad not to dash his life out on the rocks below. "But I still don't understand what you want."

The kalting had released his arm as soon as he was safe. Now she crouched between him and the gorge and turned a look of enormous impatience on him.

"The only idea I have," Beneban offered, "seems quite foolish. I've heard of people who ride kaltings, but not wild ones. Perhaps you want your dinner to ride to the table?"

Still he hesitated. The kalting hissed impatiently and nudged him again.

His frozen mind slowly remembered the insistent 'Wait' command. It seemed the kalting was what he'd been bidden to wait for.

He climbed cautiously to his knees. Again he slipped, flailed, and clutched a fist in the kalting's golden fur. At her impassive stare he scrambled awkwardly onto her broad back.

She stood at once, and he grabbed with both hands for a better hold.

Then began a bounding flight Beneban would never forget. The kalting's six powerful legs propelled them from the path to a jutting boulder, through drifts more than head high, and across bottomless chasms. As he clung with his last strength, Beneban found wonderment in this fantastic journey. He was faintly regretful when, at last, the kalting ducked beneath a ragged tree and into a snug hidden cave.

The kalting tipped him without ceremony into a piled nest of evergreen branches and fur. Then, stunned, he saw her leave the shelter again.

When she reappeared, the exhausted wizard struggled to fend off two kalting kits. They seemed convinced that their mother had brought them this strange creature as a plaything.

With a growl and stout cuff on each head, the mother made her offspring leave Beneban in peace. She dropped a mountain farsel, freshly dead, in front of him, and settled in to nurse the kits.

The wizard gazed quizzically at the fat rodent she offered. "No fire, no utensils. Another adventure and not as pleasant." Then, as the kalting lifted her head in question, he quickly added, "To my need, madam, this will be a welcome feast." Indeed, a short while later, he had used his sword as an awkward knife. He lay back on the bed pile. Food warmed his stomach. He was weary and weak, yet he felt a fragile return of strength.

The kalting stretched her long neck and nuzzled him closer into the furry pile of kits. He huddled gladly into the warm bodies. Adrift on the edge of sleep, he felt the brief touch of the stranger's mind he'd dismissed earlier as a hallucination. But now, as exhausted sleep dragged at him, he could only register warmth.

CHAPTER 2

The unusually severe winter piled snow in head-high drifts on the mountain and in the settled plains of Larlion. In the Estates, the ruling lars had sufficient food, but an effort to move it to aid the small towns and rural villages baffled their logistics. It was generally accepted that the wild North Country would have a bitter time. At length, however, the desperation of the people reached even the capitol of Larlingarde. Urged by some of the lars, the rulers of the Estates, it finally gained the attention of Lyolar, Grand Lar and ruler of all Larlion.

Lyolar was not a compassionate ruler. Now, however, he conceded the need. He organized and sent a unit of his troops, together with carts and wagons of food to help the most desperate.

The captain he chose for this unpleasant effort was a man he disliked. He would, in fact, be glad of Captain Glaynar's absence. Yet the choice would have a strong effect on the future.

Captain Glaynar was a man who enjoyed the authority to make his troopers, except for a few favorites, miserable. It was with some distaste, and only under orders from Lyolar, that he accepted a new recruit. An Ogdol, his name unpronounceable but shortened to Trog, was told off to be part of his contingent.

"No better than a beast," Glaynar hissed to his second in command. "Look! ...covered in fur... who could consider that as an intelligent..."

"Shh, he might hear..."

Glaynar whirled to see one of the three great Ogdol eyes fixed on him. "You! Trog!" He bellowed to disguise his nervousness. "Help load those wagons."

Speaking again to his subordinate, he added in a lower voice, "At least he can do that. He's got muscle to spare..."

The two men moved away as they laughed.

This, too, would have unforeseen consequences.

ZTAVIN WAS EXHAUSTED by his spiteful working of the sztaq, the wizard storm he had flung at Beneban. His fury at losing the young wizard whom he had considered his acolyte left him struggling for a way to get vengeance. It did not calm him to sense his student's escape. Not in death, which he could have accepted, but saved by a magic he did not recognize. A wild, green power, one that was very strong.

For a time, he was forced to rest. While he recovered, he began to scheme. There must be a way to reclaim the youth.

At the moment, Beneban was beyond his ability to

sense with his magic. The only certainties were that he still lived and that he had promised Ztavin to accomplish an impossible feat.

He was unlikely to fulfill the bargain of finding the Larstone. After all, it had been undiscovered for several generations.

"Still," Ztavin snarled, "there must be a way I can make the odds greater against that ungrateful whelp. I *will* have him *back,* and in my power..."

He struggled out of his chair and went to the map of the Estates. He must find a subject to use... Who owed him help?

His hand hovered over the map, then dipped south beyond the shore to an island kingdom; the refuge of the Mergols, long banished from Larlion.

There was one there who owed him whom he could turn to his need, the younger sibling of the Mergol king. The lad had the magic of shifters, and he craved power.

What was his name...?

He had it. Now energized, the black wizard sped down the stairs to his dungeon workshop. He dragged three hapless wanderers who were his captives from their chains. He cut each throat and collected the blood to paint a powerful hexagon of summoning.

Lighting a black candle at each point, he sent his power outward, searching, searching... Ahh!

A mist began to form within the summoning figure. At first only a foggy shape, it slowly solidified until it stood, fully formed into a young Mergol princeling. A long white mane of hair cascaded down his back. His webbed feet grasped for purchase on the stone. The gill slits beneath his ears flared in panic, but the green slanted eyes shot fury at the wizard.

"What is this, Ztavin?" the Mergol hissed. He lunged forward but a shock of black power kept him within the sigil.

For a moment their eyes locked. Then the prisoner tossed his head, but lowered his gaze.

"What do you want? I told you I would pay when I..."

Ztavin interrupted, and his voice was brusque. "I have a job for you, one I believe you will enjoy. It will redeem some of what you owe me. Come, Prince Kentan." He broke the dark sigil and held out a hand. "Come and plot with me."

CHAPTER 3

High on the mountain, Beneban's strength slowly returned. At first content with food provided by the kalting female, he ate, slept, and ate again. He felt secure. Surely Ztavin would think him dead; and so he healed. As his energy increased, the wizard began to wander from the cave to explore his surroundings.

The kalting kits grew rapidly. Their mother—Kati, as he came to call her—was soon hard pressed to provide for them all. Now the young wizard sought to repay Kati for his rescue.

Short trips from the den through the deep snow strengthened him. This distance was soon extended by a roughly made pair of snowshoes. Then he contrived a set of throw-stones that helped bring down fair-sized game for the larder.

Tired of eating raw meat, Beneban used a small wizardry to make a fire, but he tended the flame with care. Making fire was one of the first things he had learned as a student. He was glad of cooked food but Nigeran, his first master, had told him, 'Never spend wizardry to do what preparedness, hard work, or forethought can achieve. Wizardry will cost you far more in the long run.'

Beneban, newly recovered from the spell battle with Ztavin, understood at a deep level the wisdom of Nigeran's words. The rest of that lesson was yet to return to him, however.

One evening, on the hunt for food, he found a bush of tasty barberries and hurried to pick them as dusk fell. A magic spell sent the thorny branches whipping about as though alive. They snarled him until, at length, he stood trapped and helpless. How had he been so hugely stupid as to become so entangled?

Now Nigeran's voice came to him with one of the last lessons the old man had to offer. It had also been in regard to fire, but it certainly applied to this puzzle.

The lesson posed him then was to build a fire with magic to warm the room. Excited to demonstrate his ability, the young Beneban grabbed power greedily into his clenched fists and flung the spell with abandon about his head.

Flames shot from his fingertips. Draperies flared. The clothing of two Worfs flashed fire, and even Nigeran's comfortable chair smoldered. His magic was out of control.

Only the rapid intervention of the older wizard saved them all from serious injury.

Now Beneban remembered the shame he had felt. Trapped in the bush, he recalled his master's words.

You are too fond of power, Beneban. Do not seek to solve all problems by force. It will bring you grief. Watch as the weaver untangles her fellan. If she yanks impatiently, the knots tighten beyond help. Instead, with a gentle push, a tiny tug, great patience, she undoes the knots.

Tug gently on the power that is yours. Don't burn down the house to build a fire in the fireplace. Now try again.

Caught fast in his thorny thicket, Beneban recognized this recurrent truth. He had barely left Nigeran's keep when Ztavin, with lures of power, snared him the way an ursyn cub, greedy for sweets, falls to the hunter's honey trap.

Beneban had paid with ten years of pain for that greed. If he could not find the Larstone, he might pay much more.

A particularly vicious thorn stabbed him and brought him back to this present predicament.

With renewed patience, he carefully moved one finger, then another. A hand was finally freed then a scratched and bloody arm. Night fell as he untangled the last stubborn thorn and was free. Only the rags of his scarlet cloak remained tangled in the bush.

"There hang the remnants of the old Beneban," he vowed. "When I next wear a wizard's cloak, the wizard beneath it will be less impetuous."

That night, snug in the warm cave, he contrived a cape of hoarded farsel skins. He cut them with a flint knife he had shaped and used a bone needle and sinews gathered from past meals to piece them together.

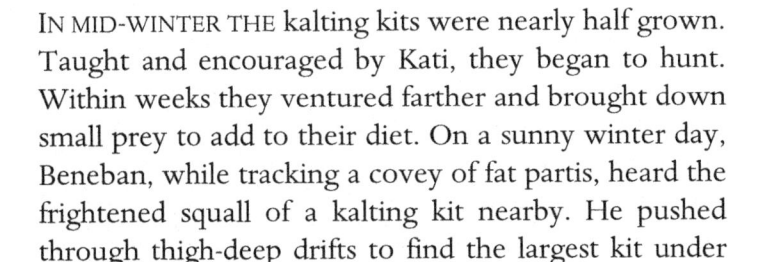

IN MID-WINTER THE kalting kits were nearly half grown. Taught and encouraged by Kati, they began to hunt. Within weeks they ventured farther and brought down small prey to add to their diet. On a sunny winter day, Beneban, while tracking a covey of fat partis, heard the frightened squall of a kalting kit nearby. He pushed through thigh-deep drifts to find the largest kit under attack by several alviari.

Backed against an outcrop of rock, the kit fought with slashing claws, but the predatory black birds' razor-edged beaks and talons outmatched his young skill.

Beneban tore Heldenhaft from her sheath and plunged into battle. The sword keened her war song. Her amber light flared gold.

Her song thrilled through the wizard as the largest bird beat upward. While the others pressed their attack on the kit, the lone alviar dove on him. Heldenhaft marked its course and thrust.

The bird impaled itself on the green-gold blade. Its huge wings beat wildly. Though mortally wounded, it fought to lift free; and to drag Heldenhaft from Beneban's grip. Metallic wing feathers sharp as razors drew blood from the wizard's cheek.

Three alviari swooped to join the fight as Beneban's foe shrieked its death. With nearly human shrieks, they deserted the kalting kit to aid their failing mate.

Beneban fought vainly to free Heldenhaft from the dying bird as it thrust fiercely to free itself. The wizard's foot slipped in frozen blood. It brought him to one knee as the second bird dove. The kalting kit struggled to recover and come to his aid.

Abruptly several things happened to change the tide of battle. An icy shadow chilled the air. A shriek stunned all ears, as Kati, speeding to save her kit, leapt and flattened Beneban.

Giant wings froze sweat on the wizard's face, and another cry deafened him. The alviari scattered, and two were lifted away on – on –

Beneban struggled to his elbows, and saw a scatter of rainbow light from ice-blue wings as their savior soared away, an alviar clutched in each claw.

"A... Kati, let me up. Look! It's a *vardraken*, an *ice dragon*."

Reluctantly Kati let Beneban squirm to his knees and went to inspect her kit while the wizard limply sat and stared after the creature he had thought a myth. Finally he returned to the present.

A shudder shook him. That had been a very close call.

"Thanks, Kati." Beneban forced the words between gasps. He pushed the dead alviar from Heldenhaft with a shaking foot and cleaned her blade with handfuls of snow.

Kati's rough tongue rasped his injured cheek. Then she examined her kit and licked his minor injuries.

Thanks to the wizard's intervention, there were no serious wounds. One huge maternal paw cuffed the cub in admonishment, and she nudged him toward home.

Beneban, holding snow to his slashed cheek, followed. If he turned several times to scan the sky, Kati hissed to speed him along. Vardraken were a threat to any creature that moved.

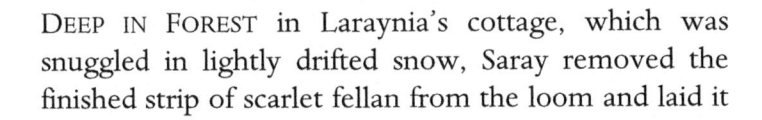

DEEP IN FOREST in Laraynia's cottage, which was snuggled in lightly drifted snow, Saray removed the finished strip of scarlet fellan from the loom and laid it out carefully. Watched by the curious eyes of the Worf twins, Dap and Dal, the old woman began to cut and sew.

"This will soon be needed," Saray said. Laraynia nodded, but her eyes were distant, knowing Beneban was in battle.

She'd sought for help but knew that it was not her doing that saved her wizard. What *was* the creature who had changed the course of the battle?

She... Forest Lady... was believed to be a myth by all her world. Yet this, a vardraken, a creature of myth, become real?

As the battle with the alviari ended, she nodded again, this time, with satisfaction. Her choice of Kati as guardian for Mygyn had been a good one. Perhaps they would remain together, though it was unlikely with a wild kalting. Still, she sensed closeness between the two. Soon it would be time for Beneban to return to his true destiny.

THE KALTINGS SLEPT from dusk to dawn. This time left Beneban wakeful for several hours each night. It gave him leisure to examine the fifty years he'd spent to reach a wizard's young adulthood. His shimmergreen hair, copper skin, and tall slender build gave him the appearance of a young noble of Larlion. Only his eyes told straightly of his wizard blood. Not the green of a Larlinga, they ranged from pale gold to dark amber. They were wiser yet more innocent than the eyes of a young courtier.

His challenges had been other than those of court life. First had been his study with Nigeran.

Thirty years in study withdrawn from the world, first with Nigeran and then in bitter bondage to Ztavin, had made Beneban strong. Yet, lack of experience left him more vulnerable than any young noble.

The old white wizard, banished some three hundred years previously from the royal court, had furiously removed himself to the most distant Kalds. There, ringed about by mountains, Nigeran set up virtually impassable barriers with his sorcery. Vicious beasts that must be defeated by magic, impenetrable mazes, and others.

The young Beneban was determined to study with Nigeran, long known to have powers and skill few other wizards could boast.

He had stubbornly used his already considerable power to penetrate so deeply into Nigeran's obstacles that Nigeran was forced to choose whether to let him die in the final trap he'd penetrated or to lower the barriers and accept the talented youth.

Nigeran relented.

Thus began twenty years of exhausting work for Beneban, days of practice under the stern teacher, weary nights of study, and steady, cautious awareness of increased ability and growing strength.

Sometimes during the long nights, a fragrance would penetrate Beneban's focus. He would become aware of his master's presence, and a cup of hot, sweet karven would be set by his elbow.

At other times, if Beneban grew careless enough through inattention or weariness to endanger others, Nigeran would remonstrate with an electric jolt to a negligent hand or vulnerable ear.

Yet in a time much shorter than a normal apprenticeship, the old man declared that the student had outstripped his teacher.

"Your powers are the greatest I have known. But remember," the old man said in their final meeting, "though minor illusions and magic cost you little, you cannot change the fabric of the world, or especially of life, without paying a price."

"There is still much to learn. Let me stay longer, Master," Beneban had implored.

"You have all my lore. One day, if you choose wisely, you may far surpass me. Experience teaches wisdom. That door may be unlocked only with great courage. One lesson I have yet to teach and one gift to give. But time moves in the world outside. Soon you will be needed."

IN THE DARK cave he shared with Kati, Beneban sat straight up at this memory. Winter dangers had passed away. The scent of spring, green and enticing, wafted up the mountain. What had the voice said as he hung by a thorny bush on the edge of destruction after his escape from Ztavin?

You are needed. Fight!

Nigeran had not sent him away to remain in this comfortable hideaway.

At his sudden movement, the kaltings stirred and grumbled. The mother's great head lifted. Her green eyes questioned.

"Peace, Kati. It's only my restless mind. No danger threatens."

The kaltings settled back into a sleepy heap, and Beneban returned to his thoughts. Curious, he sought mental contact with that will which had dragged him from death.

He had reached it only twice, always on the edge of sleep. This time it was waiting.

"Soon you will be needed." The thought entered his mind, echoing Nigeran's final words.

"You have grown strong. Now you have a destiny to fulfill. You must be in Larlingarde in the spring." Then the contact fled like a bird which nears the hand and takes fright.

"Wait! Who are you?" But there was only emptiness and the spicy fragrance of flowers.

THAT NIGHT HE slept restlessly and wakened to one word: "Larlingarde." The powerful capital of Larlion, once home of the Larstone. That was also where the voice had sent him. He would go there to seek the prize which would free him from Ztavin. The court of the Grand Lar was there. That powerful ruler could afford a wizard. He possessed the wealth and costly materials of wizardry.

If indeed Beneban had a part to play in the future, Larlingarde was surely the stage to which he was called.

The decision made, he slept soundly until Asolum lighted the shelf outside the cave.

IN FOREST, WITH the greening of spring came also a thread of darkness. At first Laraynia ignored it. Yet she was fretful as a wrongness nipped at her mind. This place, her Forest, was still her shelter and her duty; yet something had changed.

Saray, busy now stitching her scarlet fellan together, shook her gray head with concern. "I must hasten with this."

"You are making a wizard's cloak." Laraynia's tone was curious, aware it would go to Mygyn.

"He will need it. It will remind him who he is and will show the world what he is."

After many hours, with a final snip of thread, she stretched her weary back.

"It is finished now."

Saray wrapped the cloak and several other items in a small pack. "I'll return as I may, dearer than daughter." With those words, the old nurse disappeared through the door into the darkening Forest.

THE SNOWS HAD melted. Only drifts were left. The kits now hunted alone. One day they disappeared for good, and it left a surprisingly empty cave.

"I must leave too," Beneban told Kati that evening as they lounged outside the cave. The sharp smell of the small supper fire felt suddenly very dear. "I'll—I will go at dawn."

The great beast yawned cavernously and laid her

head across his legs.

"How can I thank you, Kati?" He rubbed the itchy spot behind the golden horn. "You saved my life, provided shelter, food, self-respect... Do you understand at all?"

Kati stretched and moved toward the cave, reaching back to nudge him.

"Yes. If I'm to start early I must rest." He smothered the fire he had nursed so carefully and followed her into the musty darkness that had been home for several turns of the moon.

Drifting to sleep on this, his last night with Kati, he remembered the final day with Nigeran.

The old white wizard had brought him to a chamber he had never seen and had shown him Heldenhaft. "This sword is a legacy," Nigeran had said. "One of the few things saved from Sartenruhn School when the curse of the Grand Lar's ancestor sealed its doors."

Beneban gaped at the weapon couched on a pedestal of rosy argentim from Sartenruhn—that ancient school of wizardry where so much of wizard lore lay buried. A gift kings would envy.

"Here are the runes, lad," his master continued, indicating arcane markings below the pedestal. "If you can decipher them, take the sword. If you are strong enough to take it, use it well. Follow the way of Eratim and it will aid you in battle and strengthen those who follow you. If you fail in honor, the penalty will be severe."

He barely heard the warning. He didn't notice that his teacher had gone. Beneban read the runes with ease. In the rocky chamber deep beneath Nigeran's keep, with the flicker of spell light, he reached a sure hand toward the great sword. It came to him as though crafted to his fist and blazed with clear amber light that chased the shadows. He swung it once, hesitantly, then again with more assurance. Its high song keened and sent a thrill down his spine. He ran above to the keep to show Nigeran, disappointed his mentor hadn't been there to see this feat.

The old wizard was nowhere to be found. Beneban raced through the keep. He startled Worfs in the kitchen and mice in the attic, but Nigeran had vanished.

Returning crestfallen to the entrance, he thought to leave at least a note. He couldn't just go without a word from or to his master.

A sheath that fitted the sword lay on the entrance table to the keep. It hung from a tooled leather belt. There, also, was a packet of food and the scarlet cloak that confirmed Beneban's graduation to wizard. This was Nigeran's final message.

The great door stood open. There was nothing to do but leave.

CHAPTER 4

As Beneban neared the bend that led sharply away from his winter home, he turned to catch a last regretful sight of the cave. Kati had gone before he awoke and had not returned. He would like to have said goodbye, to thank her. His vision blurred once and again. He rubbed angrily at his eyes.

"Don't be a fool," he muttered. "Wizards have no heart. It's a well-known fact. This is the way it should be."

He strode along, kicking crossly through piles of snow. The brisk air cleared his head. With a conscious effort, he straightened and lengthened his stride to its normal, distance-eating pace. Soon his steps dragged again. He felt a sense of impending menace.

A few late snowflakes drifted through sunbeams that shafted down through a winterfruit tree.

Shielding his eyes, Beneban watched a redbird, gay with the promise of spring and mating, flip through branches still clothed in the brittle shell-green leaves of winter.

"You are cheerful. You must have a pretty lady hidden away somewhere." Beneban whistled a few notes, enjoying the light shining through the clear wing feathers as the bird cavorted beside him.

"Don't follow me too far. Your lady will worry."

His thoughts returned to Kati. Would she worry to find he was gone? He had the sudden urge to turn back. He needed to say thank you to his savior and friend.

Instead he simply warned again, "Don't go too far."

As though heeding this caution, the small red acrobat exploded into the air. An abrupt and savage weight cannoned into Beneban. It flung him headlong into a drift. His ears thundered with a ferocious snarl. Twisting with difficulty, he glimpsed a large male kalting crouched over him, its teeth bared.

Before he thought of his belt knife or knew its futility, a golden body streaked through the air.

Kati crashed into Beneban's assailant, knocking him away. She crouched over the wizard. The rumble low in her throat was clear to the male kalting. This prey was hers. She would fight if necessary.

The male paced and hissed. He wanted to challenge her but finally retreated before the formidably larger female.

"G-good timing, Kati," Beneban gasped as she moved delicately from his back. He got slowly to his knees and wiped snow and pebbles from his face. His hands shook with the near disaster. He struggled to his feet.

"I'll m-miss having you to drag me out of peril." His words shook slightly.

A purr rumbled in Kati's throat. Beneban laughed at her anticipatory expression.

"No, girl. We aren't. Or I'm not, at least. No hunting today. Thank you for everything. I won't return to the cave. I'm heading down the mountain." He bent and rubbed her head briefly then started away.

Kati loped ahead and plunked down in his path.

"Try to understand, Kati. I must go." He moved around her and took another few steps before turning back around.

"I will miss you…"

Again, he started forward. Again, she outflanked him and crouched at his feet.

Holding her warm silken muzzle in his hands, he stared into her emerald eyes. "I don't want to ride, though I thank you. The time will come when I miss that comfort. Walk with me a bit, if you will."

This time as he started off, she rose to move at his side. He kept one hand on her warm neck, sad in the knowledge that she could not stay with him. Her life was here in the wild. His was somewhere with different perils to be met.

Three times as the day aged, Beneban tried to send her back. Once she darted suddenly off the path. There was a squeak as her breakfast came to an untimely end.

When she didn't reappear after a few moments, the wizard walked on. He ignored the way his feet seemed to drag.

Surely, he thought, this depression was caused by the clouds rolling damp gray fog down the mountain's slope. But when an hour along the trail Kati again caught up with him, even the cold drizzle failed to dampen Beneban's suddenly lightened mood. Trying to brace against the certainty that she must eventually leave for good, he accepted the kalting's return with the joy of loneliness deferred.

When the early mountain night fell, she curled beside him. They shared the small fire, and she added warmth to the hastily constructed lean-to he made. Once in the middle of the night, she roused and growled. Some large creature crashed away through the brush. Beneban could only be grateful for the protection she offered.

Two days' trek through the trackless mountains brought them to the foothills of the Kalds. Each dawn Kati disappeared briefly to hunt. Each day she rejoined him before long, licking her whiskers. Once she brought Beneban a fat parti for his supper. It was a pleasant change from the dried fruit and berries he had hoarded through the winter.

On the third morning they looked down on the green, rolling roof of Forest, laced along its edge with a finger of silvery water. It was, he thought, dredging up memory of a map he had seen, one arm of the Lingar River which also bordered the Settled Plains.

"Some people call that the Ariling Forest." He indicated the seemingly endless treetops below them. "It sits on the edge of Ariling, one of the Twelve Estates that are vassals of Larlion."

He often talked to Kati as they climbed a hill or stood to look out on the path ahead.

"Usually it is merely called Forest. It is a strange and mystical place. I've heard that there are those who, lost in its depths, return entranced but unwilling to speak of their adventure."

Kati sat at the top of the rise, ears cocked. She seemed to enjoy it when Beneban talked to her, though he wondered how much she understood. Since he was ready for a breather, he continued.

"A woman, an enchantress some say, or perhaps only a recluse, is believed to live there. Many call her Forest Lady, and they believe she bewitches those who wander into her realm. If I didn't feel an urgent call to Larlingarde, I would perhaps spend time seeking her..." His voice faded away.

"Well, that must wait for another time."

He forced himself back to the present.

"We should get along. In another day, perhaps two, we might reach Larlingarde," he said hopefully.

Unforeseen events would make it a longer trip.

THAT NIGHT THEY camped beneath the edge of Forest while the Lingar trilled a liquid song at their feet.

"Well, Kati, we have the river for drink, but I'm out of food. Either I must stop and hunt or find a homestead that will trade supplies for work."

Kati, relaxing by the fire, suddenly snarled and lifted her great head. Her green eyes stared into the darkness of the trees behind them. Beneban leapt to his feet. He kept one hand on Heldenhaft as a heavily cloaked figure shuffled into the edge of the firelight.

The wizard sprang forward, but Kati rumbled a warning. She grabbed the edge of his fur cape in her teeth and pulled him back. Startled, he nearly toppled into the fire.

Unwillingly he waited, forced to heed Kati's growl. He watched as a withered hand pushed the dark hood from snowy hair as the bent figure neared. The intruder was a tiny old woman. Flickering firelight picked out a bundle on her back.

She stopped and leaned on a stout walking stick. At first there was silence.

"Well, madam?" Beneban took his hand from his sword but remained wary. "What do you do so late at night on Forest edge? Aren't you afraid of Forest Lady's bewitchment?"

The beldame chuckled softly. "I don't believe every tale I hear, young sir. I have dwelt in Forest for many a year. Here I stand, unbewitched."

"Perhaps *you* are Forest Lady," Beneban suggested.

"Nay, I'm not she. If Forest Lady there be."

"Still, so late at night, shouldn't you seek your bed?"

"So I will, when our business is finished."

Again Beneban's hand touched his sword hilt then fell back. "What business might that be? What have you to do with me, old wife?"

"Wife I've never been. Mother I am and am not. My name is Saray."

"Then, *Saray*," Beneban sighed, and struggled for patience. "What does your business have to do with me?"

"Ah, you are young and impatient of course. Now be a good lad. Help me off with this pack. Then my business will be half done."

Beneban glanced at Kati. She was alert, interested but not nervous, so he relaxed a bit.

"Tis good to heed your kalting," his visitor said. "Listen to her. T'will save you much trouble." The old woman loosened the ties, and Beneban moved toward her.

He lifted the pack from her back. At her nod, he carried it nearer the fire.

Saray remained in the shadows but watched alertly.

"What is in the pack, Saray?" Beneban demanded.

"Open it," she said. "Then you will know."

"Is this pack your business with me?" He stared from her to Kati.

The kalting yawned and relaxed even more. Reassured by her acceptance, he set the pack down. After checking once more on the old woman, who stood quietly, he knelt beside the pack. When unfolded, the wrapping became a cloak of fine scarlet fellan, warm and soft beneath his calloused hands. He stared, stunned.

"Is this... Can this be for me?"

Saray moved to him. After an instant of tension, he let her approach, and she hung it about his shoulders, standing on tiptoe to reach his great height.

Woven of much finer fellan than the one he had left shredded in the thicket, he now wore a true wizard's cloak. It hung warmly, fell exactly to the ground at his feet, and fit his lanky body as Heldenhaft had fit his hand in that first instant. It boasted an ample hood and a multitude of pockets. The fastener at the throat was a spun shimmergreen leaf the exact color of his hair.

"Aye!" Saray nodded contentedly. "The cloak is my business with you. The contents of the pack are a gift.

From Forest Lady, if you believe in such."

She fastened the pin beneath his chin and began to drift away.

Beneban took a quick step after her. "Wait! Who are you?" But he was too late. The old woman had melted into the dark beneath the trees before he could reach her. "Come back. Why do you bring me gifts? Kati! Bring her back."

Kati yawned enormously and stretched to the fire's warmth.

Bewildered, Beneban stalked a few paces in pursuit. Beneath the trees, the air suddenly thickened to quicksand. He could barely move his feet. There was no sense of danger, only, as each step dragged more slowly, a sense of wrongness.

Forced to stop, he peered in frustration after Saray. The blackness was as heavy as a bag thrown over his head.

He turned. The glow of his fire beckoned with Kati's golden shape resting beside it. In every other direction was a dense nothingness through which he could not wade.

In a temper he flicked his hand. Brilliant green flame burst from bunched fingers.

The flame glowed brightly. Obedient to his will, it illuminated the space around him. Then slowly, inexorably, the blackness tightened. The green flame was extinguished.

Furious now, he brought the flame back. It died almost as it was born.

In his mind he heard a voice, cool as shadow in hot summer. "In Forest, wizardry does not exist except as I will it to be so." Beneban thought of a counter-spell. He could show his power. He would...

Kati growled impatiently and half rose to a crouch. Thus, she had warned the kits if they headed into trouble. If ignored, she would pounce and cuff them—or him—severely.

"All *right!*" The wizard, angry and frustrated, stamped back to the fire. "The old woman is gone, even if I could lift the spell." He knelt by the pack.

"Besides," he added, and pushed away his irritation, "I'm curious to see what 'gift' Forest Lady—if I believe in such—has for me."

He jerked loose the twisted vine that bound the smaller package. Wrapped in nearly waterproof Worf cloth were court clothes of fine silver-gray material. Old-fashioned but elegant, the style was from a time many years earlier.

They would be a near fit, Beneban discovered, as he held their silky length against his lean body. There was also food in the pack, travel food. In the very depths of the pack, green Worf cloth wrapped a pile of small flat cakes made of ground nuts, fruit and meal pressed together and dried. He nibbled one curiously and resisted eating the whole delicious thing. No doubt it might better serve his need later.

Utterly stunned and curious now, he opened the flask. The scent was reminiscent of the mystic help he had received in the blizzard. He resealed it for future need.

Kati yawned and stretched beside the fire then stared expectantly at Beneban. He chuckled at her nudge.

"Yes. We must sleep now. Tomorrow we head for

Larlingarde." As he drowsed beneath the warmth of the scarlet cape, a sudden thought burst in his head. He sat up.

Could the old woman actually have been Forest Lady? He had pictured her as young, beautiful... But no. The warning voice had not been hers.

The voice, that touch of mind that had kept him from death on the mountain, had that been Forest Lady? She was rumored to have strange powers, and here, in food and raiment, was physical evidence of her interest in him. But why?

He knew the danger she had saved him from. What danger did she see him about to enter? Or was he imagining too much?

He stilled his thoughts and reached gently for that quiet mind touch that had brought him help, peace, and well-being. This time his reach had more specific direction. He sought toward Forest.

With nearly physical pain, he met a wall of resistance, a mind block he could not pass. He knew it to be the same will that had bolstered his when he hung on the cliff near death. It wavered only once as he continued stubbornly trying to reach it. Then it strengthened.

To his insistence that they meet, there was flat rejection. Even if he could break through the barrier, it would injure one who had done him only good.

Exhausted and bewildered, he withdrew.

Much later as he drifted toward sleep, he felt the wall relax slightly. There came a scent of flowers and a thought; Now, he was needed in Larlingarde, but at some later time, Forest might not be forbidden to him.

The wizard slid into dreams.

CHAPTER 5

THREE RAINY DAYS later, Beneban perched on a boulder beside the Larlingarde Pike. A raindrop that hung from the leaf of a winterfruit tree caught his attention with its sparkle. He lifted a hand to see it darken, then let the light shine again as he touched Kati's wet head.

"See, Kati? Even this pale light touches color in a drop of water."

Kati grumbled crossly and groomed water from her sodden fur. Bad weather had followed them from the edge of Forest, and the sullen sky showed no sign of a return of Asolum.

Beneban smiled at his cranky friend.

"Spoiled beast. Last night we sheltered at an inn."

The great kalting hissed, and scratched one shoulder reminiscently. They had gone astray and ended up in the border town of Torgarde when night fell.

"All right, an inn *stable*," Beneban conceded. "And the hay was verminous and sour. Torgarde surely has better inns and more reasonable innkeepers. I doubt *that* stable was cleaned since last winter."

Kati snarled her displeasure at the memory.

"Kati, look at my hands," Beneban protested. "I chopped a year's supply of wood to purchase that shelter for us."

The kalting nudged her wizard friend repentantly.

The host of the Landed Fish was a surly Othring half-blood. He took one look at the soggy travelers and claimed his house full. When Beneban persisted, he grudgingly let them sleep in the stable, but only in return for work.

"And no food," the innkeeper had snarled. "Tis bad enough your kalting will upset honest carrier beasts. Cost me business. I doubt not I'll regret my generosity."

"There must be food at least for Kati," Beneban had insisted stubbornly. "Or she might help herself to one of the 'honest carrier beasts.'"

By the time he had mucked out stalls and chopped the required wood, Beneban was too weary for hunger. A nibble of the last travel cake followed by a sip of the liquid in old Saray's flask revived him enough to let him sleep.

The wizard had preserved the food the old woman had brought when they camped by Forest for moments of need. It provided strength and lifted his spirit above any wine. Even the fragrance, like that which came with Forest Lady's mind touch, helped clear a fuddled brain and strengthen weary muscles.

He and Kati had been glad to put the unfriendly village behind them. Since then they'd passed by fields already misted with green and land dotted with the farmsteads and villages of Torling Estate.

Inhabitants of the country towns were poor, but less desperate than those they had seen in the city.

Though they had taken a wrong turn from their

Forest camp, the trip through this part of Larlion had proven interesting. Now, however, Beneban was eager to reach the capital.

They reached the great Tor Bridge on the main road between the Estates of Torling and Larling as evening neared. There, weather had been a persistent drizzle all the day. It had ended at last, and the two travelers stopped to rest.

At each turn of the road, Beneban looked eagerly ahead in hope he would glimpse the towers of the capitol, Larlingarde. Still the road wound ahead, empty past the next turning.

A stream purled beside the road. On the landward side, steep cliffs surged to the High Tor, the wide grazing land of Torling Estate. It was rumored to be so rich that it would bring a flock of felle to market size in a month.

Just here the road narrowed to twist past a steep cliff. A patch of grass offered ease to tired feet and was out of the chill wind. It was a good spot to eat a bite and sleep until morning.

Kati pounced on a stray field farsel, licked her catch dry, and gulped it down. Beneban bent over his pack seeking to chase down the final crumbs of travel cake.

Suddenly the kalting snarled and sprang to her feet. Her golden ruff flared. Startled, Beneban choked on a crumb. He sprang to his feet too.

"What is it, Kati?"

A confused clamor came around the bend.

"Travelers. Not our business, girl." The abrupt clash of weapons and a woman's anguished cry changed his mind. Heldenhaft in hand, Beneban and

Kati raced forward. A few bounds brought them round the cliff.

They were instantly in the midst of a fierce battle. A glance showed them an attack on a small and outnumbered group.

Several liveried men-at-arms lay dead. Three unarmored men fought desperately to hold the attackers away from their people. Beneath a huge tree, a lady knelt. She lifted her fallen lord's head into her lap.

Beneban and Kati didn't pause. They leapt forward. Strength surged through the wizard as the sword flamed with a golden light that chased shadows from the glade. Heldenhaft's eager battle song joined Kati's rumbling war cry as they plunged into the fray.

Before the attackers could turn, two of the would-be assassins lay wounded on the ground.

Heldenhaft flashed and bit, her power contagious. Encouraged by the sudden reinforcement, the followers took new heart. Now the embattled men used their weapons with determination.

Two assassins quickly fell to them. Three more fell to the great amber sword.

Kati's horn gored one, and her huge paw knocked another assassin to smash against a tree. He slid to the ground, broken. The tenth attacker broke free and ran. He was quickly overtaken by two of the defenders, who dragged him back.

Suddenly a small figure, unnoticed previously by Beneban, exploded forward with a screech. He pushed one of the men roughly aside.

"I, Calibe, claim this captive's life," he howled. "He has killed my mistress."

Beneban made an unsuccessful grab for him. Before any could intervene, the Worf thrust a small rapier into the prisoner's heart, once, twice, and again as the hapless man slumped between his captors.

"Grab him," Beneban cried, as the Worf darted behind the men-at-arms.

"See," he shrieked in apparent hysteria. "See what they did. They have killed my larya." Half hidden by the light ground mist, the tiny creature scuttled behind the big tree where the battle had centered.

In horror, the defenders realized that the Lady had now slumped forward across her husband. Beneban knelt to help her. He would tend to the Worf later.

They had been too late. Blood poured from a wound below her shoulder. It slowed as he lifted her limp body and laid her gently back. He tucked a hastily rolled cloak beneath her shimmergreen hair.

This was a lady of the pure blood, a Larlinga.

Her eyes, green as Kati's, fluttered open. With effort they focused on Beneban.

"Tell Torlarl..." She gasped. A trickle of blood ran from the corner of her mouth.

"Torlarl is her son," one of the retainers murmured from behind Beneban.

"I'll tell your son, my larya. He shall know justice has been done on those who..."

"No!" She fought for breath, eyes holding his. "My... brother..." She coughed, and a spray of blood spattered him. She died there between his hands.

Beneban closed her sightless eyes and shaken, wiped the blood from his face. He sat on his heels to assess the scene.

Heldenhaft lay bloody where he had dropped her to care for the lady. Her consort was also dead. The Worf had disappeared, as had Kati. Near him were only the three living arms men. The elder bandaged his comrade's wounded arm.

The third, Beneban saw, was a mere boy. The lad stood, white of face and paralyzed by the same shock the wizard felt at the sudden violence.

Beneban reached within for calmness. He lifted the great sword and began deliberately to clean the blade with a handful of leaves. His voice was steady as he asked the lad his first question.

"Who are you, son? Who were they?"

The lad shook himself. In a moment he managed to answer.

"They, the Torlarya and her husband. They are... were... We all came from the OathGive at Larlingarde, my lar."

"I'm not a lar." Beneban discarded the stained leaves and rose to sheath Heldenhaft's pulsing flame.

"But your hair—and such a sword..."

Not a lar!" he repeated firmly. "I am merely Beneban, a wizard, at your service."

By this time the other man's wound was bound and the two retainers joined the group.

"I... I am Borno," the lad said. His voice shook. "These are Daram and Rad. We are—were—arms men to the Torlarya."

"We traveled home to Torgarde," said the oldest of the three, Daram. "Young Tor, the larya's son, stayed behind to enjoy the Oathweek festivities. How we're to tell him of this, I don't know." His head drooped.

"The telling will wait," Beneban said firmly. "You can't tell, Tor, is it? That must wait until you reach him. There are more immediate things to see to. First, where have your animals gone?"

"The bandits chased 'em off. We'd just dismounted for a rest," Daram explained.

"They won't have gone far. My companion is gone too, it seems. And that little fellow... Who is he? He has also slipped away."

"A Worf, sir," said Borno. "He was given to our mistress by the Lady Meriel because he amused our larya."

The older men-at-arms began to gather the cavalcade's scattered property. They straightened their comrades' bodies and piled the dead attackers in a rude heap as Beneban prowled the clearing. Borno stayed close at his heels, helping as he might.

"Given?" Beneban spoke as he walked. "The Worf was a slave, then?"

Beside the tree where the royal couple lay, he bent and eased something out of the dead woman's hand. He slipped it into a pocket. The son might want the bauble.

"Not really given," Borno corrected himself. "The Worf served Lady Meriel, and she sent him to serve our mistress..." His voice broke on a sob. He leaned against a tree and stared at the river through tears that ran stubbornly down his cheeks.

"We'll send a troop back from Larlingarde to get them decently below ground," Rad said, getting Beneban's attention.

The wizard turned to him.

"Yes," he said, "but where is the Worf, Calibe, I believe he named himself? Where has *he* gotten to? And where did Kati go?"

As though in answer came the soft sound of hooves. Eight kelsh trotted into the clearing.

Borno and Daram quickly gathered the beasts' dangling reins. They spoke quietly to calm them, while Beneban walked to the head of the path. At once he heard an angry, squeaky voice.

"Let me down, you monstrous myth. You know not the danger you court to maltreat Calibe like this."

In a moment, Kati, with her head held high and her jaws clamped on the seat of Calibe's britches, crossed and dropped the Worf at Beneban's feet.

Calibe sprang to his feet. He hissed curses. He shook with fury and tried to draw the sword that was no longer at his hip. Water dripped from his hair and clothes. Finally, surrounded by the men-at-arms who looked with amusement on his antics, his furious sputter drew to a sullen close. He glared at them.

"You will not always laugh at Calibe," he hissed.

"I am not laughing now," Beneban said soberly when it was obvious the others waited for his lead. "Where did you disappear to, Calibe?"

"I went! To be alone with my sorrow, I went." He peered at the wizard and embellished the story.

"To find the kelsh I also went. You see! I started them back. Then your beast snatched me up." He waved a fist at Kati, but darted behind Rad as she snarled.

Beneban quieted her with a touch. Her hide was damper, he realized, than the drizzle would account for. She had been for a swim.

"How did you get so wet, Calibe?" Beneban looked from him to the kalting. "You appear to have been fished from the river. Did Kati help you out of it?"

Calibe fizzed up like a small kettle on a hot fire. "NOT so; *not* so! The woods are wet. The trees, the grass, *all* is wet for a short person." He scowled up at Beneban's lean height.

The tree behind him loosed its burden of water, drenching Calibe and Rad in an icy shower as though to prove his point. Beneban, about to question him further, hesitated at Daram's next words.

"Shh, listen!" The man held up a hand and prowled to the edge of the road. In a moment the group plainly heard the approach of a mounted troop.

"Kelsh," Rad whispered, and after a moment, "foot troops, too."

"Probably not bandits, then," Daram murmured.

"More likely some of the Grand Lar's men-at-arms," Rad agreed. "I know he's had his troops out to check into…" Daram nudged Rad's arm, and the younger man gave a startled glance at the wizard. He finished lamely, "…into a rumor. They were to distribute food, and keep an eye on things."

Beneban looked curiously at the two men. What secrets would they have from someone who had just saved their lives? Before he could inquire further, Kati leapt up with a snarl.

Beneban's hand went to Heldenhaft, but to little purpose. He, Daram, Rad and Borno were quickly surrounded by a troop of men-at-arms.

CHAPTER 6

THE MOUNTED TROOP with their blue and silver pennons fluttering should have been a reassurance to the Larlinga's bereaved retainers. Here was the help they had so desperately needed not long before. Instead, directed by the captain in charge, the contingent officiously surrounded Beneban and his small group of allies. The officer in charge of the troop pulled his sword in menace as a body of foot soldiers trotted into the clearing behind them.

Among the infantry towered a being that so transfixed Beneban's attention he missed the first sharp exchange between Daram and the captain. Eyes wide, he stared in awe.

Bringing up the rear of the troop was a creature that stood nearly eight feet tall. It was shaped like a tetrahedron on legs. The triangular shape was softened by dense white fur. On the side facing him, Beneban noted a bulging eye centered above a slash of mouth. There was no visible nose, but a tuft of longer fur at each edge of the face suggested ears.

Kati nudged Beneban to bring his attention back to the now furious captain.

"Answer me!" The captain, red of face, roared at Beneban. "Who are you? What had you to do with this vile deed?"

He was a bulbous little man with pudgy cheeks and a petulant mouth. Now he impatiently repeated his first words to the wizard. *"Who are you?"*

Beneban resisted wiping the outraged officer's spittle from his face. He answered with forced calm. "Captain, I am Beneban. I..."

"Beneban!" The pudgy officer snorted. Now he reared up on his kelsh in vain effort to intimidate the wizard. "You say 'Beneban' as though that explains your presence. Beneban *who?* Where do you come from?"

Kati yawned. She sat at Beneban's feet and continued to clean her fur, but her golden eyes looked a warning at the kelsh. It settled and backed a step.

"Beneban is my entire name," the wizard answered calmly. "I wintered in the Kalds and am traveling to Larlingarde."

His quiet words failed to calm the choleric captain. The situation worsened when Calibe leapt forward in a fury. He hopped up and down, making the officer's kelsh rear and back farther away.

"Yes! Ask him," the Worf shrieked: "Why was he here just now? Perhaps *he* directed the attack. Perhaps..."

"Not so!" Borno interrupted. His young face reddened beneath the captain's hard look, but he persisted.

"Sir," he stammered, "this man f-fought with the strength of ten. Without him we would all b-be dead." Overcome with his temerity, he ducked his head and grew silent.

The captain ignored the boy's words. His attention

fastened again on Beneban.

"Answer me!" he demanded. "Why were you here?"

"Why is one ever in this place instead of that?" Beneban replied in mild amusement. "Kati and I travel to Larlingarde. We stopped for food around that bend. You passed our campfire just now. When we heard the sound of battle and a woman's scream, we came to help.

"Young Borno is too generous," he continued, as the captain sputtered irately. "The Larlinga's retainers were badly outnumbered. Kati and I had the advantage of surprise, which altered the odds."

The captain slid down from his beast. He tossed the reins to a hastily dismounted trooper and stalked close to glare up at Beneban.

"'They fought bravely, like ten men,'" he hissed. "And still, my lar's sister and her consort lie dead. And *who is Kati*? I see no other woman here."

Beneban was stunned. There was more malice and anger in the words than made sense. He reached within to find a calm core for his answer.

"Kati is my companion." Beneban touched the kalting's head.

"How did *you* come by a kalting? Only the Grand Lar's special force has such a mount. Did you steal her?"

Finally Beneban was angry. He stiffened and loomed over the arrogant little man. His amber eyes sparked dangerously.

"I do not need to steal!"

Kati's neck fur bristled into a golden ridge at Beneban's tone. She snarled and paced a step forward, standing almost on the captain's shiny boots.

The captain backed up quickly. He bumped into his kelsh, already skittish at the closeness of a wild kalting. The kelsh reared and Captain Glaynar fell abruptly to a seat in the mud.

Quick action by the nearest trooper pulled the frightened steed away before it could trample the arrogant officer or bolt.

Beneban ducked his head to hide a smile. It was impossible not to be amused by the abruptly dampened ego of the arrogant little man, but by the time the captain struggled to his feet, all emotion had vanished from the wizard's face.

Unfortunately a murmur of amusement from the troopers was audible. They turned away to hide their laughter.

"Come, captain," Beneban said, trying to calm the strangely choleric man. "Could anyone steal an unwilling kalting? I do not own her, though she may own me. She seems to believe so. For a time our road is the same. We are simply companions."

The captain shrugged his tattered pride into place. He masked his anger and humiliation with a cold air of authority that failed to hide the strange hatred in his eyes.

"I am Captain Glaynar of the Grand Lar's Service. You, Beneban, are both witness and participant in this evil event.

"Until your presence here is explained," he continued, "I place you under guard. You will testify before His Mightiness regarding your share in this business."

"There is no need of a guard. I am, in any case, going to Larlingarde and..."

"Until you are cleared of suspicion," the captain interrupted icily, "you will remain under guard."

Now he bellowed, "*Trog*, get forward!"

The enormous white tetrahedral creature rolled into motion. Troopers and beasts backed quickly out of its path. Beneban watched as it—*he*, the wizard decided—moved rapidly on the three trunk-like legs. As he drew near, a second eye appeared on a second flat plane of its body, though beneath it no mouth was visible in the white fur. The Ogdol, for it was indeed one of those rarely seen beings, thudded to a stop and saluted with one of his three arms.

"Er, Trog," the captain growled, seeming uncomfortable at his closeness. "This man and his kalting will travel to Larlingarde. They are required to testify to this event. You will guard him. Go, now!"

He turned back to Beneban. "My officers will give the Torlarya and her consort fitting escort back to the capitol. The troop will bury this carrion and follow when they finish."

Diverted, Beneban realized that while the Ogdol was giving full attention to the Captain with one eye, the creature's second eye was examining him.

The Ogdol's voice was a deep rumble, as if one of Kati's purrs emerged in words, rough, yet without threat. "Must I take his sword?" he asked.

The mention of his sword instantly ended Beneban's mild amusement. The wizard loomed suddenly taller and his hand moved swiftly toward Heldenhaft. His amber eyes sparked with gold.

Daram, the oldest of the larya's men-at-arms, saved them from a threatened confrontation. He shouldered aside troops and kelsh to face down the officer. "This is wicked, Captain Glaynar. You know *me*! I've served my larya's household for thirty years, longer than you are alive. I attest that this man fought for us. To take his sword is to dishonor him as well as myself, who speaks for him. I pledge my honor he will appear at court as he says."

The captain's face became a furious purple mask, and he sputtered angrily. Then his second in command touched his arm and whispered quietly.

A sly expression replaced fury with cold calculation. For a long moment, Glaynar and Daram locked eyes.

The captain turned from Daram to exchange a few words more with his officer. He stood in apparent thought. Attention riveted on the scene, no one moved.

At length Glaynar returned his attention to Beneban. "This dire event has us all overheated," he said. His previous fury was suddenly replaced with a bothersome affability. "You, Beneban. Do you give your word to travel directly to Larlingarde?"

"Certainly. As I've said."

"Trog will accompany you, just so you don't... lose your way or be set upon by brigands yourself."

The captain turned away in apparent boredom with the wizard. His attention shifted to delegation of the burial team. The kelsh litters for the larya and her husband were quickly arranged.

"Thank you, Daram." Beneban touched the old

man on the shoulder.

"It's only right," Daram growled quietly. "Nor would I care to see that sword in the hands of a wrong 'un like him." He moved sadly away to the grim chore awaiting him.

"That's a good fellow," Beneban murmured. He turned to find the Ogdol watching him curiously.

"We seem to have become companions," he said softly. "What think you? Do we start now or follow a decent distance behind?" A twinkle lighted Beneban's eyes.

The purring voice was reserved as the Ogdol answered. "We will start ahead. Captain Glaynar will overtake us before we arrive."

"Come on then, Kati."

Beneban swung onto the path toward Larlingarde so suddenly that kalting and Ogdol scrambled to catch up with him. The wizard's long free stride carried them quickly out of sight of the grisly scene, but the grim sound of shovels digging graves for the dead followed them a distance down the road.

The three traveled in silence for an hour. Now the trees thinned, and the High Tor flattened into low rolling hills.

As they went, Beneban became aware of a strange mix of feelings. A lighter mood seemed to come from sun, air, and fewer trees. Yet it was lessened by an odd sense of pressure. After a time, he halted and stared toward the bare-topped hills on their left.

The Ogdol turned to him. "We travel beside the burial place of Larlion's past. Great heroes, rulers, both honorable and evil, all lie there, I am told. Many died in battle, some of treachery. They sleep, but not deeply."

"You feel the pressure too?" Beneban looked keenly at his escort. Undisturbed, Kati sat licking one great paw and rubbing it over an already immaculate ear.

"I feel it. The pressure will lift as we near the bridge. It is not far now." The Ogdol stared behind and watched the wizard. He waited for... something.

"Your name is Trog?" the wizard asked after a moment.

"My name is unpronounceable in the language of the Larlinga. For convenience, they call me Trog."

"How do you come to serve in the army of the Grand Lar? In my years of roaming Larlion, I've never met one of your people. I understood that Ogdols stayed in the mountains beyond the High Kald Desert."

"I serve where I am called to serve." Now Trog's tone was sharp and cut off further conversation. "Come, it will soon be dark."

Beneban moved a reluctant step along the road. He was suddenly unsure of the path he had begun.

A thunder of hooves behind them heralded the passage of Captain Glaynar and the litter-borne noble corpses.

Beneban, Kati, and Trog moved off the road as they trotted past, pennons carried low in respect for the dead. Captain Glaynar ignored them, while Calibe, perched high on one of the litter-bearing beasts, sneered.

"That is the most unpleasant Worf I've ever met," Beneban commented. "They're often mischievous but are usually merry company."

Trog silently eyed the passing troop. As the last

kelsh passed, he absently groomed mud spatters from his white fur.

"Calibe is pleasant to those he serves," he said, his voice flattened. As soon as the dust cleared, the Ogdol started along the road again. Beneban and Kati followed in silence for a few moments.

"Trog, you always seem to say less than you mean," the wizard said when he caught up with his escort.

At first there was no answer. Then the Ogdol spoke words that seemed to change the subject.

"The eagle comes to the arm of its master," he said at length. "The wild kelsh will run its heart out for a master it learns to trust. Ride your beast now," he added. "I walk too fast for you. She will match my pace if you wish it so."

"Three legs travel faster than two," Beneban agreed. He mounted Kati. "But don't you worry that we'll run from you?"

"You have walked this far so that I need not fear. If you wished to escape, you would have ridden your kalting miles ago." They trotted in silence for a while.

"It is truly said, Trog," Beneban broke the silence, "that the eagle comes to his master. The saying about a wild kelsh is also true. What has that to do with you and me?"

The Ogdol stopped and turned one eye fully on Beneban. "I do not know yet. Many things are not clear to me. As the river finally reaches the sea, so in time I will know what we have to do with each other. Now come," he commanded, setting a faster pace. "Tor Bridge is just past those trees, and beyond is Larlingarde. Asolum races us down the sky. If we beat her not, we must camp outside this night or bribe the gate guard with much gold."

CHAPTER 7

Beneban and Kati had nearly caught up to the Ogdol when he suddenly halted again. Kati, with a lithe twist, managed not to crash into him.

"Now what?" the wizard asked.

"I think there is a problem." Trog's normal deep voice became sober. The Ogdol sank down beside Kati, who promptly sat. They had ridden on for some time but had not yet reached the bridge.

Beneban was unseated by the kalting's abrupt move, but quickly gained his feet. Trog looked like a small furry mountain that had suddenly erupted in the middle of the road, the wizard thought, mildly amused. Then he was concerned by Trog's words.

"Perhaps Kati has injured a paw?" the Ogdol rumbled. He reached out a hand and touched Kati's right front leg. "This paw perhaps? Show me, Kati."

Quickly, Beneban knelt beside him in concern. "I didn't notice her limping. Kati, are you hurt?"

Kati's green eyes stared into Trog's black one. Then she sat and held up her right forepaw for Beneban to examine.

"I do not find an injury," the wizard said. "Are you sure she was limping?"

Kati stood and walked a few steps, limping badly.

"I think it is not serious," Trog said as the kalting sat down again.

"I didn't even notice. Well, I'll walk the rest of the way," Beneban said as he straightened.

"It would be good if Kati rests here tonight."

Beneban stared at Trog. "I can't... I *won't* just leave her here."

"No. You, too, must stay. The rain has stopped. It will be pleasant to sleep beneath the sky."

"Captain Glaynar will be certain I've escaped," protested Beneban. "Will you travel ahead? Explain, and tell him we are coming more slowly?"

"I do not wish to appear before the captain without you." Trog spoke slowly, as though he were pondering each word. "No. I believe I must stay with you. Tomorrow is time enough to reach Larlingarde."

"You're doing it again, Trog, saying only half of what you mean."

As the Ogdol remained silent, Beneban shrugged. "We'll camp here then, though it's uncomfortably close to the barrows."

"The dead will not disturb us. We will camp at the end of the trees within sight of Larlingarde. There the pressure eases. Come! You must see this."

"See what?" Beneban demanded. But Trog had hurried ahead with Kati limping after.

Beneban caught his companions as Asolum, Larlion's primary sun, flung her last rays across the horizon. Where the trees ended, the ground rushed away to the river's edge. Here, where the river widened in a rush to embrace the sea, Tor Bridge's ivory span soared up and across to rule over the torrent. The graceful arch carried the eye to the walls beyond. They were tinged with pink by the setting sun and crowned with towers of rose and ruby, incarnadine buttresses that propped pinnacles of carnelian and scarlet spires, all webbed together by skywalks crimson against the deepening blue of the sky.

The last pink faded from the sunset, leaving the towered city gray against the purple night. Beneban drew a gasp of air into his lungs. He had forgotten to breathe in awe of the sight.

He moved stiffly, stretched a little, and looked for his companions. "I have never seen such beauty made by man, and the gates..." His words fell away.

Kati stretched full length in the cool grass at the road's edge as she casually cleaned the day's mud from her golden pelt. Trog still watched the city with his forward face. Another eye considered Beneban, and the third kept watch behind them.

"The gates are a gift from my people to yours. Yet, like most visions, the reality is flawed," Trog said. "Within the walls are poverty, pain, and all manner of evil." In the near dark, Trog was a furry gray blur.

"Still," the wizard offered, "it is a good vision. To see a garden is a first step toward moving a dung hill."

"It is good to wear tall boots if one must move a dung hill," the Ogdol said. Then, with a rumble Beneban interpreted as a laugh, he moved toward the trees.

"Come. A fire would be of comfort." He picked up sticks he seemed to find as easily in the dark as by day.

Beneban flicked a fingertip light to aid his vision. For a moment the green glow drew him back to the edge of Forest and the touch of another mind. That touch had vanished when they started south. When he woke each night he listened, reached out, only to sink back to disappointed sleep at its absence.

Kati stretched with a noisy yawn. She slipped smoothly into the trees to hunt. Her movement interrupted the wizard's thoughts. He watched as she disappeared, then he resumed the search for fuel, and soon a blaze crackled merrily in a ring of stones.

Kati slid back into the firelight with a brace of partis for Beneban and Trog. She dropped them by the fire and sat licking her lips where a stray feather still clung from her own meal.

The birds were quickly cleaned and spitted. Their fat sputtered into the hot coals as they roasted. Suddenly, Beneban was ravenous. He and Trog pulled the birds from the fire when they were barely cooked. They dismembered the meal in companionable, if greedy, silence while the kalting lazed by the blaze.

"That is better!" The wizard sighed in contentment of a good meal.

Trog idly dug the last meat scrap from his bird.

Beneban licked the grease from his fingers as he lounged across the fire. The heat on his face with chill night at his back made a pleasant contrast. He tossed a bone to the fire and asked the question that had puzzled him.

"Why didn't you want to reach Larlingarde tonight, Trog?"

For a moment the Ogdol was motionless. Then he chewed, swallowed. "The beast's foot..." he offered tentatively.

"Gave her no trouble when she left to hunt. Nor did she limp until you suggested it. Do you speak with animals, Trog?"

Trog tossed a final bone to the fire. "By some, I am considered a beast."

Beneban refused that thought with a shake of his head. He waited.

"I have some skill with animals, yes."

Beneban's eyes stayed steady on the Ogdol's single eye. "Why?" he asked.

"When the escort passed us," Trog said at last, "none of the Torlarya's party rode with them, save only Calibe."

"Calibe, who is no friend of mine," Beneban said slowly into the silence.

"Captain Glaynar," Trog continued reluctantly, "bears responsibility as leader of the patrol troop. He is charged to keep the Grand Lar's peace. In this case, he obviously failed that responsibility."

"It won't help that one of the victims was related to the Grand Lar," Beneban said.

"His sister." The words rumbled, followed again by silence.

Beneban waited quietly. Wizards were familiar with silence and not uncomfortable with it. Silence filled the darkness that surrounds the creation of spells. Silence was the root of concentration, and concentration was the mother of wizardry. So Beneban waited.

At last, the Ogdol continued. "The captain needs a scapegoat. Also, he dislikes you, though you have never met. It would be wiser to not arrive before those who bore witness to your actions."

"Did Glaynar leave the others behind with that in mind?"

This time Trog did not answer. After a bit, Beneban rose to pull his fur cloak from his pack.

"Would you like one of my cloaks for warmth?" At first, he thought there would be no answer to this either.

When Trog finally spoke, his voice was as rough as thought a bone had caught in his throat. "Thank you, no." Then came his rumble of laughter. "If you lie on your fur cloak and cover with the fine one, you are still less protected from a chill than I. My people wear a cloak only in the bitterest mountain winters."

Beneban's eyes met the single dark orb across the fire. *He has such long lashes,* the wizard thought inconsequentially. *His eyes are – kind.* Impulsively he held out a hand.

Time, and his hand, hung suspended...

Then Trog clasped his arm gently just below the elbow. The Ogdol's huge hand, with its two opposing thumbs, dwarfed Beneban's lower arm, and the wizard's grasp reached scarcely halfway to Trog's elbow. But the giant's hold was only firm enough to not give offense. The wizard realized absently that Trog's elbow was double jointed, able to bend in either direction.

Trog released Beneban's grip. He turned slightly so that no one eye looked at him directly. "Come. Sleep now. Tomorrow will carry its own share of time."

As Beneban crawled beneath his cloaks, Trog became simply a tetragonal shadow in the flickering light. The wizard stretched out, pillowing his head on Kati, and thought warmly of the old woman—Saray, had that been her name?—and the gift of the scarlet cloak.

For a moment, he thought he caught the scent of flowers. Then the long day plunged him into a sleep of disturbed and violent dreams.

IN FOREST, AS Laraynia passed beneath trees a distance from her cottage, each leaf shed a cool green glow. Though dawn was as distant as supper, she walked in as much light as dwellers here ever saw.

"Saray can't have gone far," Forest Lady murmured to Gorba, the giant ursyn that paced at her side. "She only went to gather moonherbs."

Arav, who rode on Gorba's back, spread his black wings and screamed as Dap and Dal tumbled too close. Quickly the Worfs darted to Laraynia's other side.

"Look, lady." One twin pulled at her cloak and pointed overhead. Now the trees had dimmed to faded gray. They no longer responded to Laraynia's presence, though behind there was still a flicker of light. It cast faint radiance into the sudden gloom.

"The dark grows closer each day, Dal." She put a hand on his little shoulder. "Hush now. Listen for Saray. If she has come this far, she may be in trouble."

They stood silent in the dim, ominous darkness. About them, Forest, too, was still.

"There are no nightbeasts afoot, not even harkowls. Nothing is stirring tonight. But why?"

The alviar half-mantled his wings with a metallic rattle of feathers.

"Listen." Dal darted a few steps ahead of Forest Lady and stared into the dark. The sound came again, a low moan.

"It's Saray." Laraynia rushed forward, hand at her throat. The green stone gleamed in answer. As if in reluctant response, the nearest trees produced a fragile ghost of the light they had left behind.

In the dim glow, they discovered the crumpled figure of the old woman. Her green cloak had been torn off and cast aside. Wounds covered her arms and face, not clean wounds, but cruel torment that channeled blood down wrinkles in her ancient skin. Laraynia, appalled at this deliberate infliction of pain, was oblivious to her surroundings. She knelt by her old nurse.

Gorba's great head swung side to side as he watched over them, and the alviar rattled his metallic plumage. A whisper of noise made Dap and Dal flank the Lady closely. Then the grolling attack was upon them.

With a roar, the ursyn towered to full height and lumbered forward. Arav flapped upward as Gorba swatted right and left. Two of the skulkers smashed into nearby trees and slid lifelessly to the ground. The alviar stooped screaming on a third. He hit it just behind the head to avoid the poisonous bite. The scaly body whipped back and forth at the end of the snake-like neck, even after Arav's knife-edged beak severed its head.

Laraynia was standing over Saray. "Bait... trap," the old woman murmured. Forest is not safe, Rayni."

Dal and Dap flanked her, and their long flat feet

braced as they rapidly fitted smooth stones to the slings always fastened at their belts. Wherever the stones flew, a hiss or howl arose, and another lizard-like grolling nursed a broken limb, or died with a crushed skull.

Arav dove again. This time his victim fell into the clearing, thrashing its six legs and horny tail as gray blood oozed from the stump of its neck.

"That pack try to ring us, Laray," Dap cried. He sent another accurate stone at the shadows that slunk between the small band and the lighted trees.

"They did this to Saray." As if wakened from a trance, Laraynia's eyes began to glow. Their cool gray sparked now with green. The stone at her neck flared as her hand tightened on it. Sudden thunder rumbled overhead, and the trees tremblingly brightened their reluctant light.

Gorba lay shaking a grolling which clung with its suction-cupped forefeet from one of his mighty clawed front paws, grolling but not before it had sunk its teeth into him.

In response to Forest Lady's anger, thunder crashed above them. Bolt after bolt of lightning blasted between the trees until the darkened Forest was brighter than a sunlit noonday. Trees burst into flame. In the blaze, the ursyn's gray-blue coat gleamed with an eerie luminescence.

The grollings, night prowlers with lidless eyes, shrank from the glare. They disappeared as suddenly as they had come, leaving their fellows' bodies behind.

"Lady, they go." One twin pulled at her cloak as another bolt exploded among the trees.

She stared at him as at a stranger. Slow awareness returned, followed by contrition as she saw the damage around her. They stood within a fort of broken trees. Some were aflame. As the light faded from her stone and from the trees still standing, the bodies of the grollings gleamed with the sick phosphorescence seen in certain poisonous fungi.

"We killed so many?" Her voice shook, but Gorba growled a satisfied affirmative, and Arav preened his metallic feathers in pride.

"It need to be, lady," Dap said.

"They not friends," Dal agreed.

"But why?" she murmured, as stunned as though she awakened from a deep dream. "They have never before been unfriends, though they hold aloof. We have even traded sweetbarb to them for herbs. Why?"

Saray groaned. Gorba's bitten paw was swelling. Laraynia, shaken, turned her attention to her friends. When they were safely home, when she had healed their wounds, then there would be time for thought, she decided.

FOREST LADY AT last sought her bed. Herbs were set to draw the poison from Gorba's paw. Saray's many wounds were washed and dressed. Laraynia's care and a soothing drink had lulled her old nurse to drowsiness.

"They sought you, Rayni," The old woman whispered her childhood name for the girl. "This," she held up one torn arm, "was diversion while they waited."

Forest Lady tossed restlessly on her cot that night.

She rose at first light and stepped carefully over the twins on their pallets to reach the door. Only Arav saw her go. A finger to her lips held him from following.

As the day's light grew, she moved to the edge of Forest where once Beneban had camped. Now she stood and watched Asolum rise. Here the remains of his campfire lingered with some sticks of unburned wood. Her mind relived the events of the night. It also reached for contact with the wizard, as it often did in unguarded moments, as indeed it had in the midst of battle.

"I've never even seen him. Why does he remain in my thoughts?" she wondered aloud. "Why, since I first touched his mind, have I felt so alone?"

"Because you seek a partner," Saray said as she moved quietly from the trees.

"Saray!" Laraynia whirled, startled. "You should be in bed."

"I am well. Only old and shaken." She watched as Forest Lady considered her words.

"I'm not alone, Saray. I have you, Dap and Dal, Gorba, and Arav."

"And many other friends in Forest for whom you feel responsibility," her nurse agreed. "That is different than standing shoulder to shoulder with the man you love."

"Love? I have never seen his face."

"You know his mind, his heart."

"He may find me unattractive. And why would I choose a wizard to love? Everyone knows wizards have no hearts."

"Everyone 'knows' Forest Lady bewitches unwary

wanderers. So Beneban told me."

"No! You tease me, Saray."

"I do not." The old woman sank to a fallen tree. "Remember, your parents left all they possessed to have each other, and your father was a powerful wizard."

"You've rarely spoken of my parents." Excitedly, Laraynia turned gray eyes on the old woman.

"Nor do I now, except to show that what 'everyone knows' is often fool's wisdom."

"Were they important, wealthy?"

"They possessed all one could ask for of the worlds' things. Had wisdom ruled them, they'd not have loved each other. One does not choose love, child; one is chosen by it."

"Then why? If you believed this about Beneban, about me, why did you have me send him away?"

"He has no power, no position to offer you."

"What matters that to me?" Laraynia asked, and anger turned her away from her old nurse.

"It will matter to him. You are Forest Lady, and more." Saray rose stiffly. "Now, I shall go and rest. Don't remain too long alone. Even in daylight, Forest is less safe than it was." She turned and hobbled toward the trees.

"But when, Saray? When can we be together?" Laraynia demanded, scowling after her old nurse.

"To push time, Rayni, is to break the hourglass. Be patient." The old woman disappeared into the trees.

Laraynia sank to the grass beside the campfire's ashes. She poked idly with a twig at their gray remains and considered the evil which walked more frequently in the depths of Forest. It grew stronger. Her protected place was threatened by a wickedness she did not understand. But why?

Unaware, her hand caressed the pale green stone that hung on her breast. A spark flared within. It echoed the glow in her eyes as she relived the terror of Saray's still body, the grolling attack, and her violent anger. Her anger that had destroyed more than she intended.

"Beneban," she murmured, "if you do not come soon, we may not survive."

BENEBAN WOKE ABRUPTLY. The red gleam of rising sun blinded him for a moment. His nightmare of fighting, danger, and blood returned. He sprang up, Heldenhaft unsheathed as Kati bounded from the trees.

"Whuff!" Trog grunted, rising to one elbow. "Is there an attack?"

Kati skidded to a stop and peered about, puzzled.

Beneban also stared about in confusion as awareness returned. Now he remembered where he was. Embarrassed, he returned the great sword to its sheath. As the golden gleam vanished, he shook his head.

"It was a nightmare, I think. Yet someone cried out for help. All night I dreamed of battles and blood and grollings. Do you know anything of grollings, Trog?"

"No." The big Ogdol had begun fishing travelcakes from a pouch which hung unnoticed around what would have been his waist had his furry shape permitted of such a concept. "Grollings are lowlanders.

They shun our cold mountains."

"I suppose so. They are ugly beasts, narrow heads on skinny long necks, and they have a poisonous bite. They run in packs, but I've never heard of them molesting people. Why would I dream of fighting them?"

"Come have breakfast. A full belly may sharpen your wits and help you interpret your dream."

"Yes, alright." Another moment and he stood, looking about. "Thanks. I'm probably only hungry. Kati seems already to have eaten."

"Kati," the Ogdol said, looking into her eyes, "you must remember, please, to limp a little today."

Kati sat and held up her right front paw with a little whimper.

"Yes, that's excellent."

"Trog, I'm not sure it was a dream. It was so real..."

"What could it be, then? Do you know anyone who bides there in danger?"

Beneban thought about Forest and the voice that had spoken to him. Remembering the barrier that had not allowed him to even to make a light, he shrugged. "No. I guess everyone I know of can take care of themselves."

Later, as their walk slowed to accommodate Kati's limping gait, Beneban admired the daylight view of Larlingarde from the peak of the Tor Bridge.

"Even in full light, it is a beautiful city, Trog."

"It is well conceived," the Ogdol agreed, "and blessed by the High Priestess Azarta's own hand, as well as that of her predecessor, and so back into...

Look. The remainder of Captain Glaynar's troop is about to overtake us."

In moments they were surrounded by the foot soldiers of the burial detail. The young adjutant in charge shouldered arrogantly up to Trog.

"You, Trog. Why are you still on the road? The captain ordered that man to be in the city last night."

"My beast has a wounded foot," Beneban offered mildly. Kati obligingly sat and held her paw up, looking as pathetic as a healthy kalting can seem.

"I know how scarce kaltings have become, sir," Trog added. "I felt it would exceed my instructions to allow this one a permanent injury."

"Captain Glaynar won't be pleased." The adjutant bustled to the head of his troop. "You two! Fall in at the rear there," he added officiously to Trog and Beneban.

As the troopers marched by, Rad and Daram nodded to the pair, and Borno grinned widely as he passed.

Even eating dust at the rear of the troop didn't spoil Beneban's appreciation of the beautiful city walls, opalescent in the sun. Though the walls appeared to be near the Tor Bridge, it was in fact an hour before they moved between the enormous gates of rosy adamant, that rare stone of such perfect hardness that nothing had been known to damage it.

Beneban gazed in awe at the runes of protection, radiant on the surface of the polished stone. The ability to quarry and shape it was a secret known only to a few Ogdol craftsmen. These stayed hidden in their distant homeland, shunning the outside world.

"Are they not beautiful?" Trog halted at the wizard's side to stare up at the gates, four times the height of the Ogdol. "Our artists have been offered great treasure to teach this craft. The Othrings have even tried abduction, but it is not a skill which can be taught to those outside our race."

"The color seems to ripple and change. They are nearly transparent. It's hard to believe they are so strong," Beneban said.

Trog mumbled what seemed a pleased agreement. "We have fallen behind the troop," he rumbled. "The adjutant will join Captain Glaynar in displeasure."

They passed through thick walls, and were abruptly plunged into such a maelstrom of life as the wizard had never experienced.

CHAPTER 8

INSIDE LARLINGARDE ON the streets and alleys nearest the walls, throngs of beggars in bright rags pushed, shoved, and begged for pistas from every passerby. An occasional grolling slithered past. Once Beneban spotted a giant Kalden, nearly as tall as Trog and dressed in rough skins. Tiny Worfs darted underfoot and slipped through every break in the crowd. Rough stands lined the streets, manned by vendors of all imaginable goods and services.

Here was a stall with an oven to cook for those who had no kitchen where one pista bought a bowl of grain with vegetables. There stood a used clothing stall with tattered merchandise marginally better than what clothed most of the mob.

One stall boasted pottery bowls and cups. Carved wooden utensils hung from hooks in another.

Over it all hung the odor of massed humanity. It was unlike any smell Beneban had yet experienced.

At every third stall, or so it seemed, a yellow cloak hung curtain-wise to proclaim the presence of a magician. These conjurors did a lively business in the good luck amulets that hung about every citizen's neck. Portents of the future were eagerly sought by the credulous, as well as charms of love, fertility, and sometimes more ominous spells. Nearly every magic-worker had customers in line to wait for his or her time.

Long lines of people carried various containers and waited patiently at the wells. At one, several of them turned away with empty jugs.

Trog saw Beneban's curiosity, and said, "There is not enough water for all."

"Surely more water can be brought. Or found?"

"Indeed. Ka'amfer, an important Othring, has begun a waterway, a long pipe to funnel water from Great Lar Lake into the city. Then he will sell it to those who can afford his price."

"Sell? Water? But all must have it to live," Beneban protested.

Trog didn't answer but pushed ahead through the crowds.

Now they passed stalls open to air and insects. These sold poor quality food for those who had a place to cook. Beneban watched in horror as a stooped hag in verminous rags bickered with the proprietor of the fish market. Money changed hands. The worst of the bugs were shaken from a small slab of fish, and the crone hobbled rapidly away. She hid the prize among her rags as she went.

"She will be fortunate to reach home without having it stolen," Trog said grimly. "Come. The quality of merchandise is better near the palace, and the air is breathable."

"Is Larlingarde always so crowded?"

"No. Many country people have come for the OathGive festivities. There would be a carnival tonight if not for the death of the Torlarya."

As the first shock of the crowd began to fade, Beneban graduated from seeing the mob as one entity. There were the Worfs, tiny, fragile, and seemingly more impoverished than most citizens. They flitted through the mob. Twice Beneban saw one make use of his race's well-known dexterity to relieve a more prosperous citizen of some small valuable.

As in all major cities of Larlion, the majority of the population was Othrings, or the increasingly common Larlinga/Othring mix. Their short sturdy build and dark hair and eyes marked them plainly from the true Larlinga.

Beggars of every race clutched at Beneban's clothes or, wary of the kalting, whined for pistas at a safe distance.

Suddenly a hand darted out to grab Beneban's ankle. Half falling, he angrily shook his foot. The Worf child held on grimly. He whimpered and peered upward. Enormous eyes in an emaciated face stared pathetically at the wizard.

"I have no money. Let go!" Beneban snapped. Then he noted the hollow eyes and distended belly of starvation. He fumbled for the piece of travel cake he had saved from breakfast.

"Here," he murmured and thrust it at the pathetic Worf.

Fragile fingers clutched it greedily. The child gave a loud yelp and scuttled back into the crowd. As if summoned by his cry, beggars of every size suddenly swarmed in on Beneban. They pulled his hands, dragged at his robe, and cried out, "Pista, pista, lar."

Trog and Kati had disappeared ahead.

"I have no money!" Beneban tried to retreat, but people ringed him tightly. His voice was drowned by the rising clamor.

A sharp push between the shoulders made the wizard lurch forward. Hands snatched at his pack. He struggled for balance and tried to clutch his few belongings. One hand fell to Heldenhaft.

With a snarl, Kati charged through the crowd to Beneban's side. Her bulk sent people flying in every direction. Her teeth bared, she struck right and left. The kalting's heavy head, flail-like on her supple neck, beat the mob back.

A rumble like thunder heralded Trog's arrival. He hoisted two wretches on the outer edge of the mob and used them to batter a path to his charges.

"This man is a wizard," Trog roared. "He is under protection of the Grand Lar."

The mob growled, loath to be cheated of its prey. For a moment longer, they pressed forward. Beneban saw the animal hunger in the mob of faces and smelled the desperation for anything that would relieve their misery.

"Draw your sword, sir," Trog muttered urgently.

Beneban dragged Heldenhaft from her sheath and swung her over his head. Amber lightning shimmered along the blade's length. She keened, and her song cut through the noise of the crowd.

"Wizard," began the whisper. "Magic sword." The words flew from person to person.

The crowd melted away, slowly at first, then in clots and bunches until finally the wizard, Ogdol, and kalting stood alone but for the Worf child crouched in a doorway. The waif carefully picked the last crumbs of travel cake from its rags.

As they stood, breathless, the child looked up. The emaciated face was split by a bright smile of thanks, untouched by the near-tragedy it had caused.

"Thank you for coming back," Beneban said to the Ogdol, as he slowly sheathed the mighty sword.

"I did not wish to face the captain without you," Trog rumbled and glanced slightly aside. "If ever you are alone in this area, remember that you might better dam a flood with a pebble than try to feed one child among so many."

"I'll remember," Beneban agreed fervently.

"Stay close now!" The Ogdol trundled off, not backward, the wizard reminded himself, for no direction was truly backward to this remarkable new acquaintance.

LARLINGARDE WAS BUILT on a massive terraced hill, and the hill was topped by the royal palace. As they climbed, hovels gave way to neat cottages. Businesses looked more prosperous, and the people they passed were dressed in better clothes. Once, a Larlinga noble trotted by, followed by armed retainers. He rode a fine kelsh, and his rainbow cloak of Worf cloth fluttered in the breeze as he passed. Many nobles moved from place to place on the covered skyways. Only the young who sought adventure or those who started a journey, descended to the streets.

They passed several large brick buildings that lined one side of the road. Their doors and windows were open to the spring day. Such a clamor emanated from these that Beneban stopped to peer through an open door.

"'Ere, you! Get out o' there. No'un don't need your nose inter Ka'amfer's business." Beneban was shoved sharply, and a burly Othring with coarse features thrust himself between the wizard and a brief glimpse of huge, noisy machines. The guard shook a stout club and made as if to grab the intruder.

Kati spun at his first words and thrust herself between Beneban and the Othring. Her snarl stopped the guard's reach for her friend.

"We mean no harm." Trog had reversed direction again. Now he stood behind Beneban. "This is my friend's first visit to the city. He is merely curious about your mill."

"Don't need curtiotissy 'ere, we don't," the guard snarled. He backed away, lowered his stick, and disappeared as the comrades moved on.

"Trog, I'd never survive my first day in Larlingarde if it weren't for you," Beneban said when they had climbed in silence for a while. He noticed that Kati's limp had mysteriously disappeared when the Othring had threatened. Now, at a touch from Trog, she resumed her supposed injury, and used the slower pace to rubberneck about, both curious and watchful.

"You grew up in the north, did you not?" asked Trog after a bit.

"Yes, in Andeling. How did you guess? I'm more familiar with plains and mountains than cities. But about the mill... What kind of mill? Why was that guard so belligerent?"

"It is a fabric mill. What do you know about Othrings?"

"Not much." Beneban stepped aside as three young nobles pranced past on frisky kelsh. They didn't glance at the pedestrians and scarcely curbed their steeds' high spirits to a pace more suitable for city travel.

"Not much," the wizard repeated once they were safe from being trampled. "I know that Othrings landed on Larlion in strange ships several generations ago. Lost from their home country, they settled here. They brought mechanical knowledge foreign to the Larlinga and diseases which wiped some of the native population out until crossbreeding developed stronger stock and immunities developed." Beneban continued, as though quoting from a book. "They have no magic, nor do their cross-blood descendants. They are shorter than typical Larlinga, and stouter. Genetically their blood dominates so that, though offspring are taller and more slender, and sometimes of darker skin, hair and eye color is usually the ordinary Othring brown..."

"Stop!" A rumbling laugh shook Trog. "I forgot that wizards are also scholars. When you say, 'not much,' this means the Othrings are not your special field of study?"

"Well, yes." Two frown lines etched between Beneban's brows.

"So you know all the history. What do you know of their character?"

"Very little." Under Trog's expectant gaze, Beneban flushed. "Say rather, nothing at all. I talk too much."

Again he heard Trog's laughter rumble. "To know about a wild kalting, you must understand teeth and claws. To know about Othrings, you must understand greed. To lack this knowledge, in either instance, is to become prey."

"Then please inform me about greed, Trog," Beneban said with a trace of humility, and the Ogdol laughed once more. "And what, please, is a mill?" the wizard added.

"It is a place to make cloth. Not such cloth as the Worfs make, beautiful, tightly woven, nearly indestructible, rather cloth like the rags those by the gate wore, making up in garish color what it lacks in value."

"But who would have such when Worf cloth is available?"

"Many people. Othrings are good not only at machinery, but at making others want what they sell. Many people now want different dress for every day of the month, each of different cut and color, because the Othrings have made it fashionable."

"These mills, they make cloth quickly?" Beneban's glance showed a dawning awareness.

"The machines make in one day more bolts of cloth than a whole Worf family makes in a year.

"I see." Now they passed through neat narrow streets overhung by deep green arcal trees. High walls encircled small estates. Beneban glimpsed luxurious homes behind the open gates, elegantly landscaped with fountains and green lawns.

Kati stretched her neck toward the gates. She smelled the green life closed away from them. The wizard scratched the place beneath her horn. "I think she misses the wilderness," Beneban said.

"Yes. A different sort of wilderness is here," Trog said.

"But then," Beneban pursued Trog's previous comments, "If the mills make rapidly what the citizens want to buy, why do they need guards? And who is Ka'amfer, whose mill is so well guarded?"

"These questions need many words. Briefly, all the money from the mills goes into the owner's pocket. The workers make starvation wages and work day and night. One day a month is all the time allowed them to spend with their families."

"But that's slavery."

"Less or more than slavery; they are paid a pittance. Also, no one cares."

Ahead, the road was blocked by a glorious wall of rough blocks of rose quartz and crystal which sparkled in the sunlight. Behind it the spires and pinnacles of the Grand Lar's palace soared to the sky, washed by Asolum's light.

"Come," Trog said. He led the wizard along a path that followed this wall. "We will reach the barracks through the back gate."

"All right." Beneban and Kati kept pace on the wide path. "But tell me, Trog, why don't the mill workers rebel? Couldn't they sabotage their work place?"

"Most of them are too beaten down to cause trouble on their own. There are some who hold that if they band together they could get a decent wage. These organizers, they're called, would cause destruction to make mill owners listen."

"And Ka'amfer is a mill owner?"

"Ka'amfer is a member of the Advisory Council. He is Advocate to the Grand Lar, and the largest mill owner in Larlion."

"And therefore a prime target for the org-anizers?" Beneban stumbled over the strange word. "But surely one would not walk up to the mill in daylight to do damage?"

"No," Trog agreed. "But the mills have caused many Worfs to become beggars or, as is more to their talent, thieves to survive. Worfs would rather steal than beg. They would prefer to earn an honest living and sell Worf cloth than either. Some would like to cause trouble for the mills."

Trog rounded a corner of the wall and tapped three times at a small gate. It was opened by an old fellow in a guard uniform.

"Eh, you be in trouble, Trog, when th' cap'n sees you. He thinks you and this 'un have scarpered. Ehhh! Look at 'er now." The guard went down on one knee before Kati and held his hand out, palm up.

Kati grumbled in her throat. She nosed at the hand and then permitted it to move up to scratch the base of her horn.

"We will be in my quarters, Gorm, if anyone asks you. You seem to have made a friend."

"Eyahh," the old trooper sighed. "I never seen a prettier lady nor her since my Kenda was killed. Is she yours, now, Trog?"

"No. The kalting belongs to my companion. Beneban, meet Gorm. He tends the gates and helps in the stables."

"Hello, Gorm." Beneban smiled at the old guard.

"Then your Kenda was a kalting?"

"Aye. I was a member of the Grand Lar's Kaltingcorps when I was young. I got this," he indicated a pinned-up sleeve where one arm was missing, "and lost my Kenda in the same battle against the Baelings when I was young. Is it a new recruit you'll be, sir?"

"I don't think so…"

"We'll take Kati to my quarters, Gorm," Trog interrupted.

"O' course, sir. She'll not go to th' stable like a common beast."

Trog urged Beneban along a path toward some long low buildings in the distance, calling goodbye to the old guard as they went.

"He will talk all day if you will stay," the Ogdol rumbled. "Still, he is a good man to have as a friend."

"When you and Kati agree," Beneban answered, "I'd be foolish to argue. But continue about Worfs and mills. No one could mistake me for a four-foot-tall Worf."

One amused Ogdol eye scanned Beneban's six foot two inches of height. "No," he conceded. "You could not be a Worf. But the mills have so many ill-wishers that their guards challenge anyone who comes without authorization."

Trog pushed open a blue door at the far end of the barracks. His voice was suddenly formal. "Here are my quarters, sir."

Standing in the doorway, Beneban surveyed the large clean room. Its only light entered from a slit window high on the wall. A musty smell of old grain was overlaid by old smoke from a small fireplace.

"Are you an officer, Trog, to have so large a place to yourself?"

"Nominally, I am an officer." At Beneban's look, he continued. "By making me a junior officer, they can give me a separate room. This solves the problem that would arise should others be required to share their space with me."

The Ogdol moved to the center of his room. Though his voice was unemotional, his eye was fixed on the window. Beneban recognized a raised barrier in his suddenly stiff words.

The wizard scanned the room, scrubbed and tidy with a sleeping platform neatly made up to one side. He looked again at the white giant, motionless in the gloom. Was it reluctance to share his space, or…

Beneban made a quick decision.

"Trog, I'm not sure how long they'll leave me free to choose, but if you don't mind a potential prisoner for a roommate, Kati and I would like to stay here until they drag us off."

Trog turned a little away.

This gesture, Beneban had learned, meant the Ogdol wanted to hide awkward emotion. Trog busied himself to light a small lamp. When he spoke, his voice, always a rumble, was husky. "I will be honored to share this space with you."

An hour later they had washed and brushed away the travel dust. Now they relaxed in comfort by the cheerful warmth of a small fire. Both were startled when someone pounded on the door.

"Ah. They have remembered us." Trog rumbled to his feet from a pallet on the floor and unbarred the door.

Backed by the arrogant young adjutant, the stubby figure of Captain Glaynar slowly lowered a fist raised to pound again. His face was dark with fury. Long mustaches twitched with a life of their own. *"You! Trog! Where have you been with this prisoner?"* he snarled. "You were to report last night."

Prisoner, sir? Did I misunderstand?" Trog asked blandly. "I believed I was to escort the gentleman for his protection."

"Well... Well! You didn't misunderstand my meaning. Where have you been?"

"Kati was limping." Beneban spoke lazily from a comfortable sling chair by the fire. "She wouldn't travel. I stayed with her. As Trog felt disinclined to carry us both, he stayed also. We came on this morning, though she is still somewhat lame."

Kati waved one paw in the air and snorted softly.

"Nonsense!" the captain sneered. "What is this tale you ask me to believe?"

Slowly Beneban came to his feet. The eyes that now transfixed the captain were the deep amber of an imminent storm. "Nonsense?" he queried coldly. "Tale?"

So icy was his tone that the captain took a quick step backward, bumping into the adjutant, who hastily whispered in Glaynar's ear.

"D-did I say nonsense? I mean to say, er, Humber here says the kalting was limping this morning."

"Trog said the kalting was limping. I *also* said the kalting was limping." The wizard's voice was as frigid as the winter wind blowing off the Kalds.

"Yes, yes. I mean to say, this morning when you

should have followed Humber, the kalting... You lagged behind."

The captain fell silent, tangled in nervous explanation. He stumbled another anxious step backward. The adjutant covered a yelp as his foot was impaled by a boot.

Captain Glaynar rubbed a stiff spot where his neck cricked from staring up at Beneban. "You fell behind."

"That is correct," the wizard confirmed. "We fell behind."

"Well!" Suddenly aware of his dignity, Glaynar pulled his stout body stiffly erect. "Move back," he snapped at his adjutant. A glint of malice lit his eyes as he returned his gaze to Beneban. "You are *all* summoned to audience with His Mightiness, the Grand Lar, directly after the dinner hour, when he will be pleased to hear your defense."

"Defense for what?" asked Beneban.

"You are charged with treason," said the captain. He made no effort to hide the nasty smirk on his face.

"Treason?" Now Trog loomed over the captain, who quickly backed out the door.

"The Grand Lar commands!" Glaynar peered back in at them. "You are under house arrest until that time."

The Captain punctuated his news with a slam of the door, leaving Trog and Beneban staring at one another.

A rumble began deep in the Ogdol's chest. As it grew to a full rolling laugh, Beneban's face relaxed into a smile of unpracticed, lopsided warmth.

"At least we are invited for *after* the meal," Trog

gasped between rolls of laughter. "He doesn't plan to roast and eat us."

"We might be scheduled as dessert," Beneban said more soberly. This set sent the Ogdol into another bout of laughter. Beneban, caught up in the contagion, was forced to chuckle.

Kati stared from one to the other in solemn puzzlement. A glance at her serious stare only increased the hilarity.

CHAPTER 9

Several hours later, in a more somber mood, they opened the door again to Captain Glaynar's knock.

In the intervening time, Trog had persuaded a guard to bring hot water. Now, bathed and dressed in his court clothes and wizard's cloak, Beneban looked formidable. He was rewarded by the captain's startled surprise. The pompous officer suddenly lost his air of superiority. Beneban was pleased by the officer's sudden nervousness.

Captain Glaynar pulled himself together with a visible effort. "What right have you to the scarlet cloak?" he demanded officiously.

"The right of birth and schooling, captain. Would you like proof?"

"I... It won't help you at this court to claim such rank," Glaynar said, and backed a nervous step. "His Mightiness hates wizards."

"Perhaps, yet I am a wizard, and this is where I must be," Beneban said soberly.

"Then come," the captain ordered. A thought made him blink then smirk as he turned.

Now Trog eyed the wizard enigmatically. "I hope you are wise. My people say, 'It is dull play to wager the bones if they be thine own.'" He gently pushed the wizard through the door and followed with Kati, who again limped slightly.

Troopers, sharp in blue and silver, formed a hollow square about them. Though some cast their charges a nervous look, they marched smartly toward the glistening walls of the palace.

Beneban looked about with interest. Even on this, the lowest level where they entered, the corridors were high and airy. Walls were crafted of stone that glowed from within. From floor to floor, narrow staircases were replaced by wider flights in colored marble. The pearlescent color of these walls was spaced by drapes of richly embroidered Worf cloth.

At length they entered the expansive reception chamber that led to the dining hall.

Guards at the closed double doors dropped halberds bannered in black to bar their way. Each helm also carried a black feather, a display of mourning, Beneban guessed, for the Torlarya and her husband.

"Who approaches the Grand Lar's table?" An officer of the Guard stepped out to face Captain Glaynar. His rank was marked by the short blue cape that fluttered from one shoulder.

"I bring those commanded to appear before His Mightiness, Lyolar, the Grand Lar, at this hour." Glaynar's voice steadied on the formality of the phrases.

"How are they called?" The officer consulted a short list held in one gloved hand.

"Here are Trog, an Ogdol in the Grand Lar's troops, and Beneban, a stranger."

"And Kati," Trog added.

"Kati? I have no 'Kati' on my list!" The officer peered at the group with suspicion.

Captain Glaynar glowered up at Trog. "Kati is the kalting," he explained angrily. "She is companion to this Beneban."

"I have no instructions about a kalting, and this stranger wears the garb of a wizard. There is nothing here about a wizard."

"Well, you'd better *get* instructions," Glaynar hissed. "This wizard *is* the Beneban on your list. The kalting is his companion. I don't plan to forcibly separate them unless at His Mightiness's specific command."

A muffled rumble from Trog made Beneban glance around, but the Ogdol appeared impassive as usual.

"Wait here." The officers turned sharply on one heel, and halberds lifted to let him pass. They snapped down as he pushed through the elaborate doors. A subdued murmur from the room beyond was clipped off as they swung shut.

Tension stretched the wait. Captain Glaynar paced two steps left, right, left with his agitation increased by the wait. His heels snapped rhythmically. Kati's great head moved left, right, left to follow him until at last, with an angry curse, Glaynar stopped with his back to the group.

Trog seemed rooted to the floor. His three eyes seemed to simultaneously look at nothing and everything. Beneban's posture was relaxed. His height and natural grace lent him an air of unconcern. One hand lay on Kati's ruff. The great beast grew still at his touch. Only the twitching end of her tail showed her unease.

Guards and troopers faced each other across the tessellated floor in impassive silence. Waiting on superiors was a game at which they had practice.

Suddenly the silence was broken by a bellow from the room beyond. *"Well, bring them in, fool!"*

The noise seemed to blast the double doors open, so rapidly did the Guards' officer reappear.

"Follow me," he ordered crisply. His face shone ashen in the flickering light.

The halberds rose, and the doors swung wide. The officer's voice intoned solemnly from beyond.

"I ask to present thy servants, Captain Glaynar of the Grand Lar's troops, Trog, an Ogdol, also of the Grand Lar's troops, Beneban, a... wizard, and Kati, the kalting who companions him. Stand forward, servants, and be seen by thy master, Lyolar, Grand Lar of Larlion."

THE SMALL COMPANY entered a cavernous room and approached the open end of a U-shaped table. It had been carved from three entire magnificent trees. Each section was covered with elegant Worf cloth, finely embroidered to simulate a garden in full bloom. On the flanking walls, fireplaces spread light and heat. Overhead, huge ivory beams crossed and re-crossed at double Beneban's height. At each intersection hung lamps of faceted crystal and jewels that fragmented light into a rainbow of color.

Beneban, in his scarlet cloak and silver-gray clothes, shimmergreen hair that lifted softly about his head in the draft, had the look of a flaming lance in the shadows. He stood motionless to gaze at the scene.

Along the table they were flanked by the Larlinga, the nobility of Larlion, male and female alike. Tall and beautiful, the men had copper skins and shimmergreen hair. The women were more golden of color, also with the true Larlinga hair. Beneban's eyes passed thoughtfully up the length of one wall. He noted that each member of this exclusive dinner was dressed in black.

At length, his gaze reached the head of the room.

Here the table had been rolled away. The Grand Lar, dressed in his house colors of blue and silver, sat on an elaborate throne on a dais above the court. His gaze waited impatiently until Beneban turned to him.

With the shock of power meeting power, their eyes clashed. After a moment Lyolar turned away with a frown to talk to the man on his left.

Captain Glaynar, who had started forward, scurried back to the group. "Wait. Wait until he commands us," he hissed as though the others had followed him down the floor.

Beneban stood, relaxed, and continued to observe the people and the dining hall's magnificent appointments. Trog and Kati stood motionless beside him.

The Grand Lar whispered urgently to the only man at the table who was not a Larlinga. Short and elderly, he was dressed in a plain rough robe of black zarweave. The humble cloth contrasted with the neighboring richness. His face wore a permanent smile that showed sharp, uneven teeth. Though he nodded and bobbed in response to Lyolar's words, Beneban felt that those sharp eyes weighed him as he might an opponent.

Beyond him sat a woman, exotic by comparison to others at the table. Apparently of mixed blood, she was shorter than ladies of the Larlinga. Yet her slender form excited interest by its tininess. Her brown hair shone, a cascade that reflected every shift of the light that splattered on gleaming jewels and shining paint.

Beneban noted servants flattened along each wall, holding candelabra which flickered and danced as they breathed. The beams overhead caught and reflected the glow and pulsed with a gentle light of their own.

Still the Grand Lar ignored them, and the wizard's mind drifted. Light, vision, a gentle fragrance... For a moment he felt himself in a wooded glade before a tidy cottage. The door was about to open...

"Why should you not die here, *on this spot*, wizard?" The harsh, deep voice of the Grand Lar brought Beneban quickly back to the dining hall. "My youngest sister died at the hands of a treacherous wizard," Lyolar snarled. "Now at the death of my oldest sister, another wizard presides. Why should I not kill you where you stand?" he hissed, rising slightly from his throne to better see the small group.

"Because I am complicit in neither death, my Lar, save that I tried to prevent the second." Beneban's voice was rock steady as he refused to be intimidated.

"Assassins set upon a peaceful party that traveled the safe lands between Larlingarde and Torgarde. A strange wizard, if wizard you be in truth, appears from nowhere. When the evil is done, he alibis himself. He has destroyed the incriminating witnesses... All but *one!*" The Grand Lar's voice rose to a roar. His copper face, suffused with blood, was burnt orange.

Lyolar lunged to the edge of the dais. "I say you *lie!* I say you plot against me. Guards, slay this man!"

Behind Beneban. the door burst open.

Kati crouched, prepared to launch herself. Trog lumbered forward a step. On every side, Larlinga were leaping to their feet, reaching for weapons which had been left in their rooms.

Beneban made a gathering motion with his fingers then cast them out in a circle about his head. Sparks showered the room to alight on all present.

All motion was frozen.

The light from the candelabra was still. Fragmented rainbows hung in colored shards of brilliance.

Only the Grand Lar and Beneban himself were free of the spell. The Grand Lar darted a quick glance about him. The angry blood faded from his face, replaced by gray fright. Still he stood his ground.

"So, wizard," he hissed. The sound was loud in the absolute silence of the hall. "You prove I'm right. Your next move will be to kill me, I presume."

CHAPTER 10

THE GRAND LAR darted a quick glance about him. Beneban was stunned by the terror in the ruler's eyes but impressed that Lyolar yet held his ground.

"So, wizard," Lyolar repeated. His voice was a harsh whisper, loud in the absolute silence of the hall. "Why do you wait? Now you will kill me, I presume."

"Not so, my lar." Beneban's calm voice bounced gentle echoes in the silent room. "I come only to serve you." The wizard turned and took the sword from the scabbard of the captain frozen a few steps behind him. He reversed it, and strode back to stop before the trembling ruler. Lyolar, white with fear, had not fled, had not sought to escape. He held his ground.

Beneban dropped to one knee and held the weapon up, laid across both hands, an offering of trust and, perhaps, of life.

"What is this, then?" Lyolar's green eyes glared into the amber depths of the wizard's eyes. He was angry now, but still nervous.

"If you wish my death, it is yours. I was born a wizard, as you were born to be Grand Lar. If this fault seems sufficient, strike now. I offer you my death, but I would prefer to offer you my life. I have done nothing to deserve your hatred."

The Grand Lar grasped the sword's hilt and weighed the weapon. "You make a basic error. I have no need for a wizard."

Beneban's eyes held on his. He didn't flinch as the ruler's muscles bunched.

Beneath the table at the side, a silk-shod foot twitched.

The blade swung up, held briefly at the apex before it flashed downward.

As it passed, a breeze kissed Beneban's cheek. The sharp edge shaved the sleeve from his upper arm and buried itself in the floor an inch from his knee.

Still, Beneban's eyes met the those of the ruler. Now a flash of something else, admiration perhaps, and a touch of humor danced in the royal gaze.

"I *can*," said the Grand Lar, "use a captain who fights as ten men and fears nothing." Lyolar repeated the words of the slain woman's retainers.

"Say rather, Your Mightiness, a man who knows when it is useless to flee." Beneban ignored the warm trickle of blood that soaked the silk of his sleeve. It preceded the protest of outraged flesh.

"You were afraid?"

"Death is but a turning of the page of life. Still, I prefer to await that turn."

"You *were* afraid?" This time the challenge was a warning.

"All men fear you, my lar. If you allow me to rise, my knees will quiver as those of a maid at her first kiss."

The Grand Lar's laugh boomed, and again Beneban glimpsed a foot moving beneath the table, a tiny foot, daintily slippered.

"Then *rise*, Beneban. Will you take my commission as captain of a troop?"

Beneban rose gracefully and stood, head bowed now, before the Grand Lar. Blood dripped from his fingers to the floor in slow droplets.

"I will, Your Mightiness, if that is your wish. Though I have no training as a leader of warriors."

"Yet you inspire loyalty in those who fight with you. How do you suppose I heard that you fight as ten men?"

"Of course. Daram."

"Also Rad and Borno. Questioned separately and together, they swear to your valor. But where is the great amber sword?"

"I would not enter your presence bearing arms, my lar."

"Only such arms as a wizard bears at all times." The Grand Lar's face clouded as he glanced about at the frozen courtiers. Then, with a shake, he brightened again. "Never mind, I'll see the sword another time. Can you free my dinner guests? Or must they be set as statuary in my gardens and a new court found?"

Beneban bowed, hiding a wry twitch of his lips. "At your command, my lar," he said.

"Then *do* it!"

Beneban circled his hand once. It seemed to pull a network of sparks into his gathering fingers.

Candlelight and color flickered again. There was a stir of movement. Courtiers finished pushing back chairs then stood, uncertain of what they had been about to do.

Kati completed her crouch then growled in puzzlement. She sensed no threat now. Trog came to with a grunt. He assessed the scene and remained where he was.

The guards rushed forward. They were waved back by Lyolar. Slowly the court subsided into quiet expectancy.

"This man," said the Grand Lar into the tense silence, "has convinced me of his loyalty. I present him to the court, Captain Beneban of the Grand Lar's men-at-arms."

A surprised whisper stirred through the room. "Man-at-arms?"

"Captain?"

"Thought he was a wizard?"

"Silence! The rest of you are dismissed. Glaynar, Trog, report to me as usual at the morning briefing. Now go! You, Captain Beneban, attend me." The Grand Lar turned and disappeared through a curtain behind his chair.

Beneban looked about. Blood dripped from his fingertips. It had pooled on the floor. He met the quizzical brown eyes of the woman who sat near the throne.

"You'd best hurry," she murmured. "He can be... impatient."

Next to her, the old man in the shabby robe smirked. His eyes spoke of malevolence.

As he tried to exercise his weary control to abate the flow of blood, Beneban stepped hesitantly onto the dais and pushed back the curtain. As he swung the door behind it open, Kati sprang before him into the dark room beyond.

"Someday," Lyolar's voice came tense with suppressed temper, "you will tell me what adventure led a kalting to adopt you, wizard."

Hurrying after Kati, Beneban discovered the Grand Lar pressed to the wall. He confronted the big feline with a hand on his sword.

"*Kati!*" At the wizard's order, the kalting sat back. "Forgive her," he asked. "She has dragged me from the edge of disaster so often, she expects nothing else."

"You've a gift for inspiring loyalty, as I said." Lyolar's tone was acid.

A small boy, dressed in the royal blue and silver, slept soundly on a bench by a second door. The only light in the room was the even incandescence of the walls. Lyolar bent and shook the lad.

"Wake up, Mero. What watch do you keep at my back, so soundly asleep? This kalting could have eaten me. Up! Now!"

The boy sat up, rubbing his eyes, and Beneban noticed a slight webbing between his fingers. He abruptly realized where he was, stumbled to his feet, and stammered apologies as he dropped to one knee. Beneban smiled to see him keep an awed eye on the kalting.

"If you would be a leader one day," the Grand Lar said, "first you must learn to follow orders. Next time, stay awake!" The ruler's words were hard, but his voice was gentle. "Stand, Mero, and make your bow to Captain Beneban. Wizard, this is one of my fosterlings, the Lar Mero of Mergoling."

The boy stood with the easy grace peculiar to childhood. He bowed with the slight inclination proper from a young lar to an arms captain, bobbed up, bowed more deeply, then bobbed up again, puzzlement on his face.

"Well, Mero? Don't you know the proper homage due my captains yet?" The Grand Lar's voice was teasing.

"But, Uncle, he wears the wizard's cloak. He looks like a great lar."

"Your eyes are better than your ears." Now anger simmered beneath his words. "If I say he is a captain, then how should you greet him?"

"As a captain, Mightiness." Mero hung his head.

"And I do so say! At this time, in this place, this man is Beneban, a captain of my men-at-arms." Lyolar folded his arms and scowled at the page.

Mero quickly made the proper bow. Beneban returned it gravely, more deeply, as appropriate from a captain to a lar.

"Better. Much better."

"It is a pleasure, Lar Mero," Beneban said. "You are the first Mergol I have encountered outside of my books. Many people think your kind are legends."

"The common folk may think so," Lyolar said with a condescending sneer, "but we at Court know better." Dismissively, he turned from Beneban to Mero. "Now escort us to the Lar Tor's rooms."

"Th-Thank you, Mightiness." The small figure struggled with the massive door and braced his slight weight against it, feet spread wide, to keep it open as the others filed out.

The halls of the upper palace were narrower than those below in the public rooms. Short flights of steps down led to long flights up. They twisted and doubled back until even Beneban, with his sure sense of direction, would have had difficulty with the maze. Now weariness and pain sapped his ability.

The incandescence of the walls raced ahead of them as they climbed.

Beneban dared a look behind. He saw the light wink out within moments of their passing. He also saw in some consternation that a trail of blood marked his passing. The scratch received from the Grand Lar's test was deep.

Normally he would have stopped the blood with his will, but he'd spent his energy on the confrontation below. His power was at low ebb.

With his right hand he pulled up the torn sleeve and clasped it hard against the wound. Still, his mind was alert, observant in this new place. The corridor was lined with suites, he saw. Every fourth door was blazoned with the insignia of one of the Twelve Great Estates of Larlion.

Servants who hurried to turn down beds and lay out night garments paused as they passed. Deep curtsies hid faces that smiled wearily.

"Usually this wing is nearly deserted," Lyolar said. "This, however, is the time of OathGive. Many of my lars and their relatives are here still. Were it not for my sister's death…"

He strode on, frowning in thought, then continued.

"This is festival time. My nephew Tor stayed behind to enjoy the celebration when duty forced his parents to leave. Now he feels guilty for not being with them."

"He could not have known they would be attacked."

"No, and of course no one blames him. But you understand how the conscience stings when one is young." The Grand Lar paused before a green door bearing a golden shield. Emblazoned upon it was the ancient insignia of Torling Estate, a peganlion couchant crossed by a blazing sword.

Young Mero tapped on the wooden panel.

After several seconds it swung slowly open on a familiar face. Daram, eyes wide at the unexpected visitors, bowed low.

"Is my nephew abed?"

"No, Mightiness. He sits by the fire still."

"Well? May we enter?" Lyolar snapped the question.

Hastily, Daram backed from the door. He bowed deeply again, and Lyolar scowled.

"Don't know why Tor keeps such an oaf around," Lyolar grumbled. He brushed past the old man-at-arms. "He has a hundred servants better trained to grace his rooms."

"Perhaps he prefers honest rock at his back rather than feather pillows of false comfort," Beneban offered wryly.

Lyolar gave Beneban a sharp look then a nod. As Lyolar stepped away, Daram nodded.

They entered an interior room made bright with firelight. At Beneban's words the slouched figure before the fire raised his head slowly. Green eyes, unfocused at first, sharpened to attention.

"The stranger has the right of it, Uncle." Tor rose

stiffly. He was a lad yet, but grief carved early maturity on his face. He gave the Grand Lar formal homage, arms spread wide as he bowed.

Lyolar stepped forward, putting a heavy hand on each slight shoulder. "There is no need for formality between us, Tor, not in the privacy of your room. You are my heir, and now, the son I'll never have."

The young man stood motionless between his uncle's hands. A flush darkened his copper skin. Beneban, senses heightened from loss of blood and exhaustion, caught a brief flash of irritation that stiffened the lad.

It disappeared as the young lar backed gently to face his uncle, and Beneban was unsure where it had originated.

"Forgive me, Uncle," Tor said quietly. "Perhaps I am too recently orphaned to readily call another man father, though I thank you for the honor. Also..."

The lad turned a searching look on the wizard. "Also, we aren't alone."

"What? Oh, Beneban. Tor, this is the newest of my captains. Captain, as you have gathered, this is my nephew, the Lar Tor, heir to Torling, and one day to the throne of Larlion."

Beneban bowed low, his hand still clutching the bloody sleeve.

"You are welcome, Captain... Beneban? A strange name for a soldier, surely? But I'm not sure I understand, Uncle. Why you have brought him, a stranger, at this time..."

Lyolar sighed. "Tor, Captain Beneban and his kalting came to your parents' assistance yesterday, or tried to."

"You!" Tor grabbed the wizard's hands and plunged to one knee. Gratitude poured from the lad, girded by grief and weighted with such shame it nearly swept Beneban from his feet.

"That *you* should bow to me," he stammered. "You, who were where I *should* have been, fighting to save my parents. How can I right this obligation?"

Beneban's amber eyes met Lyolar's irate green ones across the young lar's head.

"A gift for inspiring loyalty," the Grand Lar hissed.

"But my loyalty is yours, Mightiness." Beneban urged Tor to his feet. "There's no reason to kneel to me, sir. I did what anyone would do in defense of a lady."

"The lady was my mother. If ever there is aught you need... You are wounded!" Tor stared at the blood that stained his hand and reached for Beneban's arm. He rounded on Lyolar.

"Uncle! Surely someone might have tended his wounds? Do you care so little for the one who defended your sister?"

"Easy, lad!" Beneban urged caution softly. "This isn't left from yesterday. It's a scratch I got today."

"Tor!" Lyolar snapped in anger. "You will wish to ask the captain about the battle yesterday. I'll leave *you* to care for his arm."

Lyolar spun on his heel. Kati, crouched in the doorway, twitched her tail and stretched, lifting her great head to stare at him. Lyolar met her green eyes. He stopped as they measured each other.

Lyolar reached a tentative hand to the golden horn. Her great head dipped to accept his touch. Then the

Grand Lar ignored the startled bows and murmurs behind him. He stalked from the room. The heavy outer door crashed closed behind him.

Mero, asleep against the wall, sprang to belated attention.

"Oh! I've been asleep again. He'll skin me for certain."

"Wait, Mero!" Tor ordered the lad.

Poised for flight, Mero turned hesitantly to Tor. The young lar continued, "Daram, get a bottle of Torleus '32 for the boy. Take it to my uncle, Mero, and tell him I kept you behind to send this gift. It's a favorite of his. He won't believe your tale, but he won't skin you tonight, either."

Mero took the dusty bottle in hands that shook and looked his wordless thanks.

"Never mind," Tor grinned. "I used it myself as a page to escape a punishment or two."

As Daram opened the door, Mero darted away at a trot. He stopped at Tor's next words.

"Mero, do *not* run! He won't thank you if it gets shaken. Go on now."

Daram held the door for the boy.

"And Mero!" Tor snapped, as the lad turned. "Next time, stay awake."

"Yes sir. Thank you, cousin." The boy bobbed a cautious bow. He held the bottle cradled in his arms and disappeared as Daram closed the door behind him.

"Well, he forgot to say goodnight to you." Tor grinned at Beneban. "But it's his first week as page. He'll do better once he gets used to the hours kept by the court. Now," the young lar's face sobered, "we'll care for that arm. Daram, bring water, bandages, and whatever is needed to tend this wound. Captain, come. Sit here in front of the fire."

"It's only a scratch, sir."

"A scratch that's left blood puddled on my floor. You're already weak with its loss. My uncle," Tor pushed Beneban gently into a cushioned armchair, "can wear on the nerves."

Tor ignored the wizard's protests as he gently sponged the matted silk free of the bloody gash. Finally, Beneban gave up argument. The room spun gently, so he closed his eyes. The woody tang of the fire was replaced by a sharp smell of disinfectant that roused him abruptly. He opened his eyes to see Daram pour it onto his wound.

And the room tore loose from its moorings at the sharp bite of the medicine. With the sudden pain, the room swooped wildly, and he was flung away into darkness.

FOREST LADY PACED the boundaries of her cottage as a caged animal remembering freedom tests the limits of its confinement over and over.

"Saray, he is injured. I must go to him."

"Patience, Rayni," the old nurse soothed. "Try first to see if he is truly in need."

The girl closed her hand about the green stone at her throat. Her eyes, wide open as it flickered to life, stared across the miles.

"I can't tell," she finally moaned. Her head bowed.

"He is gone."

"Gone? Not dead?"

"No!" Then, with a breath that was nearly a sob she added, "I don't think so. It's as if... When I lose contact, it is as if he has moved to another place, one I cannot reach. He has shut me out."

Old Saray rocked and thought. Finally she spoke. "He is dealing with a new world, Rayni. He will not forget you, but first he must gain his balance."

"I know." The girl sank to the floor at her feet and looked up at the kindly scarred face. "But he is so far away. Won't he change? A new place, a new life. How will I know him? I hardly know him now." Tears filled her gray eyes. Her shimmergreen hair cascaded across her nurse's knees.

The old woman's wrinkled hand hovered then rested lightly on the young head. There was a long silence.

"Saray? Is loving always pain?"

"Child, you have hardly touched pain," her nurse said firmly. "This is only waiting."

Rayni wept softly, her head on her nurse's knee. Saray let the sound hang in the air a while before she spoke. She drew memory from a time in her own past.

"Child, love is excitement, like a mountain of presents on Greening Day, and the surety your heart's desire is in the pile. And somewhile it is pain, too, to tear the heart from your body and leave you to go on, bereft. But if it is true, if you be lucky, it is also moments of joy when every leaf and flower is painted more brightly because two of you see it together. Flowers perfume the air just for two. The sunrise colors only for you and your love. If you know only a moment or two of such joy, Rayni, 'tis worth all it may cost."

The old woman's words fell softly. When Saray finished speaking, the gentle echo of two women, lost in reverie, filled the room.

CHAPTER 11

Beneban wakened to the sweet smell of wine. He sensed he was in an unknown place. He stayed motionless, eyes closed, and sought a memory of where he had come to. The last time consciousness had deserted him had been...

"You have a nasty gash," said a cheerful voice at his elbow, "but nothing vital seems to be severed."

The wizard turned his head slowly against soft cushions. A young Larlinga, slender and tall, clothed in sober mourning, lounged across from him. In one hand he held a goblet carved in intricate patterns from some pale green crystal. This was... "The Lar Tor," he croaked.

A nod acknowledged his name. "You've been far away, captain. I take it your wound was a *test* by my uncle? He could have killed you."

Beneban's wide mouth quirked as memory returned. "Nay, had he tried to dismember me, he'd have succeeded. I offered no defense."

"But why, then?"

"The problem seemed to be that I sought the position of Court Wizard."

"And?"

"He prefers inept officers to competent wizards."

"I should have attended this evening's meal," Tor said wistfully. "To miss the beginning of a legend is a heavy penalty for choosing my own company tonight."

Beneban chuckled. "You exaggerate, I think. I am no legend, merely a wizard seeking work, sir." He struggled to get to his feet and offer a proper bow to the young noble.

"Stop!" The young man straightened in his chair and reached a hand to restrain his guest. "You remind me of my uncle's reason for bringing you. Between us there can be no 'sir.' To you I am, forever, just Tor, the grateful son of those you tried to save."

"Your uncle won't be pleased with that," Beneban said wryly. As the young man's face gathered into a scowl, he added hastily, "I am honored, Tor, but..."

"In light of the service you've done my house, no one can object to our friendship. Unless... you don't wish to be my friend?" Though Tor was a man, for a moment an insecure lad shadowed his countenance.

"Nonsense." Beneban was strangely moved. "I said I would be honored, Tor."

"So that is settled." Tor reached across to touch the wizard's arm where it lay along the chair rest. "Now, will you tell me about... my parents?"

"It's a short, unhappy tale. I'd stopped for early supper when your lady mother screamed. Kati and I..."

"Kati? Oh, your beast."

"Is she?" Beneban looked at the kalting reclining before the fire. "Or perhaps I am hers. In any case, we raced around the road's bend into the midst of battle. Your father was down, your mother holding him.

"Several of her retainers were down," he continued. "The three left were holding off eight remaining assassins with difficulty. Kati and I and an Ogdol named Trog, with the advantage of surprise, turned the battle. But there is one thing I don't understand."

"What?"

"Your mother... She was holding your father strongly as I arrived. She seemed unharmed. I swear no one approached her. But then, as the battle ended, she was mortally injured."

"Could she have taken the wound earlier?"

"The wound would have killed a strong man quickly, or so I thought. Yet I see no other answer."

After a little silence, Tor, with an effort, seemed to push away gloom. He sprang to his feet.

"I forget the duties of hosting. Let me pour you some wine. It's the same Torleus '32 just sent to my uncle. Well worth tasting."

"Nay, Tor. I'll never find the barracks if I take wine. This place is a maze to me cold sober."

"Nonsense. One glass will strengthen you, and Daram will see you safely home."

The young noble filled a crystal goblet from an encrusted bottle and brought it to the wizard. Beneban's fingers delighted in the shape, a cupped blossom. His eyes followed the dancing bubbles of the wine, a delicate green. The aroma was the fragrance of late summer, ripe fruit, the buzzing of greensters in sunlit orchards. He sipped appreciatively.

Tor sank into the other chair with his refilled glass. "It's fortunate my uncle got your left arm. You'd have trouble wielding that great sword Borno raves about, otherwise."

Beneban chuckled wryly. "Trouble enough, Tor. Wizards are left-handed. Being named captain by your uncle doesn't seem to have changed that. Between this wine and my arm, I'll be fortunate to get out of my clothes tonight, much less wield a sword."

"Your servant?"

"I have none."

"That's quickly mended. Daram?" Tor raised his voice, ignoring Beneban's startled protest.

The old man-at-arms appeared quickly in the doorway to the next room. "Sir?"

"Rouse Borno from his bed. I've an assignment he'll be glad to take."

"Aye, sir." The man disappeared, ignoring Beneban's attempt to reason with Tor.

"Tor, I can't afford a servant."

"If that were true, I'd lend him to you until you could. However, a captain's pay is ample to support several servants. You must have at least one or lose face with your peers. Besides, Borno would cheerfully serve you for nothing. Your name and deeds have been ceaselessly on his tongue since he returned."

"Boys are easily impressed," Beneban said. Suddenly the hair pricked on the nape of his neck. "Tor, someone else is in your sleeping chamber." Kati's snarl confirmed his suspicion.

"What?" The young lar leapt to his feet and whirled, a wrist dagger in his hand as though by magic. Then, with a small laugh, he relaxed.

"Come in here, you scamp. 'Tis only Calibe," he explained as the strange Worf edged into the room from the dark beyond.

"Only Calibe," the Worf whined. "Only Calibe, who waits to serve his lar. Calibe, forgotten by everyone now that his mistress has been killed by an *unknown* assassin!"

The misshapen figure scuttled over to the fire and crouched there with a nod of his head to Tor. He darted a malevolent scowl at Beneban and Kati.

The kalting raised her head and stared at him. Calibe quickly moved farther from her.

"Forgotten? Nonsense," Tor said impatiently. "You have a pallet in my own bedroom. You are hardly forgotten. He was so woebegone," Tor explained to Beneban, "I saw no solution but to give him a place with my followers."

"A generous act. I can see it is the only solution for one so supposedly loyal to your mother," Beneban said wryly.

"Supposedly! Supposedly?" Calibe screeched. He leapt to his feet and pulled his small sword from its sheath. In fury, he hopped up and down. "Does the wizard bardack suggest I am less than loyal? I? I, who alone slew my larya's assassin." He darted toward Beneban.

The wizard lurched to his feet and groped for a sword removed before the supper. Calibe scrambled around and leapt onto Beneban's chair.

Kati leapt toward the Worf and her master in an explosion of snarls, but Tor was quicker.

As Beneban spun to meet the threat, the young lar was already behind the chair. He grabbed the small figure by the back of his vest and hoisted him into the air where Calibe kicked and howled. Tor's face was flushed with anger.

"You *dare* to attack my guest?" he demanded as he shook Calibe. "This man is my trusted friend. No one calls him *bardack* or *any* manner of evil without feeling the weight of my anger, Worf!"

Over the creature's kicks and squeals, Beneban's calm voice lifted.

"He didn't actually harm me, Tor, and he says only what all men know of wizards, to call me a 'bardack,' a motherless son. I take no offense," Beneban added quietly, as with one hand on Kati's neck, his voice calmed the sudden furor.

"Offense was intended," Tor growled. He gave Calibe another shake.

"P-pardon, lar." Now tears poured down the Worf's cheek. "Forgive a poor creature, demented by his great loss, d-demented, I say, b-by…"

"*Enough!*" Goblets shivered on a corner table at Tor's bellow. "No one ever accused your people of excessive wit, but if *I* am not demented by this loss, surely *you* can retain the little sense you own."

Kati decided her help was unnecessary. As Tor dropped the now limp Calibe to the floor, the kalting sat, idly licked a paw, then pulled it over her ear. Her eyes, however, never left the chastened servant.

"Yes, Lar. Yes." The Worf groveled at Tor's feet. "If the noble wizard, who just *happened* to appear before your mother's death, is your friend, *your* friend, I say, then…"

"*Be still!*" The young lar roared.

The inner door of the room was flung open as Daram and Borno rushed into the room, swords drawn.

"What is it, my lar?"

"We heard you call out." Their eyes searched the room for a threat. They finally focused on the Worf where he cowered at Tor's feet.

"It is nothing," Tor growled. "Only this pestiferous creature of my mother's. Daram, he will sleep in the guardroom with you tonight."

Calibe howled grievously. "Don't banish me, great lar. Do not send Calibe away, or I perish."

"If you survive till morning, you may return to my service, but if I hear another word from you tonight, you'll perish sooner than you expect. Daram, take him down. When you return, you and Borno will escort the captain to his quarters.

"Aye, my lar. Come, you." The old warrior bundled Calibe briskly through the door, which slammed behind them.

Now Tor turned to Borno. "Put your sword away, lad. I've an assignment I think you will enjoy." He turned and saw the wizard's pale face.

"Beneban, sit down before you fall, man. Come, we'll finish our wine while Daram is gone."

The young man-at-arms, on being told he was assigned as body servant to Beneban, broke into a face-splitting grin. He stationed himself behind the wizard's chair and darted forward to hand him the goblet of wine or replace it each time Beneban twitched, until finally the wizard could stand it no longer.

"Suppose, Borno, you wait in the outer room until I'm ready to leave. You'll want to say farewell to your fellows, I'm sure," he offered.

As his new servant plodded dejectedly from the room, Beneban turned amused eyes on his host.

"Now what have you wished upon me, Tor? That child will have my nerves in tatters if he stays on the jump to intercept my every move."

The wizard reached for his wine. Pain wiped the laughter from his face, and he gulped a bit of his drink quickly to hide it.

Beneban finished the pale wine with relish. He winced again as he set the goblet on the fireside table. At the movement, Kati stood lazily, stretched, then moved to his side.

"He's young, but youth is something we all outgrow, and loyalty isn't so common a quality. But would you prefer Rad? Daram?"

"Nay!" The refusal came quickly. "I feel guilty enough taking this youngster. Nor would the others be pleased to leave your service."

"Then Calibe?" Tor suggested. An impish grin removed the lines of grief from his face for a moment.

"Gods, no! You mention loyalty. I'd never sleep a wink with him near."

Tor nodded sober agreement to that. "Then it will be Borno," he continued. "Well, I'd hate to lose Rad or Daram, to say true. They guarded my first steps and pulled me out of the watering trough when I was a toddler. Most of my meager talent with arms I owe those two."

"I thank you for the excellent care and hospitality, Tor. Now I must go. Young Borno can guide my shaky steps, and if the halls obligingly light our progress as they did our arrival, Kati and I will do well enough."

Borno, evidently with his ear against the door, popped into the room and stood at attention.

"They'll do that," Tor said. "The wizard Nigeran helped Lyolar the First, this Grand Lar's father, to build this palace. It's some wizardry of his that reacts to movement."

"Nigeran. The wizard that was banished from court by our present Grand Lar?"

"Aye, banished. And he took this Lyolar's young sister with him. In effect, he stole two treasures from under my uncle's nose. It has been a long time past, but Lyolar doesn't forget. So you must sympathize with his suspicion of wizards."

"Two treasures?" Suddenly alert, Beneban asked quickly: "What besides his sister?"

The outer door burst open. Daram hurried in before Tor could answer.

"Sir, if we're to get you to your quarters, we'd best be going. There's a right storm brewing."

"You don't need to get soaked on top of your wound," Tor said quickly. "Goodnight, my friend. I'll see you soon again. That story is an old one. It can wait for another time."

"Goodnight, Tor. I'm much in your debt. For nursing me, for Borno..."

"The debt between us will forever go the other way, my friend." Tor turned to his servant.

"Take him safely, Daram. Borno, you young scamp, serve him well, or I'll have him turn you into a swamp creaker. Begin now by getting his cloak."

Much later, with Borno settled on a pallet and Daram returned to his master, Beneban lay awake in the dark of Trog's room. The Ogdol had roused briefly to provide bedding, then he and Borno quickly joined voices in sonorous snores.

Too tired to sleep, the wizard's mind was filled with the strangeness of the day. It flung itself from question to unanswered question.

How had Tor's mother been killed? What significance, if any, did the silver fish brooch that he had taken from her hand hold?

Why hadn't he returned the brooch to the young lar? Well, he'd been wounded, unconscious... Simply forgotten...

His thoughts wandered to the Grand Lar. Was he bordering on true madness? Or was he only power mad?

But the most important question he pondered had to do with his own mission. Where was the Larstone? Was it one of the treasures Tor spoke of as being taken by his old teacher, Nigeran? And if so, where did that leave Beneban?

Restlessly, he eased his wounded shoulder into a less painful position.

Kati lifted her head at his movement. She peered through the dark, alert for danger. As her companion settled, she stretched silently at his feet, and closed her green eyes.

Beneban's mind was less calm. Three years. So little time to find so small an object. So huge a penalty for failure. The loss of his name, his being, his will to the evil wizard, Ztavin...

Panic flared then died as the wizard forced his mind through control exercises he'd learned long ago. Slowly he curbed the restless thoughts. He remembered his master's words:

Without self-control, a wizard's mind is a monster waiting to be loosed.

Nigeran's voice, hard and steady, was as real to him as though he were here in the room. Obediently, Beneban mentally turned off one switch after another until, finally, his mind rested in a safe cave high in the mountains, protected by Kati, with snow drifting silently down.

As he drifted, his mind reached, as it often did before sleep, for the scent of flowers. He saw, instead, a tiny silk-shod foot that twitched with impatience beneath the table at Lyolar's dinner.

His own spell had turned the whole room to statues. Why was this one figure, this young girl, immune to the magic which held all, people, animals, even the candlelight, frozen in place?

As darkness fell at last on the palace in Larlingarde, a wizened figure sat up from his rough pallet. About him was only the even breath of Tor's servants. He slipped from the bedding and crept softly to the door, which remained open in case the young lar needed something.

A cough made him freeze in place. Daram tossed and growled in a dream. The old man sat up, and the tiny figure crouched, motionless. The guard coughed, rolled over, and sank back to sleep.

Now Calibe slipped from the room and darted through the royal palace. He came, at length, to a quiet office he had noticed before. Sliding through the unlocked door, he moved to the fireplace. He knelt and pulled an object from a bag at his waist. Next he drew runes in the ashes. At a muttered a word of command, the runes gathered light until a dull purple gleam lit the wizened face.

In the cold fireplace, blackness rose like smoke. It swirled and the shadow became a dark face.

"Why do you call me," it hissed. "What of Beneban? Is he slain?"

Calibe hunched to the floor and shook his head, mute.

"Obviously not. Then explain."

As Calibe told of the supper, coldness gathered in the room. At his news of the wizard's promotion to the Grand Lar's Troops, black spirals smoked about the dark figure. Finally, at his own removal from Lar Tor's room, an implosion of bitter cold caused soot to whirl in spider webs that curled about the small figure and burned where they touched. As the silence gathered at the end of his excuses, Calibe sank with hands over his head.

"You have failed me." The words hissed like steam. "Your debt grows. Do better."

The blackness sank until there were only ashes. Slowly, Calibe stopped shivering. He carefully stowed the silver leaf pin in the bag at his belt. Quiet as a shadow he slithered through the halls and regained his pallet.

Though all about him were the whispered snores of sleeping servants, he shivered in fear at the debt he had incurred.

SOMEONE WAS BUILDING a fair booth, no, a scaffold, maybe a mansion inside his head.

Bang! Bang, bang! The noise increased as Beneban winced.

A catapult pounded the walls of the beautiful crimson-towered city. *Bang, bang!* Or was it...

Beneban, yanked from unremembered dreams, swore by the seven symbols as his wounded arm pulled and scraped against the covers. Pale dawn light filtered through the window slit.

Now Trog rolled from his bed to lumber toward the door. In the corner, Borno sprawled in the abandoned sleep of youth.

Kati reared her head. With a sigh she stood to pace behind Trog as Beneban struggled to an elbow, shaking off sleep.

"A minute, a *minute!*" Trog rumbled as a renewed bout of pounding threatened to shatter the door. "What is it?" he growled, pushing it open. "Oh. Gorm! What do you *want*, man?"

"Eh, Trog. I be needin' you, or more like your wizard, to come t' the gate. I be havin' a problem there."

"What problem requires our presence at this hour?" Beneban's sleepy grumble came as he struggled to sit up.

"It be a younker, one o' they little folk, see…"

"I do *not* see," Trog said impatiently. "A child is at the gate? Or a Worf?"

"Aye, Trog, a lit'le 'un, a younker," Gorm repeated. "It wants 'im." Gorm pointed at Beneban. "Nor it won't go off, jus' keeps whingin' sumpin', over and agin."

"I'll go, Trog." Beneban struggled carefully into the breeches that Borno had hung from the corner of his bunk.

"Your arm, my friend. You were badly hurt?" Trog rumbled.

"No: It is painful, but not serious."

"I do not remember what happened."

"The Grand Lar decided to test my courage. He came closer than he intended… I think."

Beneban swung his scarlet cloak around his shoulders against the early morning chill but winced at the pull on his shoulder.

"Let me help." Trog settled it on the injured arm and hooked the silver clasp. "Who sleeps so soundly in the corner?"

"That's Borno. Do you remember? The youngest of the Torlarya's men-at-arms?"

"Yes, but why does he…"

"He's my new aide. Young Tor assigned him to assist me by way of saying thanks."

"Pard'n, sir," Gorm interrupted, "but I be overlong from me gate."

"I'm coming, Gorm," the wizard said impatiently as he turned to the door.

"I am curious as to the nature of this problem,"

Trog said. "May I accompany you?"

"Always, Trog. Yet I can't think it's for me." Beneban shrugged. "No one knows me here."

Asolum's dawn rays just touched the towers to crimson as the party reached Gorm's rear gate. Gorm unbarred it then cautiously put his head out and peered around.

"Here it be then," the old guard muttered disgustedly and stood aside.

As Beneban moved past him, an emaciated little bundle of rags sprang forward. It began wiping the wizard's boots with a scrap of its shirt.

Beneban jerked his foot away with an oath. The Worf dodged, expecting a blow. Then it reached out to mop a tear drop from the shiny leather.

The wizard stared down at the tiny tear-streaked face. He bent to gain eye level with the scrap of humanity, and spoke softly.

"Have I... I've seen you before, haven't I?"

The tiny creature bobbed its head. The large gray eyes fixed hopefully on Beneban's face.

"It is the Worf child you gave a cake to, is it not?" Trog had trundled up behind them. The child peered nervously at him and shrank close to Beneban, clutching a corner of the wizard's cloak.

"I believe so," Beneban agreed. "Now listen, child. You can't stay here. Go on home." The wizard pointed down toward the city.

With a wordless wail the little Worf fell to the ground and clung to Beneban's ankle.

"Let go! Now stop that!" the appalled wizard cried. "What do you *want?*" He pulled the child to its feet and sank to one knee to peer into its eyes.

"I don't understand what you want," he said more gently.

The child gasped for breath and began a strange pantomime. He brushed Beneban's clothes with one hand, polished his boots, ran back and forth in frantic activity, and repeatedly touched his own bony chest, then Beneban's, still bare beneath the cloak.

Finally the wizard's hand closed gently around the matchstick arm and held the child still.

"It wishes to be your servant," Trog said. "Also, it seems to be mute. Can you speak, child?"

The Worf shook its head and opened the tiny mouth wide. There was only a ragged stump where the tongue should have been.

Horrified, Beneban sprang to his feet. "What monster did that?" he cried furiously. The child sensed only his anger. It flung itself to the ground, eyes tight shut, but still grasped one of Beneban's ankles.

"Many children are maimed by their owners. It is an attempt to make them more *productive* as beggars." Trog's eyes were stony.

"But I can't keep it, him…" Beneban laid a gentle hand on the head of the terrified Worf. "He must belong somewhere."

The wizard looked from the child, now firmly attached to his left leg, to Trog, then to Gorm, who watched from the gate. A radiant, if toothless, smile split the guard's old face.

"I doubt the child has a home, captain." Trog squatted and turned the small creature toward him. "Your mother will worry about your absence, little one."

The small hands made a violent negative motion.

"Your father?" Trog tried. The movement was repeated. Trog stared across the youngster's head to meet Beneban's amber eyes.

"I already have Borno," the wizard sputtered. "What would I do with a child?"

"This one could fetch and carry, do things young Borno would think beneath him. Or, of course, you could return him to the one who maimed him." Trog stood, impassive. The Worf child slumped like one that awaited certain doom.

One tiny hand still clung hopefully to Beneban's left ankle.

Beneban gently loosened the waif's hold and moved to the gate. He stared out across the city.

At length Trog joined him. The Ogdol was quiet for a moment. "I would not pressure you, captain," he said finally.

"I know!" the wizard snapped. Then, more quietly, "I know. My plans don't—didn't—include dependents. That's all."

"Soon we must attend morning briefing."

"Yes. Well, there is no real choice, is there?" He turned. "Come on, child. See that you behave." Beneban stalked back toward the barracks. The tiny Worf scampered behind. One hand clutched an edge of the red cloak, while the other wiped tears from his dirty face.

Trog trundled sedately in the rear.

As he re-barred the gate, old Gorm chuckled. "Aye, he be a right-un fer 'citement, that 'un," he muttered. "A kalting, a Ogdol, an' a Worf, and he's only been 'ere but one day yet."

Deep in Forest, Rayni sat on the stoop as Asolum's early light touched her abode with gentle rays. The healing pool where she had been scrying was serene now in the new morning. Saray stood patiently in the doorway. The fragrance of breakfast wafted from the kitchen within.

"He is all right, Saray. So far he has survived my Uncle Lyolar's anger. And he has friends."

"Of course. Now he must learn a new life and lessons that are more difficult, in some ways, than the study of wizardry."

"He will do it. I think he can do anything." Rayni's voice smiled as she felt the breeze, heard it reflected in the soothing movement of the trees.

CHAPTER 12

Though Gorm's assault on their door had been early, Asolum was fully above the horizon by the time they arrived back at Trog's quarters. In the distance, they heard the Troopers toss raucous comments as they cleaned their barracks or groomed the kelsh. It blended with the faded smell of the breakfast that Beneban and Trog had missed.

Trog suddenly realized that Beneban had lagged behind. The Ogdol reversed until they were able to talk.

"There is a need to hurry, Beneban," he urged his comrade.

A light morning breeze wafted the dark smell of kelsh manure and the sound of troopers' babble as they cleaned the stables. More distant but more acrid, the same effort was underway at the kalting barns.

Instead of more haste, Beneban stopped completely. The Worf child huddled between his feet.

"Trog, I don't know how... what... What is expected of a captain in the Grand Lar's troops? I don't even *have* a troop."

"First," Trog said urgently, "We must get this little one to our quarters. Then there will be some need to explain what is expected of him. After that—*if we arrive in time*—I am sure your duties will be explained. It is urgent that we not be late. Please come now."

Beneban followed and hurried, but it was not simple.

Borno instantly took offense at his new companion. "I can do all that you need!" he growled, glaring at the little Worf.

"He is under my protection," Beneban stated and forced Borno to meet his eyes. "You will not bother him."

Kati skulked about the child, who hid his head between Beneban's legs.

"*Kati! Mine!* He is *not* a new kalting toy," the wizard growled.

Kati hissed quietly and slunk to crouch in wait at the door.

"We cannot continue to call the child 'him,' Trog." Beneban turned to see his friend waited with Kati by the door.

"Later," Trog offered.

"But he is tiny, lively like a mountain farsel, one seriously underfed. We shall call him Sel. Do you understand, child?" Beneban stooped and lifted the small pointy face to look at him. "Your name, now, is Sel. Do you understand? Borno, this is Sel. You are to care for him and teach him."

The Worf listened carefully and stared at the wizard's serious face. He nodded. A tear ran down his cheek, quickly wiped by a corner of the rags he wore.

"Don't *cry!*" Beneban put an arm around him. "Trog! Why is he crying?" The wizard knelt and tried to look into Sel's face.

"Perhaps he has never had a name. Captain, we must *go*."

Sel nodded vigorously. He quickly hugged Beneban's arm where it held him.

"Okay? Okay, Sel. Now, no more tears. Here, wipe your face." Beneban pulled a cloth from his pocket and gave it to the little Worf. Then he rummaged in his pocket.

"I had... have you seen a pin... a silver leaf?"

Borno had moved to a corner and stood with his arms crossed. "He don't need a name," he said crossly. "Don't see why we need him. *I* can do for you, Captain."

Beneban started to argue but turned to rummage in his bedding. "A pin... this big... a silver leaf. Borno, the matter is closed. Sel will remain. You are responsible for him. Do *not* let harm come to him."

"We are too late to eat at the mess, Captain," Trog said gruffly, hiding amusement. "Borno has laid out your uniform. Get into it. We must go, *now!* The Grand Lar frowns on his troops being late for morning briefing, and this is not a good time to make him angry."

"Good job, Borno." Beneban grabbed the unfamiliar uniform. "But where did it come from?" The wizard ignored Trog and struggled into the new clothes. "Borno, I *trust* you to take care of Sel. Help him get bathed and find him appropriate clothes. When we return, we will discuss duties, yours, as well as Sel's. Now, quickly, find us something to eat while we go."

Borno's smile returned. "The Lar Tor sent the uniform, sir." The lad quickly handed them each half a loaf of the day's fresh baking, which he had gotten in their absence.

At Beneban's thanks, the lad wriggled like a happy pup. "I'll take care o' the younker, sir, no worries," he said, cheerful again.

Beneban tore off bites of the fragrant, crusty bread as they hurried away. Other troopers had disappeared around a square building ahead of them.

"It seems, Trog, that time to eat isn't built into my life just now," the wizard grumbled. "And I imbibed too much of Lar Tor's excellent wine last night. My head... I would have preferred to sleep late this morning, but instead, I'm on my way to my first report. This is a job for which I have little talent and absolutely no understanding."

Trog rumbled sympathetically. "It was necessary for you to dress. The job of captain will not be as difficult as you imagine. It was good that you made your intention clear to Borno. He would have disposed of the small one before our return."

"Disposed?" Beneban spun to face his companion.

"Not with violence." Trog patted the wizard's good arm and gently turned him back to the path. "He would simply have pushed him back out the gate."

"But why?" Beneban swallowed the last crust and brushed crumbs from the blue and silver cloth, the unfamiliar uniform of the Grand Lar's men-at-arms.

"Why would Borno chase the child away?" Beneban asked again.

Trog had swallowed half his loaf in a single bite. A shake rid his white pelt of the last crumbs.

"Borno will need to train the small one, the little

Sel. He must keep him in order," Trog answered. "He must be certain the child is clean and teach him manners. Sel has lived as a wilding. Now Borno must be sure he does not embarrass you. Misbehavior would be blamed on your older servant. Also, the lad resents competition for your affection."

"Affection?" This time Beneban stopped in sheer amazement. "Surely that presupposes that I have more human feelings than wizards are given credit for?"

Trog stopped too and considered the wizard gravely with one warm dark eye. What might have been a smile twitched at the slash of a mouth. Finally he turned slightly away. "Say, then, your *approval*. Now, come. We shall be late for report."

As Beneban and Trog approached the square building of rosy stone, Captain Glaynar and Lieutenant Humber pushed through a small group of officers to enter the building. Two more troopers, who wore orange shoulder capes, hurried around a corner to join those still outside.

"Officers of the Kaltingcorps," Trog rumbled as they reached the door themselves.

The officers fell silent and turned to the newcomers. Trog saluted gravely and waited as Beneban studied this new group.

"Well, Trog." The tallest captain, a Larlinga in appearance, broke the silence. "Is this the new man we've heard so much about?"

"Yes, sir. May I present Captain Me'ekalar, first officer of the Kaltingcorps, also Captains Ayngos, Doryl, and Ranald. Gentlemen, Captain Beneban."

"Gentlemen." Beneban bowed slightly, as did the others.

"Your reputation precedes you, Captain Beneban, like fire in a ripe grain field," said Me'ekalar, obviously the leader of the group. "Is that the famous amber sword you wear?"

Beneban touched the hilt lightly with his right hand. "Famous? It is my sword, certainly."

"May we have a demonstration, Captain Beneban?" asked Ranald, a short sharp-faced man with a ginger beard and the brown hair and eyes of an Othring.

"Another time, gentlemen. As you see, I've sustained a slight injury." Beneban indicated the sling Trog had insisted he wear to protect the left arm.

"Forgive me, sir," Trog interrupted. "If we would not be late, we must enter." He moved inexorably forward. Beneban followed, and reluctantly the others made way and closed in behind them.

As in the palace, the windowless walls were lit by an internal magic. The room the officers now entered was bare of adornment but for the banners of the Grand Lar's troops hung upon the stone walls. Benches filled the central space, seats for perhaps twenty captains. They were identifiable by small formal shoulder capes of varying colors.

"Trog," Beneban asked softly, "the capes, do they denote different branches of service?"

"Yes," Trog murmured.

Opposite the entrance, a raised platform held a podium and a bench. Behind these on the back wall of the room, a door was emblazoned with the Grand Lar's coat of arms.

"This building abuts the palace. There is a closed passage for the Grand Lar's use," Trog explained quietly.

While lieutenants of the different services moved to sit on benches at the side of the room, Beneban, at a nod from Trog, took a place in the rear of the center section. He felt conspicuous for his lack of a shoulder cape.

Me'ekalar surprised the wizard. He left his companions and slid in to sit beside Beneban. At his easy smile, Beneban suddenly felt less like a target for the curiosity of the others who had craned discretely to stare at him. Next to Me'ekalar he felt accepted.

Trog saw this, and moved silently to a place with the other junior officers. The wizard noticed two lieutenants edge away from the Ogdol, who ignored the obvious insult.

Angry for his friend, Beneban started to his feet.

"Wait!" Me'ekalar touched Beneban's sling urgently. "Lyolar..."

Before he could move, the blue door swung open and the Grand Lar entered, preceded by Mero and followed by Tor.

"Gentlemen, all rise! Here cometh Lyolar, Grand Lar of Larlion, Lord of the Twelve Estates."

Mero's young voice, stretched around the formal, outdated words, was nearly lost in the clatter of benches that pushed back as everyone leapt to their feet and saluted, left arm out straight then snapped back with a clenched fist above the heart. Beneban winced as he slipped the sling off and followed the unfamiliar salute. He held it with the others until it was returned by Lyolar.

"At ease, gentlemen," Lyolar grated. "Be seated." The troops subsided with a clatter.

Lyolar turned to his nephew. "Tor…" He gestured for the young lar to stand beside him.

"As you are all aware," Lyolar continued, "assassins have slain our beloved sister and her consort. My nephew, the Lar Tor, long my heir, is now rightful Lar of Torling Estate. Though I will be his regent for Torling until he comes of age in three years, he will begin today also to take his rightful place as my heir and second in command."

As Lyolar halted, Mero cried out, "Gentlemen, salute Tor, Lar of Torling, Lar of the First Estate, and heir to the throne of Larlion."

Again the assemblage sprang to their feet to salute, and this time there was an enthusiastic undercurrent of voices. It was obvious to Beneban that young Tor was popular. It was also obvious to the wizard that Lyolar wasn't best pleased at the enthusiasm shown his nephew.

"Enough," growled Lyolar. "Sit down, gentlemen. Tor, take the duty." The Grand Lar handed Tor a scroll then sat stiffly on the marble bench while Tor called the roll of captains. Each stood as he was called and presented the report of his troop. At the end of the call, Tor saluted his uncle and handed him the roll.

As Lyolar returned to the podium, Beneban realized that Captain Glaynar had not been called. The man stood, as though sure he had merely been forgotten. Instead, young Mero stepped forward again.

"Captain Beneban," Mero piped, "you will please approach the dais."

Taken by surprise, Beneban jumped up after a brief pause and strode forward past the agitated Glaynar.

With a hiss, the ignored man sank back on his bench.

Now the Grand Lar stared silently at the wizard until Beneban realized what was expected. He snapped a reasonable salute, managed with only a tiny wince, though his left arm had begun to ache fiercely with the activity. He had slipped off the supportive sling and laid it on the bench after the first salute at Lyolar's entrance.

Lyolar returned his salute gravely, but the Grand Lar's eyes held a hint of mockery. He knew, better than most, why the wizard was feeling discomfort.

"You will have noticed, gentlemen," the ruler said, "the absence, on the call of L Troop. This troop was responsible for the safety of travelers on the Torbridge Road at the time of the assassination of the Torlarya and her consort. They failed in that duty. We have lost an able lar, and I have lost my sister because of that dereliction.

"As a result, I hereby declare that Captain Glaynar has been demoted to the rank of corporal in L Troop. His adjutant, Humber, is reduced to private."

Beneban heard a gasp from behind him, as if someone was in pain.

"Captain Beneban," the Grand Lar continued, "was in route to join my forces. He proved beyond a doubt his prowess and courage in defense of my citizens. As he heard the sounds of battle nearby, he and his kalting rushed to the assistance of my sister and her party. Although he was too late to save her life, he killed the perpetrators."

"Because of this heroism, I have accepted his service. He is appointed Captain-at-Arms and will assume command of L Troop. Captain Beneban, step up here, please."

Shaken, Beneban stumbled up the two steps to the platform, and Tor moved to stand beside his uncle.

"Sir," Beneban said quietly, "I deserve no special recognition for being accidentally in the right place, nor is it fair to Captain Glaynar…"

"Do you think to teach me my job already?" the Grand Lar hissed. "It would be appropriate at this moment to kneel."

Hot blood flushed his face, and Beneban dropped hastily to one knee.

"Do you, Beneban, promise to serve me loyally and bravely, to do my bidding and keep my peace, on your honor as a… a man?"

"I do, Mightiness. On my honor as a man and as a wizard." The Grand Lar scowled at the words.

Mero, unaware of Lyolar's anger, stepped forward.

He handed something to Tor. Tor's face warmed in a smile. He shook out the short blue cape of a captain and fastened it to Beneban's shoulder.

"Rise, Captain Beneban." Tor turned him to face the benches. The assembled officers leapt up and saluted him, but Beneban saw only the angry, ashen face of Glaynar directly in front of him.

"There's still one piece of business," growled Lyolar. "You, Captain Beneban, must appoint a new adjutant. You'll want to wait until you've gotten to know the troop."

"Please, my lar," Beneban said quickly, "I know who I want."

"You do?" Lyolar, already turned away, looked

back in surprise.

"Yes sir. I'll have Trog as my adjutant."

"The Ogdol?"

A murmur ran through the crowd.

"It is unusual, you know, to appoint an Ogdol as your adjutant," Lyolar said quietly. "You may be unaware of the reaction of the other men. He is... different."

Beneban held his gaze steadily. "He is different, Sire, as am I."

"Well, nothing you do seems typical," Lyolar muttered. For the first time, the ruler didn't appear to be bored. "Very well. Trog, you are promoted adjutant to L Troop. That's it then." Again, he started to turn away.

"Please, Mightiness." Trog's rumble as he trundled toward the platform caused Lyolar turn around again.

Trog reached the dais and his voice carried only to those upon it.

"I ask a favor, Mightiness," he continued. "Let Captain Beneban take time to reconsider. He is unaware of the problems this will cause him."

Lyolar stared in disbelief at the Ogdol then speculatively at Beneban.

"He's right, you know. You'll have a good few problems without the need to overcome the prejudice against Ogdols. You should, perhaps, reconsider?" A hint of a sneer twisted Lyolar's mouth. His eyes seemed to ask if Beneban was afraid of the challenge.

While Lyolar waited, Beneban looked long at Trog, who refused to meet his gaze.

"No sir." Beneban now met the Grand Lar's eyes.

"With respect, I'll not reconsider. Trog is my friend and a capable officer."

"So be it," Lyolar snarled.

The Grand Lar spun on his heel. He nearly stumbled over young Mero, who was slumped against the wall drowsing. The lad scrambled for the door as the officers snapped disordered salutes.

Tor followed his uncle, but he threw a hasty smile at Beneban. Then he pulled Mero through the door and it closed on Lyolar's angry lecture to his young lar.

CHAPTER 13

"So, Beneban, this is where you disappear to when you aren't busy exhausting L Troop." Tor stood, hands on hips, and stared about the book-lined room in a mostly forgotten corner of the Grand Lar's palace. At length his thoughtful gaze returned to the pool of light at the end of one long table. It had been two weeks since Beneban's surprise appointment as Captain of L Troop. Now the wizard's face was furrowed with lines of concentration as he frowned above the pile of books, both open and shut.

Beneban blinked at Tor's words and smiled a welcome to the young noble. One slender hand marked a place in the massive tome he held open.

"Have you any idea, Tor, how little a wizard's education fits him to be captain of a troop of soldiers?" He sighed and indicated a pile of books as yet untouched.

"The word in the barracks is that a wizard's education fits him to be a slave driver in the mines," Tor said with a grin. The young noble paced forward to stand at Beneban's elbow. He lifted a tome, glanced at the title, wrinkled his brow, and replaced it. *"Order of Troop Movement?"* he wondered.

"L Troop is virtually untrained," Beneban sighed.

"As am I. I had not intended to become... Well, so I try to learn and to teach." The wizard rubbed his eyes and continued.

"I realize that Glaynar couldn't be everywhere at once, but he deserved a demotion for incompetence. The troop is badly trained and worse, lazy. I intend for that to change. I will *not* be incompetent if I can avoid it. Besides, exhausted men have less energy to cause trouble."

Tor's keen eyes took in the weary lines on his friend's face, the heavy eyelids nearly hiding the amber eyes.

"You certainly understand exhaustion at any rate." He bent to look more closely. "Have you slept or relaxed at all since my uncle gave you the appointment?"

"I... Well, I..."

"Don't think to lie," Tor laughed. "You average three hours sleep a night and you eat on the run. When you aren't showing your men how to ride, or wrestle, or shoot, or polish gear, you are in here in an effort to become an overnight expert on military tactics."

"I rarely lie," Beneban protested mildly.

Tor looked at his drawn face in concern.

With a twisted smile the wizard added, "This, books and study, is a practice that wizards *do* understand, my friend. Long hours, short rations, and minimal sleep. All must be expected, to become a wizard. Although the content of study is quite different.

"As for my work with the men," he continued, "I learn as much from them as I teach. Mainly it's just not allowing them to slack off."

Tor snorted. "No one has bested you at wrestling, even with your injured arm. If you aren't the top at riding and practice with the spring bow, you're close enough to keep everyone on their toes."

His friend rose and stretched. Tor heard abused muscles snap stiffly.

"My arm is better," he said. "The wrestling is merely a different style than they are used to. Herdsmen on the North Plains use tricks you southerners rarely see."

For a moment the wizard sagged, prepared to resume his seat. Eyes already on an open manuscript, he reached a hand out.

Tor paced the round of the table and grabbed his wrist. He ignored the sudden tension of Beneban's muscles and closed the nearest volume.

"I plan to save you from yourself, my friend. You'll study better after an hour in the gardens. The books will await your return."

Beneban stiffened then relaxed and nodded. "Perhaps you are right." The wizard sighed and gathered his cloak. He marked a place in his book. His eyes followed Tor to a gap in the shelves.

"Observe," the young lar announced. "This room was built with an eye to the relief of weary scholars." Theatrically, the lad pushed open an unobtrusive small door. Brilliant afternoon sunlight stabbed the dark room.

As they exited, a small figure wriggled out from under the table and squeezed through the door behind them.

"What's this?" Tor demanded warily. One hand

went to his sword. Then he recognized the intruder.

"This must be the Worf child you've taken on. Is Borno so lazy you needed another helper?"

"Nay," laughed Beneban. "Borno is most eager. He hovers over me continuously. He'd be twice as industrious if he thought it would get rid of Sel here. The two are as jealous of each other as two hounds with one bone between them, and I, the bone. Ahh!"

The wizard drew in a deep breath of the fresh, fragrant air. His arms stretched, then reached high. "You were right, Tor. Air is what I needed to clear my head."

"Excellent. Now clarify for me, is it true you rescued this child from some horrible fate in the city? And why did you call it Sel?"

"Therein lies a tale." Beneban began to stroll along the stone pathway. "I made the tactical mistake of giving him some crumbs. I never imagined... Well, I was virtually mobbed for my trouble. Thanks to Trog, I survived with a lesson learned. I didn't think of it again. However, the child must have followed me to the palace. He pestered old Gorm and refused to be moved from the gate until I was found. And so..."

The wizard stretched in the warm light. He moved a few steps further. At Tor's hand on his arm, he continued the story.

"I call him Sel because... Well, he is small and as lively as the mountain farsels, and also as silent, perforce. Someone tore out his tongue."

"But why?" Tor stared at the wizard in horror.

"A question for which I've no satisfactory answer. Trog says these things happen. I hope, one day, to meet the one who did it." Beneban's tone was dark.

They walked in silence for a few steps before Tor continued. "So because he was handicapped, you added him to your ménage." Tor stopped to touch an ivory bloom on an espalier against a rosy wall.

"It was simpler than convincing him to leave, or it seemed so at the time," Beneban said.

Tor looked skeptical. "If it weren't so well documented that wizards have no hearts, one would suspect yours of being overly soft." He held up a hand, laughing, to ward off Beneban's protest. "Never mind. It was merest expediency, then. How did you decide it—pardon me, *he*—was a male?"

"*Assuredly* expediency, Tor." The wizard's eyebrows quirked into exclamation points. "Think of the complications if he weren't."

At Tor's roar of laughter, Sel scuttled to shelter beneath Beneban's cloak and peered out fearfully. The wizard gently detached him, and they walked on in silent enjoyment of the lovely day. Finally, they relaxed on a stone bench beneath an arbor of the sweetly fragrant ivory blooms.

Sel crept from beneath Beneban's cape. He sat close and piled pebbles into a tiny building as they talked.

The wizard cupped a bloom in a careful hand. "See how the petals curl about each other, Tor?" he murmured. "As the flower opens, each layer pulls away until, at the heart, is the secret beauty of the blossom, studded with tiny scarlet stars." Beneban gently released the bloom to its place and leaned back against the wall.

"A lesson in how a life should be lived," he mused. "Each layer unfolding more perfectly than the last, and with old age, the culmination of grace and wisdom."

At Tor's astonished stare, Beneban laughed sardonically and added, "Not that one is often given the chance, of course." He stiffened. "Someone is coming."

A murmur of voices reached them across a tall hedge. One was unmistakably the Grand Lar's, though his tone was softer than was its wont. The other, light and musical, was female.

As the ruler rounded the hedge, Tor and Beneban rose quickly to await his approach. Lyolar's companion was the foot-tapping lady from the banquet hall. She chattered at the Grand Lar with a hand on his arm and peeped up from beneath long lashes. Her other hand lifted a dainty skirt from the ground just high enough to show scarlet satin slippers.

Sel shrank beneath the bench, out of sight.

Beneban and Tor bowed as the couple seemed about to pass without noticing them.

"Why, Tor." The woman stopped as though suddenly aware of their presence. A scowl flashed across Lyolar's face.

The woman, *no girl*, Beneban thought. Then, *no, definitely a woman.*

Her full attention was on the young lar.

"I haven't seen you for a week, Tor. Mightiness, how can you permit this young man to absent himself from court so long? And who is your friend, Tor?"

Lyolar turned reluctantly to the group. "The boy is in mourning, Meriel," he rasped.

"Oh!" Pretty confusion was followed by a slender

hand that moved to rest gently on Tor's sleeve. "Of course. I am so sorry, my dear."

Tor reddened with embarrassment at the familiarity, while his uncle glowered.

"Well," Meriel insisted, ignoring the tension in the air, "You must introduce me to this lovely stranger." She peeped up to look at his face.

"Wait! Yes! It *is* you." She clapped her hands. "Here is the wizard who froze us all the other night."

She turned a look of piquant entreaty on the Grand Lar, whose face melted in response. "Now, Sire, you must introduce me to this lovely stranger." She held out a hand to Beneban.

"If you wish, child," Lyolar grumbled. "Though you need no additional advantage." He sighed. "I present to you the newest of my captains, Beneban, of L Troop. Captain, this is the Lady Meriel, daughter of my Advocate, Ka'amfer."

"An honor, my lady." Beneban bowed over her tiny hand, touching only her fingertips and releasing them after the briefest possible time.

He stared at her curiously, then rubbed his eyes. Why did her figure shimmer slightly in the warm, fragrant light? Too many hours of study, he decided as she prattled on.

"Nay, sir, you have the wrong of it. If you knew how the court schemes to get your presence, you'd know how delighted I am to have this chance. Oh, please, my lar, invite him to supper tonight as my special guest!"

"And next Starday, sir," she added, again to Beneban. "My father is giving a small supper in honor of

Greening Day. Tor is invited, and my dear Lyolar, of course, but you must join us. Oh, and do bring your Ogdol!" She gasped in seeming excitement. "You *must* bring him along. *No* one has had an Ogdol to supper."

"My lady, I'm overwhelmed." Beneban's courteous answer was less than enthusiastic.

"Oh, Lyolar, *please!* Do make him accept." Meriel grabbed the ruler's arm with her small hands and looked charmingly up into his face.

Lyolar stared down at her for a long moment as one mesmerized.

"We will expect you at the banquet tonight, Captain Beneban," he growled at last.

Lady Meriel smiled gleefully.

Lyolar continued gruffly: "And of course, you will accept the Lady Meriel's invitation for next Starday. Now, my dear, I must go. Even rulers may not dally all the day away."

Meriel pouted prettily, but Lyolar had grown sulky now, no longer the center of her attention. He continued, to the others: "Several of my lars have not attended OathGive. Two messengers who should have returned with news seem to have disappeared. There are rumors of trouble to the east and disaffection to the north. In short, I must return to work. Good day, gentlemen." He strode away without acknowledging their hasty bows.

"How sad and how lovely," Meriel crowed. "Now you must escort me." She took an arm of each man as she moved along. "Now about the supper," she prattled. "You and your Ogdol can come with Tor. He knows our house, of course."

"You are kind, my lady," Beneban said uncomfortably, "but you are mistaken."

"I *beg* your pardon?" Amused disbelief lit the gaze she turned on him.

"Trog, the Ogdol," Beneban explained, "is definitely not 'mine.'" He rubbed his eyes with a long hand. How curious that they kept blurring.

"Oh, but everyone says you are inseparable," Meriel said.

"Everyone is proven wrong at this moment, my lady," he pointed out gravely.

"Why, that's true. How odd." Meriel gazed about as though expecting to find Trog lurking beneath a nearby bush. Her brow wrinkled charmingly at his absence. "But you will bring him, won't you?"

"I shall certainly extend your invitation," Beneban hedged.

"And Tor, you won't let this tiresome thing with your parents turn you into a hermit, my dear. I expect to see you tonight at the banquet. Court suppers are boring in the extreme when you fail to attend."

A flush of pleasure struggled with shock on Tor's face at her callous words. Pleasure won out as she clung to him and stared adoringly into his face.

After a few more steps, she spun lightly away then turned again to them.

"Here is the door, and I must go. A tiresome fitting. Besides, someone is coming to find you. I knew," she crowed triumphantly to Beneban, "that you two were inseparable." She skipped away as Trog trundled up to them.

"Captain, Lar Tor." Trog saluted the two men

formally. "The Lar of Ariling approaches the city. Our troop is to escort him from the gates, Beneban. The men are forming up."

"Ari!" Tor cried. "He's my foster-father. Beneban, may I ride with you?"

"Of course, if you wish." Beneban was already trotting toward the garden gate. "Trog, I must get into uniform. Will you see to the troop?"

"Yes, sir. Borno is laying out your uniform. I will meet you at the parade ground. Pardon me, my lar." Trog crossed in front of them and held open the gate.

"Of course. Thank you, Trog," Tor answered. "I've just heard on excellent authority that you and Beneban are inseparable. I'll hope to make your better acquaintance at another time."

A wordless wail reached them as the gate swung shut. Sel, left behind by the quickly moving men, now pushed with all his tiny strength against the heavy portal.

"What a pest you are," Beneban muttered. "Here, then. Hold on." He swung the waif up to his shoulder and trotted toward the barracks, ignoring the knowing smiles on his friends' faces.

A BRIEF TIME later, outfitted in his uniform, Beneban approached the parade ground at a near run. Tor paced at his shoulder with Borno and Kati following. From ahead came cursing and angry voices, the sound of a crowd cheering for a fight in the making.

Rounding the corner, Beneban pushed roughly

through a wall of uniformed troopers. Abruptly the men fell silent as they saw him.

In the center of the rough circle Trog faced Humber and two more of Glaynar's cronies.

"We don't got t'do what you tell us. You ain't even human," Humber yelled. His fists were cocked and ready. The two behind him growled agreement, and Beneban felt more than heard a rumble go through the troop.

Neither Trog nor the defiant troopers had yet to see him. Beneban gestured to his companions and watched to see what would happen.

The fight was short and sharp. Humber's fist swung a metal bar at the Ogdol.

Trog barely moved. One giant Ogdol hand flashed out. Massive muscles bunched, and Humber was lifted a foot from the ground by his hair.

"Little man," Trog boomed into the reddening face with its popping eyes. "If to be human is to be like you, I thank the One that I am not. I am, however, adjutant of this troop. You *will* obey the orders I give you, or you will suffer the consequence." He dropped Humber to the ground. "Mount up, L Troop!"

"Except," Beneban's voice crackled, freezing the sudden flurry of movement, "for Humber and you, Gawl, and you, Morden."

His amber glare pinned the rebels where they stood.

"You three will clean the stables. By the time we return, I wish to be able to eat from the floor, if I so desire, without concern for dirt. Now *go!*"

The three scrambled backward through the crowd

while the rest of the troop shuffled restlessly. Beneban frowned, looking slowly around the circle.

"I believe, gentlemen, I heard Trog give you an order," he suggested quietly.

There was a rush for the riding beasts. In record time L Troop was mounted and at attention. Beneban, riding Kati, took a moment to inspect them.

"You *could* be a good troop," he said finally. "And you are *going* to be. When we return, all gear will be cleaned and polished. The beasts, of course, will be given an extra rubdown special attention to claws and hooves. Lodar, take the point. No running over civilians."

L Troop made good time through the upper city with Trog rolling along at the edge of the troop. Riding beside Tor, Beneban noted that banners were beginning to festoon walls and trees.

"The banners welcome the second sun," Tor said to the curious wizard. "There will be festival for a week, celebrating the coming of spring. It culminates with Greening Day. For the country folk, it is the last chance to relax before the heavy duties of farming."

"Ah," Beneban said, "that explains the party at the home of the Lady Meriel. Actually, at Ka'amfer's home, but his daughter will be the hostess, of course. Do people no longer make pilgrimage to the high priestess Azarta's temple? Where I grew up..."

Tor nodded. "I forget. You must have grown up on the plains in the north. For most people here it would be too far. Look, I think I see Ari's flags below."

"You say this lar, Ari, is your foster father, Tor?" Beneban asked. "I guess I assumed the Grand Lar..."

Tor chuckled. "My mother felt I would get less preferential treatment at a different fostering. Indeed, for the first few weeks I was terrified. Then Ari found me cowering in a corner with some of the fosterlings tormenting me."

"But why did they want to hurt you?"

"Oh, not *hurt* exactly, well, not much. They were determined to show me that Tor of Torling was no one special. I'd about decided I'd *rather* be anyone else in the world," he chuckled. "Then Ari found me. He saw to it that I had instruction in self-defense. Before long, I was holding my own. He convinced me that I *was* special, and that only meant more was required of me. The punishment if he discovered *me* to have picked a fight makes me shudder still."

"He sounds like a remarkable man. Yet you mentioned serving as a page at Larlingarde."

"Yes, for a year, as all heirs to the Twelve Estates do. I missed Ariling far more than I ever missed my own home at Torgarde."

The crowds were thicker now, slowing the pace of the troop. Down several side streets, fair rides were being set up. High swings and round-a-wheels. And the booths of the lower town were expanding, gay with bunting, paper flowers, and other symbols of the season.

Suddenly, from a doorway someone shouted, "Look! The wizard."

The cry was taken up on every side. People pushed into the paths of the kelsh.

"Show us the Great Sword."

"Wizard! The *wizard!*"

"The Magic Bowl..."

Trog moved up beside Kati. "Sir! Someone will get hurt."

"But what do they want? All right." Beneban called the halt. Then, holding one arm high, he waited as the crowd quieted.

"The Great Sword is only drawn in time of need," he cried loudly and waited as the murmur of disappointment died away. "We are on a mission for your Grand Lar, but we would not trample any of you. Please, stand back so we may pass."

There was grumbling, but slowly the throng pushed back until the road lay clear before them.

"Thank you," Beneban called and motioned the troop forward. Behind them, a cheer arose. The words *wizard*, *sword*, and *kalting* sounded above the clamor.

"I don't understand that," Beneban muttered uneasily to Tor as they approached the great gate of the city.

"Ah, rumor has it that you rescued Sel from some dire fate. That plus the fact that Larlingarde has been long without a wizard, and you seem to have gained instant popularity with the people."

"Yes, but that's not good. Our Grand Lar is already less than pleased that I attract friends so easily. Well, there comes your foster father's cavalcade."

Tor rode eagerly ahead, leaning to embrace a tall, rugged lar who sat firmly astride an enormous charcoal-gray kelsh despite one arm held in a sling.

"Tor, lad. I'm right glad to see you!"

"Ari! What happened? You've been injured, and we missed you at OathGive. Here, let me introduce you to

Captain Beneban, head of your escort and my good friend. Beneban, I present my foster father, the Lar Ari of Ariling."

Beneban bowed from Kati's back, checked that the troop was drawn up to attention, and looked back to see the older man's sharp gaze sizing him up.

"If you're Tor's friend, you are mine," he said simply at length. "You'll forgive my handshake, I've only one for my mount."

"Yes, what's happened, Ari?" Tor broke in.

"Let's be riding while I tell you, lad. I'm over late for OathGive already. Besides, I'm ready to be off this beast."

"Trog," Beneban ordered at once. "Take half the troop. Clear the way. Lodar, form the remainder up behind. Move out when you're ready, Trog."

He watched for any trace of resistance to Trog's commands while Ari and Tor talked quietly. Soon the troop was on the move again, more slowly, engorged by the addition of Ari's folk.

"But Forest has always been a safe place, Ari," Tor was saying as Beneban brought Kati alongside the two Lars.

"Aye. Always until this spring," Ari said. "Folk believed that nothing bad could flourish near Forest Lady. Whether 'tis the bitter winter or something else, I'll not guess. There's a change now, and not a good one, either."

"Is there trouble in Forest, sir?" Beneban asked with alarm.

Ari studied him curiously before answering.

"Some folk have always been afraid of the place,

but never 'til this year have I heard of any coming to harm there. Even when some fool wanders in and gets himself lost, he turns up safe in a day or two with tales of being saved by a lady or an ursyn or Azarta knows what. You'd think there's a whole city hidden there to hear the variety folks come up with."

"But it's different now?"

"Aye, Captain. It is." Firmly the older man reined in his mettlesome steed to the pace of the troop. "This year some who stumbled in have not reappeared. The grollings, do you know of them?" At Beneban's startled nod, he went on. "Well, there've been raids on small farmsteads and evidence of grollings being responsible."

"They've never caused trouble before, have they, Ari?" Tor asked.

The older lar shook his head.

"Unpleasant beasts, they are, and I'd not care to run into them alone and unarmed, Tor. They run in small packs. There are rumors they'll take off a lone traveler if the chance is right. But no, to answer plain, they've not been worrisome before." He nodded at his injured arm and continued. "I got this beating off a pack of them, right enough, on my way to Forest Tower. You know it, Tor?"

"One of the relay chains from Bardling. You mean the one on the eastern edge of Forest?"

"That's it. Not even a walled tower, not properly. Just a stone fence around it to keep riding beasts from straying. Though, mind you, that's a fault I've set about correcting."

"Was it a large pack, sir?" Beneban asked.

"About twenty, Captain. There were only five of us. We came on 'em unawares, or they'd likely not have attacked an armed band. They were finishing off a small farmstead as we came down on 'em. This," he indicated his sling, "I got from the pack leader. He was in a corner and knew I wasn't about to let him run. Nor did I. It was vicious what they did to those poor folk. Evil."

"My uncle will be interested in your report," Tor said. "He was just speaking of some missing messengers. I wonder if you don't bring part of the answer."

Ahead, the escort separated to either side of the palace gates and held their mounts to attention. Guards pushed back the huge portals as the three men rode up.

"I'll leave you here, sir," Beneban said. "Tor has much to say to you, and I've a stable to inspect."

"But not to eat at," Tor called laughingly after him. "Remember, we're invited to the banquet tonight."

"Eat? At a stable?" Ari asked, looking from one to the other.

"I'll explain as we go, Ari." Tor chuckled reminiscently. "Until this evening, Beneban."

"This evening," the wizard nodded. "I'll hope to see you there, sir."

The Larlinga disappeared through the gates, followed by Ari's people. Beneban saw the troop held at attention and spoke quietly to Trog. "Take them to the parade ground and work them out for an hour or more. If you have a problem, well, you handled the last one excellently. But let me know who's involved."

"Yes sir." Trog looked up with what might have been a grin. "But as my people say, 'When a rock has hit you on the head, even dullards learn to watch out for landslides.' I don't expect trouble."

A rarely seen smile crossed Beneban's face. "So, you are the rock?"

"I am certainly one rock, sir. At this point, I think *you* are seen as the potential landslide. *Fall to,*" the Ogdol roared. He motioned the troop forward, falling in beside them.

"Borno." Beneban stopped his aide. "I'll need you. After I've inspected the stables, I'll want a bath and clean clothes. I've nothing fit to appear at court, unless this uniform will pass. You'll need to freshen it."

"Sir, the Grand Lar has sent clothing to replace the ruined things. I hadn't time to tell you before."

"He... what? Now *that* surprises me. I suspect Tor's fine hand. Well, no matter. Get that bath ready. The Lady Meriel's nose would be offended by the smell of honest dung."

CHAPTER 14

Later that evening, Beneban wandered silently up a softly lighted hallway, twitching uncomfortably in his unfamiliar clothes. Surely the guard had indicated this direction for the Grand Salon, the pre-dinner gathering place. He smoothed a silky gray sleeve and was saddened by the thought of the old-fashioned court clothes hopelessly ruined by the Grand Lar's sword. Those, though not made for him, had fitted like a second skin. These of richer material and current style seemed to bind in unexpected places as though they resented him.

He reminisced as he walked of the simplicity of his time with Kati, the comfort of a fire in the evening, and the rich green smell of Forest. Why, he wondered, had he come to this complicated, difficult place that seemed to fit him as poorly as the elaborate new clothes?

"What nonsense," he muttered to himself. Saray and Forest Lady, were behind him now.

Ahead, a murmur of voices caused him to hurry. Perhaps he might find the Grand Salon yet.

"...could have ended it at one stroke," an oily voice was saying.

"Not so. We would merely have exchanged one for the other," a woman replied. Her voice faded as though she had turned away then came strongly again. "...seeds of dissension first, and half the job... Oh!"

The Lady Meriel's hand flew to her cheek as Beneban appeared in the door. For a moment, white faced, she stared. Then she hurried forward with a strained smile.

"Captain Beneban, how pleasant that you've arrived early."

"I'm surely not early, my lady? I've been lost in these halls for half the evening seeking the Grand Salon." He looked ingenuously about the magnificent room with its priceless tapestries and other works of art. "Have I found it? Or must I wander on?"

"You have arrived." Meriel placed a small hand on his sleeve. She seemed to relax at his words.

She continued. "Oh, I'm so pleased. Now I can make you known to my father. This is Captain Beneban, sir, of whom I've told you. Captain, my father, Lord Ka'amfer, Advocate to the Grand Lar."

"My Lord." Beneban bowed. He straightened as the old man scuttled forward. Meriel's father was dressed in a rusty black robe of poor quality. A staff assisted his steps. The staff, the wizard noted wryly, made up for the lack of ostentatious dress. Carved by a master of black ebonium, the priceless wood was topped by a huge zeltenstone. It shone a sullen purple in the flickering candle light.

Poor robe or not this old man, the same who sat on the Grand Lar's right at the last dinner Beneban had attended, had his share of vanity.

"Ah, yes." An ingratiating smile spread on the wrinkled face. "Here is the young wizard who so bemused us... or should I say, *bewitched* us, a few nights ago."

The smile, Beneban noticed, never reached the old man's eyes. They were a cloudy, lifeless black. Lord Ka'amfer reached out a gnarled hand and patted Beneban's arm, peering up at him. His hunched, nearly crippled posture made him seem shorter than he actually was.

"Now how *long*, I wonder, were you standing out there trying to decide if this was indeed the right room? Heh?"

Unexpectedly, Beneban felt a tug at his mind. Simultaneously an alarm jolted within him and defenses slammed into place.

Almost before Beneban was sure of the attack, the old man sensed his withdrawal. He backed away, both mentally and physically, scuttling back to stand beside Meriel. When he turned, his eyes were bright with malice.

Gathering his mind, Beneban answered: "Moments only, sir."

"Ah! And I understand we are to have the pleasure of your presence on Starday next, at our small supper, eh? May we also anticipate the attendance of your Ogdol friend?"

"Providing I'm not on duty that day, I'll be there, sir. I haven't yet checked with Trog, my lady." He turned from the uncomfortable gaze of the old man.

"Oh, but I'm counting on you *both*," Meriel cried.

Voices from the hall interrupted her, quickly followed by new arrivals.

Three Larlinga nobles entered and were greeted

effusively by Meriel. Before introductions were complete, Tor and his foster-father, Ari, arrived.

Then two Larlinga noblewomen swept into the room, their shimmergreen hair piled in elaborate court fashion, each elegant finger tipped with long jeweled nail shields. They quickly separated Meriel from the crowd of men and formed a sparkling clot in one corner.

"Beneban," Tor hailed him. "I sent Daram to escort you, but you'd gone. You found your way, I see."

"With difficulty," he admitted. "Good evening, sir." Beneban bowed to Ari. "I expected to get lost though, so I left early."

More people wandered into the room, some drifting over to greet Tor and Ari. Tor introduced Beneban to them. Young Lar Ande of Andeling, and his larya, an attractive Larlinga not so tall as most and modestly dressed; Va'arlan, Arms Master of the Grand Lar's troops and an illegitimate son of a noble family, whom Beneban had already met; and others whose names rattled in the wizard's head like bones in an empty box as he tried to keep them straight. Soon the room was full to bursting with a sparkling company.

"My uncle is coming," Tor whispered just as Mero popped through the door and announced him.

A sudden hush fell on the room.

The Grand Lar entered, dressed elaborately in his habitual blue and silver. Everyone bowed low as he crossed to Ari, ignoring the rest.

"I heard you were here, Ari. We missed you last week at the OathGive."

"You didn't doubt I'd come when I could, I hope, Mightiness?"

"No formality between us. We've been comrades, slept in the same tent. Of course I didn't doubt. I'm only sorry I didn't have time for you this afternoon. If you aren't too tired from your journey, attend me after supper?"

"I look forward to it, sir."

"Excellent. Excellent!" Lyolar started to pat him on the shoulder, saw the sling suddenly, and stopped. A frown darkened his face. "What's this? You've been injured?"

"The reason for my lateness, sir. I'll explain after the meal." Ari indicated the courtiers beginning to fidget at this prolonged dialogue.

"What! Oh, they'll wait. What else are they here for?"

"But I find I'm ravenous, Mightiness, if you will humor an old friend who has traveled far to be here this evening."

"Hardly old, you're my age. But I was thoughtless. I suffer from impatience."

"So do we all, sir," Ari answered smoothly. He, Tor, and Lyolar had already swept from the room by the time the ripple of laughter took his audience.

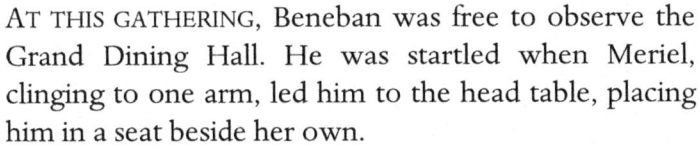

AT THIS GATHERING, Beneban was free to observe the Grand Dining Hall. He was startled when Meriel, clinging to one arm, led him to the head table, placing him in a seat beside her own.

"This surely can't be my place, my lady," Beneban protested.

"You come at my special invitation. Why should it not?" She smilingly indicated Borno, shining with careful grooming, standing behind the indicated seat. Startled, he realized that Kati sat alertly at the lad's feet.

He saw others with personal attendants behind their chairs, and at some places, great wherhounds crouched, waiting for bones from their master's table.

Young attendants stood with lit candelabra against each wall, and light fragments splashed from the jeweled overhead beams. The hearths were cold tonight.

Beneban turned to his page with a scowl. "Borno," he said sternly. "This is no place for Kati!"

The boy's face fell, but Meriel laughed merrily.

"Of course it is. Think of the prestige such a pet gives you. No other at this table owns a kalting. It was at my direction that she and Borno be here."

"She is not, however, a pet, nor do I own her," Beneban said. Ignoring her pout, the wizard stared about the rapidly filling room then bleakly at the great beast, somehow diminished in these surroundings. Yet the kalting's head was high. Her green eyes took in the bustle about her. Once, when a wherhound ventured too near, Kati's quiet snarl convinced the creature to lose interest.

He sighed as Meriel touched his arm.

"How strange," Meriel murmured uncomprehendingly. "I've made another mistake, I gather. But it's too late to take her back now. What harm can it do?"

Feeling cross, Beneban took his seat. He was pleased to find that Ari was situated on his other side.

"Well met again, Captain," the older man said

softly. "I understand you have some familiarity with Forest?"

"Not really, sir. I camped at its edge for only one night on my journey to Larlingarde. Yet I had a strange adventure that night. I think I have friends who live there."

"Strange adventures. Are there any other kind on the edge of Forest? Yet you intrigue me. To my knowledge, no one lives there, unless you believe in Forest Lady."

"I met an old woman named Saray, who claimed it as her home. As for Forest Lady…"

Beneban's words were interrupted by a fanfare of trumpets. The dais door opened. Young Mero, barely visible, struggled with the weight.

Tor entered the room to stand by a second, less ornate chair that had been installed by the Grand Lar's throne. The trumpets blared again, and Lyolar strode to his seat as the assemblage surged to their feet.

Snarling deep in her throat, Kati tensed. Beneban spun to see her crouch, ready for a leap.

"Kati! *No!*" he commanded, thinking for a horrified moment that she was about to attack Lyolar. Then he spied the bent figure of Calibe cowering behind Tor's chair. "No," he repeated in a soft growl. "Stay!"

"Are you quite finished ordering your beast, Captain?"

The icy voice of the Grand Lar woke Beneban to realize that all the room watched with rapt attention, and watched not their royal master, but his own difficulty with Kati.

"Forgive me, Mightiness. Kati should not be here."

"We concur in that opinion, Captain." Lyolar turned and seated himself. He motioned for the court to do the same and remained in cold silence until the first procession of pages bearing food made their way into the room.

Beneban, left standing awkwardly, saw a grin on Tor's face. With a last check on Kati, who now reclined peacefully, the mortified wizard obeyed Meriel's tug on his sleeve and sank back into his chair.

"Never mind, lad," Ari said. "Why, I recall when Lyolar's father ruled..." and the lar was off on a long tale about the past which successfully distracted him.

The feast wore on. There was more food than Beneban had seen in his lifetime. Dainty greens were heaped in enormous crystal bowls, and great jellies of molded fish and vegetable preceded steaming tureens of rich broth. An army of servants whisked used dishes from the table. A cavalcade of pages replaced them with clean tableware.

"Captain." Meriel's voice interrupted Beneban's contemplation of heaped roasted meat on enormous platters parading down the center of the room. "Do tell me about your fight with the assassins. Have you no idea who they were or why they did such a deed?"

"No, my lady." Bemused, Beneban turned from the sight of meat being heaped on his latest salver.

Meriel's lambent eyes were fixed in apparent fascination on his face. One dainty hand, its nails tipped with silver that matched her gown, clasped his silk-clad arm.

"I thought we had one of the villains to question," Beneban perforce returned his attention to her, "but the Worf killed him before we could stop it."

"The Worf?"

"Calibe, my lady. Your little servant."

"I protest, sir, you are too formal. You know my name. And I shall call you Beneban."

"As you will, my lady." Aware of the Grand Lar's malevolent stare, he gently removed her fingers from his arm. He lifted his fork to pick at the heaped meats.

"But how could such a little creature finish off a desperate criminal, Beneban?" Meriel persisted.

"He, the assassin, was held firmly by one of the men when Calibe sprang upon him with a rapier. The Worf took a great deal of initiative on himself, if he was not directed."

"I believe you blame me," Meriel said indignantly. "Surely the Worf is a creature of impassioned loyalty. He was demented by grief."

"So it seemed, my lady." Beneban put a bite in his mouth, hoping to end the subject.

"It was surely robbery. The lure of riches is great to those who have nothing." Again, her small hand took imperative possession of his arm.

Reluctantly, Beneban turned to her. Steam from the hot food, candle smoke, and the rich scent of rare wines seemed to fog the air, even in this high-ceilinged room. Yet he didn't think it explained how his eyes seemed to blur her face slightly.

"Yet Tor tells me," she persisted, "that something bothers you about the death of his mother."

"Does he, my lady?" Beneban rubbed wearily at his eyes. "It is only that her wound should have been instantly fatal, yet she was alive when I entered the clearing. I swear no enemy approached her after that, only the Worf. But when the battle finished, she was dead. And there was a brooch..."

"Captain Beneban."

Uneasy at Meriel's quickened attention, Beneban turned with relief to Ari.

"Sir?"

"You say you passed Forest on your way to Larlion. Where do you come from, then? The North Plains, I wager."

"You'd win your bet, sir, though it's many years since my childhood there." Beneban nodded at the guess. "I had recently finished an apprenticeship and made my way through the Kalds with Kati's help to find a place at court."

"Through the Kalds. Tell me, did you see sign of the Kaldens arming?"

"No sir. I spent the winter in the mountains but somewhat west of their usual range."

"Did I hear you mention the kalting-herders? What do you know of them, wizard?" Lyolar's deep voice boomed from Tor's far side. It cut through the hum of conversation and left a sudden silence.

Beneban, aware of Lar Ari's sudden sharp look, reddened slightly.

"I don't know of them, Mightiness," he stammered. "I've never seen them, save for one or two here in Larlion."

"Yet you own a kalting." The flat statement did not invite a repeat of Beneban's denial that Kati belonged to him. "We have been unable to meet with the Kalden leaders in many months. I wish to arrange for replacement kaltings for my Kaltingcorps and to enlarge the corps, if possible."

"Mightiness, Kati is a wild kalting who chose to befriend me. I have no contacts among the Kaldens."

Lyolar's face darkened in obvious disbelief, but before he could speak, Ari broke in. "Mightiness, this perhaps fits in with some news, or say rumor, I bring you of the Kaldens readying themselves for war."

"With whom?" Lyolar demanded.

"I have yet to verify the rumor. Yet it reached my ears from several sources. I hope to tell you more when we talk later."

"Yes, later." Lyolar turned away after a final glare at the wizard. Gradually the hum of conversation returned.

Beneban's nearly untouched plate was whisked from the table. A page peered unbelievingly into his still-full goblet, and trotted off to fill those of less abstemious guests. Fresh tableware appeared before them. Mounds of fantastic pastries paraded down the room, interspersed with flaming puddings and carved sorbets, already melting in the muggy air.

Meriel laid a small hand on his sleeve. As he reluctantly turned toward her, Ari leaned across.

"Forgive me, my lady. I would finish my conversation with the captain before the meal ends."

For a moment, a steely look about her usually soft brown eyes made Beneban think she would dispute his attention. Then with a pout she released him.

"Never mind," she murmured. "We'll have freedom to talk next Starday." She turned to Tor and began to chatter animatedly.

"So, you *are* a wizard," Ari said quietly. "I've been calling you lad. If the apprenticeship you spoke of was in wizardry…"

Beneban nodded, a small smile lighting his golden eyes.

"Then you'll be at least my age…"

"…but much younger in wisdom and experience, sir."

"Well!" Ari sighed slightly and lowered his voice. "At least I'm wiser in the ways of rulers and courts. If you'll listen to a man who's seen more than he likes of both, stay away from the lady on your left. Unless I'm wrong, Lyolar has an eye for her, and she'd not hesitate to use you to heighten his interest."

"Thank you, sir. Yet he makes it difficult for me to do so without insult to her, and thus, himself."

"Ah, well. Do the best you can. How comes a wizard to be captain of…"

A sudden roar cut off Ari's question. Behind Beneban, Kati had knocked Calibe flat. Before the wizard could react, the kalting grabbed the Worf by his belt. With a tremendous leap, she sprang to the ivory crossbeam above the table.

The assemblage leapt to its feet as horror moved them back away from the table.

"Kati," cried Beneban in dismay. "Bring him *down!*"

"Kill that beast!" the Grand Lar roared.

The double doors burst open and armed guards rushed in. They quickly pulled back their spears but hesitated. If they missed, Kati was directly in line with the Grand Lar. The giant Kalting shook her prey slightly, and brought him into line with any weapons.

"Kill that animal," Lyolar roared again.

CHAPTER 15

"*S*HOOT THAT BEAST!*"* the Grand Lar bellowed again. Guards bumped into each other as some rushed from the room to seek different weapons. Others stumbled about to seek an angle that would allow the shot without danger to other guests.

"Kati!" Beneban roared in dismay. "Bring him down at once."

Guards dashed back, now armed with deadly spring bows. In a hurry to load them, darts scattered on the floor.

"No, *no!* I'll be killed." Calibe gibbered in fear. He swung high above the diners' upturned faces. Many guests leapt to their feet and felt for the weapons they could not bring to court functions.

Kati shook Calibe ferociously.

"Kati. Come down here!" Beneban bellowed.

The kalting ignored him. She shook Calibe again, and a large object fell from the Worf's hands. It narrowly missed a standing lar and landed with a splat between the tables. Guests stretched to see it or craned to watch the desperate Worf.

Everyone froze, even the enraged ruler, as a young wherhound, ignored, left its place down the hall to nose at the object. It was a fine meaty bone. The wherhound settled down to gnaw the unexpected prize.

"Please, Master," Calibe wailed as the court stirred. "Get me down. My lady, help me." Kati crouched motionless on the beam now.

One of the guardsmen with steadier nerves than his fellows fitted arrow to bow and brought another wordless shriek from the Worf.

Beneban held an urgent hand up to Lyolar and watched as the hound gnawed its prize. "Please, Sire…"

Lyolar motioned the archer to wait.

"Well, Captain?" His face was hard as springstone. "Why should your beast not suffer the penalty? He has disrupted my meal and attacked one of the guests…"

Beneban didn't need to answer.

The wherhound suddenly dropped the bone. It stiffened then gave a strangled howl, tried to rise, and then fell heavily. As it thrashed in agony, noble guests leaned closer to stare in horrified disbelief.

One lar stepped to the floor, his face stony. He laid a hand briefly on the hound's head, then approached Lyolar.

"In mercy, may I borrow your weapon, Mightiness?"

Kati was motionless now, and Calibe hung silent.

Wordlessly, Lyolar unsheathed the ornamental dagger at his side and passed it to the Larlinga. The noble quickly knelt beside his agonized animal. He laid his hand on the great head.

The hound quieted. As it met his master's eyes with trust, the man drew the merciful blade across its throat.

Wordlessly he summoned servants and indicated the removal of the hound. The knife he cleaned on a hastily offered hand towel. He returned the blade with a deep bow, hilt first, to his ruler. His face was grim as he returned to his seat.

There was stunned silence then a burst of noise, as neighbor turned to neighbor to suggest, ask, or demand what had just happened.

"Quiet!" Lyolar's roar stopped the incipient panic. "Be seated." And as the company slowly obeyed his order, he turned to Beneban, who still stood beneath Kati and the Worf.

"The meat was poisoned." The Grand Lar stated the obvious.

He looked up where Calibe now hung silent in the jaws of the kalting. "Bring him down, Kati," he ordered.

The kalting leapt lightly to the table then the floor and dropped the Worf at the royal feet.

"Sir!" Borno tugged urgently at Beneban's sleeve. "He did it. He t-tried to poison her, the kalting. I mean the Worf. I... he... I saw..."

"Come here, son. What are you trying to say?" Lyolar's voice was gentler now, aimed not to frighten the nervous boy even more. "Calm yourself, and tell me what you know."

"Mightiness." The boy sank to his knees. "The Worf... He tried to f-feed Kati that bone. He wanted to poison her. She must have sensed it."

"Not so, not so," howled Calibe. He groveled at the Grand Lar's feet. "I only try to make her my friend. Always she growls when I come near. The bone... I found it on the floor, on the floor..." He fell on his face and sobbed piteously.

Lyolar scowled down at him. Finally he turned to Tor, who stared in horror at the creature. "He is, I believe, your servant now? What do you suggest?"

Before Tor could speak, Meriel pushed past him to peer shyly up at Lyolar.

"Please, Mightiness. He was my servant for many years. I cannot believe he would do this thing, but if he did, surely it was out of terror of a beast that threatens him at every approach." Seeing the Grand Lar's face grow hard, she continued, but shifted direction.

"Yet even with such provocation, I do not believe it. If there is no one to say he did *not* find the bone on the floor, surely you will not condemn him?" She turned from Lyolar, to Tor, and back, her face soft and wistful.

"He is your servant, Tor," his uncle repeated coldly. "What is your decision?"

Tor's eyes held on Meriel's anguished face for a long moment.

"I would not condemn him from such scant evidence," he hesitantly said at length. "Yet whatever his motive, I have no doubt he did indeed try to poison Kati. Forgive me, Lady Meriel. He may no longer serve me." Tor turned in disgust from the Worf.

"And you, Lady Meriel? Will you have him back?" Lyolar asked.

There was a long pause. About the room, guests began to shift, uncomfortable from the fumes of food, blood, heat, and tension.

Finally, Meriel wrinkled her nose in distaste and

said firmly, "No, Mightiness. One cannot have a poisoner about, however he may have been provoked. Cast him out to find his way, away from this court." She bowed her head and turned sadly away.

"You hear your doom, Worf," Lyolar said stonily. "Consider this our mercy. You will be escorted to the outer gate and released. Do not appear at this court again, or you will answer on pain of death. Guard!"

As the sobbing Worf was led away, the nobles drifted in twos and threes back to their places. At the door, Calibe pulled loose long enough to glare viciously at Beneban.

"I think you have not made a friend, Captain," Ari said softly.

"Neither have I lost one," the wizard responded dryly.

Lyolar turned grimly to Beneban. "It seems, Captain, that whenever you come to dinner, this court has food for gossip for many weeks. Ari, Tor, attend me. Supper is ended!"

The Grand Lar flung away from the table. For once, even Mero was alert. The door pushed quickly open, and the three disappeared. Lars and nobles were left to stand awkwardly. Some sank back to their seats; others stumbled away from the table. None resumed their meal.

The pages, who now held un-tasted pastries and melted bowls of sorbet, turned back to the kitchens. They had gained an unexpected feast; a gluttony of the sweets craved by the young and so seldom provided in such quantity.

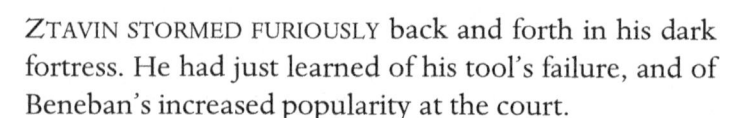

Ztavin stormed furiously back and forth in his dark fortress. He had just learned of his tool's failure, and of Beneban's increased popularity at the court.

"A *'captain,'*" he hissed. "Nothing goes as I plan," he howled.

He kicked one of the helpless drak to crash against the wall. Its fragile shell cracked at the impact, and it lay whimpering.

The drak, an infant vardraken, had been brought to Ztavin by a hunter in the frail hope of favor from the black wizard. It was one of two or three that Ztavin enjoyed using as servants. There would come a time when they would be useful, when the Varkinde queen…

The creature wailed in pain. Impatient with the noise, Ztavin kicked it down the black stairs, where a drak sibling crept to comfort it.

"That wizard *idiot* is now ensconced as a captain of Lyolar's troops. What *ails* that pathetic excuse for a ruler? And my spy, that worthless tool of a Mergol princeling, has been banished from the palace.

"Blast *Beneban!*" This was roared with the force of a viable curse. It bounced from the black wall, narrowly missed Ztavin's head, flew across the room, and shattered two crucibles before it slithered to the floor.

Ztavin paced from wall to wall. Then he circled the room three times as he thought.

"There must be a way to pollute his rosy life. I will…" The black wizard stormed to his work room. With candle and blood he sent a summoning.

"Come on... come on..." Finally a trembling face appeared in his room.

"You, *Calibe*," he hissed, "have failed me."

"I did as you bade. It is *not* my fault that..."

"The interest on your debt grows large," Ztavin interrupted. "Now, here is what you must do. There is one officer who hates your enemy more than you. You will go to him, and..."

"I cannot. I dare not be seen."

"No one will know you are not one of the regular kitchen staff. Just make yourself useful. Glaynar is a willing tool. You had best also be helpful, or..." Ztavin wrung his hands together and was pleased to hear a pained shriek from Calibe.

With a violent crash he closed the sending.

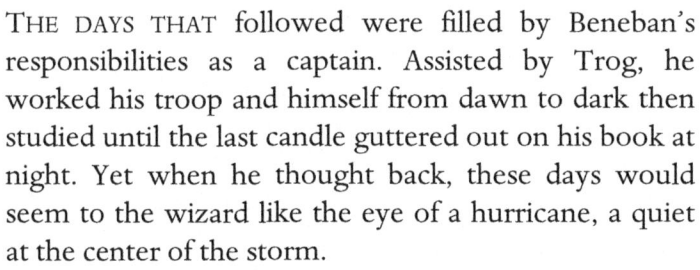

THE DAYS THAT followed were filled by Beneban's responsibilities as a captain. Assisted by Trog, he worked his troop and himself from dawn to dark then studied until the last candle guttered out on his book at night. Yet when he thought back, these days would seem to the wizard like the eye of a hurricane, a quiet at the center of the storm.

There were omens, had he been wise enough to read them. Yet even in retrospect, he could not see how he might have avoided the dangers ahead.

One night, as he looked up from the book that had absorbed him, he met Trog's steady gaze.

Beneban looked about, but saw only the neatly cluttered room. Borno sat cross-legged in one corner and stitched a tear in the wizard's uniform coat. Clothes lay folded in neat piles. Sel's tiny pallet nestled beside the wizard's neat one.

"Trog! Why do you put up with me?" he asked. "You've gone from having a large private room to one with barely enough space to move without tripping over someone."

Trog, as he polished a piece of harness, stiffened slightly. His voice was noncommittal. "Do you wish quarters of your own, sir? As a captain, you..."

"Stop that!" Beneban scowled at the Ogdol. "You *know* I'm happy here, only I should think you'd want more space. But..."

He indicated Borno then the little heap beneath his cot that had become Sel's preferred sleeping spot, and Kati, curled beneath the table where he studied. "Surely every captain doesn't live with his attendants under foot?"

"No. But few are so well served." Trog hesitated then continued. "It is pleasant to me to have these companions. But it might be more suitable to your position if you had a suite of your own."

"'My position?'" Beneban hooted at the thought. "A *suite?* I don't have *that* much position, Trog. Besides, I am comfortable here with friends about me. No, if you won't kick us out, then you're stuck with us. Now who's that?"

The quick *rat-a-tat* was followed by Tor's cheerful face.

"Ah-ha! As I thought, your nose is in a book, Beneban. Evening, Trog. Wizard, I've come to introduce you to some things you won't find in a book. You've been here nearly two Stardays and have yet to sample the pleasures Larlingarde offers. Close that musty old tome. Borno, fetch his cloak." Tor heaved the heavy book carelessly to the other end of the table, ignoring Beneban's squawk of protest, while Borno hastened for his master's red cloak.

"Come with us, Trog," Tor said cheerfully. "This wizard will make a hermit of you unless you resist."

"I thank you. But no, sir, if you will pardon me." The Ogdol smiled at the young lar. "I have the early duty tomorrow."

"Another time, then." He turned as Beneban scowled and reached to retrieve his book.

"No use protesting, Beneban. You're coming with me." Tor pulled the book away and idly read the title. "Treasures of Larlion? Why are you reading this?"

The wizard grabbed the book to look for his place. It was lost. With a sigh, he thumped it down. Borno had brought the wizard's cloak and began carefully folding away his mending.

"No, Borno, continue with your mending," Tor said. "I'll take care of Beneban. Tonight we don't need witnesses."

The young lar flung the red cloak around Beneban's shoulder. "Will you ride Kati? Or shall we get a kelsh?"

Kati, unasked, paced to the door and stood waiting.

"Answer enough," Tor laughed. He pulled the wizard out to where his own mount waited. Soon they left the royal compound to make their way through dark streets toward the lower town. One of Tor's servants trotted ahead with a flambeau. Sel, who had scampered through the door at the last moment, perched behind Beneban on Kati's broad rump.

"The court has missed you these last several nights," Tor said when they'd traveled in silence for a way. "Supper has been dull."

"Your uncle hasn't missed me, I warrant."

"Well, he hasn't mentioned it," Tor admitted wryly. "Do you *still* spend every minute in study? What treasures were you looking into?"

"Idle curiosity," Beneban said quickly. "You mentioned once that Nigeran had run off with two of Lyolar's treasures. I wondered about the second. Wizards always want to know more. From knowledge comes strength."

"Ahh." Tor rode in silence for a minute. "Well," he continued. "The second treasure was a gem of some sort, handed from mother to daughter in the Grand Lar's family. Green, I think. I'm not even sure if it was valuable."

"Hmm. Was it a named stone?"

"I don't know. Never thought much about it. Gone is gone."

Beneban rode in silence, wondering, *Could the green stone possibly be the treasure he needed? But where, if not in Larlion? Did Nigeran still have it?* Well, at any reach, Tor didn't seem to know, and was looking at him strangely. The wizard changed the subject.

"I know I spend a lot of time with the books, Tor. You've spent a lifetime of preparation for your position. I've been pitched into mine headlong."

Tor laughed wryly. "Yet rumor says you outdo all comers in strength and skill. I hear that you ride as though you were part of your beast."

Beneban snorted. "So far I haven't been challenged to the wrong thing. As for riding," he stretched wearily on Kati's back, "I grew up on the North Plains, where herding kelsh is a way of life. An orphan saves many a weary trek when he learns to stick to a wild beast's back."

"You were an orphan?"

"All wizards are so far as I know."

A group of townspeople that moved in a knot slowed the riders' pace. One looked up at the sudden light of the flambeau.

"Look! The wizard."

"Beneban of the golden sword."

"See, the Worf is with him."

"Clear a path. Let them through."

The crowd pushed against the walls to let them pass, and there was an outburst of cheers as they went by.

No one noticed the ragged figure that lurked in the alleyway they passed. Calibe, for it was him, snarled in fury. He scuttled further back, where a pile of rags served as a bed.

Calibe had been marched to the palace gate, not given time to collect his few belongings. He was furious and frightened. As a Mergol princeling, he would have been armed. Now, as Ztavin's creature, he had no defense. Disowned by those who thought of him as 'their Worf,' he had been summarily chased from the palace gates with only the clothes he stood up in. There was only one place he could think of to go.

He would find the river. Once in the water, he

could return to his natural form. He scuttled from shadow to shadow as Asolum sank lower. This area was not friendly to the helpless.

"Psst." The whisper came from between two run-down buildings. Calibe shied like a frightened kelsh and scuttled further into the street.

"Calibe! Prince…" A shadowy figure beckoned. "Come with me. My master sent me to help you."

"Who…"

"Come. My Lord Ka'amfer sent me to find you. He has a plan for your revenge."

Calibe took a step closer to the whispered words. If Ka'amfer would help him, Meriel wouldn't really let him be disgraced. Quickly he moved to the hidden voice, and soon there was only the sound of footsteps. These, too, disappeared in moments, and darkness filled the alley.

CHAPTER 16

"THIS IS RIDICULOUS," Beneban muttered when they were finally past the throng. "I don't understand."

"Don't you?" Tor asked. "How many pays have you collected so far?"

"One. Well, plus a bonus for the troop that made the best show of skill with the kelsh. Why?"

"Have you heard of a place people name the Magic Bowl?"

There was silence. Finally, Beneban asked, "The Magic Bowl?"

"It is a room in the lower town, so I've been told. A place where a child, or any person who is hungry, can come and eat his fill. There is no charge, just a donation if the patron is able."

"I hadn't heard the name," Beneban said evasively.

"It must seem like magic to those who've never had enough to eat," Tor said.

"It isn't magic." For a moment they rode in silence. Beneban sighed and continued. "The food is left from palace suppers." He shrugged. "After the cooks and servants eat their fill, they still throw away baskets full every day. The scullions are glad of a few pistas extra to collect it. For a hundredth of my own pay, two Worfs run the place, and they're better paid than they would be in the mills. But I make it plain that the largess is from the Grand Lar's table."

"Why? The idea would never occur to Uncle Lyolar," Tor said.

"I hope that if he hears of it he'll see it's a cheap way to earn his peoples' loyalty. Someday he may need it."

"Again, why? Why make my uncle this gift?"

"In my own self-interest," Beneban offered. "If your royal uncle thinks I'm trying to win the peoples' loyalty for myself, it could get very uncomfortable for me at court."

"I see." Tor chuckled sympathetically. "Well, you'd better spread the word more efficiently. As of now, the credit is strictly yours." He changed the subject abruptly. "Say, you do remember that tomorrow is Starday?"

"Yes. I saw you with the Lady Meriel in the garden today when I was on duty."

"She is quite anxious for you and Trog to attend her father's supper. She asked me to remind you."

"It appeared as though she'd never miss me if you attended the feast."

"Nay, you mistake her." They turned into an inn yard. In the light streaming from the door and window, Beneban saw Tor's face had darkened with embarrassment. "She is only interested in my uncle. The rest is mere playfulness. She sees me as a boy."

"Forgive me this question, but how does your uncle see you? It is none of my business, true. Yet the lady's *playfulness* could get someone's throat slit. Lyolar regards her as his property."

"Yes, as do I." Tor dismissed his torch bearer. He dismounted with a sigh, and threw the reins to a waiting servant.

Beneban alit and patted Kati. "Stay here, girl. Sel, watch out for her."

Tor continued in a low tight voice. "I wish the lady looked on me with favor, yet my uncle would make her his consort. No sane woman would consider my suit with that possibility before her."

Putting an arm around Tor's shoulders, Beneban broke the tension with a wry chuckle. "I can't pretend to speak for a woman, sane or otherwise. But I know which of you I prefer. Now, if you would introduce me to the delights of the city, tell me where we are."

Tor shrugged away his momentary depression.

"Welcome to the Laughing Mergol, Captain," he exclaimed. "See, here is a courtyard for the animals, and the owner has come to greet us."

A plump jolly woman had appeared in the doorway. She peered out to see who had arrived at her rear door.

"My stars, Lar Tor!" she cried. "Ye've been too long away, my darling lar. And who's your handsome friend? Come in, come in. Wash the dust from your throats."

"Maggie, my love, let me present Captain Beneban, newly of His Mightiness's Troops."

"Oooh-er!" The lady clapped pudgy hands in delight. "You 'aven't brought me the wizard captain the whole city's gabbling about? You do be welcome 'ere, Captain!" She led them quickly through the busy kitchen, filled with aromas that made Beneban salivate.

"Stolpan!" Maggie clapped her hands sharply: "Two mugs o' the best. Right quick now!" A Worf, bent and gray with years, scuttled toward the kitchen.

"Come in, come in. Sit ye down, loves. What'll ye 'ave for supper, now?" An Othring of uncertain age, Maggie's flaming hair belied the wrinkles on her face. Her warm welcome, however, easily explained the crowd in her main room.

"Or do you want a private room now?" For a moment, worry clouded her brow. "They're all in use, but..."

"No need, Maggie darling." Tor took her hand. "We're here for a bit of revelry. A spot at a table will do nicely."

"Ah, ye're my own sweet lad, Tor, so ye are. 'Ere, then!" She pushed a bench of ancients closer together to make room for them. "I've good roast gorsan or suckling eberveh, meat pasties, too."

"All of 'em, my love," Tor said cheerfully. "This man barely remembers to eat. We'll fatten him up while we have the chance."

Soon the table was piled with food, tastier, Beneban declared, than any delicacies that graced the Grand Lar's banquets. He got a decided agreement from Tor.

"Perhaps it's the company," he added, as a merry band pushed into the room. Among them were Glaynar and several captains. Beneban recognized Me'ekalar, Ranald, Doryl, Ayngos, and others whose names he had forgotten.

Soon waves of golden ale filled drinking mugs, and as sobriety sank into the mellow sea, the level of merriment rose high.

A sudden trill of music silenced the room. On a dais near the kitchen door stood a stalthinger, a traveling singer. He was a slender youth, graced with the shimmergreen hair of the Larlinga, yet dressed in wanderer's rags. His long fingers swept again across the strings of his staltin.

"Ravel!" The cry arose. "Play for us, Ravel."

"Of course," laughed the boy. "Why else have I come? What will you have, noble gentlemen?" The crowd named song after song, and as the fine-boned face turned from one to another, Beneban realized with shock that those eyes, blue as ice that glinted in the sun, were blind.

"Enough," cried Ravel. "Let me play these requests. There will be time for more."

His lack of sight didn't lessen his expertise. He swept the strings with authority into the bawdy drinking songs the crowd demanded then silenced them with the poignant ballad of a wanderer, far from home and loved ones. This was followed with a rousing battle song that brought the men to their feet with a roar at the end.

In the silence that followed, Ravel seemed to speak to Beneban's mind, though the wizard knew that was unlikely. Yet as the urge came to him, he felt the need to name a song for the stalthinger.

"What else, nobles and captains?" Ravel asked softly. His head turned toward the wizard. His blind eyes touched the wizard's face.

"Do you know "The Ballad of the Black Heart"?" Beneban named a story song, famous on the North

Plains, of a legendary leader who turned to black deeds in bitterness for the loss of his beloved.

The lad started gently, sang it well, and swept with strength to the climax where the hero, dying, realizes he has lost his beloved, not only in his present life but due to the evil he has done in his despair:

> *And Naraban,*
> *As death his eye did darken*
> *Saw once again*
> *His love, Larlinda fair.*
> *Tears starred her eye,*
> *And though she reached down to him,*
> *The blackness of*
> *His life*
> *A high wall built*
> *That none should reach*
> *Him from above.*
> *"Forgive me, love,"*
> *He cried aloud,*
> *And died."*

Voice and music whispered into the silence of the room. Ravel's slim hand stilled the final vibration of the staltin. He sat, head bent over the instrument.

There was a scatter of applause. One or two of the more besotted customers pounded a mug and clamored for more, but the mood had changed. Ravel excused himself with a promise to return, and disappeared through the rear curtain that led to the courtyard.

"My aunt's name was Larlinda," Tor said softly.

"She was the one who eloped with a wizard?" Beneban stared at him and shrugged. "Different names are given the protagonists in different versions. Was her wizard named Naraban?"

"Close enough. It was…"

In the corner, Glaynar leaned to whisper in Me'ekalar's ear. Beneban's eyes were abruptly drawn to the scene. He watched as the disgraced ex-captain refilled his companion's cup with a generous hand. Me'ekalar, the Kaltingcorps captain, seemed dazed. He had propped himself on the table with one arm. The other lifted the cup unsteadily to his mouth.

"Wizard's names are often similar. It's only coincidence," Beneban answered absently, watching the interaction between Me'ekalar and his companion. "Tor, What happens if Lyolar's captains get drunk in town?"

"If they start trouble, they're disciplined. Same thing if they don't return to quarters in time for report. Why?"

Tor's eyes followed Beneban's to the corner table. "Oh, Me'ekalar. Normally he outdrinks everyone, but not tonight, I think."

"Glaynar's been more than liberal. He's kept the lad's cup full and poured poisonous words in his ear, I think," the wizard murmured.

The demoted captain of L Troop whispered again in Me'ekalar's ear. The latter glared across at Beneban.

"I think we should slip out, Tor," Beneban urged. "Trouble is about to start."

"Surely not…"

Tor watched as Me'ekalar lurched to his feet and

pushed a citizen roughly out of the way. The young lar stood, unsteady, and glared about the room. Beneban was already moving.

"Nay! I see you are right." Tor pulled Beneban to the rear of the room.

"Let's remove the problem to the courtyard. The less witnesses, the better. The door behind the stage is closest."

Tor and Beneban barged through the crowd around the empty stage. They dodged cooks and bustling scullions and won passage through the kitchens, fragrant with good food, to the back entrance. As they slipped into the dark beyond, Kati stood, alert and ready. They hurried across the courtyard.

From the inn came a startled yell followed by a clatter of pots and pans.

"We are too late," Tor growled.

The kitchen door slammed open. Light sputtered across the cobblestones. Tor snatched the reins from the attendant who roused slowly from a nap against the wall and swung the beast to mount as Me'ekalar lurched toward them.

Beneban ignored the captain. He started to mount Kati but was slowed by the wail of Sel, still half asleep in the corner where the kalting had waited.

Now the drunken Me'ekalar grabbed a handful of Beneban's scarlet cloak and spun the wizard to face him.

"Where do you go so fast, Captain Wizard?" he snarled. "Why do you run away?"

In the calm tone Beneban used to settle restless steeds, he answered, "I don't run, Captain. We plan to return to the barracks. Will you ride with us? The hour grows late."

The easy invitation befuddled Me'ekalar. He released Beneban's cape and stared about as if puzzled at what had become of his companions. For a moment it seemed he might ride with them.

A shout from the inn recalled Me'ekalar to his grievance.

"Where now is the golden sword we hear so much of, wizard?" He pushed Beneban. "Are you afraid to fight me then?" he demanded angrily.

"Why should I fight you, Captain? We have no quarrel."

"He who calls another 'bardack' may expect to defend his words with his sword." The drunken officer fumbled for his weapon.

As though by accident, Tor turned his beast to bump the drunken captain. The officer's sword clattered to the ground.

"No doubt you are right, Captain Me'ekalar," the young lar said soothingly. "Yet who has called you such a name? Not my friend here."

"You should pick your friends more carefully." The befuddled captain bent to fumble for his lost weapon in the spastic shadows of the cloud-spattered moons.

"I won't fight him," Beneban said softly to Tor. "He's too drunk to see, much less have a chance against Heldenhaft."

"Yet, what *can* you do?" Tor asked.

Me'ekalar, rearmed, stumbled up and swung wildly about. He spied Beneban, pointed his sword in the approximate direction of the wizard's midsection, and bellowed, "Defend yourself!" Then without waiting for the wizard to draw his sword, the besotted captain lurched forward.

Beneban waited until the last instant. He heard a shuffle of feet behind his drunken antagonist.

"Tor, 'ware behind you," he cried. He saw a flash of movement near the door. He stepped outside Me'ekalar's drunken thrust, then hit him a short hard clip on the jaw.

The Kaltingcorps captain straightened. He staggered backwards and fell. There was a cry and a musical clatter. They heard the sound of wood splintering.

"It's the singer." Tor disentangled the sprawl of arms and legs and helped Ravel to his feet.

"The idiot fell right on him, and Me'ekalar is unconscious, Beneban. With luck he'll forget what happened when he wakes."

"*My staltin!*" The blind lad knelt to fumble beneath the fallen captain. A servant cracked open the door to see what caused the noise.

The dim light showed Ravel, who clutched the shattered instrument to his thin chest. "How now shall I earn my living?" He sat cross-legged on the cobbles and cradled the broken shards as though they were an injured child.

Tor looked back at the inn, the door now closed. "What's to do? Beneban, come on. Those who pushed Me'ekalar into this have gone, I wager. If we leave him here, he'll be on report for some time. He won't bother you soon again."

"We can't leave him to that. The quarrel was

caused by another." Beneban bent over the fallen captain and touched his forehead lightly with his Omera to deepen his unconsciousness.

"We'll take him along," he said to Tor. "By morning he may have forgotten, or perhaps I can reason with him once he is sober. But what about you, lad?" Beneban knelt beside the singer.

The boy's face was that of one who had suffered a mortal wound. He was silent, in shock, and seemed to expect nothing.

"He'll be alright. Someone will care for him." Tor turned to his steed.

"Tor, it was not 'someone' who did this to him." Beneban stood lost in thought for a moment. "Kati can bear Me'ekalar and me. Will your beast support the lad?"

"My kelsh? Yes. But to what purpose? You can't take him home to Trog, can you?" Tor swung up on his beast.

Beneban looked up at him in thought then said, "Perhaps I shouldn't. I already have more dependent on me than..."

"I shall not be your dependent, my captain!" The boy's blind eyes stared defiantly toward Beneban's voice.

"Yes, yet because of my trouble, you have been robbed of your living, Ravel. Well," Beneban sighed as the boy backed stubbornly away, "for tonight at least, I know of shelter for you and food for the morrow. Up, lad. We've much to do before dawn." He pulled the lad up and saw him mounted behind Tor. Then he heaved Me'ekalar's limp body across Kati's broad back.

"Come, Tor. We'll see if they sleep soundly at the Magic Bowl. They will give the lad shelter. Now where has Sel gone?"

The Worf child scampered from the shadows where he'd huddled, safe from the big peoples' fight. He leapt to balance precariously on Kati's broad rump.

As they sped through the back gate, the sound of the Watch came to their ears.

"Our friend Glaynar leaves little to chance," Tor said wryly. "He's alerted the guard to the fight. Ah, Beneban," the young lar said cheerfully. "Life is never dull when you are around."

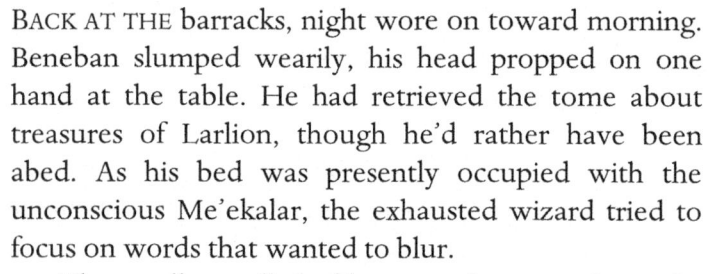

BACK AT THE barracks, night wore on toward morning. Beneban slumped wearily, his head propped on one hand at the table. He had retrieved the tome about treasures of Larlion, though he'd rather have been abed. As his bed was presently occupied with the unconscious Me'ekalar, the exhausted wizard tried to focus on words that wanted to blur.

The candle smelled of hot wax. It guttered near its end and barely lighted the table.

Trog, Kati, and Borno slept soundly, as did the unconscious Kaltingcorps officer. Only Sel had spurned his sleeping pallet. He lay on the bare floor, one arm relaxed about the wizard's ankle, his head just visible beneath the splash of scarlet cloak with which Beneban had draped him.

"Uhhh... Call me bardack..."

Beneban loosed his ankle from the Worf's grasp

and crossed to the recumbent captain. He laid a cool hand lightly on the sweaty forehead. "You'll be all right now, Me'ekalar."

The Kaltingcorps captain's eyes fluttered open and focused on the face above him. He spun from beneath the hand and swung his feet to the floor. He grabbed for the wizard's throat and fell with a crash as Beneban moved easily out of his way behind the table.

With a sleepy grumble, Trog sat up. Kati half stood and growled a deep alert. Me'ekalar looked from Trog to Kati. Now he stared about in bleary puzzlement.

"Where am I? Did I dream?"

"You are in my quarters, Captain," Beneban offered. "You have been asleep these many hours. If you mean our quarrel, it was real, though falsely started. You tried to skewer me. I rendered you unconscious and brought you here to sleep it off," the wizard continued. "Tor said the Guard takes and ungenerous view of captains too sodden with drink to return to barracks."

"Our quarrel was *real*." Me'ekalar surged up from the floor. With the tenacity of a wherhound on the trail of prey, he stuck to what he saw as the issue. "Then you still owe me satisfaction."

"With swords? I think not. If I use Heldenhaft, even your skill wouldn't save you. With a less magical blade, you'd whittle me into kindling. Swordplay isn't in a wizard's course of study. I have no desire for either result."

"You cannot call me bardack and refuse to fight." Me'ekalar stuck to his point like a glompet fish.

"I could, but I didn't. As I told you, the quarrel was

falsely started. If you wish evidence, I can only say that as a wizard, if I wished to insult someone, I'd hardly pick a term that fits me better than it possibly could anyone else."

Me'ekalar stood, weaving from side to side. "I don't understand."

"I knew neither mother nor father. If the tales speak truth, I was hatched from a spell on a wizard's workbench. The complete *bardack*, if you will." Beneban chuckled. His eyes invited the other man to share his amusement.

With a weary sigh, Trog relaxed, convinced his friend was in no danger.

Me'ekalar's mouth curved reluctantly at the edges. Finally he subsided on the bed with a sigh. "If you really disliked me, you'd have left me for the guard. Instead, you've tucked me cozily into a bed..." He looked about the room. "*Your* bed, in fact. Well," he said and brushed a lock of hair from his eyes, "then *I* owe *you* an apology."

His face grew greenish. Beads of sweat popped out on his forehead. He clapped a hand to his mouth and looked about wildly.

Beneban hustled him outside. He held Me'ekalar's head until he finished vomiting. Then he led him back to the bed and brought him a cool cloth.

Me'ekalar wiped his brow and lay back with a weak smile. "I owe you more than an apology," he said. "Drink never takes me like that."

"Certainly your companion worked to be sure you lost your wits," Beneban said. "Beyond that, I do not know."

"Well," Me'ekalar said stubbornly, "still, I do owe you..."

"Never mind," Beneban interrupted. "Just remember that whoever has told you tales about me..." As a stubborn look crossed Me'ekalar's face, Beneban continued. "Just remember, they don't wish me well. I don't ask their names. You'd feel you betrayed them. Besides, I could guess well enough." Me'ekalar stared owlishly into the amber eyes. "You're serious," he concluded at last. He sat up cautiously. For a moment his face paled. Abashed but relieved, the lad continued. "Still I am in your debt. How may I repay you?"

"The only thing I want of you is your friendship, which must be earned. If you must have a price for this night, teach me to fight with a sword."

"You mock me." Anger flickered across the passionate face. "Your swordsmanship confounds us all."

"Perhaps, but Heldenhaft is responsible. You *use* your sword. I am used *by* mine."

Me'ekalar sorted through the words. "Then I'll be honored to teach you, certainly. But the sword is my joy. To teach it is no penalty. Name me a service."

"If the service I ask is joy to you, then it serves me doubly. There is nothing else." Me'ekalar stood, stubborn and silent, and Beneban had a sudden thought. "Stay: There is one thing more. If you chance across a staltin at a price that would not beggar me, I would be grateful."

"A staltin?" Me'ekalar shook his head in bemusement. "Do you play?"

"No. I owe a debt," the wizard said simply.

"Then I shall watch. Now I'll return your bed to

you and seek my own." He tried his feet, found they held him and that his eyes had stopped seeing double.

"There's no hurry, Captain Me'ekalar. It nears dawn."

"An hour in your own bed is better than none. But if you truly hold no grudge, call me Me'ek as my friends do." With a wobbly smile, he made a shaky way to the door.

Beneban watched until he had rounded the corner of the barracks. Wearily he kicked off his shoes.

"That was well done, Captain," Trog said softly. "I'll wake you in time for report."

"Please," Beneban mumbled, and then he slept.

CHAPTER 17

"SWORDPLAY IS EXCELLENT exercise," Beneban groaned as he rubbed himself down with a piece of rough cloth. "Me'ek is a fine teacher." The weary wizard had kept his appointment with the Kaltingcorps captain. Though he awoke feeling that exercise was the last thing he wanted, he felt the relationship with Me'ekalar was important, so he dragged himself to the meeting. He had been pleased to start on this new skill and found that rather than being exhausted, his energy level had improved. "It stretches muscles I've never used," he added, reaching for the clean clothes laid out on the bed. He watched Borno carry buckets of dirty bath water away.

"Did the lesson go well?" Trog asked.

"Yes." He pulled on a silky white shirt and the gray court breeches as he added, "I wish this evening at the Lady Meriel's supper might be as enjoyable. I think you should go, Trog, and let me take the duty. I'm sure the food will be excellent, at least, and she did invite you specifically."

One large eye gazed unhappily at the wizard. "I will go, if you order me, Captain," Trog said stoically. The idea plainly did not attract his friend.

"No, of course not." Beneban touched his friend's

shoulder. "You are obviously averse to the idea. But why?"

Reluctantly the Ogdol explained, "The Lady Meriel boasts that her parties are 'different.' They often are, in the fashion of a freak show at Festival. I prefer not to be the freak she puts on parade."

"Only a fool would think of you as a freak, and though she hides it carefully, the lady is not a fool," Beneban protested. "But if her purpose *is* to use you as entertainment, we will foil her. Take the duty tonight, Trog. She'll have to manage with a wizard."

"Thank you, sir. But..." The Ogdol hesitated.

"Well? What else?" Beneban asked with a smile. His friend was rarely as undecided as he seemed at this moment.

Trog continued with an uncertainty rare for him. "It may be a mistake for you to go, rather than..."

"Nonsense. If you do not wish to go, Trog..."

"I have been laughed at before without damage. For you, there may be some danger."

Beneban shook his head. "The lady endangers young Tor. Being neither young nor infatuated, I am not in danger."

The Ogdol rubbed a large hand through his fur and left it on end in a sign of worry.

"What?" Beneban demanded impatiently. "What *is* it, Trog?"

"Sir, the fact that she does not attract you... She may see that as a challenge. As you have said, she hides her true nature." Trog paced to the wall and back then laid one great hand on the wizard's arm. "Be wary, sir. Guard yourself. My people say, 'A helpless female can bring down a warrior invulnerable to a troop of swordsmen.'"

"A wise saying. Your peoples' words are worth attention, my friend. I shall be alert for danger. But remember that Tor will be there too. He is a good companion."

"He approaches now." Trog's hearing was keen. He hurried to admit the young lar. Tor was a striking figure that evening, handsomely clad in the forest green-and-gold uniform of his house.

"Good evening, Trog. Do you join us tonight?" Tor asked. He committed one of his hands to the enormous grasp of Trog's six fingers.

"Not this time, sir. I will take the duty tonight."

"Ah. We'll miss your company. Beneban, my friend," he turned to the wizard. "It's a fair distance to Ka'amfer's residence. We must go. Do you ride Kati?"

"No." the wizard said. "I'll not leave Kati in strange quarters for the duration of a long meal. Borno will find a kelsh for me. In fact, here he is." Beneban stepped toward the door, but something snagged his foot. He looked down. "No, Sel," he said. He bent, and gently unwrapped the waif's arms from his ankle. "Stay tonight. I trust you to care for Kati."

He would remember later that, in a look over his shoulder, he saw Kati and the little Worf crouched mournfully together in the open door. They watched as the friends rode off. Beneban lifted a hand to them, but neither responded.

CELEBRATING REVELERS PACKED the streets nearly to the gates of Lyolar's palace. This first day of summer, when the green sun, Zartum, rose in the sky to join Asolum, was called Greening Day. It was the beginning of summer, of warmth and the promise of plenty. Gifts were given and received. Troths were exchanged, as houses great and small planned to be united, though marriages would come at the end of the growing season. It seemed that the entire city celebrated, and the crowds were rowdy.

Free food and drink decked long tables at every crossroad, replenished as they emptied. Much of it was largess from Lyolar, though some businesses set out food and drink as well, hoping for customers. Jugglers, mimes, and acrobats performed wherever you looked. The cheerful, drunken push and shove of the mob blustered against Tor's and Beneban's kelsh. It was a struggle for them to stay close.

"The party," Tor called to his friend across a cavorting juggler, "at Ka'amfer's home, the celebration... less chaotic than... this."

Beneban sincerely hoped Tor was right. He dodged a flung globefruit, avoided stepping on a mime, and edged closer to the young lar, glad of his guidance. "How much further?"

"We are arrived, my friend." Tor had paused at tall bronze gates. Now, at the rap of his crop, they swung open, and the companions entered a walled garden that surrounded Ka'amfer's house. The gates swung closed with a hush. It left an abrupt silence that was disorienting.

"Which way?"

Before Tor could answer, Worfs serving as grooms in Ka'amfer's livery, scurried forward to take their mounts. They shied away in fear as Tor offered a coin to one to give his animal a rubdown. At once an old Worf, a steward also in livery, hobbled forward. He hissed words too soft for the newcomers' ears. The grooms cringed away from him but quickly took the reins of the newcomers' kelsh.

"These ones will of course, sirs, give your mounts proper treatment," the steward assured them. "No gifts are needed."

Ignoring Tor's protest, he turned away. "Come, my Lars. Follow me." Without pause to see if they obeyed, he led them along a path of crushed shell through the gardens and an orchard, toward a sprawling house of coralstone. Its doors were flung open to the breeze. Now Ka'amfer materialized from a side path. At an impatient gesture from their host, the steward bowed and scuttled away.

"Ah, the noble Lar Tor." Ka'amfer's jagged teeth bared in a feral grin and he bobbed over his stick. "Heh! So good that you could attend my humble gathering. And here is our wizard Captain... or Captain Wizard? No matter," he chortled and turned away. "Come in. Come in. We shall have a cool drink. So warm it is when both suns ride the sky." The old man led them toward an open portal. The shadows beyond seemed inviting in the heat, yet both guests hesitated.

"Come now!" Ka'amfer urged them. "My daughter makes herself beautiful in your honor. She will attend us soon."

"So lovely a lady needs no adornment," Tor said

self-consciously. Hot color flooded his young face as he moved to follow their host. He linked an arm with Beneban and pulled him forward.

"Ah, yes," Ka'amfer chortled. "Yes indeed. Yet what lady was ever willing to abide mere nature's gifts, eh? Come. Come in here. It is so dusty on the streets. The rabble during Greening make so much noise and commotion. Yet here you are. You'll have something to refresh you?" He snapped his fingers.

A slender Worf maid, barely out of childhood, hurried from the corner at the sound. Head ducked, she began to fill crystal goblets with a cool fruit drink. Small tables were set beside their chairs. The girl placed a fragile goblet carefully on each. As she bent to set the last drink beside Ka'amfer, his elbow bumped the table as though by accident. The table tumbled. Glass shattered, and green liquid puddled on the tiled floor. The girl cowered away from them.

"No matter, child," Beneban murmured. "Only an accident."

Ka'amfer, however, made no effort to calm her. Beneath his malicious stare the girl dropped to her knees and nervously plucked crystal shards from the spreading puddle. Ka'amfer continued to glare, and she burst into tears and fled.

"Trained help is so hard to find, heh?" the old man sighed dramatically. "Well, well. Bring your drinks. We'll retire to the garden room until this mess is cleared."

He led them to a room where a small stream fell over artistically placed rocks and gurgled beneath a wall of clear thin quartz. Tubs of flowers and greenery were everywhere. One panel of the wall was pushed back so that a sheltered garden blended with the interior to form a huge space. As Beneban paused to appreciate a rare bush that flowered near the door, Meriel appeared from the garden.

"My lords." She looked charmingly confused as she dipped a curtsy to them all. "Can it be so late?" A simple coral dress clung gently to her form. The deeper rose of a wispy cloak was caught high on one shoulder with a shimmergreen clasp. The drape caressed her lush curves. Creamy blossoms filled her arms and accented her dark hair and sparkling eyes.

"Your arrival is always in good time," Tor began awkwardly. Both guests moved as a golden bloom fell from her bouquet. Beneban beat Tor's darting hand to retrieve it. Meriel touched the wizard's fingers lightly as he proffered the blossom. She smiled playfully up at him, but his eyes were fastened to the clasp of her cloak.

"Keep the flower, Captain." Her voice caressed him. "May it be a memento of what will surely be an exciting evening."

Grave and puzzled, his eyes met hers. The setting sun seemed to cast a golden mist about her. Beneban's thoughts jumped to a scene of carnage on the Great Road. *Where was the pin that clasped the cloak of Tor's dead mother? He had taken it. Where had it gone? Was this the same one? Or a copy?*

"Beneban?" Tor's voice recalled him to the present.

"I thank you, my lady," he said slowly. "Yet a soldier's life is too rough to allow for such dainty trophies. This evening's memories will keep most safely in my mind."

"Oh, well," she snapped. She shook away Tor's eager hand, and flung the flower at a hovering servant. "Then we must make your evening memorable indeed." Her voice was icy. "Now tell me," she snapped, "*what do* you find so interesting about my shoulder, sir wizard?"

For again, Beneban's gaze had moved to the pin that held her drapery. It was shimmergreen and intricately wrought in the shape of a leaping fish.

"I have seen another very like your pin."

"Have a drink, daughter," Ka'amfer interrupted. He motioned to the maid who had run away earlier but now huddled at the door. "Get Lady Meriel a glass of curraine, Carly. Have you lost your *wits*?"

The last words seemed equally to snap at the maid and at his daughter.

The maid returned quickly with a frosted glass of pale green liquid. Meriel snatched it and quaffed a quantity of the contents. For an instant, it appeared that she would leave the room. Ka'amfer clutched her arm and murmured a few words too low to be overheard. She stiffened, and a commotion at the door announced new arrivals.

Meriel shrugged off her father's hand, but turned to greet the guests. The light conversation that ensued eased the tension that had briefly filled the room.

Some of the newcomers were familiar to Beneban from the Grand Lar's dinner, though he was glad to have them introduced again. The Lar Ande of Andeling and his consort had sat on one side, just beyond Meriel, as Lar Ari had on his other. Lar Ande spoke to Beneban with a smile and introduced his shy wife, Amlia, to him.

Two court ladies, also from the Grand Lar's dinner, made a chattering arrival. He had forgotten their names, but soon picked them up in the ensuing conversation. Mylarma was tall, with the typical look of a noble Larlinga. She and Rhonde, an Othring who seemed to be her close friend, quickly moved to Meriel's side. Soon their hostess smiled and chattered with them. Her momentary pique seemed to have vanished.

Now more guests poured into the room. They filled it with color and noise. Light conversation bubbled, punctuated by merry laughter. It was abruptly silenced by a surprising newcomer.

A Kalden warrior dressed in leathers loomed in the doorway. A golden kalting skin was slung over one shoulder. "Hundak is here!" the behemoth boomed in a bellow that drowned scattered talk.

The silence which fell was broken only by a nervous titter from Rhonde. Meriel, however, seemed unsurprised. She took a pleased Tor's arm as she hurried to greet the giant. General conversation sputtered to life again.

Hot anger filled Beneban's throat. He turned to find Ka'amfer beside him, leaning on the elaborate stick, a twisted smile on his face. "My daughter charms even the wildest beasts, Captain. You needn't worry."

Beneban interrupted in quiet fury. "Your *daughter* would have needed more than charm had my comrade Trog accepted her invitation tonight. Ogdols and Kalds are mortal enemies."

"An oversight, my dear captain."

"An oversight that would have caused bloodshed,

sir," Beneban snapped.

Amazingly, Ka'amfer simply chortled. "Plans change." He turned away. "No worry, though, heh?" he added over his shoulder to the fuming wizard. "No need to patch a robe that isn't torn."

Now late guests blocked the door and crowded the room in a final rush. At the announcement of supper, it emptied even more quickly.

"Ah, the guests have all arrived," Ka'amfer said, "and my majordomo announces supper. Come."

Beneban took an angry step toward the outer door. He tired of this farce. He would find his way back to Trog and Sel...

Ka'amfer grasped his arm. He leaned heavily, as though he might fall. "Please, I am too long standing," the old man murmured. "Lend me your support. We will follow the crowd to the dining room."

The wizard was trapped. Ka'amfer leaned on his arm as though his stick was insufficient. Now he drew his reluctant guest down a hallway, with the babble of the fading conversation ahead of them. His apparent lameness caused them to fall some distance behind the supper crowd.

Unable to ignore the old man's need, Beneban watched as the others disappear around a distant corner. Then a faint noise made him turn.

A small bent figure scuttled across the hall behind them. Beneban stopped abruptly and tried to turn. "Now what disturbs you, young man?" Ka'amfer hissed. He pulled at Beneban's arm, and peered up questioningly. "My guests will await our arrival, heh? Yet we go slowly enough..."

"I thought I recognized... Yet Calibe was banished from court," the wizard mumbled. "Even your daughter disowned him." He rubbed his eyes.

"*Calibe?*" Ka'amfer hissed. "I shouldn't think so, heh? We'll have no poisoners here." The old man looked about and nodded. "You but saw another of our servants. I hire as many Worfs as I can, poor things, but you certainly didn't see Calibe. They look so much alike." The gnarled hand drew Beneban firmly down the long hall. They passed two doors before the old man spoke again. "About my daughter, Captain. I apologize for her temper. Yet any girl would be piqued who spent hours on her toilette only to have all the attention stolen by an inconsequential bauble on her cloak."

"Not inconsequential, sir. I've seen only one other like it."

"You've seen another? May I ask where? The rascal who executed that commission for me—for my daughter's birthday, you understand—assured me it was one of a kind."

"It was in the hand of the dead Larlinga. Oh!" Beneban staggered. His skin prickled as though a thousand barbittes had attacked. They were beside a closed black door. He flicked a hand to set a protective shield. Magic, strong magic. The zeltenstone on Ka'amfer's stick flared with sullen purple light.

"I forgot. Indeed, I did. Heh." Ka'amfer peered up from beady, slightly amused eyes. "You see the stone's radiation, heh?" The old man forced a chuckle. "Of course, to a powerful wizard like yourself, it is nothing, a plaything, a toy, heh? Minor magic passes dull hours for a cripple. Someday, perhaps, you'll visit my workroom. Come now, before my guests despair of supper." The old man towed Beneban away from the door. The zeltenstone faded to its normal sullen gleam, and the wizard relaxed his shield.

Before he could formulate a question, they rounded the corner.

"We have arrived," Ka'amfer announced loudly as they entered a large dining chamber.

He moved quickly now, away from his companion before Beneban could demand answers. His infirmity seemed to have passed. All eyes turned to them and made it impossible for the reluctant wizard to leave without insult.

Servants moved the clustered guests to places at the semicircular table as music trilled from a hidden alcove. Platters heaped with food were paraded into the room for the guests' delectation.

Beneban looked around for a way to leave, but a servant led him to an unclaimed seat. Reluctantly, he settled there as he puzzled over unanswered questions. He paid little attention to his food or his neighbors.

Did Lyolar know his advisor was a magician? How powerful was the old man in truth?

Uneasy and not happy in this company, he quaffed the tasty drink in his cup. His mind turned over the evening's events as an alert serving lad quietly placed a full one at his elbow.

He thought about the scene in the garden. Meriel's fish pin was identical to the one Tor's mother had clutched in her dying hand. Did Ka'amfer lie about its singularity? Or was his daughter or Ka'amfer himself connected to the assassins? And what had become of the pin?

He ate absently. The food was spicy. The drink was pleasantly cool. He failed to notice that the cup, when he reached for it, was always full. His mind pulled up another puzzle. Despite the old man's disclaimer, Beneban was certain he had seen Calibe behind them in the hall.

"You like drink, uh?" A large greasy hand slammed Beneban between the shoulders. It jolted him into the moment. "You drink like Kalden! Feel happy soon." Hundak reached across to bang the wizard's goblet on the table until a hurrying servant filled it again with the fragrant wine.

Beneban, as he took a large gulp, suddenly realized there had been several cups. How many?

"Drink, little wizard. Later, we play!" Tiny blue eyes sparkled maliciously down from the broad red face. Beneban was doubtful that he would enjoy the games this giant played.

A tray of sweetmeats offered by a passing servant distracted Hundak. Beneban sat the cup away from him and turned in response to a tug at his sleeve. The lady Rhonde goggled up at him.

"So exciting, the wrestling later," she breathed. "We've heard so much of your prowess."

"I think you've been misled," he murmured.

"Oh, surely not," she began, but a blare of trumpets interrupted.

The majordomo stepped to the center of the floor. Beneban barely listened. He was suddenly aware that his food had been highly seasoned. He had drunk much more than was his habit. Now his head buzzed unpleasantly, and the room seemed to be overly full of the hum and whistle of people's noise.

"What they have behind curtain?" his large neighbor demanded. He grabbed the wizard's sleeve as the majordomo, who spouted a spiel like a carnival barker, gestured at the draped wall opposite the table.

"A rare entertainment, provided for your enjoyment by my master, the noble Ka'amfer," the major domo finished.

Beneban pried the massive hand from his sleeve. "What?"

The curtain swept aside to reveal a glass wall. It was one surface of a room-sized aquarium. The water was brilliantly lit. It seemed empty but for a pile of boulders at the rear of the tank and one enormous dead branch. Then in the shadows, a shape moved sluggishly. An enormous snake-like appendage drifted from behind the branch and hung in the water. The green tentacle probed gently here and there. It was blotched with three suction discs. These now attached themselves briefly to the glass and pulled.

"It's an arak," a familiar voice grated from the end of the table. Beneban, startled, realized that ex-Captain Glaynar was among guests he hadn't noticed.

"Will the glass hold?" A gasp from Rhonde drew his eyes back to the lighted wall.

Now from the top of the tank a slender figure sliced through the water. It paused fleetingly on the boulders. At first, it seemed to be a half-grown Larlinga, but as it flashed away from the rocks, a silvery mane streamed behind it. The swimmer's legs ended in webbed feet.

The lithe body was clad only in a brief loincloth. In the right hand it carried a slender lance, and in the left, a net.

"A Mergol," Rhonde squealed.

The arak swirled out from its hiding place to make an angry grab at the intruder. The Mergol warrior, for such he was, slid under the tentacle and aimed a flashing jab at one of the creature's bulging eyes. He missed. His lance rebounded from the beast's carapace.

"I've never seen so large an arak."

"Look at the thing's claw. It could cut him in half."

"Mergols are said to be legendary fighters."

"*Watch out!*"

"Another tentacle!"

The guests' babble stilled to horrified gasps. As the Mergol floated away on the rebound of his lance, the arak snapped its pincer-claw. The warrior gave a seemingly lazy flip of one foot. The razor-edged claw missed him but sheared a two-inch limb from the branch of its lair. The Mergol's maneuver had brought him around in a tight circle.

Suddenly one of the beast's tentacles snapped around his ankle. It dragged him forward as the pincer-claw snapped angrily. Just as it seemed the Mergol was doomed, he flung the weighted net. It opened and tangled the other groping arm and the claw. In a flash, the silvery lance plunged forward to its target, the bulging gray eye. A gush of purple ichor darkened the bottom of the tank. The monster lost its hold on the Mergol's ankle, and the creature thrashed in agony.

As the spellbound guests watched, the arak's death throes ended and the water calmed. The Mergol shot to the top of the aquarium. For an instant, his green eyes seemed to meet Beneban's in a triumphant smirk. Then he flashed a bogus bow to the breathless audience. The tank went dark. The curtain rattled closed to shut away the death throes of the arak. Lights in the dining chamber brightened.

Rhonde and several others had moved for a better view. Now next to him and caught between vicarious terror and delight, she clung to Beneban's arm. He barely noticed as he chased a sudden thought.

Mergols are shape-changers. He lost track of the thought as he heard a whisper nearby. Ka'amfer and Meriel had moved and were only a few seats away. Ignoring the drama, Meriel spoke quietly to her father.

A break in the excited chatter brought Ka'amfer's reply to Beneban:

"All three plans in place, heh? Problem is solved."

A sudden blow on his back nearly put Beneban's face in his plate and brought his attention around to his huge neighbor.

"Now, little wizard," Hundak boomed in Beneban's ear. "Now *we* play!"

CHAPTER 18

KNEELING BY THE healing pool in front of her cottage in the late afternoon, Forest Lady frowned as she prepared a poultice. Rising steam clouded her shimmergreen hair and softened the worry that marked her face. She bent to her patient and calmed the young gazert with an ugly three-cornered wound in his flank.

His twin scimitar horns tore restlessly at the sward then stilled. Carefully she lifted the poultice and laid it on the injury. Again the gazert's horns dug a furrow in the soft sod. "Gently, friend. Soon the pain will ease," Laraynia murmured.

"For this time," Saray said in her cracked old voice. "But we cannot continue much longer, Rayni. *You* cannot continue like this. Half of Forest is dark now, and you exhaust yourself to keep the other half from being overrun. It is time to leave, child."

About them trees glowed softly, lighting the glade before the cottage against the night. "Where could we go, Saray?" The girl's shoulders slumped. The tree light flickered and dimmed.

"Anywhere. Larlingarde. You'd quickly find your place there. You have relatives there."

"Forest is my home. I've never been elsewhere."

Rayni's words were low, unsure. The gazert thrashed again. An automatic gesture quieted it. One hand touched the green stone at her throat and the trees brightened. Her head lifted, and her gray eyes steadied on the old woman's face. "Besides, Saray," she continued, "Who would care for our friends here? I can't leave them to the darkness, to the grollings, and the evil that has infected Forest."

"You can't hold it back forever, by yourself," her old nurse protested. She wanted her charge safe away from the danger. Yet, she admitted silently, the light had strengthened with the girl's determination. So far it always did.

"Perhaps not forever," Rayni echoed her thought. "But I am not by myself, and while I can help, I must. Gorba should return from patrol soon. Will you waken Dap and Dal?"

Saray shuffled reluctantly into the cottage, leaving Rayni to struggle with uneasy thoughts while one hand gentled the gazert into healing sleep.

Half of Forest was lost to the darkness now, she knew. Only constant patrols and exhaustive use of her powers kept the remainder safe for a time.

From where did the darkness rise? Grollings weren't the source, Rayni was certain of that. They were a symptom, a tool for the power that battled her own.

What of the grollings themselves? They were semi-intelligent creatures, never friendly with other inhabitants of Larlion. Yet they had not previously taken the side of darkness. Now they were increasingly bold. In nighttime forays into the country that surrounded Forest, they destroyed small farmsteads, killed the inhabitants or worse, captured them. What became of the captives, Rayni had failed to discover.

The animals of Forest, Laraynia's friends, were also in constant danger as the grollings now roamed day and night within its protective dusk.

Only at high noon did Rayni dare let down her guard of light. Even then, during the few hours of stolen rest, there was no sure safety for her friends. Saray was right, the girl admitted wearily. She couldn't continue indefinitely. Yet what were her alternatives? She wasn't built to run away. Loyalty and steadfast dependability were bred into her, blood and bone. Giving up was unthinkable. She knew she would stay as long as her strength could avail against the encroaching evil. "Somehow we must get help," she murmured.

A rumbling growl announced Gorba's arrival. Her great ursyn companion shuffled up to her and sniffed curiously at the gazert then dropped wearily by her feet. Rayni placed one hand gently on either side of the great dished face and stared into the wise brown eyes. There she read the tale of three invading grollings who would trespass no more. Also, there was a spot on the northern edge of her protected territory where the light of the trees was faltering.

Dap and Dal came yawning from the house. Dap munched a crusty roll. Dal carefully stowed smooth stones in his pouch, potential ammunition for his sling.

"Give me a stone, Dal," Rayni asked. Holding it in her hand, she thought about the trees at the spot Gorba had told of. They were youngish, probably not more than seventy-five years old, and more vulnerable to evil than the older giants that surrounded the cottage. Her hand held the pebble and dipped into the healing pool. Then it moved to the stone at her throat. Gray eyes began to snap with green sparks. A strange melody, three notes hummed over and over, filled the air. She quieted.

Her eyes refocused. She held the pebble out to the Worf twin. "Keep this stone separate, Dal," she ordered. "Gorba spotted trouble on the north boundary. Bury this beneath the roots of the tree central to the problem. But be careful! That spot is most open for an attack."

Dal examined the stone. It glowed with a gentle green light. The Worf gave a brisk nod and tucked it into his tunic. "We do it, Lady. Come now, Dap. You eat so much you be a full moon soon."

"Not so. Not so I eat too much!" Dap protested, but his brother had gone. Indignantly Dap licked the last crumbs of a sweet roll from his fingers and disappeared down the path behind his twin.

Rayni leaned wearily against the tree. Overhead the full moon lit the sky, trailed by its crescent sister. Relaxing a little, her thoughts drifted to Larlingarde, the city where she had relatives, as Saray had told her. Where, if Saray was correct, Beneban had planned to go. How long since their minds had touched? It seemed to her like an eternity. The emptiness was an aching hole in her life. What did he now do while she fought for Forest's life? Did he ever think of her? Her heart ached at his absence.

His life was filled with interesting people and new places. Had she vanished from his thoughts? Unintentionally, she relaxed into sleep, into a dream...

She was in Forest, but it was older, peaceful. She dreamed that she saw two slender figures ahead, children, she thought, on the cusp of adulthood. The great trees accepted them. They glowed with soft green light as the two passed. They were a boy, and a girl, she thought, but twins. As she watched, the girl laid her hand on one of the great trees and whispered. There was a jump. A blink. They were...

...someplace different. This was still Forest, but the trees were young. Now a small green light leapt up in front of them. A guardian, she knew, and though it was unfamiliar to her, she knew it was good.

It suddenly flared and grew huge. Coming down the path, moving toward the children, was an ancient man. He was shabby, with graying hair, and held a great staff. She knew him. No, this dream...

Suddenly, she startled awake, and her eyes flew wide with shock. Beneban was in dire danger. The thought brought her fully awake. Her gray eyes deepened to the angry green of a storm-driven ocean. Her hand gripped the stone at her neck with unaccustomed strength. A deep howl moaned from her throat as she reached for power she hardly knew she had. The sky darkened in response.

Black clouds blotted out the bright green moons as they rushed overhead. They deepened and towered. As dominance built beneath Laraynia's will, they raced toward Larlingarde.

As he removed his shirt in a corner of the room,

Beneban decided he did not like supper parties at all. Each feast seemed to increase in discomfort and peril for him. How had he been trapped into this wrestling match? He knew only that, after the battle of the Arak, Ka'amfer stood to announce a "special treat" to the assemblage as though a challenge had been given and accepted between the wizard and the giant Kalden.

For Ka'amfer's dinner guests, the wait for the wrestlers to ready themselves only served to heighten anticipation. Eager wagers were offered and accepted by Beneban's troopers.

"Fifty pazts on the Kalden. Hundak, I guess his name is."

"Only fifty? Who'll cover five hundred?"

"I'll take part of that, Ranald."

"Have you seen the wizard wrestle? I'll take half."

"Where'd you get money like that, Ranald?" Doryl said good-naturedly. "Never mind. I don't even have fifty pistas, much less fifty pazts. I'll hold the bets."

Coins rattled eagerly back and forth. If Beneban refused the match, he would be branded a coward. With so many of his troopers as witnesses, he dared not risk that label.

The immediate and enthusiastic clamor from Glaynar and his cohorts closed that door, he mused. Glaynar would like nothing better than...

Tor hurried into the room with the cup of water Beneban had requested. A worried scowl scored his young face. "You'd best postpone it, Beneban. Why did you drink so much, knowing..."

"I didn't. Know, that is." The wizard smiled wryly at the disbelief on his friend's face. "But I can guess who did. My troopers, Glaynar and Ranald, are eager to take advantage of what they believe to be my imminent demise."

"Death?" Tor's voice cracked, pursuing Beneban's thought. "Surely that's too strong a word?"

"Kaldens are quite total about wrestling. The sport is dedicated to their ancestors, and it is done to the death. The loser gains merit with his ancestors by going unprotestingly to his doom."

Beneban knelt to tighten his laces and was aware of muscles that had stiffened since his lessons with Me'ekalar that noon.

"But you... But he can't..."

"Let's hope you're right," Beneban said grimly. Then, a twinkle growing in his amber eyes, he added, "As I have no discernible ancestors with whom to gain merit, I don't intend to join their nonexistent ranks without extreme protest." He folded his silky shirt and laid it neatly by his boots and scarlet cloak. "May I have the water please? And if you would stand between me and our fellow guests?"

Beneban held his Omera in one hand and the cup in the other. He stared into its liquid depths. Muttering quietly, he brought the two slowly closer until the Omera just touched the water's surface. There was a tiny flash. The air nearby filled with a scent of fresh herbs. The wizard quaffed the fragrant liquid and turned to pass the cup to Tor. He was surprised by the look of disappointment in the young man's eyes.

"What is it, Tor?"

"You would use magic to win the fight, Beneban?" Tor asked. He visibly tried to speak without censure.

"Wizardry, my idealistic young friend," Beneban confirmed, "but only to clear my head of the result of unwitting overindulgence. I can't spare the energy for more, even were I so unscrupulous."

"I didn't say..." Tor fidgeted.

Hundak's boomed challenge that echoed from the wall forestalled a response from Beneban.

"*Come*, little wizard. Your destiny awaits."

"I'm coming," Beneban called. He stood and stepped toward the giant. Briefly he turned back to Tor. "If something goes wrong, see to Kati and Sel?"

"Of course, but I don't need that waif around my neck. Or ankles," he added, drawing a faint smile from his friend. "See to it that nothing goes wrong!" Tor's tone was determinedly light.

For a moment longer the wizard looked at him. He realized, surprised, that he felt gratitude for this unexpected friendship. It mattered to him. With a light tap on Tor's arm, Beneban strode to the center of the floor.

Hundak towered over the wizard. He was stripped to tight leather breeches and a brief leather vest. His blond hair was clubbed back into a leather wrapping, but mats of yellow covered his arms and visible chest. "Now we play, little wizard," the giant Kalden roared. "I shall speak good things of you to your ancestors when I send you to join them."

"It may be your own forebears who are about to receive a visitor."

Beneban side-stepped a sudden rush and slipped a quick foot in the giant's path. Hundak went down with a thunderous crash and skidded across the room.

Beneban pounced after him like Kati on the hunt. He grabbed one massive leg and brought it up with him as he landed on the other man's back. The air whooshed out of the Kalden's lungs in an agonized roar.

"I don't suppose there are any particular rules to this sort of match," the wizard grunted, levering the huge leg around.

"Only to win, wizard," Hundak wheezed. He gave a tremendous heave and flipped over, groping for Beneban's head. With a bound, Beneban was away. On his feet, he ignored the tension in his legs as he circled. It was imperative that he stay away from the other's ursyn-like arms or risk being crushed.

Hundak was on his feet and stalked his opponent. He crouched, hands nearly at the floor, and made a sudden leap. Prepared for the move, Beneban flashed away from the Kalden's lunge. He spun, leapt, and thudded both feet against the side of Hundak's head. Had he been wearing boots it would have been a killing blow. As it was, the Kalden sprawled sideways and shook his head foggily.

The wizard darted in. He reached for leverage that would give him a death grip around the Kalden's muscular neck.

One trunk-like arm swept into his path with the effect of a brick wall suddenly arisen in front of him. Beneban, winded, was slowly dragged into the unbreakable embrace Hundak wanted.

His reflexes temporarily gone, Beneban's senses worked overtime. Everything around them slowed down. He had time to notice the gleeful expression on Glaynar's face and the deep satisfaction that Ka'amfer was showing.

Tor watched in wide-eyed horror. As the room began to darken, Beneban saw with surprise that Meriel's hand was pressed tight against her lips. Twisting minutely, Beneban managed a rasping gulp of breath, and a bit of strength flowed back into his body.

He began the only move that could release the Kalden's inexorable bear-hug and hoped it wasn't too late.

A sudden gale billowed the curtains. It extinguished candles and blotted light from the room. For the tiniest moment, the Kalden's grip faltered. Beneban gave a whooping gasp of laughter as his feet found purchase. He shot out of the other's hold. "I think," he breathed, "that my ancestors aren't happy to receive a visit from me."

The room was nearly black with the violent storm. Torches died or sputtered feebly.

The huge arm that grabbed for Beneban was grasped by what seemed to be a steel trap. It used the giant's momentum to carry him around and up. Beneban's foot flashed to Hundak's temple, and Hundak crashed to the floor. The wizard was on him, and suddenly the Kalden was in a deadly hold that should only end in a broken neck.

Lightning tore the sky outside. Thunder shook the city. A curtain tore loose and sailed across the room, just missing Beneban's head.

Beneban tightened his grip as Hundak thrashed. The Kalden groped desperately for a hold that would free him and give him a chance. His face was turning gray in the lightning flare. His resistance was reduced to aimless flopping.

The storm had centered above Ka'amfer's house. Lamps gusted out as fast as servants lit them. The struggle to shut the windows failed against the howling wind.

"I think, my friend, that *your* ancestors aren't ready to receive you yet either," Beneban gasped with a laugh. In the dusky light, no one saw as he slightly shifted his grip. One thumb moved to press a nerve center behind Hundak's ear. Abruptly all tension went out of the Kalden's body. The great man flopped as though boneless.

Beneban staggered to his feet, panting, then sat abruptly back on the floor to rest his head on knees, his legs too shaky to hold him upright.

Three strong servants finally secured the windows and shut out the roar of wind. Lights were lit. Darkness fled to the corners. People crowded around Beneban and his motionless opponent. He ignored them all.

"Is he dead?"

"Didn't I tell you about the captain?"

"You owe me some money, Glaynar."

Servants began to clear the debris tossed by the capricious wind to clutter the floor. Ka'amfer moved among his guests and persuaded them to return to their seats. Rich wine quickly filled eager goblets and calmed nerves. Tor finally managed to push his way to his friend. Meriel reached them at the same time.

"Have you killed him, Captain?" Meriel's face was solemn as she bent over the motionless Kalden.

"Beneban, are *you* all right?" Tor knelt beside him, overriding the girl's concerned question.

"No and yes," Beneban mumbled into his crossed arms. "He will awaken soon, my lady. You might have him carried to a quiet room. Tor, I'm alive. I need a place to clean up." He lifted his head and gave the boy a crooked smile. "It seems I'm still stuck with Sel."

Meriel summoned servants and gave orders. Hundak was rolled with difficulty onto a rug and dragged away by several men.

One offered Beneban a hand, then, as he got to his feet, led him away. As they left the room, the wizard saw Meriel turn to young Tor and lay a hand on his arm. She said softly, "Please come with me. I have something of importance to tell you."

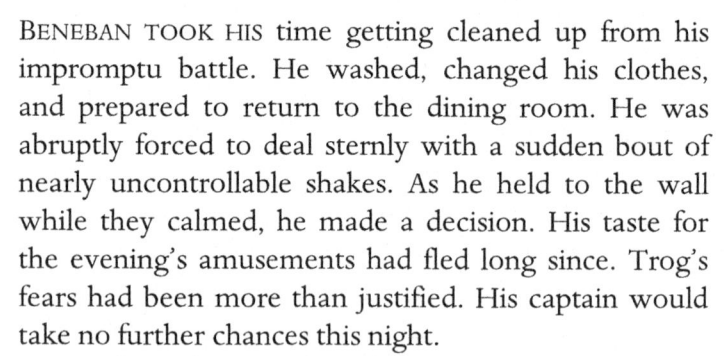

BENEBAN TOOK HIS time getting cleaned up from his impromptu battle. He washed, changed his clothes, and prepared to return to the dining room. He was abruptly forced to deal sternly with a sudden bout of nearly uncontrollable shakes. As he held to the wall while they calmed, he made a decision. His taste for the evening's amusements had fled long since. Trog's fears had been more than justified. His captain would take no further chances this night.

He found his way through quiet halls to the kitchen and persuaded a servant to help him find the stables.

The last of the storm's wind whipped Beneban's cloak wildly as he hesitated in the gateway of Ka'amfer's garden. Behind him, light still streamed from the house. Even here he could hear the excited babble of the dinner guests.

Every conversation was fueled by the wrestling match. The guests, especially those who were richer for supporting Beneban in the match, eagerly awaited his reappearance and a chance to toast the winner with Ka'amfer's fine wines.

Quietly, Beneban moved into the stable and saddled a kelsh. His own mount, he hoped. In this case he felt that failure to thank his host for a pleasant evening was a reasonable omission.

He paused at the gate. Should he find Tor? Tell the young lar where he had gone? He had left a message with the servant, but...

A raucous burst of laughter from the house decided him. His tolerance for people who considered a violent death to be a spectator sport had vanished. Hopefully Tor would understand. With a grimace, he swung onto the kelsh.

The royal palace was... That way, he decided as he slipped through the gates. He was desperate to be home.

THE STORM HAD changed the mood of the crowd. Those with a bit of money found refuge in bars and eateries that opened their doors willingly to customers. Many, however, were damp, drunk, and without funds to continue their celebration. As the free food and drink was no longer available, they had grown sullen. As the wizard sat outside the gate of Ka'amfer's estate, three citizens, more drunken than smart, shoved and stumbled into his kelsh and made it lurch sideways.

Beneban reined the beast in sharply to steady it. Then two Larlingas pushed past. They argued and shoved at each other. One crashed into the kelsh. It bucked and twisted for several steps.

Now well past the gates of Ka'amfer's estate, with a headache that pounded relentlessly, Beneban realized he was turned around. Where did the palace lay? "Uphill," he muttered and turned to his right. But a small group shoved carelessly past. The kelsh danced sideways, and Beneban was pushed into a small side street before he could rein the beast in.

"I'll go around the block," he grumbled. But a knot of drunken citizens made the wizard weave to avoid trampling them. He rounded a square, turned to the right, and a rowdy gang crashed into his mount's shoulder. Beneban swerved, but they followed, pushing and punching. One blow hit his mount on the muzzle. It was too much. The kelsh put its head down and bit the closest drunk. Dragging the reins from the wizard, it spun in an effort to throw Beneban off.

When he regained control, he was badly lost. The last two turns had carried him further downhill into progressively meaner streets. He should have observed more carefully as they came to the party. He pulled the kelsh to a stop. Neither light nor sign gave clue to where he was. He had gone far astray.

An ominous silence fell about him. The stink of garbage assailed his nose. He was in a rough, unpaved lane, lined by tumbledown hovels. There wasn't so much as a light behind the windows.

The people who lived in this squalor were undoubtedly behind him in the rowdy throng, he thought. Free food and drink were plentiful at carnival. That was a strong draw for those who often had neither. Well, he needed directions. Perhaps if he turned back...

As Beneban reined in his animal, he heard a clatter. In the empty silence, someone had kicked a stone. "Ho! Is someone there?" The wizard turned his now weary mount a little but saw nothing. The natural blackness of the alley was compounded by the final storm clouds that sullenly hid the face of the nearly full moon and her dark sister. "Is someone there? Come out. I only want directions."

Silence. It grew more oppressive against the distant, muffled roar of the carnival. There was no answer. Reluctant and weary, Beneban rode a bit farther. He wished for Kati, for a light, for home... and was brought up short against a blank wall.

Again, as his weary kelsh stopped, he heard a stealthy noise. Vermin? Certainly, this area invited them, yet... His hand went to his sword.

With dismay he realized that in expectation of attending a party, he had belted on the dressy rapier he used when Me'ekalar taught him to fence. Heldenhaft was somewhere above, in his room, out of reach. It probably didn't matter, he thought. Surely the noise presented no threat to an armed rider. Still, it was time to find a way out of this maze.

Impatient now, and angry, he flicked his right hand. A splash of light blossomed from his fingertips.

A shout rang out.

"That's done it, men. Get 'im!"

Hooded figures rushed him in the dark. Two

yanked the kelsh's head down, and it plunged wildly. One grabbed Beneban's cloak to drag him to the ground. The saddle slipped as he unsheathed the unfamiliar blade, and Beneban knew someone had cut the girths.

To take advantage of the momentum of his imminent fall, he rolled hard against someone's legs. One assailant crashed to the ground with a curse. Beneban scrambled for the wall. He muttered a command that set the wizard light steady above his left shoulder. To his dismay he saw five assailants armed with clubs and blades.

Because he was a trained athlete, because his lessons from Me'ekalar had taken root in fertile ground, and perhaps because his muscles had learned form and pattern from exercise with Heldenhaft, Beneban held them off for a bit.

One went down with a scream after a thrust clean through his belly. Another fell to his flashing foot and rolled about with a howl. A third also went down, victim to Beneban's sword, but this one proved to be the wizard's undoing. The slender rapier slid between the villain's ribs, and stuck. Beneban tugged desperately to free it. He sensed a club's descent.

The sword abandoned as a lost hope, he spun at the last moment and dove under the blow toward his attacker. The man went down beneath his weight with a grunt.

Before Beneban could regain his feet, a blow crashed into the back of his head. Brilliant light flared behind his eyes. Then there was only bitter dark.

CHAPTER 19

*H*E WAS A *wizard. A name—his name—Beneban. Cold. So cold. He soared on the sztaq, Ztavin's killer wind. No, he rode a vardraken. Its icy teeth stabbed his head. Wild wind flung the wizard up. It dropped him then, down and down, battered him against rocky steeps. Fangs pierced his head. Now pain blazed again as he soared up toward a light...*

...The light...

...Too light. A vardraken dove at him. She stabbed his head with ice. She would turn him to...

"No, Kati, run..." He struggled with a great weight that held him down, fought to understand, to reach the present. Pain stabbed as his eyes opened a crack.

"He is coming out of it, sir," a rumbling voice thundered in his ears. This voice, no threat, but how? Trog?

He tried to move, but his arms and legs were so heavy. Was he tied? Blind? Brightness stabbed as he forced his eyes open. He managed to lift a hand.

Green eyes beneath shimmergreen hair stared into his, and a face creased with worry flickered into focus. A tiny Worf perched beside him on the cot. Cot? Yes, his hand confirmed the soft scratchy warmth of a blanket. Beyond, a furry white triangle studied him with one large round eye.

"Beneban, can you hear me?" The green eyes bent nearer. Kati hopped down from his chest. Ahh... He could breathe, could move.

"Bene..."

"Don't yell," he croaked. He winced as the vibration of the words echoed in the cavities of his aching head.

This man... *What is his name*, Beneban demanded of his disordered mind. All right, *Tor*. That's better. Tor backed up a little and lowered his voice to a whisper.

"What happened, Beneban? Who attacked you?"

"Vardraken, so beautiful, but Kati... No, that was on the mountain. Is Kati here? This isn't her cave."

"Beneban!" The sharp voice brought him further into the present. He winced as his headache throbbed. The voice softened, but continued, relentless.

"Vardraken are a *myth*, Beneban, and Kati is right here. She is in the barracks in Larlingarde with us. She and Sel found you. You were unconscious when we reached you, and Kati..." He paused, then continued. "Who attacked you? Did someone follow you from Ka'amfer's? The Kalden was..."

Beneban closed his eyes against the thud of the words. Not the Kalden, but who? "No." he shook his head slightly and wished at once that he hadn't. When the pain eased, he continued. "Footpads? Thieves? I don't know."

He struggled with the pain and his confusion. There were words. Had he dreamed them? Or remembered? The words whispered in his head. *All three plans...in operation...*

Who had said them? The memory seemed important, yet all he wanted was a return to the dark of sleep. He was safe now, and his head... One hand lifted, touched, and found a lump that radiated pain.

The white hairy creature—*Ogdol, Trog,* he pulled from his brain—came over to the bed holding a steaming cup in one massive hand. One of three, Beneban realized, and then Trog raised him effortlessly. "This will help the pain," he rumbled softly.

"Beneban," the young man insisted, but Trog interrupted him.

"Until the pain lessens, sir, he will not be coherent."

The wizard sipped. Then he eagerly drained the minty concoction. Even the fragrance seemed to sooth his head. He was laid gently back. Beneban's eyes closed against the busyness of the room. He would let the potion clear the pain-clogged pathways of his brain. As he rested, as the pain backed away, his memory began to return, at first in brief flashes, then longer scenes that attached themselves to other bits.

"Sel, bring me warm water." Trog's voice was a low rumble. His hands were steady as he bathed the caked blood from behind Beneban's ear. The other man...

"Tor! It wasn't the vardraken. *Ow!* Though they *are* real, Tor. I saw one on the mountain. Not the Kalden, either."

"No," Tor affirmed. "Hundak was still unconscious when I left Ka'amfer's."

"Then who attacked you?" Trog rumbled. "Footpads are rare in this place."

"Men, several men followed me, I think. Or possibly herded me. I lost the way. They attacked me in an alley. I thought... How did you find me?"

"It is thanks to Kati and Sel," Trog said. "An hour ago, no, it is longer now, Kati grew restless. Sel was also upset. Before I could stop them, the small one and Kati were gone out the door. I followed until they went over the wall. I am not slow, but I lost them and returned here."

"Meanwhile, I, um, finished talking with Meriel." Young Tor's face crimsoned in the lamplight. "I looked for you, but they said you had departed after the wrestling."

"Tor came here before returning to his rooms," Trog added. "He was looking for you."

"I was concerned," the young lar added. "After the fight, I thought your defeat, even your death, seemed a near thing to me once or twice. And when I found you'd never reached home..."

"At about that time," Trog picked up the tale, "Sel returned. He was wild, ready to tear down the barracks, if necessary, to make someone follow him. When he agreed that he knew where you were, Tor and I went along. "We found Kati," the Ogdol continued. "She stood guard in a pitch-black alley littered with clubs, blood, two dead thugs, and of course, you."

"Two? Two bodies? I'd have guessed only one," Beneban said weakly.

"Kati had dispatched one assassin, not neatly but quite thoroughly," Trog said. "There were signs that others did not leave unscathed."

"I'll wager not," Tor laughed. "She even snarled at

us. At first she wouldn't let us near you to help. If Trog weren't so good with animals..."

"It was not necessary. Kati had no doubt that we would help Beneban. She is too sensible to stand in our way." Trog turned to Sel. "Can you find me clean cloth, Sel, with which to bind this wound?" Trog was firmly in charge of priorities.

With a pat to Beneban's hand, the tiny Worf crossed the room and rummaged in the tall storage cupboard. Finding nothing at floor level, he scrambled to the high shelf and burrowed into the clutter. A pan rattled to the floor, followed by a spare blanket and a scrolled paper. Finally the urchin gave a triumphant squeak and scampered back to Trog. He brandished a roll of white cloth.

"That is well done, Sel." Trog ripped the cloth into strips.

Tor began idly to gather the fallen items. He wrapped the pan in the blanket and shoved them up onto the shelf. Then he bent for the scroll of paper. "What's this?" he asked lazily. The heavy paper unrolled in his hand, a weight of deep blue wax pulling it down. "This is Uncle Lyolar's seal. Your commission, Beneban?" He began to read while Trog bound a pad soaked in the minty concoction over the split behind the wizard's ear.

There was a sudden snarl as Kati lifted her head from Beneban's ankles. Her green gaze fixed on Tor. The young lar stared in frozen horror from the document he held to his injured friend. His face was paler than Beneban's, and his hand went to his sword.

"I d-didn't believe..." The young lar stuttered to a

stop. "Meriel *said*, but I didn't believe her. You've been my *friend*, Beneban. And my uncle…"

"What is amiss, Sir?" Suddenly aware of the tension between Tor and Kati, Trog crossed toward him, but the young lar shoved past him and stormed across the room to glower down at Beneban.

"*Explain* this!" he demanded. He rattled the document in the wizard's face. Before Beneban could focus, Tor continued. "You can't explain! Can you?"

"I can't even see it." Beneban moaned and held his head. "What is it, Tor?" The wizard tried vainly to focus his uncooperative eyes. With great effort, he reached for the flapping document. "Here. Let me see."

Tor yanked it away. "I should kill you where you lie," he snarled, and for a moment it seemed he might. His free hand pulled his sword halfway from its scabbard.

Trog's huge fist closed about the angry noble's sword hand. "I do not know what the paper says, sir," the giant Ogdol rumbled quietly, "but I am sure that it can be explained."

"Indeed." Tor's voice was scornful. "I'd be interested to hear Beneban *explain* how he acted as my friend *after* accepting my uncle's commission to *kill my parents. Would I, then, be next?*" he hissed. "*Let me go!*" Tor roared. He tore loose of the Ogdol's restraining hand. "Don't worry, Trog," he snarled, and spun to the door before turning back. "There's no satisfaction in vengeance taken on a defenseless man," he spat. "I'll wait until he's on his feet and quite recovered. And *then* I'll kill him!"

Tor slammed out the door, leaving the paper

where it had fallen on the bed.

Beneban struggled to sit up. He fumbled for the scroll, squinted, and tried to focus through a furious headache to read the spidery scrawl.

"I can't make it out. But Trog, I've never seen this before. What is it?" His hand shook as he held it out to the Ogdol then sank back weakly.

Trog read it silently, slowly, carefully. Then, not quite meeting Beneban's anxious eyes, he said, "It appears to be a written order from the Grand Lar, Lyolar, to one Beneban, wizard, to assassinate the Torlarya and all of her party as they return from OathGive." His toneless voice gave the words the weight of a judge passing sentence.

"But it's not... I never... Do *you* believe it, Trog?" Despairingly the wizard struggled to push up on his elbows. Eyes glazed with pain stared up at his friend. Trog studied the document carefully. At length, the Ogdol looked straight into the wizard's anxious amber eyes.

"It is," he said slowly, "a very clever forgery. *This* was never in my cupboard before tonight."

Beneban's face relaxed in relief. At Trog's next words, however, he sank back in despair.

"I must wonder, though," Trog continued, "what does young Tor plan to do about you, and about his uncle, who appears to have commissioned the murder?"

BENEBAN ROUNDED THE corner from early inspection

the next day and slumped against the concealing wall. He closed his eyes to shut out the light. Asolum and Zartum seemed determined to hammer dents in the fierce ache of his head. He had discarded Trog's careful bandage before morning report. His hair, pulled into a loose tail, concealed the lump and split behind his ear.

Aware of the Ogdol's wish to keep him from a confrontation with Tor, he had rejected Trog's offer to take the duty. He would not hide like a coward.

Still, his head throbbed with every pulse of blood.

Now, at the end of this shift, the cool dimness of his room seemed as distant as his hope of attaining Eratim, that final union with the One that was promised those who fulfilled their cycle, or cycles, of time here below.

A firm hand fell on his shoulder. He spun around, reaching abortively for Heldenhaft, even while he knew that he could never use the enchanted sword against Tor.

Me'ekalar backed a cautious step. His tough face was lined by concern. "Are you ill, Beneban? We all saw your triumph with the Kalden last night, but were you perhaps injured?"

The wizard's shoulders slumped with relief. "Not then," he answered. "Later. As I traveled home, I was attacked by footpads. Thanks to your lessons with the sword, I wasn't killed, just got a knock on the head."

Beneban changed the subject to one more comfortable. He indicated the bundle Me'ekalar held. "What have you there? Is it for me?"

Smiling, the Kaltingcorps captain undid the Worf cloth wrapping to reveal a staltin, a beautifully carved instrument inlaid with a simple but elegant pattern of contrasting fine woods. "I think I've found the instrument you asked me to watch out for."

"Me'ek! It's beautiful." Beneban touched it with an appreciative finger. "But, my friend, I can never afford such a fine piece, however I might wish to."

"It cost me nothing. I charge you the same." Me'ek grinned at the wizard's confusion. "My mother wanted me to be a musician," he told Beneban. "She managed to afford this instrument, and years of painful lessons. Painful for both of us. We did without many things as a result. Yet I never mastered it. Besides, I only ever wanted to be a soldier. When mother died, I buried her and wasted no time in joining Lyolar's troops. I kept this because I couldn't sell what she'd sacrificed so much for. But now it is wasted. It serves only as idle reproach and sits covered in my room."

"You don't even know what I want with it."

"I think I do, as a matter of fact." Me'ekalar grinned ruefully at the thought. "I have a dim memory of a musical crash on the cobblestones of the Laughing Mergol. Am I correct? Was it the stalthinger's instrument I destroyed with my impious ass?"

Beneban nodded and resisted clutching his head at the pain.

"I've heard Ravel play many times," Me'ekalar said, sober now. "Since I smashed his staltin, I'd like to replace it with this one. He'll do it justice."

"It's a more than generous gift, Me'ekalar."

"Reparation, more like."

Beneban nodded acceptance. "Very well, then, thank you. Do you know where to find him?"

"Yes, if he's still at the Magic Bowl. Will you come with me?"

"I won't be free for hours. Besides, the gift is yours to give. I could never afford such a replacement."

"If I weren't convinced it is better for you to rest than to ride, I would insist on your company. Still, the sooner the lad has this, the sooner he can return to his trade. He'll be glad to finish washing dishes for his keep."

Beneban chuckled, winced, and held a hand to his head.

Me'ekalar laid a concerned hand on his shoulder. "I'll go then. Can't Trog take your place here?"

"No need. I'm sure you've worked through many a headache as bad as this."

"Aye, but I've earned them. Never mind." Me'ekalar held up a hand. "Stay at your stubborn duty. But we'll postpone our next lesson at swords until tomorrow."

The Kaltingcorps captain strode off in his jaunty fashion as Beneban returned to his troop. If he was, perhaps, a less strict taskmaster than usual, none of his men chose to test his patience. Yet over the wizard, despite his headache and nausea, the awareness of Tor's distress and fury hung heavily.

Back in his room, freed from duty at last, the wizard longed for nothing but sleep. Instead, he forced himself to examine the false commission from the Grand Lar.

In its minutest detail he found no fault with the genuine appearance of the document, save one thing; he knew with certainty that had had no part in such a plot. He had never seen it before.

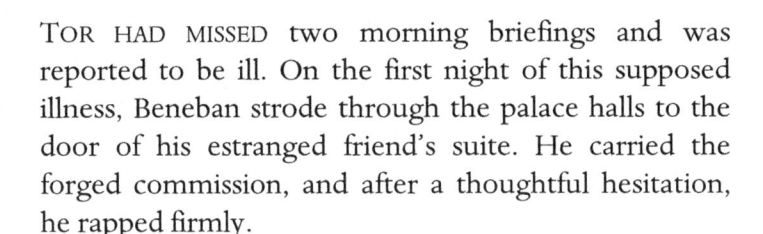

Tor had missed two morning briefings and was reported to be ill. On the first night of this supposed illness, Beneban strode through the palace halls to the door of his estranged friend's suite. He carried the forged commission, and after a thoughtful hesitation, he rapped firmly.

The heavy panel opened a crack. Daram's lined face appeared, aghast to see him.

"I'm here to see Tor, Daram. Where is he?"

The old man remained silent but blocked the way. Finally he answered, his face twisted with worry. "Best leave 'im be, Captain. He's fair rabid about you, sir."

"I don't blame him. Yet what he believes isn't true. How can I convince him if I can't talk to him?"

Daram considered for a moment. Finally he stepped out of the way. "In there, then. But I'm thinking he's too well furred to listen to you."

Beneban strode past him toward the flickering light in the next room.

Before the fireplace where they had first cemented their friendship, Tor was slumped. One hand held a goblet at half-mast. A damp spot on the carpet below showed that at least some of the wine from that libation hadn't added to the lad's inebriation.

"Tor..." Beneban spoke in the cautious voice he'd use to gentle a frightened kelsh.

Its effect on Tor was violent. He sprang from his chair, whirled unsteadily toward the door, and pierced

Beneban with a baleful glare.

"*You!*" he spat. The hand holding the goblet lifted and let fly. Had previous cups not spoiled his coordination, the wizard would have added another lump to his head. The goblet hit the wall a bare inch from him.

"Tor, *listen to me,*" Beneban spoke urgently. "You are *mistaken!* I never saw that paper until you shook it under my nose."

"I suppose you never saw the assases... ashashins... *killers* either, before you killed them so they couldn't identify you."

"But Calibe killed..."

"...and I suppose my *uncle* was also totally unknown to you." Tor overrode Beneban's attempted words. "Get *out*. Get out of here before I kill you, *now!*"

The young lar stumbled across the room and nearly fell into the fire. Beneban grabbed his arm to steady him. A mistake, as Tor pulled his sheathed sword from the mantle and whirled. He spun one way, then staggered the other, before his eyes found the wizard.

"You can't believe that I..." Beneban backed hastily as Tor whipped out his blade. The sheath flew across the room as he lunged for the wizard.

"I wish I couldn't!" The young man cried, torment in his voice. "*I wish there was another explanation, but...*" A wild slash nearly separated Beneban from his left ear and stuck Tor's sword into the wood of the door.

"Meriel was right. You are scum. Get *out!*" Tor yanked awkwardly at the weapon. He spun half around as it came loose, and he stared wildly about the room.

Beneban grabbed his arm, speaking urgently. "The document was a forgery, Tor. You must know..."

The wizard was forced to let go his arm and dodge as Tor swung a punch that spun him in a circle. Again, he stared in muddled confusion. Then with another turn, he remembered the sword he held, and swung it wildly.

It slashed the front of Beneban's uniform and was stopped only by the wide baldric that crossed his chest. The sudden stop tore it from Tor's hand, and it fell to the floor with a clatter.

His violent move spun him half around again. He turned, dove, and snatched up the sword and thrust again. Only Daram's quick grab at his sword arm kept Beneban from being spitted like a parti. The man gave Tor a light push that dropped him into his chair.

"Please go, sir," Daram whispered urgently. He tugged open the door. "Try when he's not so upset."

There was no real choice. Beneban left, resolved to try again the next day.

ON THE FOLLOWING morning Daram refused the wizard entry. He swore it was as much as his life was worth to allow Beneban in.

Unsure if Daram meant his own life or Beneban's continued existence, he retreated. As he returned gloomily to his quarters, Me'ekalar nearly ran him down. The young captain bounded around a corner and stopped with a lurch just before he crashed into the wizard.

"There you are. I've been looking for you. Trog said you visited Lar Tor?"

"I tried, anyway. Why are you so perky?"

"Just came back from a visit in town with a young lady of my acquaintance. Why are you so gloomy? Don't tell me you and Tor had a fight?"

"All right."

"Hmm?" Me'ekalar looked puzzled.

"I said all right. I won't tell you that Tor and I had a fight."

"Oh." Me'ekalar considered briefly. "Well, never mind. It won't last long, I wager. Come on now. Let's see if you've forgotten all I taught you about swordplay."

He spun away but called back to Beneban. "Say, have you heard the latest song going around town? No, I suppose you haven't been to town since Ravel returned to his music."

"Was he pleased with the staltin?" Beneban's face lightened a little.

"*Was* he? I guess *so*! He spent ten minutes running his hands over it, like you'd learn a new lady's... er... to know it. Ravel's face glowed like a warm fire in winter. Ten minutes more went to tuning it to perfection. Go on, Beneban. Get your rapier. I'll wait." The Kaltingcorps captain leaned on the door frame and watched as Beneban rummaged the slender weapon out from beneath the bed.

"*Any*way," Me'ekalar continued as the wizard rejoined him, "then he tuned it, ever so careful, he was. And then he plunked down cross-legged and composed the first three verses of a new ballad. Can you guess its subject?"

"No, I'm just glad he's back in business." The two

strolled toward the practice grounds.

Me'ekalar unsheathed his rapier and held it in the formal duelist's salute. His green eyes glittered with mischief as he stared across at Beneban, obviously waiting on his answer. "Well? The ballad?" he persisted.

"The ballad. I've no clue. Should I?" Beneban returned the salute. The two touched blades, then Beneban swept his weapon in a rapid parry as Me'ekalar attacked.

"It's all about," *thrust, lunge, recover, retreat,* "a wizard with an enchanted sword," *thrust, parry,* "who seems," *parry, riposte,* "to have," *lunge, deceive, touché,* "a heart!"

"Hold," Beneban gasped. "You've beaten me again. Have pity on my poor head. Let's rest a moment." They sank onto one of the benches lining the practice yard. "Now, do I understand you?" Beneban mopped sweat from his face. "Ravel is making a ballad about me? Why? *You* gave him the staltin."

"I couldn't pretend in all honesty that it was my idea, Beneban. Also, he's talked to the people at the Magic Bowl. The latest version, the one I heard today, mentioned the rescue of fair ladies and the ignominious defeat of a Kalden, among other things."

"I should have left him washing dishes," Beneban groaned.

"But why? Even Lyolar could envy such instant popularity."

"Indeed," the wizard agreed with a crooked smile. "And can you imagine a better way to lose favor with Lyolar? I've been too visible since my arrival in

Larlingarde. No matter how I try, I can't melt into the background. The Grand Lar didn't want a wizard at all. He certainly doesn't want one who is popular. And now..."

"Now?" Me'ekalar prompted as Beneban's silence grew long.

"Now someone has provided him reason enough to remove me, I'm afraid." On impulse, the wizard told Me'ekalar about the damning document.

His friend said nothing at first. Then his words were abnormally serious. "It seems," Me'ekalar began, "that someone is going to a lot of trouble to get rid of you. First they thought I'd dispose of you that night at the Laughing Mergol. Then there's been a murderous wrestler, quickly followed by an attack from unknown thugs. And now this thing between you and Tor, your best friend at court. Beneban, who, besides Lyolar, would have the power to arrange all that?"

"Why *not* Lyolar?" the wizard asked, not denying the logic. "But there was something I heard right before the attack. I've been trying to remember, but I can't quite catch it. Only, I don't think it was Lyolar."

"He might implicate you in a crime," Me'ek agreed. "I don't think he'd destroy his relationship with Tor by insinuating his own involvement. Of course, you've proven remarkably difficult to finish off." Me'ekalar's laughter drew a rueful chuckle from Beneban.

"Well, one thing," the Kaltingcorps captain concluded, "Lyolar won't dare dispose of you casually as he might another guardsman."

"Why not?" Startled, the wizard stared at him.

"The town would rise in rebellion, Beneban," Me'ekalar said. "Nay, don't protest. You've become extremely popular. If the old man decides to finish you, he'd better do it out of his back pocket, so to speak. If he does it openly, the lower town will rise to remove his head from his shoulders. No wonder he fears you."

"Fears me? That's ridiculous. I only want…" Beneban paused. The need to locate the Larstone intruded on his thoughts. *Was he running out of time?*

"Only want what?" Me'ekalar nudged his friend to finish his words. He noted the weariness as the wizard stammered and stopped.

"I want to be a *good* wizard," Beneban stumbled on. "Or if not that, as good a captain of L Troop as I can possibly be."

Beneban again retreated to his own thoughts. *Larlingarde is—must be—where I will find the Larstone and my freedom from Ztavin.*

Me'ekalar shrugged away his silence and slapped his friend on the knee in hope to break this strangely somber mood.

"Good luck, my friend. From all you've shown us, you are already adept at wizardry, and L Troop has never been sharper. But you seem fated to be dragged into high places, want it or no." He swished his blade suggestively. "Come, let's try another bout. Or are you too tired?"

Beneban stood and moved slowly into dueling position, but his mind was obviously elsewhere, and Me'ekalar won the round easily. Puzzled by his friend's preoccupation, Me'ekalar saluted him and sheathed his sword. "You are still tired, my wizardly comrade.

Tomorrow I expect you to give me a better match."

Beneban stood a moment, slightly bemused. He looked at his rapier as though he didn't know it then slid it into its scabbard.

"Yes. Tomorrow, my friend. I'll give you a better match. The library, there is a book there…"

Me'ekalar watched in concern as Beneban wandered away. Perhaps he should talk to Trog. He wondered whether, indeed, the head injury had addled the wizard's wits.

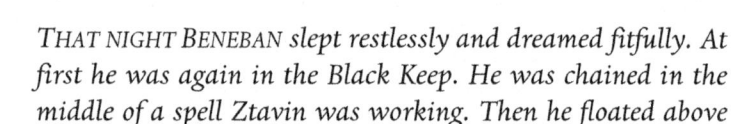

THAT NIGHT BENEBAN *slept restlessly and dreamed fitfully. At first he was again in the Black Keep. He was chained in the middle of a spell Ztavin was working. Then he floated above the carved Shadeus, forced to watch.*

A hapless wretch was chained at each point of the figure. In the corner, a dark robed figure lit a black candle and summoned.

The robed figure turned. At first Beneban thought it was himself. He groaned and tried to escape, to wake up…

As the dark figure pointed a wand at each tortured prisoner, the wretch thrashed against the chains in agony. Each, as he died, was replaced by three small figures. They were drak, mythical creatures.

Each trio of drak was herded into a small cage, but for the last of the eighteen. This one was placed in a silver cage. The cage was suspended over a fire.

"No! Beneban thought he shrieked at the black figure. At… himself?

The figure turned. One hand reached to push back the hood…

"Noooo!"

With a shudder Beneban awoke with Trog and Sel standing by his cot and Kati snarling as she paced and searched for something amiss.

CHAPTER 20

IN THE DAYS that followed, it helped Beneban to spend much of his spare time with Me'ekalar. He was haunted by the strange dream, and more, by the rift between himself and Tor. The activity of sword practice, plus the discipline of learning a new skill, kept his mind from dwelling on the continued absence of Tor. The young lar still refused to see him or to appear at morning roll. Me'ekalar's cheerful companionship kept the wizard from useless speculation about Tor's behavior.

Two days later, Beneban and Me'ekalar were again at rest on the shady bench after a hot workout, when the Kaltingcorps captain looked up. He nudged his friend. "Remember what I said about high places? Here comes young lar Mero. Two pazts say he's looking for you."

The lad arrived before Beneban could answer. Me'ekalar was proved half correct. Mero brought a summons for both the wizard and Me'ekalar to attend the Grand Lar in the palace garden.

Lyolar paced restlessly along the white shell path as the two captains approached. Meriel posed nearby upon a carved crysolate bench. A shaded arbor protected her from the heat. She was motionless but for one restless toe that tapped as the two men approached, but her eyes fixed speculatively on Beneban.

"Where have you been?" The Grand Lar glared angrily at his page. "Can't wait all day when I summon you. Do you always dawdle on my errands, Mero?"

Mero's squawked protest was covered by Beneban's hasty disclaimer. "We were at the practice grounds, Mightiness," he said, making a quick bow. "We had to dispose of our swords. Forgive our tardiness."

"Never mind then." Lyolar flapped a dismissive hand at Mero. The lad disappeared speedily as Me'ekalar snapped a sharp salute to Lyolar. The Grand Lar continued to pace and to ignore them.

At length, Beneban coughed. Lyolar spun and speared the wizard with furious green eyes that made him wish he'd simply waited in silence.

"How may we serve you, Sire?" Me'ekalar spoke quickly to deflect Lyolar's attention. "Do you have a command for us?"

For another long minute, Lyolar scowled at Beneban. Finally he cleared his throat and addressed them both.

"I am come from a meeting of the Council," he snarled. "Something must be done. This situation cannot deteriorate further."

Beneban, his mind ready for a move by Tor, couldn't think what the Council had to do with their disagreement. The Council was a body of advisors to the Grand Lar. It consisted of three Larlinga nobles, three Othrings, and an Advocate who could be either.

The current Advocate was Meriel's father, Ka'amfer. It seemed an unlikely group to be brought into a dispute between Beneban and Lyolar's heir.

"Also," Lyolar continued, "There does seem some cause for alarm. Conditions deteriorate, both with the Kaldens and in Forest. If things continue as they are, I expect to hear the vardraken have risen from beneath their mountains to pose a threat."

For a careless moment this reference to the legendary beings that had just been in his dream distracted Beneban. With a start, he realized that Lyolar was not talking about his heir. This was a different subject entirely.

Me'ekalar also seemed taken aback. He looked to Beneban for a cue.

"Suggestions, gentlemen?" the Grand Lar challenged his captains. "This concerns you especially, Captain Me'ekalar. The shortage of kaltings will undermine the strength of your corps."

"Yes, Mightiness," Me'ekalar responded. "Er, could someone be sent to discover the problem?"

"That is my plan. I've dispatched three messengers to the Kalden high chief, Kaldar," Lyolar snarled. "Two of them never found his camp."

"The Kalden are nomadic, but what of the third messenger?" Me'ekalar ventured hesitantly.

"Never returned. Vanished. And two other scouts, disguised as itinerant magicians, have also disappeared. That is why I will send you both."

Meriel yawned and covered her mouth with a dainty hand. Then, abruptly, she straightened. At her startled look, Beneban turned and saw that Tor had entered the garden from the library door. The young lar strolled in their direction. He seemed relaxed, unaware of them. Idly he stopped by a bush that bloomed generously. He bent to sniff the offered fragrance.

Beneban tried to pinpoint a difference about him, a wrongness, and yet not wrong.

As clearly as though he were back in the barracks just after Tor stormed out, the wizard remembered Trog's deep voice the night he had been injured. *What, I wonder, does young Tor plan to do about you and his uncle?*

Now Tor was only a few yards from the group. Lar Ari, who had fostered Tor as a child, burst from a distant door and raced toward the gathering. He called Tor's name, but the younger man ignored him or didn't hear.

Beneban was focused on the young lar. Tor's walk was—no, it *seemed*, Beneban thought in alarm—casual. A young man who joined friends. But there was a stiffness.

The young lar managed a strained smile for the group. Then one hand moved lazily to…

…*his sword!*

Arms were forbidden in the Grand Lar's presence, Beneban knew, and at the thought, the wizard's left hand clasped the Omera that hung always about his throat.

No one, not even Tor, was allowed to enter Lyolar's presence while armed, save only on sentry duty. This was an attack.

With the thought, Tor freed his weapon and

lunged at his uncle, and Beneban's hand moved as he spoke a command.

A flare of light sheeted between Tor and Lyolar. The young lar's sword clattered to the ground. Tor cursed and cradled his burned hand.

Ari was also stopped in mid-stride, hands spread wide in front of him, his fingers splayed against a sudden, invisible pane of glass.

Tor reached with clawed hands for his uncle's throat. Here, too, an invisible barrier blocked him from his goal.

Lyolar was frozen in shock.

"Get out of it now, you young idiot!" Beneban pushed the nearly silent command at Tor. He waved his right hand toward the garden gate. Its locks snapped open.

Meriel leapt to her feet. She moved toward the young lar but hesitated as Me'ekalar grabbed her arm.

With a snarl of frustration, Tor pounded his fist against the invisible wall. He knew well whose magic stopped him. He swore at Beneban and bent for his sword. Then, aware that his own life was forfeit for a threat to his uncle, he spun and raced for the gate. His weapon was quickly hidden beneath his cloak.

"*Guard!*" Lyolar roared, but the guard on duty could not hear his command from behind Beneban's barrier. A sudden gale whirled leaves between Lyolar and the glass wall. Lyolar yelled again, furious, and watched as the guard smiled, nodded to his nephew, and let the garden gate slip closed behind him.

"Captain! After him!" Lyolar bellowed.

Me'ekalar, inside the barrier, heard Lyolar. He

plunged obediently through the whirl of leaves, but crashed against the same invisible wall. Beneban allowed Tor another instant to be gone. Then he released the spell. Me'ekalar fell to his knees as the barrier vanished.

Me'ekalar leapt to his feet and burst toward the gate as ordered. He collided violently with Ari as Lyolar roared again for the guard.

This time the guard heard and ran toward them. By the time he understood his ruler's orders, Tor was gone beyond capture. Still, obedient to command, he raced to the gate and called for backup.

Ari and Me'ekalar untangled themselves with a struggle. They returned as Lyolar canceled the order to pursue his nephew. Beneban sank to the bench now vacated by Meriel and sat, head low, hands limp between his knees.

Ari turned a quizzical look on him but said nothing as Lyolar spun angrily.

"You contrive to let a would-be assassin of your Grand Lar escape," the ruler stormed at Beneban. "You should be hanged. Why should I not have you executed? And stand up in my presence! You failed to defend your lar."

"I contrived, Mightiness, without a weapon, to keep a would-be assassin from attainment of his goal." Beneban's voice was weary, diminished, as he stumbled to his feet. His shoulders sagged.

Meriel pulled urgently at Lyolar's arm and whispered to him as he bent toward her to hear.

"Shall I let him get away with it, then?" he demanded angrily.

Again, Meriel whispered.

Lyolar's eyes, the pale green of old ice, fastened on Beneban.

"My lady reminds me, *wizard*" he snarled, and the title was an epithet, "that you are popular with my citizens for some reason, as was my nephew. I tire of the trouble you bring. Yet to execute either of you would be unwise at this time. However..."

Beneban saw a half-smile on Meriel's face. He opened his mouth to speak.

"*Silence,*" Lyolar commanded icily.

The wizard, startled, returned to contemplation of the ground.

"I need someone to contact the Kaldens for me," the Grand Lar said after a brief moment for thought. "You, Captain Beneban, will take L Troop at first light tomorrow. You will proceed to Kaldenspeke. You will arrange for replacement kaltings and, if possible, an enlargement of the Kaltingcorps.

"Captain Me'ekalar, as one closely concerned with the success or failure of this mission, you will accompany L Troop." Lyolar spun for the palace.

"I'll ready my troop..." Me'ekalar began.

"Appoint a temporary captain to take your place while you are gone," Lyolar snapped, turning back. "Take only such as you need to herd untamed kaltings."

He had one final command. "Captain Beneban, report to me in my library after supper. I will provide you with gifts for the Kalden chieftain, just in case you manage to get an audience with him."

The Grand Lar studied Beneban for a moment and

then considered Me'ekalar. He seemed to expect a protest.

When neither man responded, he bellowed, *"Dismissed!"* Then without pause to see them obey, Lyolar spun on one furious heel and stalked toward the palace.

Meriel hesitated. Then, with a little frown, she took the arm Ari offered, and followed. The old lar was silent as they walked away, but the look of contempt he cast on Beneban lanced even the wizard's dazed fog.

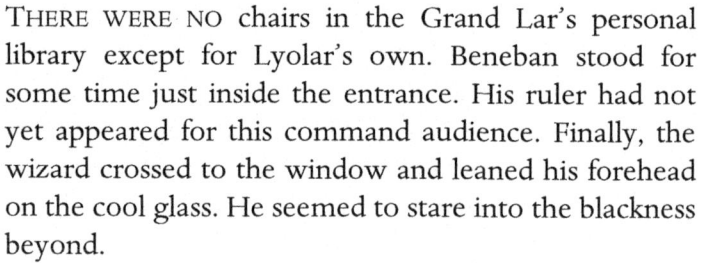

THERE WERE NO chairs in the Grand Lar's personal library except for Lyolar's own. Beneban stood for some time just inside the entrance. His ruler had not yet appeared for this command audience. Finally, the wizard crossed to the window and leaned his forehead on the cool glass. He seemed to stare into the blackness beyond.

When the library door finally clicked open, Beneban turned and began a bow to the shadowy figure standing there.

The sharp voice was not the one he expected.

"I don't understand," Lar Ari snapped without prelude. "You kept me from Tor, yet you made it possible for him to escape. Why?"

Beneban closed his eyes briefly. He opened them to their amber widest. Overuse of his magic had left him nearly blind. Now he sought to gather such light as was available.

All remained a blur. He quit the effort and forced a response to the lar whose friendship was now lost.

"Would you have gone with him, sir? Or returned to face Lyolar when he had made his escape? I thought you would choose the latter."

There was a long silence. At length, Ari said coldly, "Surely that is my business?"

"You must know I have considered you a friend." Beneban said.

"*You* must know," Ari interrupted, "that Tor told me what has come between you. I find it difficult to believe you would be so foolish as to keep an incriminating document of that type."

After a moment, Beneban said carefully, "I also would find it difficult to believe, in your place."

"Do you claim it is false?"

"If the document were true, would you keep your OathGive to Lyolar?"

"My oath *is* my oath," Ari said simply.

"And if I say the document is false, will you believe me?"

"If it is false, what evidence have you to show in proof?" the lar challenged.

"I have none," Beneban said simply. Ari snorted in disgust. The wizard winced and put up a shielding hand as he continued. "I have only a memory to offer. One from before footpads knocked me on the head. While still at Ka'amfer's supper, someone behind me said softly, '...all three plans ...in place,' and another answered, '...the problem is solved.' Three events followed," the wizard continued. "Three that would seem unrelated without those words."

He spoke over Ari's interruption. "First, I knew nothing of the wrestling match arranged for me with the Kalden. It was intended to be fatal."

"How do you…"

"Second," Beneban continued, "I received a blow on the head that followed when I left Ka'amfer's *hospitality*. An attack by footpads that should have left me dead."

"But these…"

"And finally," he spoke past Ari's interruption, "a document of dubious origin falls from storage in Trog's room. *Any* of the three should have removed me, if not from my life, at least from the Grand Lar's court."

"I leave tonight for Arilgarde keep," Ari said after several moments. "I remain true to my OathGive, but my stomach turns at court life and the people it breeds. Only the fact that you saved Tor from disgrace and probable death today stops me from a challenge to defend your honor with the blade. As I've told you, a friend of Tor's is mine also."

The old lar was silent for a long moment. Beneban raised his head a fraction. At Ari's next words, he remained motionless.

"As Tor no longer considers you a friend," the old lar said harshly, "I warn you that in all cases you must now look on me as an enemy. Save only that I shan't actively stop you from doing Lyolar's bidding."

There was no reply Beneban could make. After a brief moment, Ari stalked from the room.

SEVERAL NIGHTS LATER, and far distant from the comforts of Lyolar's palace or even of the barracks,

Me'ekalar stood concealed by the drooping branches of a dorpal tree. His men, several more than Lyolar had intended, were settling the riding kelsh. Me'ekalar listened to the ongoing bickering of L Troop. The troopers had sullenly pitched camp in the drizzle that had hounded them through Torling, along the western edge of Forest, and eastward to the head of the Little Mer River.

"What're you snarling about, Darkins? Food, shelter..." one of the men protested.

"Me, I don't care," the disgruntled trooper grumbled, "but we could ha' saved a day or more, just going through Ariling. Captain, er, *Corporal* Glaynar says..."

"Arr, stuff it," a young trooper said rudely. "Glaynar don't like the cap'n, and no wonder. But I do. Our troop can ride and fight and just plain last longer since we got us a wizard captain."

"Well, whose side's he on, though? Letting them Torlingals get away with not giving us food or shelter. Then he give Jaran such a whuppin' when Jar took them felle from that little kid."

"Jaran *broke the kid's arm* to get the beasts," Beneban's defender, a trooper named Denodar, pointed out. "He *stole* 'em! We're troopers, not thieves, and..."

Beneban came quietly up and touched Me'ekalar's shoulder as the Kaltingcorps captain gave a quiet ear to this conversation. They moved away from the group at the wizard's direction and paced beneath dripping trees to a large overhang of rock. Beneban indicated a pile of blankets and sank down beside his guest, muddy boots stretched carefully away from the bedding.

Me'ekalar took a moment to observe the neat shelter. Behind Beneban's bed roll stood a large, intricately carved crysolate box. Bound with gold and studded with precious jewels, it was both gift and container for the priceless present The Grand Lar sent to the Kalden chieftain.

The wizard leaned against the rock wall and let his eyes close. At length he opened them to peer curiously at Me'ekalar, now seated and comfortable.

"It was a bad day for you when we became friends, Me'ekalar."

"I don't complain." The Kaltingcorps captain spread his hands. "It's good to get away from the city and its intrigues. Good to be away from the heat."

"Perhaps. But you've been sent on as near as may be to a suicide mission. A tidy way for Lyolar to rid himself of a wizard he never wanted. You wouldn't be here if you hadn't been in the garden eight days ago to observe his anger."

"Ten." At Beneban's blank look Me'ekalar elucidated. "It's been ten days. Nine on the road."

"It's hard to number days that drag on forever." Again the wizard closed his eyes.

"Beneban?"

"Mmm?" the wizard asked, motionless against his bedding.

"I realize no one is supposed to notice," Me'ekalar said diffidently, "but you snapped Trog's head off yesterday when he asked if you were well. You seem worn to the bone since... well, since Tor ran off."

Still motionless, Beneban grimaced as though stricken by a sudden pain.

Me'ekalar watched him in silence. Finally the wizard shrugged into a more comfortable position and stared at his friend from dark-ringed eyes. His voice was low when he spoke.

"You don't think the need to beat L Troop into shape, being on the road late into the night and breaking up a multitude of fights, not to mention a knock on the head and a suicide mission might explain it?"

Silence was the only response.

"No," Beneban said wryly, "I gather you don't."

"Does your exhaustion have to do with... Well, when you let Tor go?"

Beneban turned his head and shaded his eyes with one hand as though the watery twilight somehow hurt them. "You are too observant," he hissed.

Me'ekalar waited, silent. Finally the wizard sighed, and answered.

"Let me tell you a bit about wizardry, my friend. Here, sit beside me. I don't wish to discuss this with the whole camp."

Me'ekalar twisted until he could lean against the tribute chest and still keep his muddy boots off the bedding, his head near the wizard. Beneban was silent.

"Well?"

Beneban was quiet for a moment more. He seemed to choose his words carefully. "Wizardry," he began slowly, "that is, *true* magic, is the transmutation of the inherent energy of one thing into another. Wizards seek to become incredibly rich because valuable items are a source of that energy."

He paused again, then continued reluctantly. "When there is no other source to draw from, the energy comes from, or more precisely, *out of,* the wizard."

After some moments of thought, Me'ekalar exclaimed, "You lose your sight!" Suddenly he understood more of the past several days. "Is it permanent?"

"My sight is the first thing to go, perhaps because I value it. It is not permanent. Not unless *I* am a fool and continue to drain my power. I am nearly well now. It was, in fact, the combination of all those events that has slowed my recovery."

"I guess I thought," Me'ekalar said slowly, "that wizardry was a *means* to wealth. I've heard that Ztavin," he nodded guardedly toward the mountains looming behind them, "is richer by twice than the Grand Lar."

"He is a *black* wizard," Beneban said tersely. Me'ekalar sat in puzzled silence. Finally Beneban continued. "Black wizards use sources of power forbidden the rest of us. As a result, they do become wealthy. And more powerful."

"I don't understand."

"Have you suddenly decided to pursue the study of wizardry?" Beneban snapped impatiently.

"No, but I have this friend," Me'ekalar said with a quizzical smile. "I'm curious what makes him act as he does."

"Mmm." Beneban grumbled. He stared into the gathered darkness for a while. "Well, pain is a potent source of power. So is life."

"You mean Ztavin uses live beings?"

"I mean it is possible to use them."

"But that... That's evil! It's against the law of Eratim."

A sudden yell arose from the camp and interrupted the conversation. Trog's voice rumbled. It was followed by a deep bellow.

Halfway to his feet, Beneban sank back as the furor subsided.

"There's another queer thing," Me'ekalar said to allow a change from the subject the wizard obviously had closed. "Hundak. Who'd have thought the Kalden would come near you after you beat him at Ka'amfer's banquet? Yet here he trots into camp two days out of Larlingarde. He claims his life is yours to use. That he will stay with you from now on. Then he jumps on your closest friend and tries to kill him."

Amused dismay colored Beneban's face as he responded. "Yes, and Trog did his best to return the favor." He shook his head. "I think," he added hopefully, "that they've accepted, if not each other, at least the need to coexist, if they are determined to stay with me."

"But why?"

"Why? Why, indeed?" Beneban snarled impatiently. "It seems I collect dependents like an overripe curranfruit collects barbittes."

"W-Well..." Me'ekalar stammered to a halt at the acerbity of the answer. He tried again. "But still, why?"

"Why did Hundak come to me? By the custom of his people, his life or mine was forfeit when we agreed to wrestle. When I refused to kill him, that custom left him to live as a bhaskie, a sort of ghost. He has no existence now with his people, and no standing except what I give him."

"You plan to keep him then?"

"I plan to let him stay," Beneban corrected. Then he angrily added, "What else can I do?"

Me'ekalar decided not to voice his thought. Many others, he knew, would let the defeated Kalden fend for himself. So he asked mildly, "Do you trust him?"

"Oh yes. Within the limits of his beliefs, he is absolutely trustworthy."

"What limits?" Me'ekalar asked, but Trog trundled up to them before Beneban could answer.

"Camp is settled for the night, sir," the Ogdol reported, saluting.

"Thank you, Trog." Beneban returned the salute. "Have you and Hundak calmed down too?" he asked. Then, impatiently, "And sit down! Don't *tower* over me."

Trog settled down on his three legs like a small mountain coming to rest, his whiteness a gray blur against the darkening woods. "Hundak is settled, too," he said complacently.

"Trog..." Beneban started up in alarm.

"Be easy, Captain," the Ogdol calmed him. "I have stationed him as rear guard. I told him you fear attack from High Aril, but that you do not wish to alarm the men unnecessarily."

"We're less than a day's march from Kaldenspeke," Beneban pointed out. "If there's trouble..."

"Perhaps Hundak may be trusted," Trog continued. "Yet the Kaldens are his people. I shall post other watch to be certain he is alert. Lodar, perhaps, in case of trouble from that direction." Trog changed the subject abruptly. "Have you eaten, sir?"

"I'm not hungry. As we are low on rations..."

"We may get food from the Kaldens if our mission is successful," Trog said. "In any case, you cannot carry the responsibility of leading L Troop if you are faint from hunger." Trog pushed a plate of bread and dried meat at him. "It is not your fault that the Torlingals refuse to sell us food. Eat."

"Did I appoint you my nursemaid and then forget?" Beneban snarled.

"If you had done so, I would remind you also of that." Trog turned his gaze slightly aside, but the plate of food stayed relentlessly before the wizard.

At length, ignoring the smothered laugh from Me'ekalar, Beneban snatched the plate.

"Sorry," he growled ungraciously. He balanced the plate on his knee and with his belt knife slit the soggy half-loaf and stuffed meat between the layers of bread. He tore off a bite and chewed unenthusiastically. Then, as his hunger flared, he ate the rough food eagerly.

Once Trog was satisfied that Beneban would continue his meal, he shifted as though to rise. "I will go now to set a watch toward Kaldenspeke," he rumbled.

"Wait, Trog," Beneban muttered through a full mouth. He swallowed. "I need to talk to you about Kaldenspeke."

The Ogdol settled back. "I too have considered the problem of my presence."

"Your people and the Kaldens are mortal enemies. Yet both serve in the Grand Lar's armies. Since they are allies of Larlingarde, will these Kaldens accept you as a member of L Troop?"

"These Kaldens owe no loyalty to the Grand Lar. They will not extend any special treatment because of my oath to him."

"You mean they'll try to capture you."

"To begin with, yes," Trog agreed.

"What happens if we, or rather, what happens *when* we don't allow that?"

"They will use what force is necessary."

"Yet Lyolar insisted that you accompany the troop."

Trog didn't comment.

"One more strand in the trap he's woven," Beneban said wryly. "Do you have any suggestions that may cause this ploy to fail?"

"I must stay out of sight for the duration of the conference."

"Yes. But how?" the wizard wondered.

"Kaldenspeke is a valley. It is ringed with rough mountains," Trog said. "I shall find a shelter just short of the meeting place." The Ogdol paused, and Beneban sensed his friend was struggling for words.

"What, Trog? What bothers you, beyond the fact that none of us is likely to return from this mission?"

Reluctantly the hairy giant rumbled again into speech. "I would not have you think me a coward who stays behind when danger threatens you. I will be not far. I will come if you need me."

"The threat becomes a certainty if you accompany us," Beneban pointed out. "Our only chance of survival is for you to stay away. I could never question your courage."

"I shall go and post the night guard." Trog started

away but stopped again. "Yet remember, sir, I *shall* be within call at Kaldenspeke. If there must be a battle, you will not be alone."

"I'll remember. But stay out of sight," Beneban warned firmly.

The giant vanished into the trees as Me'ekalar, a silent observer to their conversation, stretched and yawned loudly.

"It's been a long day," he said. "We should sleep. By the way, where did you stash the Worf child, Sel? I'm surprised he'd be left behind."

"I left him with old Gorm. No need for a child to be trapped in this," the wizard said wearily and changed the subject. "I am also ready for sleep. Will you bring your blankets under here? Unless you share the men's suspicions of caves and prefer the open and the wet. There's room to spare."

"I'll take dry every time if I won't disturb your rest," his friend said with a chuckle. He stood. "First, though," he added, "I'll check on Hundak. Incidentally, if you don't expect trouble from High Aril Tower, why didn't we stop there? The men would have had shelter, and it's just a day from Kaldenspeke."

Beneban grimaced at the memory of his interview in the library. "Lar Ari said he wouldn't stop me doing Lyolar's bidding. He also made it clear that he wouldn't help me. As High Aril is his hold, I'll not take assistance from his people without his knowledge. The long march didn't hurt the men. They'll sleep better and be sharp tomorrow."

"Indeed. The troops, yours *and* mine, are in the best shape I can remember. Of course, the Kaltingcorps can still run 'em into the ground... Ooops. Hello, Kati."

The big kalting, back from her night's hunting, purred a deep greeting as she pushed past to curl at the head of Beneban's bedding.

The wizard smiled slightly at the sound. Kati's purr and Trog's deep growl reminded him of each other.

Me'ekalar flipped a hand and disappeared as the wizard leaned back to pillow his head on Kati's flank. He shut his eyes. Now the thoughts he'd closed off pushed past exhaustion to worry him.

Several days ago, they had marched up the western edge of Forest. Beneban had called an extra rest near the place he'd once seen Saray.

It was midday. His men had been noisily glad for the unexpected break. They didn't notice as Beneban moved into the edge of the trees alone.

Seated on a sheltered log, he'd spent half of an hour in search of that mental contact he remembered, but he'd found only emptiness, and at the fringes of that emptiness, a hint of evil. Had Forest become an evil place as Ari suggested?

Had Forest Lady left her haven? Or had she joined the evil? Or been evil to begin with?

No! He ousted that last thought as merely the result of exhaustion. He'd sooner believe that Trog would betray him than accept Forest Lady as a source of evil.

He closed his eyes, and one last question arose. Why was his sleep haunted with silvery fish and Mergols?

He took another deep breath...

...and slept.

Ztavin's spies informed him of activities in Larlingarde, and particularly at his order, of anything that might concern Beneban. Disappointment in the failure of his Mergol princeling to destroy his protégé ate at him. Angry that the young wizard had neither found the Larstone nor returned to the black tower, he puzzled how to increase pressure on Beneban. If he could not be brought to heel, he must be destroyed.

When he heard that Beneban would meet with the Kaldens at Kaldenspeke, he began to plot in earnest.

After careful preparation, he flew on a bitter wind to the north plains, beyond the settled lands of Larlion. Nearly at once he had a stroke of good luck. A drak, an infant vardraken, curious as the young often are, came cautiously from its egg to investigate the newcomer. Now the little drak would have to suffer for his curiosity.

Ztavin's summoning was strengthened by torment of the hatchling. The pain of the infant would draw in his true target.

It was the next evening before Ztavin was successful. He had settled to eat a light supper when abruptly the bowl froze in his hand and the food on the spoon at his mouth grew icicles.

"Ah, Varakin, you have come, my queen." He forced tension from his voice as he dropped the spoon with an icy clatter into the bowl.

The woman who stood before him was tall, slenderer than a wood sprite. Her ice-white hair whipped wildly around her face in a wind Ztavin had not noticed. She was colorless but for her eyes. These were the deep blue of a glacier's heart.

Those eyes shot fury as she took a menacing step toward him…

Instantly Ztavin wrapped the nestling drak, hidden nearby, in another layer of painful heat. It squeaked pathetically. He was pleased to see her wince.

"Let him go!" she hissed.

"I only wish to ask a small favor of you, my dear. It is long since we spoke. Will you sit? I'd offer you food or drink, but as you see…" He indicated the frozen remains of his supplies.

"Let him go!"

Ztavin felt a thrill of cold dance along his veins. He must make his point quickly. This lady was a dangerous tool, not a weakling like the Mergol princeling.

"No? Then I shall make this quick. Let. Him. Go. Or I will freeze you where you sit."

Aware that ice water had filled his boots and drooled icicles over the tops, Ztavin stopped being amused.

"Very well, to business," he hissed. "I need a small favor of you and one of your delightful vardraken. There will be a meeting of Kaldens with a troop of Larlingarders. This is what I request, my queen…"

Ztavin's business was concluded. His hostage he released to the queen's tender mercies.

As she gathered up the infant vardraken and soothed its wounds, he continued.

"I would not deceive you, Varakin. I have others of your children at my keep. They will be treated well, so long as you do as I ask."

The blast of cold smashed him into a boulder and extinguished his tiny campfire. The water in his boots froze solid.

Then she was gone.

"Well, that might have gone better," Ztavin muttered. He rekindled his fire and propped his feet near the heat. Finding dry socks in his gear, he was finally able to change from the frozen boots. Then he thawed his supper.

He had little appetite.

He scraped the icy food onto the ground and summoned his travel wind. By the time he had regained the Black Keep, he was not happy to realize that his adventure had left him with a miserable cough.

Ill and desirous of simply taking to his bed, instead he set a search for infant vardraken in place. The gold he offered would quickly bring him hostages from the local hunters. Varakin was a powerful card to hold.

He sneezed violently and stumbled to his chair where he huddled beneath his covers.

"Now I will need to be sure I collect a few hostages for the lady's behavior," he grumbled and sneezed miserably again.

CHAPTER 21

Several mornings later, Beneban ducked out the door of his tent and into ankle deep snow. He shivered in the crisp air and stamped his feet as he stared about. On all sides loomed the fierce peaks that girded the natural bowl of Kaldenspeke. This traditional meeting place of the Kaldens rarely knew summer. Now, though it was the time of Greening in the lowlands, the peaks on the north were still snow covered. Even in this sheltered place, though there were a few patches of grass, sleet coated the campsite, and drifts of snow lurked in sheltered spots.

Only keen eyes would spot the pass in the hills by which they had arrived a couple of days earlier. A second pass exited to the south at the far side of the bowl. If Hundak had not pointed it out, it would have been invisible.

"An unpleasant trap," the wizard muttered.

Me'ekalar crawled from the tent and joined him. He shivered and rubbed his arms against the chill. "Where will the Kaldens appear?" the Kaltingcorps captain wondered aloud. "They weren't on the trail behind us. The men say the path south leads down from the heights to the plains of Ariling beyond. That's not their country."

"You've never been here?" Beneban was surprised.

Me'ekalar shook his head. "In the past, they brought the beasts down below, eager to sell their extra mounts."

"There are paths fit for mountain gazerts or Kaldens all over these cliffs, even to the north," Beneban told him. "I'm less concerned about their arrival than about our way out if things get ugly. They surely know we're here. They want us to kick our heels until we're properly nervous."

"Could be," Me'ek nodded. "If they knew you better... Look!"

Gawl came running toward them. "Cap'n, some movement on them cliffs. They're headin' in, Sir. There's a big, *big* lot of 'em. Trog s-signaled. No women or k-kids. That looks like war. Th-they..."

"Gawl!" The snap in Beneban's voice brought the panicky trooper to attention. Gawl was a big man, heavily muscled. More than once his fellows had suggested there might be a Kalden in his background. The wizard was surprised to see him so shaken. "Now," Beneban took a slow, calm breath. *"Precisely what* did Trog signal?" The wizard's eyes flickered to a spot above the southern pass where the Ogdol kept watch from the shelter of a dorpal tree.

"S-Sir." Gawl fought his nerves down. He swallowed loudly and managed to speak with military conciseness. "Trog signaled at least sixty on the way. Warriors, armed. No family groups, sir."

"Thank you, Gawl. Send me Sergeants Aylmer and Denodar. And Borno if you run across him. Have Lieutenant Reeno bring the troop to attention. Arms at rest but ready. Dismissed!"

The shaken Gawl, a bully among his fellows, saluted and disappeared into the crowd around the breakfast fire. The fire was quickly doused. L Troop was drawn up at attention, weapons sheathed but loose. They were prepared to greet the huge, golden-haired tribesmen who wound their way slowly down into the Kaldenspeke.

Beneban, mounted on Kati, was at the head of the small mounted troop. Me'ekalar and his kalting, She'em, flanked him on the left. At his right hand, Hundak prepared to translate as necessary. Kaldens rarely learned any language but their own, so he was valuable as an interpreter.

At Hundak's feet stood the richly carved and jeweled box, the treasure they hoped would pave the way for more kaltings and no battle.

Inexorably, the horde of Kaldens loped toward the confrontation. Each chief wore the golden skin of a kalting. It was hard to see where hides left off and their own blond pelts began. Mainly unmounted, they advanced with a wild, free stride across the frozen tundra. Short stabbing spears were carried loosely. War axes hung from every belt. Only the leader and two under-chiefs rode kaltings.

The head chieftain, a man as tall, Beneban was sure, as Trog himself, carried no weapon. About his neck hung countless strings of precious and semiprecious stones. The kalting he rode was larger than Kati, though a male and hornless.

The chieftain advanced quickly. He halted within a bare yard of the wizard.

As he neared their captain, the troop moved restlessly closer until Beneban gave an imperative motion that stilled them.

The narrow distance between the two leaders was anything but comfortable. Kati snarled and tensed to leap, but Beneban held her steady. He refused to give ground.

The huge chieftain held up his hand to halt the horde. He dismounted, and afoot he looked the mounted wizard in the eye.

A warrior strode forward to take the kaltings away as the under-chieftains also dismounted.

Silence filled the bowl. It pressed down on the massed warriors as the two leaders stared at each other. Each sought for a first advantage.

The Kalden chief was a veteran warrior, but his courage was of the spontaneous type. Nowhere in his past had he been so schooled in self-discipline as even a minor wizard. After what seemed to the alert troopers an interminable time, his eyes shifted infinitesimally to one side. He loosed a guttural burst of angry sounding words.

"Over-chief say, Captain," Hundak interpreted, "'It be customary for those who seek his favor to kneel.'"

"You are not kneeling, Hundak," Beneban said. His eyes remained locked on those of the over-chief.

"Hundak be bhaskie. Homage not acceptable," said Hundak. Indeed, the giant Kalden, here before his tribe, seemed oddly shrunken.

"Very well. Tell the over-chief I bear greetings and an offer of trade from Lyolar, Grand Lar of Larlion and Lord of the Twelve Estates. Lyolar's servants owe homage only to the Grand Lar."

Cringing, Hundak repeated this to the chief. Though it sounded humbler and longer than Beneban's spoken words, the Kalden leader's eyes flashed blue fire. He snarled a question, then another.

"He asked, 'Shall he then stand, while you look down on him?'" Hundak interpreted.

"What was the first question, Hundak? Did he ask why you don't wipe out your dishonor by taking me apart one rib at a time?" Beneban barked an unamused laugh as Hundak's rising color showed the guess was close.

"Never mind," Beneban said. "I'll meet him that far. Hundak, say that I invite him to sit out of the wind in my tent. Sergeant Aylmer, open the flaps. Show that there is no trap." Beneban dismounted, and Kati, with a final snarl, stalked away.

"Borno," the wizard continued, "where are you, you scamp? Ah! Break out that old bottle of baraque and the silver goblets. And take this inside." He toed the gaudy chest as though it mattered little.

"Captain Me'ekalar, take the troop!" Beneban gave the formal order. A warning glance told the Kaltingcorps captain to keep them at full alert.

The men moved sharply to obey his orders. The troop grounded their spears, but let swords hang at the ready.

With a gesture of invitation to the chieftain, Beneban turned his back on the massed horde. He moved toward his tent without seeming concerned. This left his guest, the other two chiefs, and the two hulking warriors that guarded them, to follow as they would.

The Kalden chieftain stood for several seconds and watched the troop, busy and alert as Beneban had ordered. He peered closely at the open tent.

A terse order to his horde left them facing the Larlingarde troopers. After a tense moment, they also lowered spear points to the ground. With a sharp nod to his under-chiefs to follow, the chieftain stalked to the tent.

Borno had transformed Beneban's bedroll into a rough seat, big enough for the two leaders with the elaborate chest against one wall. Now the lad produced a dusty red bottle and four small goblets of beaten silver from the wizard's pack. Beneban waved an invitation, then sat beside the high chief. After a brief hesitation, the under-chiefs squatted on the ground to the other side of their leader.

Theatrically the wizard broke the seal. He decanted a few drops of the fiery liquor into one goblet and sipped to show it wasn't poisoned. Then he poured into the other goblets and passed them to his guests.

The goblets, in their enormous hands, looked the size of thimbles. As they held them and tipped the liquid from side to side, the wizard wondered idly what degree of civilization was required before one man would drink with another whom he intended to destroy.

The over-chief, his temper now under control, burst again into speech. Hundak, who stood at Beneban's shoulder, interpreted. "He say, 'Grand Lar take our beasts, tear heart from our tribes. For this he send baubles.'"

"If the stones he wears about his neck are an example, they've been quite nice baubles indeed," Beneban said. "No, Hundak, don't repeat that. Tell him I bear a gift of such magnificence as he has never imagined." He nodded toward the jeweled chest. "Also, say that Lyolar will increase by many pazts the price for each kalting trained and delivered. But our master wants twenty kaltings to return with us immediately, and another forty by year's end."

Hundak translated this to the now impassive over-chief. When he finished, the chief muttered to a companion.

"What is his name, Hundak?" Beneban asked quietly.

"Kaldar, Captain."

Kaldar growled a few words. It seemed he wished to see this awesome gift. Beneban sent Borno, and he and Gawl returned to lug the heavy gold-bound box from the wall. It was set carefully in the center of the tent.

"Dismissed, Gawl. Open it, Borno."

The boy caught the golden key tossed by his captain and laid back the cover to display an object of such richness that few would notice its vulgarity. A huge basin of heavy beaten shimmergold stood mounted on a carved and faceted gem as large as a man's head. The whole was so thickly encrusted with jewels as to nearly disguise the original material.

The glitter scattered dancing rainbows of light across the tent. It seemed to blaze against the snowy white vevar fur that lined the case. All eyes were held as the bauble imposed a brief, awed silence.

At length, Kaldar turned to Beneban. His face was

still impassive, but a glint of greed quivered in the sharp blue eyes.

"It is acceptable," he said in understandable Larling. "But," he held one hand up, "price for kaltings will double."

"The price is high, Kaldar. Yet the Grand Lar values your friendship. He will not let so small a thing come between you. That too is acceptable."

The Kalden chief set down his silver goblet without a sip. He stood, and Beneban followed suit. Kaldar inclined his head slightly and started to turn away. He looked back and spoke a few careless words, once more in his native tongue.

"'Is one other thing,'" Hundak interpreted.

Beneban, who had begun to hope they might turn this mission into a success and cancel the Grand Lar's anger, felt a chill pick its way along his spine.

"'We send kaltings,'" Hundak continued to translate, "'So quick as they be selected. You leave with us Ogdol who is spy from cliff above.'"

Beneban's eyes darted in shock to Hundak's face. The defiance blazoned there was a plain statement of guilt.

"The Ogdol is an officer of this troop," the wizard said slowly. He forced the tension from his voice. "He camped outside our boundaries to avoid insult to the noble Kaldar."

"Ogdol is spy and enemy." Kaldar spoke in Larling, and his tone was hard. "You, your men, go in peace. He stay. Be dealt with as is custom." He spit and turned away, certain that his superior force and his willingness to provide the kaltings would carry the point.

"No."

Hundak didn't need to translate. The flat syllable from Beneban spun the over-chief around as though he'd been hit.

"Think what you say." Kaldar spoke, still in careful Larling. "Twenty kaltings wait in hills. Forty more at year end to please Lyolar. You much outnumbered. Not throw away advantage for bardack Ogdol."

"I've no idea whether Trog has a mother," Beneban said coolly. "He does have comrades."

"You what say?"

"I say," the wizard repeated grimly, "*No!*"

Kaldar spun toward the waiting horde and bellowed a command. Within the tent, his tribesmen reached for their battle axes. Before the weapons were freed, Beneban held the over-chief in a stranglehold, his belt knife at the leader's throat.

Weapons clashed outside as the squared formation of troopers was assailed by angry Kaldens. The troop retreated slowly to the tent as they fought to keep it from being overrun.

"Tell your friends here to drop their weapons," Beneban grated in Kaldar's ear.

"Not do! *Aaagh*," the chieftain groaned as the wizard's knife drew a thin red line across the other's throat. A guttural word followed. The over-chief's companions hesitated then dropped their weapons.

"Borno, pick up that flashy wash-basin and stay by me," Beneban snapped. He edged toward his embattled troop as Me'ekalar worked his way around the battle and appeared before them.

"Barbitte's nest, Captain," he gasped, wiping blood

from a shallow cut over one eye. "Any orders?"

He lunged and impaled a Kalden who had hacked his way too close then pushed the body off with one foot. "Good spot for Heldenhaft."

"Yes. Hold Kaldar a moment. Slit his throat at any interference." He passed his prisoner to Me'ekalar. "Now," he said, as he knelt by the golden basin and freed the Omera from his tunic, "let's call in some reinforcements."

Beneban touched his deep red wizard stone to the enormous jeweled bauble. His amber eyes focused on the spot where the two objects met. He muttered softly and fought to shut out the danger and draw from the air a picture of his need. As his concentration deepened, his gaze moved to the cliffs about the Kaldenspeke.

The basin beneath his hands shimmered more brightly than before. It lit the tent with its brilliance.

Something heavy fell against Beneban's back, but the wizard's concentration was unbroken.

Now the basin's edges blurred as Me'ekalar and Borno watched in amazement. It faded, and was drawn into a net of sparks, then the sparks flew outward.

From the cliffs surrounding the Kaldenspeke, great shouting arose.

"Larlingarde!"

"Larlion! And a rescue."

"Ariling! Fare forth for Ariling."

On every side of the great basin, warriors of Larlion were seen to scramble down from the cliffs. The Kalden force assailing L Troop began to waver.

Beneban leapt to his feet and dragged Heldenhaft

from her scabbard. "Rally the troop, Me'ekalar. A little push now, and this rabble will run."

He looked in puzzlement at the dead Kalden warrior tangled about his ankles. The man's head, nearly severed by a battle axe, sprawled across the cushions. The two lesser chiefs raced toward their horde as Hundak calmly cleaned blood from the edge of his weapon. He met the wizard's eye.

Well, no time for that enigma.

"Now, Me'ekalar!" Knocking the over-chief neatly behind the ear with Heldenhaft's hilt, Beneban raised the mighty sword and plunged into the fight.

"Heldenhaft and Larlion," he bellowed. "To me, Larlion!"

Heldenhaft blazed. The air about the wizard turned to amber shot through with streaks of gold. The magic sword's high song overrode the sounds of battle as she plunged fiercely into the Kalden horde. Her strength poured through the wizard in a flood of joy as she pulled him into the fight.

The Kaldens, beset by the demon with his wailing sword and threatened by massed troops of Larlinga behind, wavered.

L Troop, heartened by the wizard's uncanny power, redoubled its efforts.

Fighting along the edge of his men, Beneban was quickly in the thick of the battle. A mighty axe aimed at his head caught on Heldenhaft and slid down her length. A foiling thrust of a dagger dispatched its owner. Heldenhaft caught another blow coming at his ankles.

Me'ekalar struggled to stay with him. "Where's

Kati?" he gasped.

"No idea. She'll be with us when we leave."

"If we leave." Another Kalden fell to Me'ekalar's sword.

Suddenly the Kalden horde howled and cowered to the ground as an icy shadow overflew the meadow.

Beneban and Me'ekalar stared up. Above the fight, they saw a creature from myth overfly the battleground. Me'ekalar dropped to one knee, but Beneban stood erect. His eyes, shaded by the hand that still held Heldenhaft, followed as the ice dragon soared above the battle.

She banked, flew over them again, and her rider leaned far out. For a moment the wizard saw her. Silver hair flailed about ice-blue eyes. They met his, and magic flashed between the two. Then the vardraken banked again and disappeared past the looming mountains.

"Wh-what?" Me'ekalar was struggling to his feet, his face as white as snow.

"A vardraken. If they are come to join the battle, let's get out of this!"

As quickly as the vardraken disappeared, the Kaldens resumed their feet and the fight. One of the tribe joined his ancestors with Heldenhaft's help. At Beneban's side, Borno, eyes still wide from the vardraken's flight, parried a blow aimed at his captain, and Beneban thrust through the warrior.

Another warrior had worked in behind the little group to slash at Beneban. He missed the wizard but drove his axe deep into Borno's shoulder.

Warned by the lad's cry, Beneban whirled and

furiously took the Kalden's head clean from his body.

And the fight was over. Shaken by the flight of the ice dragon and afraid they were about to be cut off from their hidden pass to the north by the phantom troops that poured along the cliff, the Kaldens broke and fled without a command.

Beneban dropped Heldenhaft and knelt beside Borno. He ripped off his own tunic and pressed the rough pad against the gaping wound. Instantly the blue cloth turned to sodden purple.

Me'ekalar bellowed an order that halted the troop as they would have followed the routed Kaldens into the mountains. Then he knelt beside the wizard.

Hundak held the lad's hand in his huge one, his large flat face mirroring Borno's pain.

"Got to get that artery," Beneban grated as he probed with questing fingers deep within the wound. The boy, his face ashen, stared trustingly at his captain. "Me'ekalar!" the wizard gasped. "Something to tie this off."

Sweat poured down his brow as the long slender fingers, prehensile extensions of his eyes, searched the wide wound.

"Tie it?" Me'ekalar frowned in puzzlement, then his face cleared as Beneban found and pinched off the ends of the severed artery.

Quickly Me'ekalar pulled two strands of silk from the embroidery that was thick on his Kaltingcorps cape.

"This'll be strong," he said then frowned as a third enormous, gold-furred hand, delicately swabbed the blood that made everything slippery. "Good man, Hundak."

At Beneban's direction, Hundak carefully grasped the arteries. Tongue clamped fiercely between his teeth in concentration, Beneban made delicate loops in the silken strands and, one at a time, eased them into place and tightened them.

"What about infection?" Me'ekalar asked.

Gingerly, Beneban loosened one strand, then the other. He waved Hundak away and saw that the loops would hold. Finally, he looked up at his aides. His face was nearly as white as Borno's. Sweat stood in great drops on his forehead.

"There's baraque in the tent, if the bottle isn't broken. Will you get it, Me'ekalar? That is the only hope to stop an infection."

Me'ekalar ran for the tent. When he disappeared, Beneban's amber eyes fastened on the Kalden's ice-blue ones. "You told Kaldar about Trog," he said flatly. The wizard's eyes were cold with anger.

"I do." Hundak made no excuse. His tone was flat, but he stared at his feet.

"Yet you killed two of your tribesmen in the tent to save my life. *Look* at me, Hundak!"

"Yes. I do." His blue eyes moved to the wizard's angry amber gaze. For this too, Hundak offered no explanation.

"I don't understand," Beneban said. "But I will give you one more chance. Understand me in this! If you wish to stay with me, you will be as loyal to Trog in the future as if he were my very self. You do not have to like him, but you do have to cease this enmity. He will be your comrade in arms."

Amber eyes held the wild blue until deep within

them there was a flicker, a tiny change. What Beneban saw there seemed to satisfy him.

"Alright. We are agreed. Now find material for a bandage then see to a litter to carry the boy."

He bent back to Borno but looked up again as three legs like white-furred trunks halted before him. Trog towered over them.

"Trog! Good man! We need to stretch a cloak, something to transport the wounded between two kelsh to carry them."

"Yes sir! It is underway." The Ogdol said nothing about the mysterious appearance and disappearance of the extra troops. "But sir, you must hear what Kati and She'em have been up to."

At Beneban's curious look, Trog's wide mouth curved up in a rare smile. "They found the Kalden's corrals. They have a herd of some thirty kaltings gathered by the south pass of Kaldenspeke."

"They don't!" Beneban stared in astonishment, and for a moment, glee replaced concern. "I wondered where they'd gotten to."

Me'ekalar appeared, slightly out of breath, and held out the dusty bottle of baraque.

"Thanks, Me'ek." The wizard turned again to Trog. "Collect the men near the kaltings. Are any of the beasts tamed?" At Trog's assent, he continued. "Choose a pair to work as litter kelsh. Can we get the wounded down that path, carried between two kelsh?"

"For a time," Trog said. "If it becomes too narrow, I will carry Borno." He moved away, and Beneban turned to the injured boy.

"This will hurt, son." Borno, eyes dark with shock,

nodded slightly. Then, as the wizard tipped the bottle and the fiery alcohol burned into raw flesh, he gave a strangled howl. He surged up against Me'ekalar's strong grasp, and then went limp.

"So," the wizard sighed. "He's better off unconscious when we move him." Beneban deftly bandaged the shoulder. "Me'ek," Beneban asked, "how many wounded do we have?"

"Only one other that can't ride. We've arranged two slings. Eight troopers are dead," he continued. "We've tied 'em to kelsh. No time to bury them. Won't leave 'em here. Half a dozen more are lightly wounded," he finished.

"Better than I feared. There." The wizard finished bandaging the wound and lifted Borno gently to the waiting litter.

"Let's get out of this trap before the Kaldens realize our reinforcements have vanished."

CHAPTER 22

Two hours later, each trooper and his kelsh trudged head down into a driving, sleety rain. From Kaldenspeke, the trail wound along a narrow, nerve-shattering ledge. They assumed the weather to be only a normal irritant until a sudden violent gust of wind brushed one man and his kelsh screaming into the deep chasm. After that, each trooper led his mount, stepping carefully to stay as close to the wall as possible. The litters were awkwardly slung from one beast's rear to the front of another to allow for the narrowness of the path. Spare blankets had been wrapped around the wounded men to provide such shelter as was possible from the weather. For the rest of the men, there was no escape. Half-frozen gouts of rain crept diabolically beneath every collar, into every opening.

The downpour gave the sheer granite path an oily slickness. Twice a trooper, setting a foot unwarily, had slithered toward the edge. He had been saved only by a firm grip on the reins of his increasingly skittish kelsh.

Well aware of the danger, Me'ekalar edged past the weary soldiers toward the front of the troop. He nearly lost his footing as he spied Beneban's tall shape ahead and took a less cautious step.

"Easy, Cap'n!" A strong hand plucked him back to the path. Me'ekalar recognized with gratitude the young trooper who had defended Beneban in the camp at the Little Mer.

"Thanks," Me'ekalar gasped, shuddering at the close call. "What's your name, trooper?"

"Lodar, sir." With an easy grin and a flicker of a salute, he stood tight to the wall to allow Me'ekalar to pass.

"Beneban," Me'ekalar called as he came nearer his scarlet-cloaked friend. "The storm is worsening. If we don't stop, we'll lose half the troop over the edge."

Beneban peered toward the cliffs edging the far side of the pass. He gave his friend an enigmatic look. "Pass the word, Scat," he said to the young trooper who was taking Borno's place as his aide. "Five minute break. Make them sit tight to the wall." The wizard turned to Me'ekalar. "Come on, Me'ek. We can at least catch our breath." He kicked aside small stones to clear a spot and sank down. He followed his own advice and rested wearily against the towering wall. The cliff above them leaned slightly outward here, a semblance of shelter.

"Now, what's the problem?" Beneban peered at his friend.

"This storm is the problem," Me'ekalar snapped. "Or hadn't you noticed? We've already lost one man to it, and it's getting worse." Me'ek voiced his real concern. "Beneban, are you well? The 'reinforcements' back at Kaldenspeke didn't..." Afraid to put his worry into words, Me'ekalar stumbled to a halt.

"Hmm? Oh. You mean the wizardry. No, that atrocious basin provided enough energy for the hallucination. It's easier to turn reality into any amount of illusion than the reverse. No, Me'ek, I'm just wet, tired, and cold, like the rest of you."

"Well, that's what I was saying. We must stop and sit this storm out."

"That won't work," Beneban said bluntly.

"But why? The storm can't go on forever."

"It can get worse," his friend interrupted. "This weather isn't natural, Me'ek. My skin is prickling. The Kaldens are having a much easier time as they move along the top of these cliffs, I expect. We're due some unpleasant surprises up ahead."

"Not natural?" Me'ek pounced on what seemed to him the crux of the matter.

"Look across the chasm. The sky is clear over there. No, this comes under the heading of diversionary tactics, wizard hatched, just for us. Which means that unless the Kaldens have wizardry, somehow Ztavin and they..." Beneban's voice drifted off as he stared into space.

"Ztavin?" Me'ekalar squawked and signed against evil. "But why?"

"Just so," Beneban interrupted. "Why would Ztavin join forces with the Kaldens? They are unfriends at best. The Kaldens raid his supply trains, and he retaliates by contriving the, er, disappearance of such warriors as fall into his hands. It would be strange alliance, yet it seems to be a fact.

"We can't stop," he continued. "Only try to move more quickly than they expect and introduce an element of surprise ourselves. Do you know the path ahead?"

"No, but Lodar traveled it many years ago," Me'ekalar answered. "He says it pitches steeply downward not far from here. It ends at Mergol Ford."

"Is that the edge of Kalden country?"

"They've never passed it in war if that's what you mean. The other side of the ford is the border of Ariling. They don't want trouble with Lar Ari, but I thought you wanted to avoid Ariling?"

"Indeed. Yet as we were a trifle rushed, we left our tents and supplies in Kaldenspeke. Ariling is the shortest way home."

"Yes, if you cut through the eastern edge of Forest where the grollings have been raiding," Me'ekalar said thoughtfully.

"Have you a better idea?" Worried amber eyes met Me'ekalar's green ones. When his friend just shook his head, Beneban nodded decisively. "Then it's time to go. Scat?" The boy materialized at his elbow. "Has Trog managed with the kaltings?"

"Aye, sir, him and She'em and your Kati has 'em all together."

"What about Borno and the other litter case, Sherning, isn't that his name? Never mind. Me'ek, come with me, we'll check on them."

"I fear," Me'ekalar began as they edged past huddled troopers and gingerly stepped over sprawled legs, "the kelsh litters won't be safe over this next bit."

"That was my thought, too," Beneban agreed. "We'll unhitch them. Relays of the eight strongest troopers can carry the wounded. Here's Borno."

Borno tossed restlessly in a fever. Beneban stooped over the boy and touched the Omera to his head. The stone glowed gently for an instant, and a strange look crossed the wizard's face. As he straightened, the boy was quiet.

Me'ekalar, seeing the wizard's face pale in the dim light, placed a worried hand on his friend's sleeve, but it was shrugged off.

"He must lie quietly or more lives will be lost," Beneban said, straightening. "I'll be fine." He ordered the troop forward.

Beneban's prediction of trouble proved prophetic. As the afternoon darkened quickly toward gloomy evening, the weather worsened. Rain mixed with sleet to make the footing more dangerous. The pass rushed down toward the foothills and descended at an angle that made each step perilous.

As they rounded a particularly narrow bend, boulders assailed them from above. Many were larger than a man. The rumble of their descent was lost in the roar of the storm. It caught them by surprise, and two men were knocked screaming from the path before the danger had been realized.

"Against the cliff," Beneban roared, and Trog, his fur sleeked with rain and ice, relayed the order to the rear in a bellow.

"Kaldens or a natural slide?" Me'ekalar asked. The men splayed themselves against the sheer wall as the last boulder thundered into the depths beyond them.

"If it *is* Kaldens, they'll be ahead of us at the ford," Beneban shrugged. "How far would you guess?"

"To Mergol Ford? Never been there, but... An hour, perhaps?"

Young Scat dashed up to edge past Trog, who

moved to check on the rear. The lad's face was white as he reported, "Cap'n, there was two more rock falls back along. One kelsh went over, and a man's arm is broken."

"So much for accident," the wizard snarled. "Well, we have to get *to* Mergol Ford before we can cross it. The rocks have stopped for now. Let's *move!*

"*Pick up the pace. Pass the order back, Scat!*" His voice lifted above the wind. "We'll see what other jolly surprises are in store."

IN ANY EVENT, the avalanche was the end of the attacks. An increased downpour was all that harassed their final hour in the pass. Troopers slipped and slithered on the steep path, but as it reached the foothills, it widened. Soon the troop had warily bunched up, two or three together, anxious to reach the open where a potential attack would be more visible.

Beneban and Me'ekalar rounded the final bend well within the predicted hour. As they reached the flat, the rain stopped abruptly. Ahead, the evening light of Asolum shone on a lush meadow dotted with wild blossoms.

Here the cliffs widened out to enfold the grassy carpet. They curved like cupped hands, and closed in again to funnel traffic across the ford.

This meadow had been a place of meeting between Mergol and Larlinga in the past, when there was still an effort to heal the differences between them. That truce had ended many years ago, with Mergols exiled from the land. Now seemingly deserted, the water rushed over rocks in a merry song.

Mergols were rarely seen in the lands of Larlion. Lyolar's page, Mero, was known to the courtiers and nobility, but few outside Larlingarde had ever met a Mergol. Most of the common people considered them a myth, a tale used to frighten small children away from dangerous water.

Beyond the quiet meadow, the water continued to hurry over the rocks. The gentle, grassy slope of the lea was perhaps fifty yards in width. It was awash with the evening sun.

Beyond the grass lay Mergol Ford, and on the far side, Ariling. This, the only possible crossing within many miles of travel, was a dangerous passage in good weather. Now the water, swollen by the rain that had harassed their passage above, thundered as it roared across the stones.

Beneban and Me'ekalar stepped aside as the troop poured from the pass with glad shouts. Ahead was home, or at least an outpost of it.

"Perhaps we've made it," Me'ekalar said, hopefully. He gave a wry look ahead.

"I'll ask a favor of you, Me'ek," the wizard said quietly as the troop formed up, brought to order by their officers.

"Of course, but what? And why not get across the ford first? Those Kaldens are close behind us. You can ask favors after."

Me'ek turned restlessly to check the cliffs that loomed behind them. Then his attention returned to Beneban as Trog, who brought up the rear with the herd of kaltings, interrupted. "The beasts won't like that water, Captain."

"No. So we won't give them time to think. They'll cross with Kati and She'em to push them. Kati!" he called to the large feline, who had already bunched the herd of mostly young male kaltings. "Take them across, girl."

He turned again to the Kaltingcorps captain.

"That's the favor, Me'ek," the wizard said urgently to his friend. "Get on She'em and take those beasts across. Don't stop, *no matter* what happens here, until you reach High Ariling Tower. There may be more trouble here. Send reinforcements back, if you can, but *do not* bring the kaltings back."

"But…"

"Take them on to Larlingarde as fast and as straight as you can manage. Go! Please, Me'ek!" he urged as She'em crouched at his master's feet.

Slowly, Me'ekalar moved toward She'em. He half turned back.

Beneban gave him a gentle push. "Word must get to Lyolar! I'll catch up and take my share of the glory, Me'ek. But if I don't, who's to give Ravel a last verse for his ballad?" Bene gave his comrade a wry grin and a slap on the shoulder.

Behind them, a trooper gave a startled yell. As though in echo, the meadow cliffs resounded with Kalden war cries.

"*Go*, Me'ek!" But the Kaltingcorps captain, with a last look back, had already pushed the young kaltings into a full run, twice as fast as a kelsh could go. Kati seemed to understand. She nipped at their heels and didn't allow them to pause at the water's edge. By the time the front ones would have balked, the far shore was nearer and the pressure behind too strong for them to stop.

As the kaltings disappeared around a bend on the far side of the ford, a horde of Kaldens surged from the pass. Their yells were anguished as they saw their treasured beasts vanish.

Giant battle axes reflected the sun's dying rays. Muscular legs hurled the Kaldens across the springing grass.

"Take the first platoon across," Beneban yelled.

He moved to stand beside Trog and Sergeant Aylmer. Wearily he drew Heldenhaft for the second time in what had been an impossibly long day.

It surprised him when the exhaustion drained from his body as the mighty sword flamed amber. Ignoring his fatigue, she poured her battle power into him and sang her fierce song of combat.

"Joran," Beneban yelled to the man leading the first platoon at a gallop for the ford. "Get the litters across. Form up on the far side and prepare to hold the ford for the rest of us. Bows, men! And swords!"

The wizard sprang astride a spare kelsh in time to meet the first rush of Kaldens. As Heldenhaft slashed, parried, riposted, and thrust again, he felt an upsurge of what could only be termed joy.

With difficulty, he dragged his mind free of the battle madness induced by the great sword and backed his animal to check the rest of the troop.

The first platoon was nearly across the ford. The second, led by Sergeant Aylmer, had lost more men above. Now they were at the edge of the water.

"Retreat to the ford," the wizard yelled as the second troop started across. Trog's iron-bound lungs repeated the order in a bellow that carried above the crash and clamor of the fight.

An anguished yell from Gawl, one of the leaders in the second platoon's retreat, made Beneban whirl about in a fight to control his terrified kelsh. Disbelief stunned him as he watched the center stones of the ford disappear in a sudden torrent. Some troopers who had plunged toward them were swept away by the rush of water. Others whose steeds were strong swimmers managed to get all the way across.

"Get a line across. Secure that passage with ropes!" Beneban bellowed. Again, Trog's mighty voice relayed the order. Ropes, carried always at saddle, were secured. The platoon surged forward again.

Beneban's platoon, the last, was nearly against the ford, hard pressed by the Kaldens. Trog, who wielded two battle axes in his foremost hands and guarded his rear with a gigantic sword, decimated the enemy forces in swathes.

Suddenly, Beneban heard Humber's voice. It carried clearly across the roar of the water. "Come on, men! Let the Ogdol hold the ford."

Beneban whirled, disbelief in his eyes.

"Go, Captain!" Trog said. "I can hold on." He gave Beneban a quick glance. "It is good strategy."

"We'll hold it together and cross together."

A scream, almost childlike in its terror, slashed across his words.

"By the Powers, Captain, look!" Sergeant Denodar's voice, usually cool and emotionless, was shrill with panic.

Above and below the ford, slender shapes rose from the water to cast tri-pronged spears with dire accuracy at the troops still on both banks. The creatures sank briefly back into the foam. Their white-maned heads, with pale skin and gill slits, were barely human in appearance. They shimmered in and out of sight like a nightmare.

"Mergols. Shape-changers," the sergeant breathed, barely loud enough to be heard.

For an instant, Beneban froze. He had seen a Mergol. But where... Then he remembered.

It had been the first entertainment Ka'amfer presented at the ill-fated party in Larlingarde. The Mergol had fought and killed a sea monster. But something else nagged at him. The way the Mergols shimmered in and out, always with a haze.

Beneban was motionless for less than two seconds, but it was too long in the midst of battle. A well-thrown trident pierced the ground beside his mount. The beast reared, and he was afoot, unbalanced.

"Sir, Mergols!" The sergeant said urgently. He snatched the reins of the loose mount.

Beneban closed off the thought in his mind. It could be revisited at a less urgent time.

"Mergols, or whatever, they're certainly trouble. They've cut the line," he yelled. "Use your bows, men. Clear the ford!"

Trog bellowed the command for all to hear.

Some of the troopers led by Sergeant Aylmer, now safely across, began to wing daggered shafts at any

Mergol that showed its slippery hide, but Beneban saw Glaynar move from man to man and point away from the battle.

Here and there a knot of men followed him as he slid away toward a bend in the path. Desertion seemed a better option to some than death by Kalden or Mergol.

"Get another line across," Beneban yelled. Sergeant Denodar and Lodar began that operation as the Kaldens pressed forward again.

"Trog, I need one minute. Can you manage?" The wizard slammed Heldenhaft into her sheath.

Trog's teeth were visible in a wicked grin. "My people say, 'If you never dare the thunder, you never learn to tame the lightning.'" With renewed frenzy the Ogdol became a lethal buzz saw. He cleared the space around them minimally.

"Be ready to move fast," the wizard spoke quietly to those nearest him. "Pass the word."

He knelt to gather a handful of dust and touched it with the Omera as he closed his eyes.

The stone shone, softly red at first. Then as a spasm crossed Beneban's face, the gleam grew until it seemed to blaze cupped in his hand.

With a yell he rose and cast the dust east, north and west.

About his beleaguered men a protective wall of fire sprang up. It spread, not with the wind, but in a circle like cupped hands to either side of the ford path. As it touched the river it flared hungrily as though water were its chosen food, and the flames pushed the Mergols back.

"Get across *now!*" Trog bellowed and tightened the line Denodar and Lodar had flung.

Only Sergeant Aylmer and a handful of loyal men remained after the deserters had fled. Steadily, they winged shafts at the Mergol shape-changers, whose outlines blurred in and out of focus.

Beneban's flames repelled both Kaldens and Mergols. Though these latter cast some weapons through the blaze, they were aimless and harmed none of the troopers who struggled across the ford.

Trog, halfway across, turned to look for his captain. The wizard stood beside his kelsh and stared blankly into the flames. At the Ogdol's shout, he fumbled for the saddle, mounted clumsily, and then sat motionless.

His mount took an indecisive step or two away from the fire. Then it balked at the water.

Trog reversed direction. He sped back and gave Beneban's mount a mighty slap on the rump then followed rapidly as Beneban's kelsh took the one direction left open to it. As it lunged out of the water on the far side of the ford with Trog clutched to its tail, a cheer arose.

The flames began to die out as Beneban and the last of the troopers reached the shore.

All at once a platoon of men dressed in the red and gold of Ariling raced around the corner. They were trailed by most of the deserters from Beneban's troop.

Seeing reinforcements, the Mergols cast a few last tridents before they disappeared beneath the foam. One took Sergeant Aylmer full in the throat with its double-pronged blade, and he sank to the ground. The Kaldens bellowed defiance across the rushing water, but as the mounted troop moved toward the crossing, they fled to their mountains.

"Captain? Captain Beneban?" The leader of the Ariling platoon rode up and saluted at his weary nod. "Captain Linder of Arilgarde, sir." He dismounted and continued. "We met your men up the road. They said you were in need of assistance, but you seem to have things in hand. What has happened here? What do you need?" His unspoken question as to why half of this troop had fled the fight hung silently in the air between them.

The wizard straightened stiffly and turned to the other man.

"We need shelter for the night, care for our wounded, and assistance to bury our dead, sir."

"There is shelter in Aril Tower, sir, if you…"

"I thank you, but our news that Kaldens and Mergols now seem to have allied must reach the Grand Lar without delay. Tents would be better."

Beneban began to turn away, then he remembered a request. "Can you see that a messenger is sent to Lyolar? He should know where we are. We will camp here, with your permission."

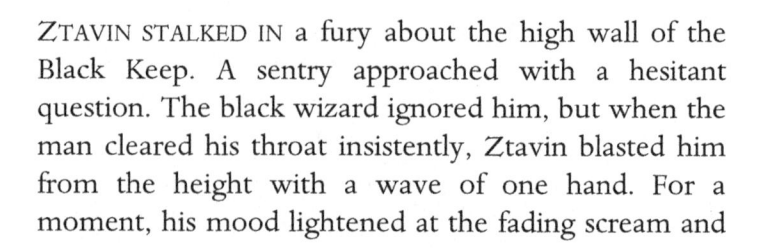

ZTAVIN STALKED IN a fury about the high wall of the Black Keep. A sentry approached with a hesitant question. The black wizard ignored him, but when the man cleared his throat insistently, Ztavin blasted him from the height with a wave of one hand. For a moment, his mood lightened at the fading scream and thud of his victim. He ignored the call for help from the dimming voice below.

It wasn't enough to content him.

Varakin had failed. She was to lead a force of vardraken and make certain that the battle destroyed that defiant upstart, Beneban.

Instead of obeying him, the ice-witch had gone alone. She reported that the Grand Lar's forces were seriously outnumbered, and most likely to fail in their mission.

She had not stayed. She had not taken more of her beasts to ensure that Beneban and his troops were wiped out. *She did not obey his orders!*

Ztavin had been forced to take matters into his own hands.

The evil wizard had ridden a bitter wind to rally the Kaldens. Then he had exerted a good deal of his own magic to send black ice and foul weather to harry the troop.

Stupid female. She could have finished it for him. Well, he now held a number of her drak, her children, in the keep and would soon have more. When she came to get them, he would have a little trap ready. He would show her that his orders were not subject to her interpretation. He would...

A cough wracked him, a return of that blasted cold that had assailed him since his first trip to the north. This was all her fault. How could she enjoy such bitter weather? He doubled over in a struggle for breath.

The next time he gave an order, she'd obey, he swore. He forced his steps toward the dungeon where several small drak waited, caged in his laboratory.

Another spasm of coughing gave him pause.

Tomorrow. Tomorrow would be time enough to torment his captives. Tonight, he needed a hot drink and a warm bed. Tomorrow he'd show the witch who held the power.

It was the next evening after the battle at Mergol Ford, and dusk fell rapidly at the edge of Forest as Trog posted a guard about a hastily erected camp. The small group, twelve counting Beneban and Trog, had moved swiftly from High Aril Tower along Forest Road. Rumors of disappearances had been frequent enough that the road was shunned by most travelers these days. Though the troop was tense and on guard, there had been no disturbance. Forest brooded, silent as death.

Dividing his men, Beneban had kept Glaynar, Humber, and Morden, the main troublemakers of L Troop, with him, as well as seven more trustworthy fighters.

The remainder, with Sergeant Denodar in charge, had been detailed to the slower road as escort to the injured men. Should some disaster befall the wizard's company, they would also serve as backup for the information that must reach Lyolar about the union of Kaldens and Mergols and the interference of Ztavin.

"The guard is set, Captain." Trog squatted in front of the wizard, who slumped listlessly against his bedroll where it had fallen after he pulled it from his kelsh. "The food is not fancy sir, but here is bread, and meat."

Beneban's amber eyes had widened in the fading light. They seemed almost to glow.

"Scat could have brought the food, Trog. You aren't my aide."

"Yes, Captain, but he is tending your animal. And you need food. I want to be certain you eat."

Beneban growled. There was no other word for the sound he made.

Without pause, Trog continued, "I have fingers to spare sir, if you prefer them, but even this stale food would taste better, I am sure."

A silence like the threat of a storm hung in the air. Then Trog was rewarded with the shadow of a smile on his friend's face.

"I understand, Trog," Beneban said. And Trog, embarrassed by the sudden certainty that the other had indeed understood, looked slightly away from his captain.

Wearily, fumbling a little, Beneban took the proffered food and began to eat.

"Captain?"

"Yes?"

"When you cast the ring of fire at the ford..."

An expression colder than any Trog had ever seen crossed the wizard's face. The Ogdol's words stumbled and changed.

"It was fortunate for us. I mean, it worked well."

The chill held for a moment. Then Beneban coughed, and a faint smile lit his eyes.

"Thank you, Trog." After a moment the wizard touched his friend's arm. "When I'm tired, my temper is abominably short. Will you send Scat to me before you sleep?"

"Yes, Captain." Trog rose to his full height. "Why did you not leave me to defend the ford? Any man in the troop would have."

"Did you leave me to find my way across?"

The Ogdol stood silent, unable to answer without reference to the topic that angered Beneban. After a moment, a crooked smile lit the wizard's worn face.

"There are two words, Trog. One is *friends*. Friends don't leave each other in trouble if there is a choice, that's all." He held out his hand and, still mute, the other grasped it and held it for a moment, before moving away.

Later, Trog would puzzle over what the second word was.

WITH A SHUDDER of revulsion, Beneban forced himself to take a bite of the hard bread. He chewed, swallowed, and took another reluctant bite. Finally he grimaced and stowed the remainder in a pocket. Then he turned and fumbled with the bedroll.

"Here, Cap'n. I kin do that." Young Scat gently pushed aside the awkward hands and made a neat couch of the bedding.

"Thank you, Scat."

"That's okay, Cap'n. Sorry t'be slow gettin' back. Yon beasts are skittish-like, being on the edge o' Forest, and all." The boy's brown eyes, enormous in his freckled face, showed his own awe of the nearly legendary place. His voice dropped to a whisper. "Is there really a... a sorta magic lady what lives in there?"

"There used to be, Scat. Now... I don't know any more." Beneban closed his eyes, and the lad took the hint.

"Anythin' else ye need, sir?"

"Nothing more. Good night, lad. Thank you." Exhausted, Beneban lay back with arms beneath his head and stared into darkness.

His thoughts skipped to Me'ekalar. The Kaltingcorps captain must be halfway to Larlingarde with the kaltings, but with only part of the information. The Mergols hadn't appeared until Me'ekalar was out of sight. At least his friend knew the Kaldens were ready for war and that they seemed to be allied with Ztavin.

That further, almost unthinkable suspicion, brought on when the Mergol warriors had misted in and out of the foam as insubstantial as fog, Beneban had shared with no one. That suspicion touched Lyolar's very court, perhaps even the future of Larlingarde. Was it possible that Meriel...

The wizard twisted restlessly, unable to quiet his thoughts. Were the grollings allied to this conspiracy? They had made no move today. Yet they were rumored to attack only small, poorly defended groups. Beneban's men were armed and had moved quickly. Even at night they should be safe so long as the sentries were alert.

Forest... Exhausted, Beneban let his mind wander. Its trees formed a pocket about them here. Strange how they gleamed with a soft green light to the west, while south and east of them was all darkness. Odd that he could even see that light. Unless his eyes played more tricks.

He hadn't noticed that phenomenon before when he camped by Forest. And what of the Forest Lady?

Too weary to attempt mind touch, the wizard finally drifted to sleep. His dreams were restless, filled with Mergols, silvery fish, and giant warriors, all whirled in a sztaq, a wizard wind.

CHAPTER 23

THE CAMP QUIETED quickly. Soon two of the sentries, weary with battle and hard travel, slept at their posts. The third, Humber, waited until all was quiet. Then he muzzled a kelsh and walked it until the camp was out of earshot before he mounted. He continued to hold the steed to a quiet walk until he was well away from the camp. Then he galloped west.

The troops were exhausted. Aware that the captain would push hard tomorrow, they slept while they could.

Someone muttered in his dreams. The sentry to the west stirred then relaxed against the giant tree that sheltered him. The camp sank into silence.

Beneban groaned in restless sleep. He tossed an arm out of the covers and rolled onto his side. In the fading light of the fire, the chain that held his Omera glittered around his neck.

Two small figures, Worfs, were crouched on the first limb of the dozing wizard's tree. They eyed the sparkle of the chain. They looked at each other and glanced again at the shiny silver as it winked at them in the thin firelight.

For a moment the thinner of the pair hung back in silent protest. Then, agreement reached, they slid down and into the shadow of the trunk. So small and light of foot, they seemed to vanish into the darkness.

The sentry heard no sound, saw no movement. Sleep enfolded him ever more deeply.

Less visible than shadows, the two Worfs crept silently toward the sleeping wizard. As gently as fog that settles on a marsh, dexterous fingers touched the chain that held the Omera. With less disturbance than a leaf makes when it drifts to the ground, the silver links slipped free into the hand of the rascal. The mischievous pair darted silently away out of the camp.

When Dap and Dal were safely away, they huddled beneath the shadow of a bush, eager to examine their treasure.

No one heard. No one saw. The camp sank more deeply into dreams. Kati, had she been there, would have heard silvery laughter. But Kati, with her hunter's ears, was near Torlingford. She and Me'ekalar, as they'd been ordered, pushed a herd of wild kaltings at speed toward Larlingarde.

THE FOLLOWING MORNING, as the men ate a sparse breakfast made from supplies shared by the force from Arilgarde, Trog paced restlessly. Within minutes they'd be ready to move, yet Beneban slept on. He was unsure what to do. His captain seemed oblivious to the commotion.

As Beneban made no move to waken, Trog finally approached his pallet. He squatted down. His captain never stirred.

"Captain. Sir. Beneban?" Trog laid a hand on the wizard's shoulder. He shook it gently, and finally as there was no response, with more force.

"Mmm? Ohh," Beneban groaned. He slowly pushed aside the bedding.

"By the Power, where did we drink last night, Trog?" he moaned and struggled to sit up. Then he clutched his head in both hands as he abruptly became aware of two important things.

First of all, he was *not* in Larlingarde after a night of carousal; he was in a glade at the edge of Forest. Second, he had only once in his life felt so ill.

Long ago, the student wizard had ignored the precise instruction of his first teacher. His carelessness had caused injury to one of the staff. Nigeran, to reinforce the importance of the lesson, had briefly taken away... Memory flared.

His hand flew to his throat. *His Omera!*

Desperately Beneban felt around the bedding. Trog was quick to understand. He, too, searched the bed roll and the ground nearby. He found no sign of it. At last he turned to Beneban, at a loss.

"Your Omera has vanished. But how?"

"Was there any disturbance through the night?" Beneban scowled, trying to force rational thought through the howl of pain in his head that threatened to flatten him.

"Humber and one animal have disappeared," Trog reported. "This was not unexpected in view of his behavior at Mergol Ford. Wait here. I will question the guards."

This, too, brought no enlightenment.

"I was exhausted, but I don't believe Humber could have taken the Omera without waking me," Beneban insisted. "It *must* be here."

"He could *not* have taken it, Sir," Trog agreed. "He was on outer guard duty. He deserted the camp during middle-night."

Again the area was searched, and ultimately, with the help of the troop, so was the entire glade. At the western edge of Forest by the tree where a sentry had drowsed, a few leaves had fallen to the ground. Trog brought them, still gleaming gently, to Beneban. He only shook his head in despair.

"It's gotter be *that Forest*," Morden growled. "It couldn't get us in the light, so it waited, 'til we was sleepin'. I couldn't keep my eyes open on duty last night, and I bet it were that *Forest* what did it."

"You slept?" Beneban snapped the words as his head lifted quickly. "Did you both sleep on duty? No punishment, but I must know."

At length, both sentries admitted to 'at least drifting off' during the first watch.

"That must be the answer." The wizard's brief animation evaporated. "Someone—or some*thing*—crept to my pallet and stole it."

"Sir, Humber's trail leads away from Forest."

"Humber didn't take it, Trog. I'm sure of that," Beneban insisted. "I feel its pull. It is in... there." His voice faded. How was he to find it when he could barely see from magical exhaustion?

"How do you get another one?" Trog looked worriedly at his captain's haggard face. Beneban seemed to have aged several years since the night before.

"Another?" Beneban laughed bitterly. "There is only one. It is as much a part of me as my blood."

"Then..."

"If I don't find it, my life expectancy is quite short. Trog, you and Hundak will have to take the message to Lyolar."

"No!"

"Yes. There can be no argument. Lyolar *must* hear about the Mergols and about Ztavin. And if I don't get back, Trog, you'll have to watch..." he beckoned the Ogdol close and stretched to speak quietly into one ear tuft.

The great brown eye that faced the wizard widened in surprise.

"Now, I'm going. Trog, I count on you. Don't let me down." The wizard stumbled awkwardly, hands out, toward the edge of Forest and lurched beneath the unlighted trees.

Trog watched the spot where his friend had vanished for several seconds. Then he muttered quietly, "There is no choice. He can't even *see!*"

Trog summoned Hundak. "I will not leave the captain in Forest alone. You keep the squad here for two days."

Hundak stared at the Ogdol. "But he said... B-But then..."

"If we do not return by that time, take the squad to Larlingarde. Tell Captain Me'ekalar what has happened. The Grand Lar *must* hear about the Mergols at the ford."

Trog ignored Hundak's stammered protest. He turned and followed Beneban's trail into Forest.

Dizzy, ill, with a head that seemed packed with demented demons, Beneban stumbled along a faint trail. He reeled into a tree trunk now and again, cling there until a modicum of strength returned, then plunged doggedly on along the faint trace left by his Omera.

The gloom beneath the thick trees belied the Asolum-bright day he'd left behind. Roots on the forest floor tangled maliciously about his ankles.

Once, as he clutched onto a tree for balance, he was dimly conscious of a slimy feel to the bark. It was as though, while still alive, the giant plant was rotting. Yet without his Omera, his senses were dulled. The concern faded quickly and left only a blind determination not to stop.

When another path intersected the one he was on, he stood for several minutes in an effort to decide which to follow. At length he continued east. It took less energy than changing direction.

Because of his debility, he never sensed the pack of grollings directly ahead of him.

Instantly they surrounded him. They began to snap and claw at his feet and his arms. He managed to clear Heldenhaft from her scabbard as they rushed him. He swung feebly at the pack. The sword's magic strengthened him slightly, and the grollings were frightened of the amber glare and the singing noise.

Warily they backed away, but one crept up from behind. It swung its odd hooked weapon and knocked the blade from the wizard's hand as he struggled to recover his balance after a clumsy thrust.

At once the pack swarmed him. They pulled with suctioned fingers and snapped with venomous teeth. Finally one steel-billed club sank deeply into Beneban's upper chest and ended the fight.

The crippled wizard fell to the ground, mercifully unconscious. At once, the snake-necked beasts swarmed over him. They tugged at his clothes and hair, poked at his eyes. They poked and peered into his mouth. All the while they hissed and clicked in their barbaric speech.

TROG HAD FOLLOWED Beneban but stayed far enough behind to leave the captain unaware of his disobedience. He caught up in time to see the wizard fall. Even with all his Ogdol strength, he knew he would need help against so large a band of creatures.

He trundled with all speed back toward the camp. Soon he reached the intersection of paths where Beneban had paused. Trog heard the sound of voices that came near. One was gentle with laughter. Two chattered merrily. None were aware of his approach.

Trog charged toward them at speed. He nearly ran down a slender girl with shimmergreen hair.

The young woman started at this sudden apparition. One hand flew to a green stone at her throat, while a gazert darted off the path and into the trees.

"Who are you?" she demanded.

"My lady," Trog bobbed a hasty bow. "I am Trog. But that does not matter. My captain has been taken prisoner by a band of grollings. Please, can you help me?"

I should have run for our camp, he thought in despair. *What help could this girl be?*

The girl's eyes widened. Her hand clutched the green stone firmly. It flared with light. She asked no questions, but her magic was immediate. A hummed threnody came from her throat. Above them the wind whipped branches against a rapidly blackening sky.

She gave a shrill cry. It might have been the hunting call of a large bird. Then she strengthened the music of her voice. It howled like wind, and rumbled like thunder.

A lightning bolt tore the trees behind Trog. He heard, like an extension of the thunder, the deep growl of a beast.

"Come," she ordered confidently. "We will rescue him." Eyes flaming with green fire, she laid one hand on his great hairy arm. "Lead us, quickly."

Again she began to hum. Not understanding what she could do, still Trog obeyed as though bewitched.

Above his head an alviar soared in with a shriek that matched her cry. Trog ducked warily. It alit on the girl's shoulder as gently as a butterfly. A large ursyn crashed through low bushes with a growl. Two Worfs leapt onto its broad blue back. Passing the girl, it humped along beside Trog. The gazert, with its scimitar horns, kept pace shyly between the trees, and soon its mate joined it.

As the Lady's melody continued, Trog would have sworn that the storm gathered strength. Three notes, and three notes again, each punctuated by the crash of lightning.

They reached the battle spot quickly. The last grollings, dragging Beneban, were about to disappear around a bend in the path.

Three fiery bolts seared the ground before the fleeing creatures. As they turned, terrified, the giant ursyn roared. His battle cry united with Trog's own bellow of rage.

The two thundered forward side by side, a formidable avalanche of fury.

The grollings were harried on the flanks by the gazerts' wicked horns. The alviar's airborne attack hit them as they tried to defend from the gazerts. Stones from Dap's and Dal's busy slings hit the beasts as they dodged and twisted to defend themselves.

Convinced they were outmatched, the grollings turned to flee. When they tried to take Beneban with them, lightning blasted their path. The oily smell of singed scales filled the air, and two grollings howled in pain. Finally they dropped everything, including the wizard, and fled in terror.

Now the storm pursued the grollings. They howled and dodged beneath the grim gray trees as lightning blasted about them.

Trog and the defenders were left beneath peaceful skies. The Ogdol moved quickly to his captain. He squatted to turn the motionless wizard over and cringed to see his Beneban's tunic soaked in blood.

"We are too late," he moaned.

At once the girl knelt to join him. "Tear back his tunic," she ordered calmly.

They saw a wedge-shaped wound that sullenly welled with blood. The girl sighed. One slim hand cradled the green stone at her throat. The other reached out, and a slender finger traced the wound as she murmured a low melody.

The bleeding stopped.

Trog gaped in astonishment as she quickly examined the unconscious wizard. She found a number of bites and abrasions caused by rough handling.

"Grolling wounds are poisoned... their teeth, and their weapons are coated with venom. We must move him to my cottage. I have herbs there to draw the poison and a healing pool." She turned to Trog. "Can you carry him?"

Trog gently lifted his captain and stood.

"Can you manage? It is a fair distance."

"I will carry him however far is needed," Trog affirmed and moved in the direction she indicated.

"Are you certain?" she repeated to the giant Ogdol.

"Lead, Lady. I will follow." There was no further argument.

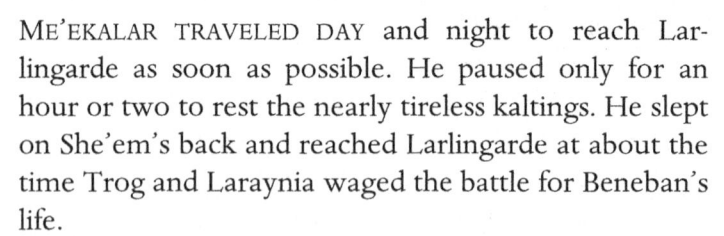

ME'EKALAR TRAVELED DAY and night to reach Larlingarde as soon as possible. He paused only for an hour or two to rest the nearly tireless kaltings. He slept on She'em's back and reached Larlingarde at about the time Trog and Laraynia waged the battle for Beneban's life.

Larlingarde was in an uproar. When young Tor had fled the court, he went north to his cousin, Lar Bori, with his tale of treachery. Rumor said that a force of Borilings were armed and ready to march from the northern provinces to attack Larlingarde. No one knew what the other two northern lars, Lar Ami and Lar Ande, would do. As they had close ties with Bori, the worst was feared.

Recruits were conscripted in Ariling and Torling Estate for the Grand Lar's armies. Each night, desertions undid most of the day's efforts. The sullen Torlingals were not eager to fight against their popular young lar.

When Me'ekalar arrived with the herd of kaltings, his news of the Kalden uprising and the alliance between the Kaldens and the black wizard Ztavin spread like wildfire. Panic hit the city as the citizens armed. Many wondered anxiously when the wizard Beneban and his mighty amber sword might return. Somehow wizard and sword had become synonymous with the safety of their home to Larlingarde's citizens.

Thanks to a quiet word from Lar Ari, the Grand Lar had continued, and even expanded Beneban's program that fed the city's poor. As a result, the people of the city grew more loyal to their ruler.

They would have risen in terror and fury against Lyolar had they known how placidly he accepted the likelihood of the wizard's death. Beneban was *their* wizard, and his well-being seemed tied to their own.

Doggedly driving his kaltings through the crowded city, Me'ekalar finally reached the palace grounds. He turned the new kaltings over to the stable for care of worn pads and headed for the palace to report to the Grand Lar.

News of Beneban's probable death at Mergol Ford, outnumbered by Kaldens and assailed by Mergols, reached the city soon after Me'ek and his report had been dismissed by a distinctly unimpressed Grand Lar.

Ma'arteen, one of Lyolar's spies who had been sent to shadow Beneban and report back, rode in on a lathered horse and was taken immediately to Lyolar. His tale was immediately silenced. Only those of the Grand Lar's Council who were present when Lyolar's exhausted spy made his report were aware of it, and Lyolar instructed them not to let it become public knowledge. Ma'arteen was given a fresh horse and supplies and sent back out to confirm the death of Beneban.

Ka'amfer, however, could hardly wait to take the news to Meriel.

"Well," he purred, as he entered the garden room of his mansion where she sat. "That scheme worked very nicely indeed. It was clever of you, my dear, to dispose of the wizard in such a way." His voice suddenly sharpened as she turned away. "Now what ails you?"

"Nothing. I am fine," she answered tonelessly.

"Surely you do not weep for that blusterer?"

"*He* didn't bluster. And no, I am not..."

"I believe you are." With a rough hand the old man grabbed her arm. He pulled her to face him.

"Take your hand off of me, you slimy worm." The girl's eyes were dry, her voice now loud and angry. "I need not hate a man to know he must be removed for the success of our plans."

"Hush. Remember, *daughter*, someone might enter at any time. What would they think, to see my dutiful child treating her old father thus."

At the fury in her eyes, Ka'amfer backed hastily

away. He held the jeweled end of his cane toward her.

The girl made a rapid pass of her hand. At once a blue sheet of light glimmered between her and the old man. Sullen purple sparks bounced from it. Suddenly the purple gem on Ka'amfer's stick flared. The wizard dropped it with a curse. He sucked on his singed fingers. The air reeked with blue smoke and the smell of charred skin.

"Do *not* point that thing at me, you hedge magician," Meriel hissed. "For good or ill we are allies, but no day passes that I don't thank the Sea Lady for the certainty that our relationship is only temporary."

"Perhaps not so temporary as you hope," the old man muttered. Then he spoke more loudly. "At least you will agree it is time to get in touch with your noble brother. He must be alerted to the rise of forces against Lyolar."

"I suspect he knows more than we do. His ears are everywhere. Still, I'll send him a message. Calibe should leave Larlingarde anyway before someone sees him.

"No one need recognize the fool if he would only change his shape."

"True," the girl answered. "Yet he is stubborn. That is another reason to send him to my brother." She pushed past Ka'amfer, but paused in the doorway. "I'll see to it then. Are there any other messages?"

"Does he know of the new waterway? He should hear that it nears completion."

"I'll include that in the message. If you will excuse me, *father*," she added as a maid scurried by in the hall beyond.

WITHIN THE COTTAGE in Forest, Laraynia sank back on her heels beside the cot where Beneban lay in deep coma. A frown etched small vertical lines between her green eyes as the afternoon drew on. The air was fragrant with the scent of healing herbs, yet none of her efforts had managed to rouse the wizard or even to stabilize his condition.

Dap carried a basin of bloody water outside to be emptied. Dal carefully retied the small bags of herbs she had used as poultices.

Old Saray rocked and wondered at Trog, who towered nearly to the ceiling beside her nursling. She had heard of Ogdols, but in her long life she'd never seen one.

"I do not understand." Laraynia pushed back shimmergreen hair with one slender hand. "The poison has been neutralized. His body is strong. In this place his wound, though serious, should heal. Yet there is pain I cannot reach. He is fading."

"Do you mean he will die?" Trog's rumble, low though he kept it, vibrated in the small room.

"If he continues as he is, yes." The girl glanced up at the Ogdol. "I cannot reach him."

"Reach him?" Trog repeated, puzzled.

"You say this is Beneban, the wizard. My mind has spoken to his. Yet now there is a block. I feel his pain, his despair, but he is closed away. He knows only darkness, and loss. He is not aware of us. Only his true name holds him from passing the gates of Mordim. I fear that it will not long suffice."

Trog paced across the cottage floor, reversed direction, and came again to Rayni's side.

"You say you can feel his loss. Could it be the loss of his Omera? It *must* be," Trog said.

"Omera?" The girl's storm gray eyes fastened on his face. "Explain."

"It is a stone he wears always about his neck. It seems to hold much of his power as a wizard. Last night, as the camp slept, weary from battle, it was stolen. Though it is difficult to understand how that could happen without his awareness. This morning he was ill and dazed. He insisted the thief came from Forest. He said that without the stone he would die. That stone is what he sought when the grollings came on him."

Rayni stared up at him with a still, clear gaze. After a moment, the Ogdol turned slightly away. He felt that she searched his very heart to find a reason why his friend had been alone.

"You *are* his friend." Her voice was clear and sure.

Trog's eye met hers again. "I am," he affirmed.

"Then why was he alone in such dire condition?" she demanded.

"He is my commander. He ordered me to take our squad to Larlingarde. I could not leave him, sick and alone, to fight for his life. Although to disobey him may be unwise, I left the squad with Hundak and followed him."

For another moment, Laraynia stared at him. Into him, he thought.

"This Omera, what is it like?" she finally asked.

As Trog described the stone, one eye glimpsed

Dap, who slowly retreated behind Saray's chair. Dal, who had been putting herbs on the shelf in the corner, disappeared into the shadows.

"But who could have taken it? Could it have been a trooper?"

"It might, of course." Now Trog edged toward the door as he spoke. "Yet the captain felt its pull from Forest."

He was just in time to catch one wriggling small figure as it darted for the opening. Trog held the tiny sprite easily by the collar to dangle in mid-air. Dal's small feet flailed uselessly against the Ogdol's bulk. He squeaked in protest as the hold on his collar half-strangled his voice.

"I think the answer may be closer than that," Trog said. "How sure are you of these imps' loyalty, Lady?"

"To myself?" Rayni asked, as she stood in alarm. "Perfectly. Yet..." One long finger touched her wide mouth as she thought. "They were on patrol last night," she said finally, reluctantly. "If they took it, it was not from evil intent. The twins are strongly drawn to any bauble that glitters. They wouldn't understand its importance. You have the door well blocked, Trog," she added with a merry laugh. "Can't you let Dal go?"

Trog set the furious Worf gently on the floor inside the room. He ignored a kick aimed at his ankle.

Now the Forest Lady spoke sharply. "Stop that, Dal. Come here. Yes, Dap, you too."

When the two stood sheepishly before her, she questioned them.

"You heard the description of the missing stone. A life depends on that bauble," she said sternly. "If either of you know its whereabouts, fetch it at *once*."

"You punish us, lady?" Dap whispered, but Dal moved quickly to the corner with the shelves.

"If I punish you or do not, it should not change your decision when a life is at stake, Dap. I am ashamed that you would ask."

Dap ran and curled into a pathetic lump on his tiny cot as Dal returned with an herb bag and silently handed it to Rayni.

Quickly shaking the heavy contents into her palm, Rayni held it out for Trog's inspection.

"Yes," the Ogdol breathed. "That is Beneban's Omera."

"Dal, join your brother. We will speak of this later." Gently, hopefully, Rayni slipped the silver chain over the dying wizard's head.

The change was nearly instantaneous. Slow color rose to the wizard's grayed skin. His harsh breath slowed and deepened. As Rayni laid a light hand on his forehead, Beneban's eyelids fluttered open.

Amber eyes stared with wonder into gray and found peace. There was healing and... more. More for which no experience gave him a name.

"You must rest," the gray-eyed girl said softly. "Sleep now. Later we will talk."

His eyes nearly closed. A movement behind the girl caught his attention. They flew wide and clouded with dismay.

"Trog!" he croaked. Even in his weakness there was anger. "The men..."

"I go now to join them, Captain," Trog said.

"You were ordered not to follow me."

"Don't berate him," the girl interrupted, angry at his unfairness. "If he had obeyed, you would be dead now."

"If he had obeyed, he would be halfway to Larlingarde, which is more important." Beneban struggled to rise on one elbow. A spasm of pain crossed his suddenly bloodless face as he collapsed on the pillows. He fought to rise again.

Trog hurried forward, but Rayni was before him. She touched Beneban's head with a light finger, and with her left hand at her throat, she made the gesture that had brought sleep to the wounded gazert.

The wizard sank back. His eyes held hers for a startled moment. His own held disbelief, then dismay, and finally, acceptance. He slept.

Rayni rose gracefully to face Trog. If there was a trace of moisture in the Ogdol's eye, she ignored it. "What were your orders, Trog?" When he told her, she smiled.

"Good. The men should still be there. Your captain will need several days to recover, even in this spot. He must have companions for the return journey."

"Do you know what he will do if I am here when his strength returns?"

"Do you fear him?" Rayni gazed curiously from wizard to Ogdol. At length, the girl was given her first glimpse of the grimace that served Trog as a smile.

"Is one who skirts the quicksand afraid, Lady, or only wise?" he asked. "Yet I shall stay at the camp if that is your will." He backed quietly through the door and disappeared.

Crossing the room, the Forest Lady watched his

mountainous shape vanish into the trees beyond the healing pool. "Gorba," she ordered the ursyn now basking outside the door. "Take the gazerts and escort him. Then do the rounds. If anything threatens the Ogdol's camp, warn me."

The giant beast disappeared behind Trog, rumbling a call that would summon the gazerts.

Rayni turned back to her sleeping patient. Then, with a sigh, she remembered her delinquent Worfs.

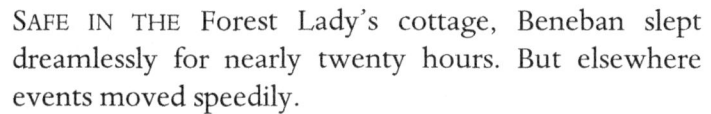

SAFE IN THE Forest Lady's cottage, Beneban slept dreamlessly for nearly twenty hours. But elsewhere events moved speedily.

In the North Plains, Bori and Amelar, lars of two of the Northern Estates, held deep council with young Tor. Eventually, they agreed that Lyolar's assassination of Tor's parents canceled the northern lars' obligation to their OathGive. They began raising an army of hardy plainsmen.

It wasn't difficult. The northerners envied their soft southern cousins' easier lives. The North Plains provided a living, but only for hard and endless work.

Lar Ore, Lar of Oreling, the Guardian of the Pass, was a blond, bearded giant of a man whose looks hinted at Kalden blood. He had no argument with Lyolar. Yet, as Bori's emissary pointed out, Lyolar was not apt to be pleased with the man who had allowed Tor passage to the north. Unsure it was wise, still Ore joined the rebels. They determined to keep the defection secret until the northern armies were ready to march on Larlingarde.

Another northerner, Lar Ande, was an easy-going young man, newly married, but he surprised Bori's agents and declared himself loyal to his OathGive until Lyolar was proven guilty of the assassination. He proceeded to imprison the emissaries. Then he armed his borders. A messenger was sent to warn Lyolar of the danger of rebellion.

A small force of Lar Ande's men, Andelingers, pushed through the northern town of Ameling and took Amel Gate seaport to hold for Lyolar.

IN THE SOUTH it was nightfall as Humber, determined in his desertion of Beneban's forces, reached Torlingford. He was nearly asleep in the saddle. He needed rest, food, and time to decide what to do next. Looking for a place to stay, Humber came across an old acquaintance. Surprised and curious to see Humber alone, this companion took him to the village inn.

Humber guzzled the ale provided generously by his comrade as he told the story of the ill-fated L Troop. He included the news that the wizard captain had not been killed at Mergol Ford.

Near midnight, a night bird dipped to examine some flotsam awash on the Little Gar River. It flapped aloft with a squawk as the body rolled in the current to reveal Humber's white, dead face.

Still later that night, Calibe, Humber's treacherous drinking companion, reached Merktan.

Merktan was Calibe's brother, and also the high

king and ruler of the Mergols. He was excited to hear that the awaited waterway had neared completion from Great Lar Lake to Larlingarde.

Calibe added the information gleaned from Humber that the wizard captain was still alive. Unsurprised and ignoring Calibe's weariness, Merktan sent him onward to another who would be interested in this news. King Merktan then set certain forces in motion himself.

On the day following, the Grand Lar announced publicly his intention of wedding the Lady Meriel.

He also set the townspeople to military drills with makeshift weapons. He ordered swords, pikes, and bows from the armorers of Terreling and Dinling to be delivered with all possible speed.

Lyolar proceeded to stock the city warehouses against siege from the north and harried the engineers who built the new underground waterway. In case of siege, it would provide urgently needed water to the city. He also had sledge loads of rock dragged from Streeling for defense of the walls.

After only four hours of sleep, Me'ekalar was instructed to begin training the new kaltings.

Kati, having completed the task set her by Beneban, disappeared from Larlingarde, taking with her an unexpected comrade.

ZTAVIN RUBBED HIS hands in glee as he watched the Varkinde queen fight for freedom. Each time she reached past the window of the tower room, the Black

Keep was filled with the pained whimper of a drak. He finally had collected a sufficient number of vardraken eggs—strange little things, alert, capable of movement and of pain, yet harmless to him—that he could bait his trap.

How simple, he thought *and how elegant.*

A message telling her of his captive drak brought her flying on a bitter wind that he admitted still made him shiver. He wouldn't want to repeat the pain of combing ice from his hair and beard.

She entered the keep, all arrogance and fury, and demanded the immediate release of her children, her drak. It was an unpleasant meeting. Yet when she realized at last that to fight him was to cause pain to the helpless drak, she swore she would see him turned into an ice sculpture to decorate her home. She whirled to go and leapt for the window... And the cries and howls of the agonized drak filled the air as her hands crossed the sill. She spun back to him.

"They will suffer until you understand your position, my dear," Ztavin gloated.

"Turn them loose," she hissed, her eyes shooting icy fury at him. Her hands curled in the start of a spell.

The air again was filled with the whimper of a tormented drak as Ztavin touched the black stone at his throat.

Finally she sank to the edge of the rough bench, far from the fire. "What do you want of me?"

"Very little, dear Varakin, and a great deal. You will lend me your power as I need it. I plan to end that upstart Beneban sooner rather than later, and I believe you will be happy to assist me. In the meantime, you know, woman's work. You may clean, serve my meals..."

As she sprang for him, fingers clawing, he again touched the Omera he always wore. A pitiful whine filled the air, and she sank back with a furious hiss.

"Ah, that is better. Now, as for your children, I believe they will make good workers here. So long as you behave, they will be fed and kept in reasonable comfort. Your room... well, for now this room at the top of the stairs will serve. A bit sparse, but it will remind you of your position."

CHAPTER 24

THE CLEAR LIGHT of noonday that fell through a cottage window onto his cot finally roused Beneban. Slowly the darkness faded from his mind. The memory of unbearable pain made him cling to oblivion until, when the agony did not return, he carefully opened his mind to his surroundings. The smell of green, of herbs seemed to pull him up, up... And he realized that the pain was nearly gone.

Suddenly he was eager to reach the light, to see again the face that had gone into the dark with him. It was near as his eyes opened.

Asleep in a chair beside him, Rayni yet kept vigil. One slender hand rested lightly on his wrist. As he stirred and opened his eyes, her gray ones were at once wide and aware. The lightest questing touched his mind. Pleasure lit her face as she saw he was truly better.

"I feel as though I've been on a long, long journey," he said slowly.

"You traveled to the Gates of Mordim, and back. Now you are much recovered. Are you hungry?"

"I could eat a kelsh, hide and tail, and it would be lost in the cave of my belly."

"I had food less ambitious in mind." The girl smiled

and moved to the low fire in the hearth where she ladled broth from a kettle. She returned to sit on the edge of his bed.

"I'll feed myself," he protested. He tried to sit up, but one light hand held him effortlessly flat.

"Let me help you this time. You are weaker than you realize, and your wound is barely closed."

As he opened his mouth to ask a question, she spooned in some soup. Her mind touched his with a promise to answer his questions when the bowl was empty. Yet though the soup strengthened him, when he had finished the meal, just the effort of being fed had depleted his small supply of strength.

"I've no energy for questions, my lady." His voice was barely audible. Pain flickered deep in his amber eyes, but stubbornly he refused to relax.

"My last full memory," he continued, "is a camp with my troop at the edge of Forest. In mercy, tell me what has happened."

Soberly, Rayni told him of the grollings and the fight in Forest. She explained the riddle of the lost Omera and its subsequent recovery. As he listened, the wizard watched dappled light play across her expressive face. When, at times, his eyelids drifted closed, it seemed as if every word she spoke was augmented with nuances of thought, as clear as if they rose in his own mind.

Steadily from the touch of her hand, healing flowed into his exhausted body.

"And so," she finished, "you slept, and so did I. Now, allow me to check your shoulder and be certain you are as improved as you seem."

Her hair, scented with herbs, brushed his face as she bent to him.

She loosened the bandages that bound his wound. Craning his neck, Beneban saw a large, raw triangle of new skin, the center still open.

"You say this happened yesternoon, my lady? I wish you'd been beside us when the Kalden cleaved young Borno. I begin to believe the stories that are told of the Forest Lady."

"This is a place of power," she answered. "The healing pool and Saray's herbs do the work, and I reap the credit. Now, how do you feel? Are you rested enough for a small journey?"

"To the Farther Lands and back," Beneban said. He swung his feet to the floor then grabbed for the cover, suddenly aware of his nakedness.

"Not so far as that." She laughed gently and handed him his pants. "If you can manage with my help, the afternoon rays of Asolum and the water of the pool will be beneficial."

Her prediction proved true. Asolum bathed his bared torso and warmed the cold core that the loss of the Omera had caused.

Small white flowers with pearly cups delicately edged with green sprinkled the grass about them. Each tiny cup held a single drop of dew. Rayni gathered several of these blossoms and crushed them into the water with which she bathed his wound as he rested beside the pool. His back rested against a large stone. The faint fragrance of the flowers that hung in the air was the same as the perfume Beneban had noticed at times of mind touch between them.

"So there *is* a mystical Forest Lady," he murmured, half drowsing beside the water.

"Perhaps, yet…" Suddenly, Rayni sat motionless. The cloth dripped its healing waters onto the ground. Her left hand touched the gem at her throat.

"What is it?" The wizard lazily opened his eyes as she stood.

"Dap and Dal must start on their rounds. You make me careless of time," she said with a small smile. "Don't fall asleep. I will return at once."

She vanished into the cottage and returned with the Worf twins.

"So, you two are responsible for my near extermination." Beneban smiled wryly at the pair.

"They really are sorry. Aren't you Dap? Dal?"

"Dal sorry. Not mean to hurt you. Dap sorry, too," Dal whispered, while his twin tried to hide behind Laraynia. "Us go guard now, Lady." The twins scampered up into a tree and swung quickly out of sight. Arav, the great alviar, flapped ahead as scout.

"How came *you*, my lady, to be keeper of those two imps?" Totally relaxed, Beneban watched them chase through the branches.

"Twins are believed to be evil fortune among the Worfs. I found them as infants, abandoned at the edge of Forest one winter morning."

Beneban's amber eyes left the Worfs to rest on Laraynia's serious face. Laughter bubbled in his throat.

"Were I parent to such a pair, I'd certainly think it evil fortune," he said. He smiled wryly and continued. "Do you habitually take in strays? Or is it only Worfs and wizards?"

A gleam of mischief lit her gray eyes. "What else shall I do if Worfs and wizards come to litter my doorstep in need of assistance?"

Before Beneban could sputter an answer, Gorba grumbled into the clearing. Searching wildly for a weapon, for Heldenhaft was still inside the cottage, the wizard sprang to his feet and pushed Laraynia behind him. He grabbed a fallen branch and had unsheathed his eating knife before Rayni was able to catch his arm in both hands.

"*Stop!*" she cried. "You'll reopen your wound. Gorba is a *friend*. You owe him your life."

At her words, Beneban let the branch fall. After an abashed moment, he sheathed his knife and leaned weakly against the tree. A wry smile lit his eyes as he looked down at the warrior woman ready to throw herself between the two.

"Gorba? You told me that Gorba fought alongside Trog, my lady, but I don't *think* you mentioned Gorba was an ursyn."

"Does it matter?" she snapped. "Is his help less valuable because of that?"

"Nay, perhaps more so." The wizard's eyes danced. "I would surely retreat before such a pair. But there are ursyns whose names are *not* Gorba, whose intentions might be less friendly."

The angry color faded from her cheeks. Her breath quieted. As Beneban watched and realized a strange delight at the sight, he wondered, if she was always so quick to defend a friend. And with the thought, he knew she would be. Gorba swung his enormous head back and forth between them. He seemed to whuffle ursynic laughter.

"Oh," Rayni cried. The storm died from her face, and her gray eyes twinkled. "My *stupid* temper. Wounded, with no weapon but a tree limb, you would defend me from a giant ursyn, and then I berate you." Her face sobered. "Forgive me, Beneban?" She touched his arm and looked into his eyes.

Laughter died from his golden eyes. They darkened to amber in a sudden surge of new warmth, of closeness.

His lungs swelled with an urgent need to escape, yet he refused to break away. After a short silence, he answered hesitantly. Words were suddenly too clumsy for communication, and mind touch seemed an unthinkable intimacy.

"There is little you need ask forgiveness for, my lady, and less for which I wouldn't give it, unasked." He touched her hand with a hesitant finger. A shiver ran through the girl. He felt it, a small electric shock where they touched. Slowly she took her hand back. Faint color stained her face, yet her eyes held his in question. Her mind had opened to him, Beneban realized. Here was a haven, offered with all bars down.

He knew, too, as a hunted bird knows it mustn't go to its nest, that as long as he stood beneath Ztavin's threat, he must refuse that offered closeness. The pain of that refusal tore words from him that later he would wish unsaid. "I've never seen this place before. I have never known a home. How, then, do I feel that I've come home, my lady?"

Rayni smiled and seemed to change the subject. "I helped to save your life," she said. "Here, just now, you would have fought for mine. It is unreasonably formal for you to call me lady."

"What then?" He fiercely rejected words that leapt to mind. *Beloved. Heart of my life.* Words he must never say so long as Ztavin's threat existed.

"You must call me Rayni as Saray does." Her eyes held his as he tried to look away.

"It wouldn't be proper, my lady. Saray would be the first to tell you so. To tell *me* so."

"I do not care for propriety here. This is *my* home. Will you not please me in this?"

Reluctant but unwilling to hurt her, he agreed. "For so long as we are in this place, then," he qualified, "and if you do truly wish it, Rayni."

"And I will call you Eban. May I?"

Feeling as though he were riding a wild kalting on a narrow path through a swamp, Beneban could not deny the pull between them. He was painfully aware of the danger inherent in agreement. Yet he could not refuse.

"All my names belong somehow to you," he answered finally. "Even that one known only to myself. You could not have reached my will in the blizzard if it weren't so. Yet if you ask my leave, I gladly give it."

Satisfied, Rayni turned to speak to Gorba.

Sudden weakness brought beads of sweat to Beneban's brow. He slid blindly down and sank to the ground against the tree. The music of the girl's voice, the sudden urgency of the ursyn's grumbled replies, made an unintelligible background to the mist of pain and fatigue that overpowered him.

Rayni murmured a startled exclamation. Cool

hands touched his face, and water was held for him to drink. The mist of pain that had blinded him cleared.

"You have done too much." Rayni's voice was filled with contrition. "Have you opened your wound?" Quick, gentle hands checked and replaced bandages.

"I'm fine," Beneban grumbled, irritated by his weakness. He pushed back to his feet.

"Yes, but it has grown cool, and I must leave for a little. Come inside now, Eban." She ignored his protest and helped him to his cot.

Soft pillows welcomed him. Before the girl had finished quiet instructions to Saray, and long before she and Gorba sped into the darkened Forest to help the small camp of beleaguered troopers, an avalanche of sleep conquered the wizard.

THE STORM WHICH soon crashed about the edges of Forest never touched Beneban's awareness. In their small camp at the edge of the great trees, his troop, aided by the magical storm and by Rayni's small band of friends, beat off the large horde of grollings that attacked Beneban's force. It was a fierce battle. Afterward, Rayni and Trog worked side by side. They patched wounds and applied poultices to draw poison from the bites suffered by some in the troop. Hundak hurried back and forth as needed. He carried water, and tore bandages from shirts over the protest of their owners.

"You must move the camp, Trog." Rayni fastened a bandage on a shallow cut in Lodar's arm and stood.

"This is a bad spot. It is too close to the dead part of Forest, and this attack was in force."

"You were right to keep us here, Lady. But the evil in Forest has grown beyond your strength. Let us help you," the Ogdol urged.

"I won't send you away, Trog. Eban... Beneban, I should say, will need your help when he has recovered." She thought for a moment. "There is a glade to the west, near to the cottage," she said. "It will be safer than this. My protection still holds there. Come. We will help you move."

Trog thought that when the Captain was healed they would have to persuade this fierce, gentle woman to leave with them. She must leave this dangerous place behind. But he left that battle for later. For the present, he collected the troop and moved where he preferred to be. Closer to Beneban.

IN THE FAR reaches of the Kalds, as the hour neared midnight, Ztavin swirled like a black demon through the lowest passages of his hold. He noted with satisfaction that his captive drak maintained even these halls in spotless order, according to his instruction. Fearing his punishment, the fire box, they did as he directed. His mind flew ahead to his plans.

A little longer, he thought. *It is more difficult than I expected to upset Lyolar's power structure and to keep from him my true intent, but soon! Soon, greater power—more than anyone has ever dreamed of—will be mine.*

Two drak squatted silently against the wall at his approach. With their lumpish bodies, gray skin and clothes, they looked like part of the stonework.

Lost in his hungry thoughts, Ztavin didn't see the malevolent gleam of icy eyes that followed his progress. Even had he noticed, he would have been unconcerned. The drak would remain loyal while he held Varakin prisoner. His plans were ripening nicely.

How foolish she had been to try to rescue her drak. Now they were each a surety for the other's obedience. Her room in the high tower was also a trap. When she had tried to leave, one of her drak had begun toasting over a slow fire. Its pathetic squeal had clarified the boundaries of her freedom.

Soft, he thought. *She is as soft hearted as a human.*

He pushed open the door to his work room.

IN THE DEPTHS of Forest that same evening, Ma'arteen was waiting. While spying for the Grand Lar, he had been diverted from his mission and captured by grollings. Wounded, tortured, but determined to survive, he bided time until Asolum left the sky. Someone *must* get news of the conspiracy to Lyolar. Now, for the first time since his capture a few days earlier, he felt a whisper of hope. For some hours his captors had been occupied with a stranger who seemed to bring news, and apparently, controversial instructions. They were too involved with this newcomer to continue their evil sport with the hapless captive.

Though most of the conference had been conducted in the rough tongue of the grollings, at one point they had lapsed into more civilized language. It allowed the wounded man to understand the nature of their discussion.

Now Ma'arteen had an urgent reason, besides that of saving his life, to escape. He had information that could mean the destruction of Larlion.

Gathering the fragile strength that respite from torture had brought him, Ma'arteen waited until the grollings were in loud dispute over some point. Then, as quietly as he was able, he slit his bonds with the razor-edged stone he'd secreted for the purpose and slipped silently into the underbrush. He worked his way west, toward the part of Forest where the trees glowed with a gentle green light. If safety was to be found, it would be there.

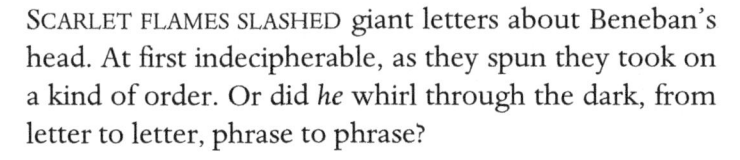

SCARLET FLAMES SLASHED giant letters about Beneban's head. At first indecipherable, as they spun they took on a kind of order. Or did *he* whirl through the dark, from letter to letter, phrase to phrase?

> *Lose my forfeit, name and will*
> *In years not more nor less than three...*

Spun dizzily through blackness that clutched and flung him, Beneban suddenly beyond hope, burst out of the nightmare and into a fire-lit room, strange at first, then as memory returned, strangely comforting.

A gentle face bent over him. Shimmergreen hair, soft as silk, brushed his cheek. A cool cloth perfumed the air with the scent of herbs. It replaced the sticky one on his forehead.

"You are feverish, Eban. Do not worry. By morning it will pass."

For a moment his mind pressed with concern against the dream. The missing Larstone, the three-year deadline, now reduced to two and one half. With a shudder, he shook these concerns away and turned to the face above.

As the past receded, he noticed a smear on Rayni's white sleeve. He captured her wrist to look more closely.

"This is blood, my lady. Have you been injured?"

"You promised to call me Rayni," the girl evaded. She freed her arm and replaced the cool cloth.

"While we remain here, I will," he agreed. "Is this your blood, then, Rayni?"

"No."

"Where did you go so urgently with the ursyn? Why did I conveniently fall asleep this afternoon?" His voice held a rising anger.

"Conveniently? I didn't... You were exhausted. I did *not* cause you to fall into sleep."

Beneban watched as her gray eyes widened. They sparked with angry green. At length, the wizard nodded. "Yet we both know you might have."

"Only now," she protested. "Only when you have been weakened by your wound and loss of your Omera."

"Perhaps," Beneban nodded. "Yet I would have said no one could mind-control me. Now I understand better the resentment some feel for wizards. Very well. I *ask* again, where did the blood on your sleeve come from?"

She turned away. For a moment he thought she wouldn't answer. Then, rubbing her head with a weary hand, she said, "The grollings attacked your camp at the edge of Forest. We drove them off. No one was killed, though there were minor injuries."

Beneban sat straight up. He ignored sudden dizziness and demanded, *"Do you mean my troop?"* The words were low, spaced, and furious.

"I've moved them closer."

"My men should be in *Larlingarde* by now!" Beneban snarled. "I thought *I* was the wizard, yet you wave a finger, and my men forget orders and duty both."

"In twenty-four hours you'll be able to ride in company," Rayni said.

"So they sit here waiting until I'm well enough to ride? Never mind. I see they do." The silence was tense with anger.

"Have grolling attacks become common in Forest?" Beneban demanded, finally. "Perhaps if we wait long enough, we may hope to escort you to safety. A day or two more will hardly matter to the *urgent* news I bring to Lyolar."

Instantly ashamed of the biting words yet still angry at Rayni's interference, he tried to touch her mind. It was closed to him.

"I shan't leave Forest. You needn't wait for *me!*" she said icily. She pushed a cup at him. "Drink this. It will lower your fever."

With every breath he took, Beneban was more aware of having hurt this lovely woman who had done him only good. He took the cup and touched her hand, seeking to apologize. She turned away. So he drank the herbal brew as a tacit apology. He remained propped on an elbow as Rayni moved about. She replaced herbs and covered the Worf twins against the chill of night.

Finally she finished all possible chores and ended beside his cot. She refused to look at him as she took the empty cup.

"Forgive me, please, Lady of Forest." He pushed up from the bed to reach for her hand, but the pull at torn muscles dragged out a groan.

"Lie down!" Rayni snapped. But her face twisted with a responsive spasm of pain, and the barrier thinned between them, though her words were sharp. "I won't have my care undone by your recklessness."

She sank into the chair beside him.

"It makes me angry to be helpless," Beneban said after some thought. He hoped an explanation might bridge the chill between them. "Also," he continued, "There *are* urgent messages which should have reached Lyolar by now. Yet none of that is your fault. Please, don't let my careless words keep you here, when you should indeed move to a safer spot."

"Your words don't affect the matter," she said coolly. "This is my home. The animals, the birds, and trees are my family." With a sigh at his stricken look, she continued. "My parents fled here to Forest when civilization would have barred their union. I won't leave when all I love is in peril. If I go, Forest will succumb to the dark."

"The dark. Is the lighted Forest the part still under your influence?"

"Yes."

"How much was lighted a year ago?"

"Nearly all," Rayni admitted reluctantly.

"Then you surely see..."

"I will not discuss it. This is my home. We hold fast for now. *I will not leave.*" Resolutely, she leaned back and pretended sleep.

Twice, Beneban tried to reopen the discussion. The girl shook her head slightly and refused answer. At length, as the wizard rested, he watched the firelight dance across her features and saw her face relax as true sleep took her.

Stubborn, he thought. *Brave, and gay, and gentle. What shall I do? I can't leave her to face the dark, but I can't stay. My duty is to Lyolar.* Forest, *indeed, the safety of all Larlion, may depend on my information.* As pain and exhaustion took their toll, he too lapsed into sleep. A wry smile twisted his face as the room faded. Perhaps the morning would bring answers.

His dream this time was of a gleaming green stone hung about an ivory pillar, just beyond his reach. In the dream, his hand stretched out to it. As he touched it, power flared in his mind. But when he held the stone, it dissolved into pain and emptiness. He held all the power there was, and it was nothing compared to what he somehow knew he had lost.

He awoke from his dream to a pain beyond agony...

A PITY YOUNG Beneban *must be disposed of*, Ztavin's thoughts drifted idly. *I could use his power. Yet he has a genius for disruption of my every scheme. Well, that will soon be finished, and the Forest witch will be ended, too. Wherever the Larstone has been hidden, I'll have to find it without Beneban's help.*

The black wizard pushed open a dull black door, sullenly rune-signed in red. The dark wizard observed the room and stroked his beard in anticipation.

Before him was a large square space. No cobwebs, beloved props of storied evil magicians, adorned the corners of this space. Here were no nameless piles of gruesome ingredients. The room, with its bare, light-absorbing walls, was as clean as terrified drak servants could make it. Each polished instrument stood in place. Against one wall stood neat shelves of labeled containers. A bucket of glowing coals stood ready by the door. And in the center... Ztavin hissed in evil pleasure.

In the center, five poor wretches were tied, each to a heavy ringbolt at the points of the graven Shadeus. The figure was sacred to the demons of Shadeum, who dwelt in the hellish depths of Malec. Two of the sacrifices were mercifully unconscious. The others watched through terror-filled eyes, and one garbled a strangled whimper as he strained to speak around the gag that filled his mouth.

Everything was prepared. He made a circuit to check the bonds of each sacrifice. Farmers and vagrants picked up by the grollings in their raids.

Under the new alliance with grollings and Kaldens, these worthless creatures were deposited in the wizard's dungeons to await his needs.

Finally, he lifted the great copper brazier to the center of the Shadeus within the smaller, deep-graven ring of protection and emptied the hot coals into it.

As the flames leapt, he stripped and ritually washed in a waiting basin then donned a heavy new woolen robe. It was entirely black, without seam, tie, or fastening for a demon to cling to.

Now the fire splashed sullen crimson light on the dull walls. Ztavin's swollen, distorted shadow leapt about the room as he took three small cloth bags from a shelf and prepared to step within the circle.

Someone pounded at the door safely sealed behind him. At his angry gesture it flew open, revealing the stunted form of Calibe.

"Are you mad?" Ztavin demanded incredulously. No one had ever willingly knocked at this door before.

"I want to help," he hissed. "I, Calibe, want to send that bardack wizard to Malec. Let the Shadeum demons feed on him there for eternity."

The gleam in Calibe's eye and a looseness about his lips made Ztavin wonder if the creature had not slipped over the border into insanity.

"He must not interfere with the attack on Larlingarde," Calibe ranted. "Merktan say 'destroy him!' Destroy, I also say. Let me help." Small hands rubbed eagerly together, and his eyes entreated like those of a child pleading for sweets.

"Only these can help me," Ztavin said coldly as he indicated the bound figures on the floor. "Will you take the place of one? I'm sure we could persuade them. No?" His voice was impatient and angry now. "Then be gone! Do not return unless you would die before Beneban."

"You must heed me!" Calibe leapt up and down in his fury. His form seemed to subtly blur in the flickering light. "I am an ambassador from your allies. I demand you allow me to observe, at least."

"You speak foolishness. From where can you observe? The only safety within this room is that circle. It is barely large enough for one. Even there, without the knowledge of a lifetime of wizardry, your life would quickly be forfeit to those I summon."

"We have magic of our own," Calibe hissed. "Generations of exile from this land have given us immunity to much that threatens land dwellers. Nor am I without power. Make me a circle of safety outside the figure."

Ztavin shook his head impatiently.

"Then shall I report to Merktan that you do not cooperate?"

As Calibe spoke, his warped shape shifted and took on a height and dignity unfamiliar to most who thought they knew him. There were those, had they been present, who would have recognized the Mergol warrior from Ka'amfer's supper party who had successfully killed the arak to entertain his dinner guests.

"Very well," Ztavin hissed furiously. "But if harm comes to you, Prince Kentan, the responsibility is also yours!"

The black wizard set the three bags he had collected on a bench and snatched up a box of carved zeltenstone. With the gray powder it contained, he impatiently marked out a small circle in a corner of the room. He muttered spells and incantations.

"There! I've made it as secure as possible. They may not notice you if you are very still. Yet you should use what warding you may for the sake of your life."

Calibe, or rather Kentan now in his true form,

stepped within the perfect circle Ztavin had drawn. He was careful not to smear the powder with his now-webbed feet. Next, he took a small bag from his own belt and sprinkled deep blue powder in the shape of a star. Each point just touched the circle Ztavin had drawn.

One of the sacrifices turned his terrified eyes to this new presence. A plea was gargled, but Kentan turned a careless shoulder to him.

Ztavin fought down his own impatience. He closed his eyes and took several deep breaths until he was again calm. He checked the bags of herbs once more. Finally, he stepped carefully into the center circle of the large Shadeus.

Flames leapt from the brazier to greet him.

As he chanted words in a long-forbidden language, he reached into the first bag and cast a handful of its contents on the fire. Instantly a thick, noxious smoke rolled from the brazier. It filled the space between the inner and outer graven symbols and rolled up to the ceiling. Yet it was contained as if within an invisible wall.

The room's temperature plunged to an icy chill that fought the flames and bit through Ztavin's heavy robe.

A second handful of herbs dropped precisely in the center of the coals. The chill deepened. Yellow tendrils smeared with oily black writhed into the air. They wove through the clots of gray fumes.

Spirits of the outer cold,
Come to my command!
Here is food more rich than gold.

Come, thou dwellers known of old,
Cast thy blight upon the land.

As he chanted, Ztavin pointed his black Omera at each of the bound figures, barely discernible in the foul-smelling fug. Each writhed upward in agony, choked to silence by the fat gags they wore.

As the tormented wretches strained frantically against their bonds, the wizard's hand dipped into the third bag and cast its contents upon the flame. This time the gouts of smudge that oozed from the brazier embraced the yellow tentacles that had previously appeared. The oily gray smoke gathered, now here, now there, into nightmare shapes. Whenever one of these phantoms neared a captive, the poor creature flung more desperately against his ropes and groaned. Then, as the amorphous figure covered the victim, it gave a last strangled cry, collapsed, and lay motionless. A bag emptied and cast aside.

The last prisoner was consumed, and in the bitter cold, the mal-shaped spirits formed and reformed. They hovered hungrily about the graven figure within which Ztavin stood. Yet each one winced away. They were unable to cross and consume the wizard as the flames leapt high.

As Ztavin clung to his Omera, he hissed the ancient words that bound the demons to his will. Then with a violent motion, he flung them through a narrow slit in one wall, the wall that faced south, toward Forest.

For a long moment, Ztavin's shadow towered, proud and black in the flare of light. Then wearily, he slumped and stared about the room as if uncertain where he was. At length he extinguished the flames, stumbled from his protective circle, and crossed to the second guardian shape. With a foot, he blurred the marks.

Within it, Prince Kentan slumped unconscious on the icy floor.

Ztavin knelt beside him. He felt for a pulse and noted the clammy skin.

"Ah, well," he sighed. "I warned you. If Beneban, worth five of you, must be sacrificed to my purpose, we can surely spare one mad shape-changer."

The Mergol stirred beneath his hand. Kentan groaned and struggled to sit up. Ztavin scowled, yet he lifted this strange ally.

"They are gone? Gone? The wizard is finished?" the Mergol gasped.

"They are on the way. Soon wizard and witch will no longer weigh in our plans."

"Are they strong enough? Are these spirits strong enough?"

"You nearly lost your life to them. You should know their strength. Come. I need warmth and food, and so do you. Then you can report to your master. There will be no hindrance to Merktan's plans for Larlingarde."

"The day grows close," Kentan hissed. "The day when my people attain their proper power in the land draws near."

Ztavin supported his unwelcome observer through the door and paused to check that all was in order.

"Yes," he murmured. "The day of power is near." Kentan leaned heavily on Ztavin's arm. He failed to note the ominous difference in the black wizard's words.

IN THE DARKEST hour before dawn, Beneban awakened. He thought he was caught in another feverish nightmare. The room leapt with firelight. On the floor sprawled a bloody, tattered scarecrow. A man near death, to judge by his total stillness. Two small figures capered from fire to body and back, like demonic imps.

Rayni entered abruptly, and all was right again. "Is everything ready, Dap? Then you two join Arav on watch while I tend this poor fellow."

The twins hurried into the dark night, and Rayni shut the door.

Seeing Beneban awake, she smiled faintly. "He crawled out Forest and collapsed on the step." She dampened a cloth and knelt to bathe the stranger's torn chest. "This poor man. The grollings had him too long. His last strength has gone to getting him here."

"Better to die here than live on amongst the grollings." Beneban struggled up and knelt beside her. "Look, Rayni. He wears Lyolar's blue and silver. He must be a messenger."

"Such rags as they left him could be from a trooper's uniform," she agreed.

Saray roused sleepily from her pallet. "Do you need help, child? Why didn't you call me?"

"I thought you needed to sleep. This night may be a long one."

"Do you expect an attack here?" Beneban stared at

her. "Has this man said anything?"

"The twins found him unconscious. I sent them back along his path to keep watch. Grollings don't easily lose their prey unless..." The wounded man jerked convulsively. His teeth clenched on a cry of pain as Rayni's cloth touched the deep wound beneath his ribs. His eyes flew open and fixed incredulously on Beneban's uniform shirt and the ranking insignia.

"Captain?" It was a breathless, incredulous question, barely audible.

"Easy, man," Beneban soothed. "When you're stronger..."

Outside the cabin there was a shout, an urgent command.

Laraynia's golden hand touched the sparkling jewel that hung about her throat to the trooper's body. It seemed to ease his agony, and he was able to speak further.

"Tell... Lyolar..." the stranger grabbed Beneban's hand urgently, straining upward with the effort to speak. "Mergols... gate..."

He sank back exhausted. His eyes closed then fluttered open once more. "Water..." His voice faded.

Saray hurried up with a cup but heard the last breath rattle from the torn body. The wizard gently closed the dead man's eyes.

From the clearing, Trog's voice bellowed, followed by Gorba's deep rumble. Steel clashed on steel.

Beneban rose then dropped to one knee by Rayni. The girl was motionless save for slow tears that ran down her face. He watched Laraynia release the pendant hanging about her slender neck. The jewel was as green as new spring leaves that sparkled, translucent beneath a brilliant sun. Suddenly his dream flashed before him. The dream of finding, of reaching to take a green stone from a slender ivory pillar, and of the pain that followed the theft. Was it even possible? He must be wrong. The thing he needed so urgently couldn't be the very thing that would destroy this person he had come to care so much for.

"Sir!" Scat gasped, sticking his head into the room. "Trog do say he'd 'preciate your help." The boy vanished, leaving the door ajar.

Fiercely, Beneban tucked the problem away. He reached to dry Rayni's tears, his hand so near the chain that held his salvation… and her destruction.

"You did all you could, my lady. With these wounds he could not survive. Here he died in less pain, among friends." As his long fingers dried her tears, he felt a path open between them. For an instant he accepted it, shared her pain, and lent his strength. The banked ember in his chest grew to a bonfire.

Saray silently cleared the rags away and watched. Her heart was torn at what she saw. Outside, the sound of weapons and shouting arose.

Beneban rose and smiled gravely at Laraynia. "Your prediction of trouble has come true, Rayni. We may all be glad you kept my troopers here." He buckled on Heldenhaft, turned, and threw an arm across the door to stop Rayni from darting outside. "Stay safe inside with Saray, Rayni."

Her wide gray eyes sparked with green fire. She smiled faintly up at him as her hand went to her gem and caressed it to life. Beneban sternly closed the door, *again*, on the dilemma that hammered at his mind.

"This battle will need us both. I am not unprotected, Eban." Rayni pushed past him. In the clearing beyond, the dark was skewered with lightning.

Beneban followed quickly. In awe, he saw tree tops whipped by a sudden gale. Continuous lightning cast the scene in a series of vignettes.

At the edge of the clearing beside the healing pool, troopers defended a hastily erected barricade against a horde of grollings. Gorba was a mountainous shape by the other side. His sickle claws were reinforced by Trog, a massive white windmill of flashing blades.

Overhead, Arav dove again and again. His wings slashed, and his razor beak repelled those grollings who survived the deadly rain of missiles laid down by the Worf twins perched in the big tree.

Buoyed by Heldenhaft's power, Beneban plunged to a threatened spot. Jaran, hard pressed, had fallen back, leaving a hole between the troopers and the gazerts, whose horns formed a fearsome V of slashing scimitars. A wedge of grollings plunged for the hole, seeking to get behind the defenders. Beneban met them with Heldenhaft's singing gold and amber flame. He dispatched three and sent the others to cover.

A cheer rose from the men at the sight of their captain and his mighty sword.

"Scat," Beneban bellowed as he drove back another charge. "Send Hundak to me." From somewhere the giant Kalden appeared. There was a brief lull as the grollings pulled back from this new threat, and from the nearly continual blaze of lightning that seemed to frame the clearing. Beneban glanced at Rayni.

She stood alone on a tiny knoll. The stone at her throat, cupped in one slender hand, echoed the green flash of her eyes, and her hair whipped wildly in the roar of storm wind.

"Hundak!" Beneban slashed a grolling. "Guard the Forest Lady. If she is injured, you'd better not survive to tell me about it."

He watched briefly as Hundak lumbered away. He saw with wonder that, as her free hand moved, lightning slashed with the accuracy of a whip wielded by an expert. It was as though the storm was orchestrated by the slender girl.

"It couldn't be that simple," he muttered and watched as she rubbed her talisman while the lightning flared in response. If this were the Larstone, with powers similar to his Omera, to take it would mean her death.

And then there was no time for thought, only for survival of the small band in Forest.

Black cold, a cold from the bitter depths of Malec, rolled the Forest glade.

Sooty shapes, malformed, the essence of evil, towered over the grolling hordes. These hissed and squealed as they fell away. They made a path for the hideous shapes to move slowly, ominously forward.

Gawl, who tried to escape into Forest, was the first to be taken. A dark figure loomed over him and enveloped him. He screamed once and collapsed, an empty bag. The demon, engorged, grew denser.

The cold deepened.

On the far edge of the clearing, pitch-dark phantoms towered before Trog and Gorba. They swelled and overhung the pair. As the stalwart giants stood their ground, they drifted away to seek easier prey.

Yet valor was not enough. Lodar and two others bravely held their position as a pitchy tide swept toward them. Slowly, stubbornly, the demons enveloped their defiant shapes. As Beneban confronted a demon of his own, he had time to see courage turn to despair then to stark terror as the three collapsed, one by one.

One demon that rolled toward Rayni's knoll fell back as a bolt of lightning flamed into a pile of brush before the girl. As little flames licked up, the creature hovered then oozed toward the trees where the Worf twins were entrenched.

Beneban saw but could not free his thought from the deformed demon that towered over him. It fed on his need and pounded self-doubt deep into his mind. Slow blackness filled his consciousness and blotted out hope. Heldenhaft's point fell to the ground, useless against the bitter strength of cold self-disgust. Ugly questions battered his mental defenses. *Who are you to let others die for you? What right have you to power over others? You, who deny other's pain and who does not want responsibility for others.*

Sel, Ari, Tor, Borno... The list of those he had failed and led to disaster pounded away at him. The cold blackness sucked away his courage, his very self, swallowed his strength. He fell to his knees.

"*Eban!*"

The frightened cry, mind to mind, cut through the black miasma of self-absorption. He fought, not just for his reason but for that other self he had only just discovered, and found a spark. Spark? *Flame!* Antithesis of cold.

One hand crept sluggishly toward his Omera and held to it as to a lifeline. Stern, hard-learned discipline pushed back the blackness. He visualized a tiny, perfect flame, the flame that had sprung up in front of Rayni. Easier to focus on something real to begin with.

He *saw* red fingers of heat lick at fragile shavings, *felt* the frail warmth increase as twigs ignited, *smelled* the woodsy smoke as larger fuel caught. No illusion, this, to fool a band of Kaldens. Only real fire, hot and fierce, would push back these demons of Malecian cold.

The dark figure cowered away from sudden flames that leapt up. Beneban, barely conscious of the soul-eater's agonized howl, held one hand to the heat of the furious blaze before him and concentrated on feeding it until it widened to burn a ring of defense around the clearing.

Trog saw the demons retreat. He rallied the troops to carry fuel for the fiery wall. Lightning called down by Rayni's will set trees aflame around the widened ring and strengthened it. Trog, Gorba and those troopers still on their feet dragged burnable objects from the cottage to feed the hungry blaze.

The grollings, never brave, always afraid of fire, danced angrily outside the barrier. The black spirits hovered at the edges of the defense in search of any weakness.

Beneban knelt in blind concentration, building an ever-tighter wall of heat and flame, but there was little natural fuel left to the defenders. The wizard's face was beaded with sweat, and Trog saw him waver. He strode over to steady him, but the Ogdol wondered what they would do when Beneban's strength was gone.

As if aware of the wizard's failing power, there was an anticipatory moan from the attackers.

Then a sudden howl swept through the massed ranks of grollings. Through the ring of flames leapt a great golden shape. It was Kati. Her curved horn and claws were stained with grolling blood. She knelt by the Forest Lady's mound to let the figure on her back slide to the ground.

Rayni stared with concern and wonder at the slender youth and the giant kalting. "Glad though we are of reinforcements," she began, "this is an evil time in which to join us."

Ravel, for it was the stalthinger, slid from Kati's back. He smiled at the Forest Lady, and pulled his instrument free.

"We thought you might use some help," he said.

CHAPTER 25

Undeterred by his blindness, Ravel moved quickly and with focus. First he pulled a small pack from the kalting's back and whipped the wrap from his staltin. Then the stalthinger stepped over to Laraynia where she stood agape.

"Forgive me, Lady," he murmured. "I shall pay you more proper homage, but first we must deal with this business." Ravel knelt, adjusted a string here, then a second. Then he struck a chord on the beautiful instrument. Its ringing tone pierced the angry air. As though slashed by arrows, the power of the dark shuddered.

Once Kati was free, she loped across to where Beneban drooped. His energy nearly spent, all his focus now was a fight to maintain control over the fire. He started as Kati nudged him for attention. One of his hands sank, stunned, to her wide head. At once the contact gave his magic a jolt of fresh energy.

Now Ravel's pure voice lifted. It began softly then rang out to fill the glade. The music increased quickly in strength.

The language was unknown to the Forest Lady, yet at the back of her memory she felt its sense and the total rejection of all that was evil. Notes soared aloft.

She saw them as clouds of butterflies and felt the wings brush her cheek. The beauty of each verse that followed beat back the blackness.

In response to the music, the exhausted flames of the barrier leapt anew. They stabbed the attackers, and where they touched, the demons howled and retreated.

By contrast, Beneban's energy grew. His head lifted to the melody. As though in response to a powerful tonic, he was infused with new strength. The weary wizard straightened. Flames leapt ever higher now, as his clasp tightened on his Omera. He turned briefly to Laraynia, and sensed union, the power her stone added to his.

Now exhausted men stirred. Those who had waited limply for their doom now stumbled to their feet and lifted weapons.

As hope stirred in the little company, a new light flamed in the east. Asolum's fiery fingers streaked the sky to join the wizard's blaze and bring the day.

It was too much. The cold demons of black Malec fled, a dark maelstrom that howled back toward the Kalds and Ztavin's keep. The few grollings who remained alive melted into Forest.

Trog touched Beneban on the shoulder. "It is enough," he rumbled. "Let go thy effort now. The enemy has fled."

For a moment the wizard's concentration did not break. Finally, he looked blindly up to where Trog's bulk blocked the sky.

"They have gone?"

"As you see."

The wizard sighed and bowed his head. The flames abated in the fiery ring his magic had built with the help of the music. Beneban sank to the ground and rested his head on bent knees. After a moment, Trog crouched beside him.

"How many have we lost?" Beneban asked wearily. His mind reached first for the Forest Lady, she for whom he had most feared. He felt her green strength as she moved to tend the wounded, and relief surged in him to the point of illness.

"Glaynar is dead elsewhere." Trog's steady voice answered. It brought the wizard's attention back. "Lodar and three others are wounded in spirit, more lightly in body. One trooper fell to the grollings, and they killed one gazert. The lady is unharmed, though Saray was injured. Kati and Ravel..."

"Kati? Ravel?" Beneban lifted his head. He stared about with eyes blind from power use, then gave up the effort.

"Kati and Ravel. They came through the fire. You did not see?" Now Beneban's eyes opened wide, seeking light, then closed helplessly.

"It was his music that revived me. It has strengthened me ever since."

"It strengthened us all. Here is Kati."

The kalting butted Beneban's arm with her heavy head, and he groped upward to scratch the base of her horn.

"Crazy kalting. You came into grave danger. You might have been killed in this. Trog," his head lifted again, "send Scat to me. Where is he?"

There was an ominous silence.

"Tell me, Trog," Beneban said. But he already accepted the dreaded answer.

"He lies at your feet, Captain." Trog's voice was carefully pruned of grief and likewise of the shock Beneban's words had given. "He brought the item you needed for the fire. Heldenhaft flamed in his hands a little when he raised her. Enough to hold the demon at bay."

"No!" Pain filled Beneban's voice. The wizard struggled to his knees. He reached out, felt the dead boy's face, and gently closed his eyes.

"The demons could not take him, Captain."

"No! They feed on lack of courage, and he had no such lack. The sword burned him out." Beneban's face was a frozen mask. "He gave me time to stir my courage, and he died of his," he added bitterly.

"Your magic saved us. You blame yourself too much," Trog rumbled.

"Do I?"

"You had responsibility for us all; he had only you."

"Yet my responsibility leaves me alive, while his has killed him. Poor reward, to care for a wizard. It is why we leave hearts to humans." Beneban's voice was bitter. He rose to his feet, staggered, and gripped Trog's arm briefly. His face lifted to the warmth of Asolum, strengthened now by her small sister, Zartum.

Trog stood silent. He knew no words to comfort his friend. Finally, aware that sympathy would shatter the fragile bonds that held Beneban together, the Ogdol said matter-of-factly, "What are your orders, sir?"

"We must reach safety before nightfall."

"Eban." Rayni had approached quietly. "Saray cannot travel. And the dead..."

"A litter will be arranged for Saray and other wounded. We will take the dead with us. Unless we wish to join them, we must reach Arilgarde before dark."

"But the wounded..."

"The wounded, my lady, will certainly die when the demons return," Beneban snarled. "Do you think they will not come back? They have weakened us. They will return with the dark to feed. We have Gorba, Trog, Kati, more riding kelsh than..." His voice broke slightly. "Than people. We will... We *must* manage."

Rayni was angry. "Go if you must," she snapped. "Take the wounded. I will not leave Forest." She turned away.

The wizard's words, hard and cold as ice, spun her around to him. "*You* will go if you must be tied and carried. We will not leave you or any other behind. Unless you wish to be responsible for all our deaths, you have no choice."

Beneban sensed her pain at his tone, felt brief defiance, and knew his anger hurt her. Momentarily his courage wavered. Then he thought of young Scat, devoted and dead. That pain reinforced his stubborn determination, and he stared fiercely at her.

Finally she turned away. "I'll make ready what I must take." Her footsteps faded.

Now the wizard slumped and struggled again to see. It was useless.

"Trog!" Beneban turned his head and sensed the

Ogdol's presence as he rumbled it. "Make ready to move. I'll be by the pool if you need me." Beneban felt for Kati's head and moved haltingly off.

With one eye, Trog watched the dejected Forest Lady enter the cottage. Another considered the wizard's uneven progress as he sank beside a large stone and dangled a hand in the water. The Ogdol's third eye closed wearily as he shrugged a shoulder-less shrug and prepared to evacuate Forest. He could not heal the pain of these humans he cared for. All he could do was to carry out orders as efficiently as possible.

His voice lifted, and he began to rap out commands.

ASOLUM'S BRIGHT DAWN was soon swallowed by black clouds and driving rain. The foul weather made the need to gather the wounded and collect such supplies as remained to them as miserable as possible for the weary troop. Laraynia had efficiently packed a small sack for each of the twins. She added a few supplies to use in care of the wounded as they traveled. The dead were bundled together and secured to one riding beast.

Now they fled as gloom turned early afternoon to evening. The bedraggled Forest refugees urged more speed from their weary mounts as they followed the road beyond the dripping trees.

Lodar and Morden rode listlessly in the midst of the remaining troopers. Lodar sported a bandage on his head, and Morden's right arm was in a sling. Neither trooper would accept a litter.

Saray, too old for such foolishness, lay warmly wrapped. Her litter followed the wounded men, swung between two spare kelsh and steadied by Trog and Hundak as needed.

The surviving gazert had knelt before Ravel and submitted to his weight. Now, without reins, saddle, or vision, the stalthinger easily balanced with his instrument on the slender beast's back.

Gorba flanked the travelers. He carried Dap, Dal, and a bulky pack gathered by Rayni. Overhead, Arav scouted tirelessly ahead and behind.

At the rear of the troop, Kati carried double. The kalting, after Beneban mounted, had crouched before the Forest Lady and waited. Finally Beneban snapped at her to mount. "There *will* be another attack, my lady. Unless you wish to assure the success of the demons, you will mount *now*."

She rode stiffly at first, still angry. But at length, exhaustion took her, and she slept safe in the wizard's stubborn arms.

The journey since then had been largely accomplished in silence, broken mainly by Trog's occasional orders to the men. Now the Ogdol, aware of the gathering gloom behind them, fell back beside Kati.

"The dark comes early, Captain."

"And artificially," Beneban agreed. "Is it normal, or…" The wizard straightened wearily. Rayni, half asleep within the circle of his arms, roused with a startled exclamation.

"How far is it to Arilgarde?" Beneban asked.

Trog replied, "I have never approached it from this direction, Captain."

Beneath a smothered yawn as Rayni studied the path ahead. "Perhaps an hour to the gates," she said.

"And how long until dark falls, Trog?" Beneban demanded.

The Ogdol eyed Beneban. The wizard's blind gaze was fixed on the Forest Lady's back. Trog glanced back at the trees, black against the darkening sky. "Less than an hour, sir."

"Can we go faster?" Beneban asked.

"I think we must," Trog said unhappily.

"Then give the order," the wizard snapped.

Trog trundled rapidly up the line to relay the order for more speed. Beneban stretched wearily. As Kati increased her pace, he automatically steadied Laraynia.

"I'm sorry I fell asleep, Eban. You must be cramped from steadying me."

Moments passed. Then Beneban answered tonelessly, "It was no trouble, my lady."

Rayni stiffened at the formal speech. She pulled away, not seeing the pain that twisted his face. "Have I angered you? We agreed formality was out of place between us."

Beneban broke another lengthy silence, still carefully polite. "Our agreement held, my lady, within your domain. Nothing can justify such lack of protocol between us in the real world."

"The 'real world,'" Rayni began angrily. "What is this 'real world' you speak of, where friends..." Arav screamed an interruption overhead, and Laraynia peered up at the huge alviar. She turned anxiously to Beneban.

"Forest is black," she said urgently. "The last light

has gone out. Arav reports that the dark follows us quickly now."

The wizard's head lifted. "Trog!"

The Ogdol hurried back to them. "We must go faster. We are pursued," Beneban said.

"The injured will suffer," the Ogdol replied.

"We have no choice," Beneban answered. "To be overtaken will mean their death. All of our deaths. Or worse."

Without argument, Trog sped forward and urged the column to such speed as was possible.

Now Ravel joined them, the gazert responding to his need. The stalthinger had heard Laraynia. With a gentle smile, he loosened the staltin's wrap. "Ride as quickly as you dare. I'll buy a little extra time, Captain."

"No," Beneban snapped. "Already I have lost Scat and Borno. Too many have suffered to ease my path. You will not join them. I'll stay."

"The strength you have left is unequal to the task, Captain," Ravel said quietly. "Also, and perhaps more important, your information must get through. Do not despair of me. I'll write more verses to your ballad one day."

The lad plucked a simple tune as he rode beside them, music that seemed to ease their resistance. Then he halted the gazert with a touch on its neck.

"Ride quickly now. I'll follow close behind," he called. Kati ignored Beneban's order to slow her pace to match Ravel's. She sped after the troopers as they rounded the next bend in the road.

Behind them, Ravel's clear voice soared to join the

staltin. As his music rose, a cloud of light lifted above them. The darkness smashed into the light. It roiled but was held back by the power of the clear notes and the sound of the blind lad's voice.

"Eban! His music is power itself," Rayni cried. She peered past his shoulder. Then, as the wizard didn't answer, she touched his arm. "He is following closely, Eban. He will be safe."

There was a shout ahead. Around a bend in the road came mounted troops uniformed in red and gold. The sturdy figure of Lar Ari led them. They encircled the beleaguered band, and Ari halted his kelsh beside Kati.

"Well, Captain? I thought we had an understanding, yet here you are on Ariling land, and as usual, trouble pursues you."

Wearily, Beneban pushed a lock of shimmergreen hair from his brow and turned his blind eyes to the angry lar.

"You said, sir, that you would not obstruct execution of his Mightiness's orders. I hold his commission, and I bear news he urgently needs. I do not ask shelter for myself. Here, though," he added, "are refugees and wounded. For them I pray your protection."

Ari stared at the girl who rode before Beneban. Curiosity and wonder lit his eyes. "Of course. But what has happened in Forest?"

"Before we talk, sir, may we reach the protection of your walls? Those that pursue us…"

"Come, then." The lar wheeled his mount and shouted an order. His men swept up the refugees and galloped for the city walls just visible down the road.

Ari paused once and stared back toward Forest. He watched in disbelief as blackness piled in mountainous billows, breaking against a wall of light.

Out of the light galloped a gazert, and on its back a slender lad rode, laughing. They paused by Ari.

"It is best to ride quickly," Ravel cried. "I've only sung them a small song. It will not hold them for long."

"Come, then," Ari said again. They swirled in pursuit of the troop as cloaks whipped the air in flight.

Behind them, the black threat piled high and higher still, held by the wall of light. The brilliance bulged outward. It stretched to transparent thinness as though pregnant with some sooty monster. Finally, curtain-thin, it split and was torn by a bolt of dark lightning. Like viscous fog, blackness poured through. It oozed sullenly down the road from Forest. With it came a spectral howl that froze the heart of all who heard.

It was too late.

The troopers, Lar Ari, Kati with her riders, and all the refugees fled safely through the gates of Arilgarde. Ari's gates had long been runed with spells sufficient to bar even this foulness.

Nothing but weather invaded Lar Ari's home city that night. An icy, driving rain assaulted its citizens, but the terror remained outside the walls.

ARI HAD SENT a messenger to speed ahead with an alert to his people. The stone castle that was his home greeted them with welcome light and warmth. Rooms stood ready. A hasty but generous meal had been assembled. Ari's physician waited to care for the wounded. The riding animals were comfortably absorbed into ample stables, wiped dry by a horde of stable attendants, and fed warm mash.

Late that evening, when his guests had retired, Ari stalked along an upper hallway toward a confrontation he'd rather have avoided. He paused, glaring at the carved door ahead.

"Get it done, now," he muttered crossly. He rapped sharply.

"Come in."

The room within was typical of Ari's home. Warm and comfortable, it belied the castle's rough exterior. It was low-ceilinged and thickly carpeted. The walls were hung with tapestries. An efficient fireplace gave heat and light.

Kati sprawled before the fire and inspected the visitor. She relaxed as Ari paused by the door.

At first the old lar didn't see Beneban. Relief surged in his chest. Yet Beneban had answered his knock...

"May I help you?" Beneban stood in shadows across the room. One slender hand just touched the wall. Ari stiffened at the cool tone.

"I came, Captain, "Ari challenged at once, "to ask what service *you* demand of me." He resisted the urge to slam something and shut the door with determined care.

For a moment it seemed Beneban wouldn't answer. Then his voice, tired but controlled, came from the darkest corner. "Hardly demand, surely. Grant me shelter for the night, if you will? I'll leave at dawn."

Ari stalked past a suddenly alert Kati. "You can't

leave for Larlingarde," he said grimly. "The Lingar and Little Lin are out of their banks with this rain. 'Tis all flood from here to Torgarde. He halted and peered into the shadows that darkened the corner where the wizard stood, silent. The old lar's hard-held temper snapped.

"What were you doing up north? How did you meet the Forest Lady? Do you have any idea who she is?" Suddenly aware of a total lack of response from his target, he barked, "Come into the light and sit down, man."

At first Ari thought he would not answer. Then his voice came, haltingly.

"Lyolar sent us to obtain kaltings for the Kaltingcorps." Beneban's voice was flat, without breath behind it. He remained motionless in the shadows. "I sent Me'ekalar ahead with the animals. The rest of us fought off Kaldens and Mergols at Mergol Ford."

"Mergols?" Ari was incredulous.

Beneban plodded on, not noticing. "Then... The lady will tell you about the attack on Forest. I *must* leave in the morning."

Ari stalked over to the wizard and peered into his face.

"Sit down, man, you're exhausted. Lady Laraynia told me about the battle this morning. You pay for wizardry like that. We can talk by the fire."

"But I seem... to have misplaced the... chairs." Beneban's voice was so toneless that at first Ari didn't understand. Then, his face set, he took the wizard's arm, pulled him across the room, and settled him in a cushioned chair. He positioned a stool for his feet, bumping the wizard's knees slightly with it until it was in use.

"You've not been hit on the head, have you?" The older man towered grimly over him. "'Tis the wizard price you pay? How long have you been blind, Captain?"

"Since the battle last night... This morning?"

"How do you think to leave for Larlingarde tomorrow?"

"The blindness will pass. Besides, Kati knows the way."

"Well, you can't leave while the way is flooded." Ari sank into a second chair. He fought down unwilling sympathy for the man before him. "Anyway, you need to know some things."

"What I already know should have reached the Grand Lar days ago." Beneban's words gained urgency. "I went through Forest to cut time from the trip. Instead, most of L Troop is either missing or dead. I'd have made better time by the main road. Now... I must get through." Beneban sagged back into the chair.

"Your men are here, the rest of your troop."

"Here? What of the wounded? Young Borno..." The wizard sat straight up again.

"Borno? The lad with the injured shoulder? Doing quite well. They got this far and were stopped by the floods. Captain Me'ekalar went through several days ago. He'll be safely to Larlingarde by now. Why didn't you send the information with him?"

"I gave him what I knew. Since then there have been Mergols and more. I've pieced some things together. May I tell you? If I don't reach Lyolar, someone else must know, someone to whom Lyolar will listen." Beneban's eyes closed then opened wide again as they tried to gather light they couldn't find.

"This blind spell... and there was one in Larlingarde, the night I left, wasn't there?" Ari demanded. "How many others have there been? How long can you push yourself before the blindness is permanent, lad?"

"It was very minor at Larlingarde. I'll manage for long enough, I think." Beneban nearly smiled at the reluctant concern in the old lar's voice. "With luck, I'll find less need for magic in Larlingarde. Lyolar keeps insisting he wants no wizard."

"Well," Ari sighed, "You'll not leave tomorrow, but tell me your news if you wish."

Ari listened with increasing agitation as Beneban explained the apparent alliance between Kaldens, Mergols, and the black wizard Ztavin, the appearance of a vardraken, and a connection with the grollings. When he tied them together with the link he'd seen between the Mergols and Meriel, the lar swore a startled oath.

"Lyolar plans to marry the wench," he exclaimed. "He'll not welcome that news, even if it's true. How sure are you?"

"I'm sure there's a connection. Calibe was Tor Larya's servant, given by her to the Lady Meriel. No one but Calibe was close enough to have killed Lyolar's sister. Beneath her hand was a fish-shaped pin. It was unusual in workmanship, but identical to one worn by Lady Meriel on another occasion.

"Then," Beneban continued, "A spell I cast that

froze all the court except Lyolar, whom I deliberately left free, failed to hold Meriel. Her father, if such Ka'amfer truly is, traffics with Mergols." The wizard sighed.

"And have you ever seen the shape-changers? When I look at Meriel, it is like peering through a mist as it was with the Mergols at the Ford. Not proof, but suggestive." Bene leaned forward and held his head. His voice was muffled as he continued. "However it angers him, Lyolar must be warned."

"Yes." Ari sprang up to pace the room's length. Returning to the fireside chair, he sighed. "If something happens to you, I'll pass your suspicions along. What does she want? The Mergol wench?"

"I don't know," Beneban said. "Ztavin seeks power. He seems to be connected to the Mergols. Where the Lady Meriel fits in, I'm not sure. Is she, in fact, a Mergol? Does she act for her people? Does Ka'amfer seek to overthrow Lyolar for the Mergols or for himself? And where do the Kaldens come in?"

Ari groaned, and Beneban continued. "No one of these threats is so ominous alone," the wizard said. "Yet this unlikely union, added to the neat separation of Lyolar from his heir, adds up to an ominous plot. Someone as yet unseen must exercise considerable power to set this all in motion."

"It makes sense," Ari said. He stared into the fire then added, "Have you heard this news? Young Tor has stirred up Ameling and Boriling against his uncle. Torling, of course, is ripe for rebellion. Tor was a favorite there."

"I didn't know." Beneban sighed and held his hands

to the fire. "So with Larlion already divided, an enemy finds the battle half won," he added.

Someone tapped on the door. At Ari's call, Laraynia entered. Dap and Dal hovered at the door. They held bandages and a pan of steaming water. Herbs wafted their scent into the room with the steam.

"Come in, my lady." Ari leapt to his feet. He frowned when the wizard remained seated. "Forgive the captain. He can't—"

Rayni seemed to ignore Beneban. "Forgive *me*, Lar Ari. The captain was wounded recently. I've come to check that the day's activities haven't reopened his injury."

"My shoulder is well enough, my lady," Beneban interrupted. "How are Saray and the others?" He turned an urgent look on the lar.

Ari fell abruptly silent, unwilling to give the support the wizard sought.

Rayni moved forward and stood over him, hands on hips. "Unbutton your shirt, please. Or shall I do it for you?"

"I'm not a babe, Lady Laraynia," Beneban snapped.

"Then don't act like one. If your shoulder is well, show me. I'll leave the sooner."

Beneban sighed and undid buttons so she could ease the shirt away. Silently, Rayni removed the bloody bandages and confirmed the wound was unharmed. She ignored his protest as she bathed and rewrapped the wound.

"Will you tell me about Saray, my lady?"

"She'll recover with time." The girl's voice was remote. "The ride was less than helpful."

"What would you have had me done?" Beneban snapped. "All our lives forfeit that she not be moved?" The Worf twins scurried from the room at his tone, pushing each other to escape first.

"Will you sit down, my lady?" Ari intervened.

"The captain would prefer me to leave," Rayni said. In spite of her intention she waited for him to deny it.

"Close the door when you leave," Beneban said wearily. "There's a draft."

Ari's angry oath covered the girl's muffled sob as she ran from the room. "*I* will close the door on my way, Captain," he snapped. "Be certain I shall tell you as soon as you may safely go."

Beneban winced as the door slammed behind the angry lar. He leaned his head down to his knees. "I think, Kati," he said, his voice strangled against his breeches, "that Lar Ari and I might be friends if people would leave us alone."

KENTAN HUDDLED ON the hearth in the main room of the Black Keep and tried to feed the fire. The hungry black wind howled around the walls and shrieked its fury. It sought for any crevice to enter and sucked away the fire. Kentan shivered and huddled closer to the blaze.

"Why does it howl so?" the Mergol prince cried. "What does it want? Make it stop!"

"It seeks food. Its proper prey has escaped," Ztavin hissed angrily. "Why don't you go out and talk to it.

You might satisfy it for a time, Prince Kentan"

Kentan cringed away from the furious black wizard. "I don't... It won't... can't come in, c-can it?"

"It never has so far." Ztavin scowled. "It will stop with tomorrow's dawn. Stop whinging, or I might just toss you over the wall as an offering."

Varakin, huddled in a corner away from the heat, looked from one to the other. That they were unwilling cohorts was plain enough. Perhaps if she...

"Quit thinking, woman. Go and make food for us unless you would like to hear one of your puling drak cry," Ztavin snarled. He yanked her from the corner by the hair and shoved her toward the kitchen.

"As for you, my soggy princeling," Ztavin continued, "I suggest you not disturb me further. Food for us will be ready soon. In the meantime, sit somewhere I needn't see you and be silent."

Never a hero, the Mergol prince slunk away and settled nervously in a cool, damp corner of the great room. A cold draft slid down wall. When a drop of icy water lit on his neck, he leapt away from the corner with a terrified howl.

Ztavin sank down in wild laughter that joined the feral howling of the black demons that sought entry.

"You won't always find me funny," Kentan snarled at the black wizard who had convulsed in amusement at his guest's panic. The Mergol prince stalked into the kitchen and slammed the door.

"Not always funny," Ztavin gasped "but until better entertainment arrives, you'll suffice, my soggy princeling. You will do."

Two mornings later, Beneban stood at a small window overlooking the sunny Arilgarde castle garden. In one hand he held a book, a finger marking the page from which the view had drawn him.

The door opened, and Lar Ari entered. He paused to observe the obviously stronger wizard. Then he noticed that Beneban clutched the window frame so hard with his free hand that the wood had splintered. Ari cleared his throat.

"I hope you'll forgive my invasion of your library, sir," the wizard said instantly without turning. "I'm surprised to find so complete a section on magic."

"I've experimented with it. I'm not power-hungry enough to pursue it far. Surely you aren't in need of a magician's hocus-pocus?"

"This book?" Beneban turned. He released the wood and stared at the volume he held in his hand as if curious how it came there. Then, suddenly focused, he answered, "No. I wanted to refresh my memory of Mergol history."

"Mergols have no cause to love Larlion," Ari said. "The fact that they made a way of life for themselves after they were banished from the country doesn't lessen the bitterness they feel."

"Were they true Larlinga? They are so different now," the wizard said. "Even their magic is different than ours and contrary to it."

"They were Larlinga," Ari confirmed. "But they dabbled in a different power than was common. Even then, they looked to the sea."

"It was very long ago."

"Yes, but they've never made treaty with us, nor even talked for long to that purpose. They grabbed for control of Larlion and missed. Now it seems they hunger still for that power," Ari noted.

"Yes." The wizard set the book on a table and turned fully to face Ari. "I gather you sought me, sir," he said soberly. "I am well enough to leave, as you desire."

"Wait, I have news..." Ari stumbled to a stop, appalled at the visible strain on the other's face. "Beneban, have you slept at all? I've seen men wounded to the death who looked less worn."

Beneban blinked at Ari's unexpected concern. He forced a small smile. "I'll manage, but thank you. The study of wizardry encourages the ability to go without sleep. What news, then?"

Ari took an impatient step away then turned and continued. "You are stubborn."

There was no reply but a nod.

"Very well, you need this information. My foster son, Tor, has raised an army from Boriling and Ameling. Stree, the young idiot, is riding the wind. He has Larlingarde under siege. He never was long on brains, and as my fosterling, was always quick to try to impress Tor."

"Stree is the Lar of Streeling?" Ari nodded. "What of the other estates?" Beneban asked.

"They hang back on one excuse or another until they see where their advantage is. Except for Ore, who holds the pass against the northern army, and young Lar Ande, who has taken Amel Gate. It borders his land, so at least we have a sea gate open in the north, so long as he remains loyal."

"Streeling isn't much of a threat by itself," the wizard mused. "Yet if the Torlingals throw in with them, or the Mergols enter the picture…"

"…then Lyolar is in trouble," Ari completed the thought. "He has grown somnolent. He doesn't understand that some of the lars find his petty tyrannies unreasonable. He may awake now with the threat at his gate.

"But there is more," Ari added. "Mergols have also been seen in the rivers near the capital and have attacked some small river villages."

"Ah." The wizard nodded. "I doubt we've heard the last of Ztavin either," he added. "With a coalition of Mergols and Ztavin, with the Kaldens evidently ready to go to war, I think we must force Lyolar to understand what is at stake. Larlingarde must be strengthened. Not only Lyolar, but the people of the capital will become fuel for Ztavin's lust for power. Every soul he takes strengthens him." Beneban turned to the door. "I must ride! Are the floodwaters down?" Now he turned again to the window as though drawn and stared out. For a long moment there was silence. The wizard thought again of the Larstone, of the price he would pay if he failed to get it and the price Rayni would pay if he took it. But that puzzle must remain unsolved a little longer.

He must leave for the capital. If he didn't save the people of Larlingarde, the black wizard would have power too great to be resisted by anyone. He had no choice but to leave now and see what chance might offer.

Ari's response interrupted his spinning thoughts. "The floods are down. A messenger killed two riding beasts to get here to demand aid for Lyolar. It was speed, not the floods, that did for them. If you are going to leave..."

Beneban turned quickly, his task clear before him. "Yes. I'll go at once and take what is left of L Troop. May I leave the wounded here?"

"Of course. Trog is gathering your men. Three troops of mine will go with you. I'll follow with the remainder of my force as soon as I've secured things here."

"I will travel more quickly alone. Sir, you asked me once," Beneban said, changing the subject abruptly, "if I knew who Forest Lady is."

The wizard paused, wondering whether to continue. It was a painful discovery. Still, he trusted Ari. He thought it likely the information wouldn't be news to him in any case. And of course, his host wouldn't know the horrible choice the stone held for him.

"If I am right," Beneban finished, "she is Lyolar's niece. The stone she holds must be the missing Larstone, the second 'treasure' you mentioned that was stolen by the wizard, Nigeran." The wizard still gazed through the window.

He wondered if Lar Ari knew how important the jewel was to him. How important the Forest Lady was to him.

"She is, and it is. I, along with half the court, was in love with her mother, Larlinda. Lyolar was no exception. He intended to follow the royal tradition and marry her. When she eloped with Nigeran, Lyolar was apoplectic. The girl is the image of her mother. I remember Saray, too, who was Larlinda's maid."

"Did he really love her? Lyolar, I mean."

The wizard turned and rubbed one long hand idly up and down the window frame. His hand, his entire body, seemed to yearn through the window, Ari thought. What drew him so?

"Yes," the lar answered in the matter-of-fact way Beneban seemed to need. "But intermarriage also keeps the power of the Larstone within the royal family." The older man started away, but changed his mind. "It's none of my business, but the girl saved your life. How can you dislike her so much?"

Beneban turned, and in the dusky library his eyes were wide and golden. For an instant Ari was so certain the wizard was in pain that he took a quick step forward. Yet when the wizard spoke, his voice was light, almost flippant. "Dislike her? No, that doesn't describe my feeling for her at all. Say, rather, she terrifies me. I am running for my life and my honor. Keep her safely here, for both our sakes. I'm on my way." The wizard pushed quickly past Ari and hurried from the room.

Lost in speculation, Ari crossed to the window. He was curious to confirm what had held Beneban's attention so strongly, and he'd thought aright.

In the garden below, Laraynia knelt beside a fresh patch of dirt. About her skirts lay a small bed of neatly planted green. As he watched, she gently firmed in more clumps of tiny white flowers, the laril she had found time to dig from beside the healing mere in Forest.

Ari watched her for several moments in thought. Then he turned to stare at the door through which Beneban had disappeared.

A slow smile creased his face. He nodded once, decisively, and went to begin his own preparations.

CHAPTER 26

Beneban's breath plumed in the cold air as he knelt on the knoll overlooking Larlingarde. It was three days since the wizard had spoken with Lar Ari in the quiet library. Though this should be the height of summer, a bitter wind had blown down from the Kalds. Beneban was glad of the heavy cloak the old lar had pushed into his pack when he left Arilgarde. He knelt at the edge of Little Larwood, a small forest that often served young nobles as a favorite place for al fresco meals. In this bitter wind, however, it was not an auspicious day for idle outdoor activity.

Hard riding had brought Beneban and his small troop to this spot in that short time. They had bypassed the easy route to Larlingarde. At Lingar Tower Ford they had crossed the Lingar River. Then, in order to avoid contact with the rebels, they drove straight south. Stops for food and rest were brief.

Beneban shuddered as an icy drop found passage down his neck. He shivered again at the ominous scene below.

On the wide plain before the Great Gate of the city, an army moved busily. The area resembled a barbittes nest that had been kicked. Lar Stree, the brash young Northern lar and an ardent follower of young Tor, was encamped there. His pennant flaunted his presence.

The gates of the city, normally flung wide to all, were fast shut against the rebel force.

Stree's troops were vivid in the scarlet and black of his house colors. They moved briskly to tie down tents against the wind and shelter small cook fires. It was, beyond hope, an army.

Sword practice clashed at one end of the camp. Near the cook fires, knives chopped food with crisp whacks. The scrape of weapons on whet stones drifted ominously to Beneban's keen ears.

Even on this tall knoll, the light breeze brought a smell that made Kati, crouched beside the wizard, snort softly. It was the smell of incipient violence.

Now Beneban's force rested and checked their gear. The wizard stole a moment to consider the situation below. "Pretty quiet at the moment, girl," Beneban murmured to Kati. "It looks like they don't expect much opposition. I doubt they'll let us just ride down and send them home, though." He sighed heavily. By tomorrow, many would lie dead for a quarrel that should never have begun.

"What are your plans, Captain?" Trog had come silently up behind the pair. He shaded one eye and peered down at the attackers.

"I think..." Beneban paused and looked up at the Ogdol. "I've got an idea, but we must get a message into the city tonight. The people must know to expect our support and be ready to open the gates. Who can we send?"

"There is Lodar, sir..."

"I left Lodar at Arilgarde. He was weakened from

the battle in Forest..."

"He is much improved," Trog said. "Also, he followed behind until we were more than halfway here. He thought to avoid your order to go back."

Beneban smiled wryly as he considered the rebellious trooper. "Do you think he's up to it, Trog? He's trustworthy and obviously determined. Well, send him to me. This assignment may at least keep him from the worst of the battle. We'll rest here for the night," he continued as Trog turned away. "Cold camp, no fires. We'll surprise them tomorrow," Beneban added as he slid away from the exposed hilltop.

No one but Beneban and Trog saw Lodar drift from camp that night. His mission was to alert the Grand Lar and Larlingarde's forces to Beneban's plans. The wizard intended a two-pronged attack. He hoped to catch the Streelingers in a trap between the city troops and his force, a trap that would, perhaps, minimize the slaughter.

As THE FIRST fingers of Asolum brightened the next morning, the Great Gate of Larlingarde burst open unexpectedly. Troops of the Grand Lar spewed forth, led by the Kaltingcorps. Behind them hurtled an angry mob of citizens. These waved knives, pokers, and other such weapons as could be found.

Lar Stree's men were literally caught asleep. They were, however, a well-trained army. Awakened to their danger, they collected wits and weapons with equal speed. At once they formed the tight knots of trained soldiers to resist the untrained mob from the city.

Me'ekalar led his force well, and quickly overran the largest force, but the city folk were less able. It seemed at first that Stree's troops would succeed in pushing the Larlingarders back to the city walls and possibly even to press on through the city's massive gates.

Then Beneban's small army poured down from the Larwood and hit them hard from the rear. The great sword keened her battle song. L Troop and the men from Ariling, fresh from a night's rest, drove deeply into the body of the beleaguered Streelingers.

The townspeople rallied with a roar. Cheers of 'the wizard' and 'the golden sword' spurred them on.

Caught in the pincers between Beneban's men and the city force, the rebel army fought hard as Asolum went from dawn to midafternoon. They expected bitter terms if they lost this battle. Lar Stree himself, astride his great black kelsh, was at the forefront of his force. The fight surged like the ebb and flow of the tide. The advantage of Beneban's surprise attack was gradually offset by the desperate determination of the rebels who fought for their brave young lar.

Stubbornly, pace by pace, Beneban and Kati fought their way closer to the rebel leader. Finally, only a knot of Stree's own household guard separated him from the wizard.

The battle surged back and forth. It was nearly at the gates when an arrow felled Stree's mount.

Stree jumped clear of the dying kelsh as Beneban's cohorts, Trog and Sergeant Denodar, engaged the rebel guards. They left Stree and Beneban face to face.

The wizard slid from Kati's back to even the fight. He swung Heldenhaft up in a hazardous parry as the young lar lunged at him.

"Lay down your weapon. Surrender," Beneban gasped. A fierce sweep of Stree's broadsword slithered down Heldenhaft's length.

"Why? To lie in *prison*?" Stree lunged. "Or worse, at Lyolar's doubtful mercy," he grunted as they slashed and parried. He dove aside as Heldenhaft whistled golden sparks down the length of his blade.

"But you'd be *alive*." Beneban drove him back, the great sword invincible in the wizard's hands. His eyes widened momentarily. With renewed intent he drove the young lar, step by bitter step, toward the Great Gate. Several times he ignored a chance for a fatal thrust.

"He'd pardon you, eventually. Just one more s*tep*!"

Trog, poised directly behind the rebel leader, silently reached out and imprisoned Stree in his enormous embrace. His third hand removed the young lar's sword.

"Good work, Trog," Beneban gasped and stood with Heldenhaft at rest, his hands on his knees.

With Stree's capture, the last resistance faded from the rebel army. Those who were still able fled. The rest laid down their arms.

"Believe me," Beneban said, his breath harsh as he wiped sweat from his face. "It is good, to be alive."

"Not a problem this rebel cur will have for long!" Lyolar's strident voice overrode young Mero, who tried to proclaim his ruler's presence in shrill, excited tones. The Grand Lar, astride a restless white kelsh, paused in the gateway to survey the battleground. "Captain Ranald!"

The ginger-haired captain edged his mount past Lyolar's and whirled to salute him.

"Take Stree *and* his fool officers." Lyolar indicated the men standing under guard of Sergeant Denodar and two others. "Hang them from the walls as a lesson. Retribution for rebellion will be harsh under this Grand Lar," he added pompously.

"Mightiness." Beneban shoved quickly through the throng of prisoners and guards. "Mightiness, I gave him my word..."

"Just wait 'til the waterway gate opens," one of Stree's men cried as two of Ranald's guard dragged him away. At his words, Beneban froze to listen.

"*Shut up!*" Stree roared and struggled to reach the man. Beneban lunged to stop Ranald, but he was too late. The officer hit Stree on the temple with the hilt of his sword. The man slumped, stunned.

"What about the waterway gate?" Bene bellowed. It was too late. The wizard bent over the fallen lar and shook him urgently. It was no use. Stree had gone down like a felled tree.

Furious, Beneban turned to his ruler. He strove for control of his voice. "Mightiness, I ask your patience. It is urgent that we question these men. I promised Lar Stree mercy. As you value your honor..."

"Be careful, wizard." Lyolar's voice was frigid. "You have already incurred our displeasure. Consider yourself under barrack arrest until a court can be convened tomorrow."

"Mightiness, you can't..." began Me'ekalar, who

had just trotted up on She'em.

"I can't do this. I mustn't do that." Lyolar's face had purpled with fury. "*I* am the Grand Lar. I shall do as I choose."

Beneban ignored them all. His thoughts flew to assemble pieces of a puzzle.

The scattered words of the dying courier, and now the words of Stree's man. *Mergols... the waterway... gate opens...* Now they coalesced for Beneban. The Grand Lar and his capital city were in dire danger. The rebel attack at the gate was a distraction from the true threat. The threat posed by the new waterway.

Now, hopefully not too late, the wizard realized what Stree's army had waited for. But there was no time to explain to the impatient Grand Lar.

"Me'ekalar," Beneban shouted. "Bring your troop. Follow me to the new waterway."

"Not so fast, Captain," Lyolar roared to his retreating back. "You're under arrest. You're to be tried for treason."

"Your treason is closer to home, Mightiness," Beneban shouted. He leapt onto Kati and spun toward the gate. "The city is about to be taken by the Mergols. Meriel is a Mergol."

Unsure his words had even been heard and before Lyolar could answer, Beneban and Kati disappeared into the narrow maze of streets in the lower town.

"Meriel?" Lyolar roared. "What new treason is this? After him."

Me'ekalar was already in pursuit at Beneban's words with half the Kaltingcorps and a mob of eager townsfolk on the chase.

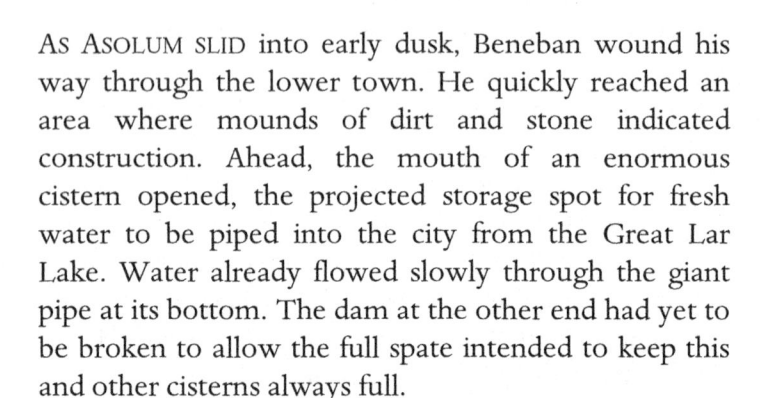

As Asolum slid into early dusk, Beneban wound his way through the lower town. He quickly reached an area where mounds of dirt and stone indicated construction. Ahead, the mouth of an enormous cistern opened, the projected storage spot for fresh water to be piped into the city from the Great Lar Lake. Water already flowed slowly through the giant pipe at its bottom. The dam at the other end had yet to be broken to allow the full spate intended to keep this and other cisterns always full.

Through the gloom, Beneban saw that the locked steel gate, which normally barred entrance to the new waterway's mouth, had been forced. The broken lock lay beside the pry bar that had shattered it.

On the edge of the enormous reservoir, a slender, hazy figure stood watch as it filled.

"Lady Meriel," Beneban called softly.

Meriel spun toward him. Her face, a mask of shock, was instantly covered with a look of nonchalance.

"Captain Beneban. Whatever brings you here?" she asked innocently.

"You steal my very question, mistress." The weary wizard slid from Kati's back and climbed awkwardly down. He stumbled over clods of dirt and slipped once in the mud. "This is hardly where your friends at court would expect to find you," Beneban said. As he neared, he noticed a ladder that led down to the mouth of the pipe. "How soon will they open the water flow? There seems already to be a largish stream within the cistern."

"I... don't know." she stammered. Her face turned pale as ash as her confidence faltered. Her eyes darted nervously, first to the flood of water, then to her interrogator.

A shout rose behind them. The cry of the Kaltingcorps sounded clear in challenge.

"Oh no," Meriel cried and covered her mouth with a tiny hand. "What have you done?"

"The rebels of Streeling are defeated, my lady. The plan for Mergols to conquer Larlingarde has failed. Was Stree to then be destroyed, as well? What did you plan for the citizens?"

"My brother... he would be... they would become..."

"Slaves?" Beneban demanded in a cold voice.

"No!" Meriel backed closer to the edge as Me'ekalar and his troops thundered into the square. Below them, the water in the cistern swirled more deeply. Barely visible in the dark, Beneban saw heads with manes of silvery hair break the surface. Slanted eyes peered up at them, and an arm drew back with a flash of metal.

Beneban, already with one hand at his Omera, flicked the other in a command as a three-pronged spear flew at him. It bounced harmlessly from his invisible shield.

Me'ekalar saw the weapon. At once he, and a dozen of his troop galloped to surround the wizard. Bows quickly drawn, they fired arrows into the swirl of water at the invaders.

"You think you have won, but we have just begun," Meriel cried. She peered in despair at the troops.

With a cry of misery, she changed. Brown hair became a silver mane that grew from brow to nape. Her features slimmed, and her eyes slanted in her pale face.

Me'ekalar, who had dismounted from She'em on a run, grabbed for her, but Beneban's shield blocked him.

Meriel touched her hands above her head and dove into the water. A swirl, a splash, and the surface of the water below stilled to mirrorlike blackness. She was gone, as were the invading Mergols.

"You should have held her, Beneban." Me'ekalar peered in amazement at the dark water. "It would have proven your loyalty to Lyolar."

"Do you think so? I don't. Not unless she confessed. And now?"

Me'ekalar looked miserably at his friend.

"Yes, never mind. I'll go with you. I recall some words about being under arrest." With a twisted smile, Beneban walked slowly beside his friend toward the waiting kaltings. He mounted Kati and rode, surrounded by Me'ekalar's men.

As they reached the Great Gate, a yell arose from the crowd. They looked up to see a body, silhouetted against the last pale light, pulled into the air to hang, legs kicking. Soon it hung motionless beside two companions.

"If His Mightiness won't tolerate rebellion from a fool like Stree, how then will he punish treachery from one as close to him as Meriel has become?" Beneban wondered.

Me'ekalar just shook his head. For a moment, the Kaltingcorps captain paused. He laid a hand on Kati's head and looked slyly toward the open gate.

"No, Me'ek. I thank you, but I will not end your career that way. Besides," Beneban added, as he rode slowly on toward Lyolar, "the gate is blocked."

In a flare of torches, outriders in red and gold appeared. Me'ekalar and the wizard had just enough time to hear Lar Ari of Ariling being announced before Captain Ranald and ten men surrounded Beneban.

"Captain Beneban, you are under arrest for treason by order of the Grand Lar. Drag him from that kalting, men." Ranald's face twisted in smug pleasure.

Two burly troopers reached upward but winced away as contact with the wizard sent a sharp shock up their arms. Kati snarled a threat, and they retreated rapidly.

"I'll dismount myself," Beneban said quietly. "Me'ekalar, you will care for Kati, yes?"

"Of course," Me'ekalar responded quickly, his words nearly drowned by the Captain's furious shout.

"Tie his hands. Tie his hands," Ranald screeched. "He'll escape again."

The wizard eyed the vituperative little captain. "Why don't you do it yourself?" he asked and held his wrists forward. Ranald backed nervously away.

"No," Beneban said. "I didn't think so. You will always lead from the rear. Come on then," he said as he turned back to the troopers, hands held out. "I won't give you more nasty surprises." After a moment, one soldier stepped forward. He quickly dragged Beneban's arms behind him and lashed his wrists with rough rope.

As the wizard was dragged away, he heard the cheers of the crowd. He twisted around and saw that

Lar Ari had reached the gate.

Trog spoke urgently to the old lar, and Ari's head reared back in disbelief. Ari urged his kelsh through the crowd toward Lyolar.

The last thing Beneban saw as he was roughly yanked around a corner and dragged toward the castle dungeon was a glimpse of the Forest Lady's pale face. Hooded and cloaked, only her enormous eyes were really visible and one slender hand that rose to touch the stone at her throat.

At length he stood before the heavy open door to a dank cell. A hard blow to his head by Ranald removed even that fair memory as he tumbled helplessly into the dark.

THE DUNGEON, BELOW ground level and windowless, was intended to hold prisoners likely to be executed in the near future. The only nod at an amenity was a noisome hole in one corner. The ceiling was too low to allow a prisoner of the wizard's height to stand erect. A rough, pest-ridden pile of rags served as a pallet. As Beneban regained consciousness in the dark, he found it difficult to mark time.

At first he thought he had finally gone completely blind. His head ached miserably. There was no light nor dark, no way to measure the time that passed.

Eventually, a door panel slid back. The flicker of light made sudden, unexpected hope flare as he scrabbled toward the opening.

A bowl of meatless slop was shoved carelessly

through the hole. It tumbled to the floor, and half the contents were lost.

Beneban had little appetite but knew he needed to keep his strength up. The rank smell of the food made him gag. As his hands were still tied, he could only eat as a wherhound might, so he lapped at the swill.

He considered using magic to escape this trap. Dungeons were merely a hole in the ground. His powers could overcome this. Yet, if he escaped, then what? His choices were poor.

He drifted into a half-sleep, his mind unguarded.

"Ah, Beneban," A voice, gentle and sad, pushed itself into his awareness. "What have they done to you, my lad?"

Beneban tried to see who spoke. The voice was familiar.

"Come, son. This is poor pay for your efforts. Why accept this ill-treatment? Just come to me."

Beneban's mind said, "I cannot. I am a prisoner."

"Only reach out with your mind, Beneban. I will take you away from this. Give me your will, and we will be gone from this place. The price is small, and you will be free."

"I will *not!*" Beneban roared, and his own voice roused him from the trance of sleep. How had Ztavin found him there? He stared into the dark that surrounded him. There was no one to be seen, but he knew Ztavin had found him somehow, had thought him weakened enough that he would accept...

Slavery. It would be a complex slavery, one that seemed to offer power. And he, the slave, would eventually be bent to the will of that evil mage.

He would not pay Ztavin's price. The Larstone would give the evil wizard unimaginable powers and was certain to be used for evil.

In Beneban's mind rose the clear gray eyes and

quiet courage of the Larstone's rightful owner, Laraynia, the Forest Lady, her home now closed to her. Would he... No, he could never try to take the gem.

Yet without that treasure, his freedom would also be gone. Beneban would owe far more because of his naïve oath to have his own will and strength subverted to Ztavin's fell purpose.

At least if he were executed for treason, Ztavin's threat would be crippled. He, Beneban, would no longer be tempted to betray the person he held close in his... Well, in his heart, he admitted, though wizards were thought to lack that organ.

Beneban gagged down the next swill they shoved into his cell and hoped his doom would not be too long in arriving.

By his best measure, six days passed before he heard loud steps approach in the stone passageway outside. The door creaked open, and a flare of light made him wince. His eyes no longer expected light.

He twisted awkwardly to his knees. When he could see, Me'ekalar stood in the doorway.

"Captain Beneban, you are ordered to appear before the Grand Lar." His one-time friend spoke with cold formality. The wizard made out two burly guards, mere shadows to his abused eyes, who lurked behind Me'ekalar.

"Follow me," Me'ekalar ordered. He backed a step. He left Beneban to struggle to gain his feet, as the wizard's hands were still tied behind him.

Neither Me'ekalar nor the guards offered to help, though the wizard could not stand straight in the low-ceilinged cell. Awkwardly Beneban staggered forward and stumbled through the door.

Once in the passageway, he was able to stand nearly erect for the first time since he had been thrown into the cell. Me'ekalar remained stern and silent as he stalked ahead along the corridor. One of the guards gave Beneban a shove.

Beneban followed his lead. With an effort he straightened as his bound hands allowed and stumbled silently behind the Kaltingcorps captain.

At the dungeon's exit, Me'ekalar paused. "I will take charge of the prisoner from here," he said brusquely to the guards.

"He's dangerous, Captain," one of them objected. "His magic..."

"He's half starved, and his hands are tied. How could he harm me?" Me'ekalar snapped.

He shoved Beneban in a stumble through the door ahead of him. Then he shut the heavy door of the dungeon on the guards' worried looks.

Silent still, he led the way through increasingly wider passages until they reached a distant wing of the castle. Once, when Beneban started to speak, Me'ekalar shook his head sharply and shot a warning look at the wizard.

Finally, they stopped before a green and silver door. Before the wizard could decipher the heraldry, Me'ekalar took a strangely shaped key from his pocket and opened it. The Kaltingcorps captain stood aside as

Beneban entered the room beyond.

Me'ekalar followed wordlessly. He shut and locked the door behind them. Then suddenly his tension disappeared. With a great sigh, he snatched his knife from its hip sheath, grabbed the wizard's hands, and slashed the ropes that bound them.

For a long moment, Beneban stood motionless. Then he moved his raw wrists and held them before him as though they were still tied.

"What did they do to you, man?" Me'ekalar demanded, horrified. He reached out to touch Beneban's wrists and winced at the raw skin there.

Beneban tried a rusty smile. "It all goes to improve concentration, Me'ek." With a little shudder, he lowered his hands then raised them again and began gently to massage one with the other. Sharp pain shot through them as circulation returned. He forced his attention to his friend.

"By the Powers, it's good to see a friendly face, Me'ek, but where are we? What is this all about? I doubt His Mightiness has decided suddenly to set me free out of the goodness of his heart."

"I don't know what he intends. What I said back there is true; you *are* to appear before Lyolar. I thought you might appreciate a bath first and some clean clothes. You have an hour. There is soap and hot water. Be quick. I'll guard the door from the hall."

PRECISELY ONE HOUR later, Beneban waited in the small private library of the Grand Lar. Clean in body and clothes, he fought to stand erect.

"I could grow to dislike this room," the wizard murmured and stared around him. There was a flurry in the hall outside. Young Mero pushed the door open. *He's grown taller*, Beneban thought.

"His Mightiness, Lyolar, Grand Lar of Larlion and Lord of the Twelve Estates, and the Lady Laraynia, Heiress to the Title," Mero intoned.

At the sound of Rayni's name, Beneban's head lifted quickly. Lyolar entered first. He strutted in his blue and silver finery and turned back to hold a hand out. Laraynia entered, accepted his arm, and walked with him to the twin chairs that now stood at the end of the room. Neither of them looked toward Beneban.

The Forest Lady was gowned in green and silver. Her shimmergreen hair was piled high on her head and green jewels at her ears echoed the familiar one about her throat. Her gray eyes were not visible. They focused firmly on her folded hands, and she did not look at Beneban.

"Come forward, Captain." Lyolar beckoned imperiously.

"Mightiness." Refusing to move stiffly, he strode forward, bent a knee before the ruler, and waited for permission to rise. It wasn't given.

"You have displeased us, Captain."

"I regret to hear it, Mightiness. May I ask—"

"You may speak only if I permit it," Lyolar snapped.

Rayni's head jerked and almost lifted. Then her eyes returned to contemplation of her hands. Angry color blushed in her cheeks.

Beneban continued to kneel silently and averted his eyes.

"No! I am not pleased with you," Lyolar repeated after a moment. "You have brought nothing but trouble. Since you first appeared at our court, there has been disorder." He held up one pudgy hand to enumerate. "First, my sister, the Torlarya, died."

Beneban's incipient protest was silenced by a wave of the royal hand. "Next," the ruler continued, "my nephew, the heir to the throne, was alienated from me by a rumor in which you were implicated.

"*And,*" he again overrode the wizard's protest, "when he tried to kill *me*, you allowed him to go free. Since then Tor has fomented rebellion among my otherwise loyal subjects, and Larlingarde itself has been under siege. You showed my betrothed to be a traitor. Can you doubt that I am angry with you?"

"I doubt my guilt in the incidents you mention, Mightiness."

"*Be silent,*" The Grand Lar snapped and then paused in apparent thought. He looked sideways at Rayni. She still wordlessly contemplated the richly carpeted floor. Her head lifted slightly, and one hand touched Lyolar's sleeve.

Lyolar turned back to the wizard. "However," the ruler said reluctantly, "you have achieved some good for the realm. You procured, with the help of Captain Me'ekalar, the kaltings we need. Also, I am informed that you are in some way responsible for the safety of my niece. She claims you removed her from danger, and brought her to this court. Therefore you shall, of my mercy, not die as a traitor... yet. I shall give you one more chance."

Laraynia tugged at his elbow.

"*What?*" He bent his head impatiently to Laraynia's whisper. "Yes, yes," he sighed. "My niece reminds me that you also razed the siege of Larlingarde and defeated an attempted takeover of the city by Mergols, though no one saw them except you."

There was a pause. Beneban held his tongue and refused his aching knees permission to ease their position.

"As a reward," Lyolar added pompously, "I shall give you one more chance to prove your loyalty to this throne."

Bene continued to kneel in silence.

"Well, Captain Beneban?" Lyolar demanded angrily. "Have you nothing to say?"

Startled, the wizard lifted his head. "I hardly have words to express my... gratitude, Mightiness."

"I can easily believe it," Lyolar agreed. His lips puffed out smugly. He was unaware of the irony, but for the first time, Rayni's eyes met Beneban's, and in them, brief laughter sparked.

"We have a mission for you, Captain. As you know, there is unrest in the country. We have received news that tribes of Kaldens gather on our border. Furthermore, Mergols invade our rivers. They have initiated hostilities. In the north, there is rumor of the Baeling, the undead, arisen. The Varkinde have moved south from the Farther Lands and threaten us from the north. Our nephew, Tor, has raised armies in the Northern Estates. We need him and his allies to stop turning on us and, instead, to protect our northern border. In short, Larlion stands in grave danger. This is not a time for us to fight amongst ourselves."

Lyolar fidgeted in his chair. His silence seemed to demand an answer.

Finally, cautiously, Beneban spoke. "I can only agree, Mightiness. Can you, perhaps, convince your nephew that you are not responsible for the death of his parents? It would be a major step to reconcile him to the throne."

"That, Captain, is the mission I have for *you*. Find Tor. Return him, repentant, to my side, and I shall forgive your other faults."

Abruptly Lyolar rose, held a hand out for Laraynia, and started from the room. Laraynia stood motionless until he turned back.

Lyolar's eyes met Laraynia's and held. He then added a reluctant boon. "In order that you have sufficient status to be our ambassador to the rebels," he said pompously, "I hereby name you Lord of Sartenruhn. You shall have the ancient title and the keep of Sartenruhn."

Stunned, Beneban lifted his head, unable to speak. And again, Rayni pulled against Lyolar's hand as he would have departed.

"Yes, yes," Lyolar added petulantly. "In addition, all the confiscated goods, both property and real, of our traitorous former Advocate Ka'amfer shall be yours."

Now Lyolar turned from the stunned wizard and towed Laraynia through the door. With only an instant left, she cast on Beneban a smile that made his heart leap into his throat. The smile and the jewel that hung about her throat, green as springtime, green as hope, nearly wiped out his awareness of the Grand Lar's questionable generosity.

Beneban knew beyond hope that Laraynia wore the Larstone, the price of his freedom from Ztavin. He also knew he could never take it from her. He had nearly died from the loss of his Omera. Surely the loss of this greater stone would wreak havoc upon this fierce and gentle woman who had saved his life and the lives of so many of his troopers.

The door swung softly closed on the new Lord of Sartenruhn. He struggled to stand. His knees creaked and his head spun. For a moment his legs shook so badly that he considered the empty royal chair. The thought caused a shudder of distaste.

With a return of will, he stumbled toward the door. Freedom was best affirmed in open air. But before he reached the door, it crashed open!

Beneban looked about wildly, thinking that Lyolar had played a cruel joke on him, and here were those who would return him to that foul cell. He would run... hide...

Then Kati was there. Her great paws rested gently on his shoulders. She licked his face thoroughly with her rough tongue and sneezed in disgust. The wizard choked out a laugh and took her great head in his hands.

"Do I still stink of dungeons, Kati?" he asked.

Then Me'ekalar was there. His strong hands grasped his friend's shoulders.

"You are free. I just passed Lyolar. He says I am to escort you to your new home. New home? Where is that?"

His voice unused to speaking, Beneban croaked, "Ka'amfer…"

"I don't understand."

"I'll explain later, Me'ek."

Beneban's voice strengthened with realization that this was not a return to the cell.

"Take me first to my *real* home. I would see Trog, Sel, and Borno and see that they are well. My friend," Beneban grasped Me'ekalar's arm, "take me there first."

Buoyed by Kati on one side and Me'ekalar on the other, long unused muscles began to remember how to put one foot in front of the other. His eyes winced at the unaccustomed light. The clean smell of open air made him shiver, and Me'ekalar turned more than one worried look at him.

"I'll be fine, Me'ek. The news the Grand Lar delivered has me still in shock."

"News?" Me'ek scoffed. "It's more likely lack of decent food and light and freedom."

"Perhaps," Beneban agreed. Overwhelmed, he would tell all at one time.

As they approached the barracks, Trog burst from their room and trundled toward them on his three tree-like legs. He enveloped Beneban and lifted him from the ground.

Underfoot, little Sel jumped up and down. He squeaked his mute excitement then grabbed the wizard's ankle in an unbreakable grip.

"You are back," Borno cried, nearly as excited. "Where were you? Are you hungry?"

"Come in, come in," Trog rumbled. He still held

Beneban off the ground.

"Get him inside," snapped Me'ek in a tone that demanded instant obedience. "He needs food before you batter him with questions."

Borno rushed back to the barracks. By the time the others had entered, he pushed a bowl of fragrant soup at Beneban.

"Let me sit down first. Thank you, Borno. This smells wonderful."

In short order, the soup disappeared together with a heel of bread used to mop up the last drops. Tears suddenly leapt into the exhausted wizard's eyes. He ducked his head to hide them. This warm welcome had unmanned his stern visage as a heartless wizard. He couldn't bear to share such weakness, even with these friends. Yet little Sel, snuggled next to his feet, reached up and patted his knee as if he understood.

Trog hunkered down patiently in front of him while Kati pushed Sel to one side to lay across Beneban's feet.

Borno took the bowl and offered more soup.

"Thank you, no, Borno." Beneban blinked away the tears and looked up. "An empty stomach must get used to food again."

Me'ek sitting on the edge of one cot, sprang up in horror. "You weren't fed?" he exclaimed. "I'm an idiot. I never thought…"

Trog rumbled angrily, and Beneban tried to reassure his friends. "There was food. At times I was even hungry enough to eat it."

"But your hands were tied. How?"

"Yes, like a dog, Me'ek. Never mind." He stretched

his arms wide to include this place, these friends. "Now I am free."

Trog rumbled angrily. A tear dropped from Sel's eyes to Beneban's feet. Me'ekalar saw his friend wanted to change the subject.

"You spoke of your new home, Beneban," Me'ekalar said. What new home?"

His friends all turned, curious to hear his answer.

With a laugh, Beneban told them his news. "It seems, my friends, that the Grand Lar still has use for me, even, perhaps, some gratitude. I am ordered to return Lar Tor to the fold. Once I convince Tor of his uncle's innocence and he repents of his rebellion, it seems all will be forgiven the two of us."

"How will you do that?" Me'ekalar asked flatly.

"Yes, that *is* a question, since Tor thinks I collaborated with Lyolar in his parents' murder. However, Lyolar has not left me without some resources, should I be able to use them." Beneban shook his head, still distracted by the news he must impart to these friends.

"He gave you money?" Trog asked.

"He gave me Ka'amfer's estate and named me Lord of Sartenruhn.

A barrage of questions flew at Beneban. He held up his hands, and his friends quieted.

"I have all the same questions. I do not have answers, neither the why nor the how. The Forest Lady was there and is named, if I remember it right, as Lyolar's heir. What she had to do with my sudden rise in fortune, I can't begin to say."

Someone pounded suddenly on the door.

Trog rumbled across the room and yanked it open,

ready to deny entrance to any further threat to his friend. The two palace guards who stood there reeled back nervously.

"L-lord Beneban," one stuttered, trying to peer past the huge Ogdol. He lifted the document he clutched and read with a shaken voice, "Y-you are required to come with us to an audience with Lyolar, Grand Lar…"

"*Required?*" Trog rumbled. The guards shuffled nervously.

"Never mind, I'll go with you," Beneban interrupted, standing wearily.

He detached Sel from his ankle and pushed past Kati. "*Don't…*" the wizard spoke urgently to his friends, "do anything rash."

"Th-Then you *will* come with us?" the guard asked more confidently. "We are to *escort* you," he added nervously. "We have kelsh ready."

"Am I to go to prison? If so, I would like to make…"

"N-No. I mean, it is an audience with the Grand Lar," the guard said with an eye on Trog.

"I will see you all later," the wizard said to his friends with more confidence than he felt.

Beneban followed the guards, both curious and trepidatious about why the Grand Lar would demand to see him again so soon. His companions were unsure what they should do. Finally, as the guards disappeared with his friend, Trog closed the door with a crash that nearly ripped it from the frame.

CHAPTER 27

THREE KELSH WAITED near the palace gate. The guard captain motioned Beneban to mount one, and with an escort behind, the officer moved them rapidly through a town much quieter than before the wizard had been imprisoned.

The gates stood open at Ka'amfer's estate. Beneban stopped as he realized that this property now seemed to be his, a puzzling gift from Lyolar.

"Yet here I am under escort to face... what?" the wizard muttered.

The captain urged him toward the house. Several Worfs stood at the edge of the path and bowed nervously. Beneban nodded to one that he recognized as they took charge of the riding beasts. The officious steward had disappeared.

The guards led the wizard to a small room in the main house, just within the entry. He was overwhelmed by the idea that this room, with its elegant vulgarity, belonged to him. He began to believe he wasn't returned to prison.

Between richly patterned drapes, Lyolar stood looking out the window.

The senior guard began... "Lyolar, Grand Lar of..."

"*I* know who I am, as does *he*. Dismissed." As the

guard hesitated, Lyolar turned sharply. *"Leave,"* he bellowed. *"You*, wizard, close the door!"

Beneban obeyed. He turned, back against the door, and eyed the choleric ruler.

"Well, come in, *come in*. This is your house now. May I sit?"

"Certainly, Sire. May *I* sit?"

"Yes, obviously. Don't loom over me." The small room filled with strained silence. They spoke at the same time.

"About Tor…"

"About Laraynia…"

They eyed each other like duelists. Beneban waited for Lyolar to continue.

"What about Tor?" Lyolar asked finally.

"My task. I'm to bring Lar Tor back, repentant. Sire, forgive me, but I must ask first, *did* you order the assassination of his parents?"

Lyolar's face reddened. He snorted. "You do trust in your own invulnerability, I see."

"Not since my recent imprisonment." He held out his deeply scarred wrists, and Lyolar winced.

"Still," Beneban persisted, "the question stands. Am I to bring Tor back to you as merely another body to hang from the gate, or…"

Lyolar leapt up. "And if I should say that was my intent, would you?" He took two sharp steps away, then back. "Don't answer that. I was angry. Young Stree… I made a mistake in that. One I'll never admit to outside this room."

"Still, my question…"

Lyolar held up a hand that stopped Beneban's

words. With a heavy sigh, he answered. "My older sister, Tor's mother... She and her consort had plotted to have *me* killed. She always wanted my place, and her consort backed her. But I have no wish to hang young Tor. He's like a son to me, or was."

"Then you... Your sister..."

"No! I hoped that by making Tor my heir, my sister would cease her scheming. I did not..." For a moment Lyolar's throat closed, and he turned away. "I *did not* have my sister killed," he said with visible anguish.

He turned back, his voice hoarse. "So, will you be my agent in this?"

"How shall I bring Tor back? Do you have any suggestions, Sire?"

"You'll need troops. Young Me'ekalar and his Kaltingcorps and whatever others you think necessary. Torlarl has joined other hotheads, Amelar, for one and possibly Borilar. And Stree's troops have taken Oreling Pass.

"The rebels are well armed," Lyolar continued. "Weapons, armor, arms. With Tor to lead them, we could lose the Northern Estates entirely."

"What of Lar Ore?" Beneban mentioned the staunch Lar of Oreling. "Has he also..."

"I don't know." Lyolar followed Beneban's thought. "Dead, possibly, if he wouldn't join them, or captive."

Beneban hesitated. "You mentioned the Forest Lady, Sire."

"Forest is dark. Her place is here." Lyolar paced to the window and back. "She is the daughter of my younger sister. Since Tor's defection, she is also heir to my throne."

He turned and fixed Beneban with an icy stare. "As such, wizard, you will have nothing more to do with her."

"I... But, Sire..." Beneban stammered. Dismay darkened his eyes.

"That is an *order.* Nor will you, in any manner, allow her to know that I am the reason. *Guards!"* Lyolar bellowed.

Beneban's escorts dashed in, swords half drawn from their scabbards.

"I will leave now," Lyolar snapped. "Bring my beast to the garden."

The Grand Lar stalked past Beneban. The guards stumbled quickly out of his way. After a startled glance at the wizard, they hurried behind their liege. Beneban was alone. It was a different prison, but no less a trap.

WHEN BENEBAN WAS recovered from the Grand Lar's visit, late evening had dimmed the world. Asolum had set and left only a green wash of light from Zartum, the second sun. Stunned by Lyolar's orders, Beneban sought the peace of the twilight. He needed solace, needed Kati.

Cheerful voices brought him to his feet. His friends had just entered the gate. Borno rode uneasily on a kelsh. Me'ekalar carried Sel before him on his kalting, while Trog trundled beside them. Kati weaved around them as though to herd them.

When they saw Beneban, Me'ekalar and Borno dismounted. They stood for a moment. Then

Me'ekalar saluted gravely, head bowed while Borno went to one knee. Even Trog seemed about to attempt a bow. Only little Sel dashed forward and fell to hold Beneban's ankle in a death grip.

Bene was stunned. "Stop that. Stop right *now!*" the wizard roared in his best parade voice. Then he added in a shakier voice, "How could you think this is necessary?" His head drooped. "Why *would* you?"

A grin spread slowly across Me'ekalar's face. "We fooled him." Then they all leapt forward to wrap arms about Beneban, or grasp his hand, or pat his back. "It was a joke, Bene. We came to be sure you weren't back in prison, to see that you are... That you are *well*."

This time the wizard didn't bother to conceal the tears in his eyes.

"So," Trog rumbled, "you now own all of this?" One hand waved about them.

"It seems so, Trog, and I have no idea yet what 'all of this' entails. And now I must ask you, my friends, a most uncomfortable favor." Eyes studied him as he chose his next words carefully, but Me'ekalar understood at once.

"You are overwhelmed. How can we help?"

"As yet, I do not know. I need time. What do I do with... all this?" He waved a hand. "And these..." A number of the household Worfs had gathered. They clung shyly to the edge of the path to watch with huge eyes. "These are... are *my* people? I've never had servants, only Borno as my aide."

Beneban gave a deep sigh. "I would rather spend the evening with you, my friends, but yes... Thank you, Me'ekalar. I ask that you give me time, a day maybe, to make sense of this 'gift' and to remember who I am. I don't…"

Me'ekalar punched him lightly on the shoulder. "Come on, all, back to the palace. We will visit tomorrow, or if tomorrow is too soon…"

"Yes, tomorrow!" Beneban agreed firmly. "By then I may even have a clear thought in my head."

Me'ekalar collected their mounts. Borno drooped silently on his kelsh. Trog detached a stubborn Sel from Beneban's ankle and carried him away as the waif wailed.

Only Kati remained. As Beneban headed back to the mansion, the great kalting slid through the gate and bounded ahead of him. She stopped, turned, and sat stubbornly staring at him until, with a small smile—the first in many days—he scratched the rough fur at the base of her curving horn.

"No questions, though," he warned. Then he actually laughed. He roughed her ears, and the kalting shook her head indignantly. The wizard laughed again and began to make order out of this new responsibility.

First he gathered the servants. Some were absent, but there were still twenty, including a pompous cook.

"Have you eaten," the cook demanded, as Beneban began to gather names. "Never mind, you haven't. I will bring food."

"But what is your name?"

"Name is Cook! I see to meals for all, but need two of these as scullery help." Assured that no meal was required that evening, he disappeared. Moments later, he returned. He set a tray with soup and bread before Beneban and said, "Eat!" He dropped a bone with meat in front of Kati with the same order. Then he vanished again.

Beneban asked the names and duties of each Worf and found his wizard's memory could retain them. Then he dismissed them for the evening. He tasted the soup and ate hungrily before he moved further into the mansion.

Kati carried what was left of her treat and paced by his side. She hissed when they passed the magic room, but Beneban, his mind absorbed, didn't notice.

They passed a library and found an office. The wizard sat for a time at the wide desk. Pens and ink were at hand, so he scribbled documents to free the servants and to provide them some funds. It must be their choice to either remain there as his staff or to find other employment.

He had returned to the garden when he was surprised by a visit from Lar Ari, led to Beneban by the gatekeeper.

"Sir." Beneban stood quickly and bowed. Ari clapped his shoulder. When Kati nudged the lar, he scratched her head.

Ari carried a large bundle wrapped in cloth. "We must talk, Beneban. Somewhere more private if you know such a place yet in this warren."

The wizard nodded. "The office should serve, sir. If you will follow me..."

"I'll walk beside you, son, if I may." Beneban was startled by the words, but he nodded, pleased.

"I believe... Yes, this is right." Beneban led him into the room he had recently left. He indicated a pair of chairs away from the desk. "Please, be seated, sir.

Would you like something to drink? I can find a servant, I'm sure."

"No need." At the stricken look on Beneban's face, Ari spoke sharply. "Beneban, I'd gladly drink with you. But I can't be away too long from the palace, and we need to talk soberly."

As acknowledgement of passing time, a clock on the mantle chimed eight times.

Air continued. "First, I return this to you. Lyolar appears to have forgotten to do so. I wrapped it in your cloak, as you see. Your court clothes seem to have disappeared. I'll keep after them." He held out the wrapped bundle.

Beneban knew instantly what it was. His hands shook as he unwrapped it.

"Heldenhaft," he whispered. The sword flickered to life at his touch. "How can I thank you, sir?"

"You can begin by calling me Ari instead of sir," the old lar said wryly.

"I'd be honored, Ari," Beneban said with the smile he rarely shared with others. "But what more?"

"I'd like to know what Lyolar said to you today," Ari said bluntly. "I do have a reason."

"You need none. But which time?" Beneban asked. "He said I'm now owner of this property and that I am, for some reason, the new Lord of Sartenruhn."

"Yes, yes. That was this morning, an apology of sorts for inexcusable behavior to the hero of Larlingarde. What did he say when he visited you *here?*"

A short silence followed. Then Beneban decided that if he couldn't trust this man, he needed to know that now.

"I'd not intended to share the subject of that meeting, sir, but..." he added quickly as Ari looked impatient, "he wants Tor to return. And he ordered that I not see or meet with Forest Lady."

"The Lady Laraynia will not be pleased about that. And he wants you to go north?"

"Indeed. I am to 'bring young Tor back, loyal and repentant.' And while I'm at it, to settle the rebellion there, I gather," Beneban said wryly.

"Ahh, only that?" A smile lighted Ari's face. "Lyolar must think you a wizard indeed."

"I'll need to be more than a wizard, sir. I did get his assurance that he doesn't plan to hang Tor, should I manage to bring him back."

"I suppose he assured you he had nothing to do with the death of his sister and her consort?"

"He did. Lyolar *said* that his sister plotted to kill him. He also said that he made Tor his heir, so she would stop her plot. I believed him, sir."

"As I guessed. Then someone else had her killed. Well," Ari pondered, "then what will you do? Think carefully before you answer that question."

Startled, Beneban watched as Ari stood.

"What I really came to say is this..." Ari added, waving the weary wizard back to his seat. "Be sure that I will help you however I may. I apologize for doubting you, Beneban. I was a poor friend when you needed one. I intend to do better in the future." He started away but then turned back. "One more thing. When do you leave for the north?"

"Kati and I will be on our way tomorrow, sir. I am ordered to take Me'ek and part of the corps, but we'll travel more quickly alone." He left unspoken his fear of causing more death, more wounded men, more destruction. "Perhaps if Kati and I go alone, I can talk to Tor and reason with him."

"Perhaps. But if help offers, don't turn it down. Goodnight, Beneban." Before Beneban could move, Ari clapped him on the shoulder and was out of sight on his way to the stables.

After Ari had returned to the palace, and after the servants had refused to leave when Beneban read to them the papers that freed them and instead promised to serve their new Lord, and even tried to kiss his feet... Beneban was finally alone with Kati.

The exhausted wizard searched the halls until he discovered a room with a large bed. He climbed into it and closed his eyes, but it was too soft for sleep.

Restless, he left the bed and paced the room as Kati watched. When she yawned impatiently, he finally rolled up in his cloak and settled on the thick soft pile of the carpet with his head pillowed on the kalting's warm flank.

At last he slept.

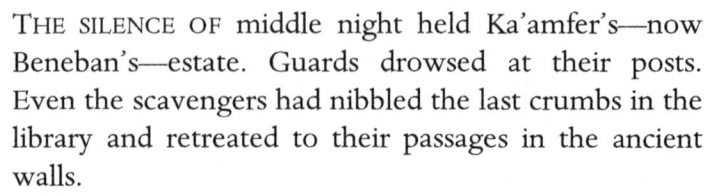

THE SILENCE OF middle night held Ka'amfer's—now Beneban's—estate. Guards drowsed at their posts. Even the scavengers had nibbled the last crumbs in the library and retreated to their passages in the ancient walls.

Inside the door of the magic room of the mansion, runes began to glow on the wall. At first there was only a whisper of movement, less than a night breeze, had any waked to notice. Then, in the seemingly solid wall, a shadow became a crack. It widened. A lithe figure slithered through. Darkness more solid than night hid it completely as it moved to sit cross-legged behind the bulk of the desk.

The intruder cupped his hands and whispered a word. A purple light glowed deep between his fingers, and Calibe, for it was the Mergol prince again in guise of the Worf, whispered a second word.

The air chilled. Within the purple light, darkness swirled and gathered. A face flickered into view, thin and crested with a mane of white hair where solid wall had been. Sharp teeth glinted as the figure spoke.

"Well? Is it done?" The purple lips formed the words audible only to Calibe.

"Nay! I was nearly, nearly successful. Lyolar blamed the wizard for Meriel's failure. The wizard was condemned as a traitor. He should have died in the dungeons."

Calibe's alibis for his failure to destroy Beneban tumbled over each other. "It was the Forest Witch. She must have enchanted Lyolar. He blamed the wizard for everything until she came. Now Lyolar has freed the wizard and given him wealth."

"Wait!" Merktan, the face in the light, closed his eyes. A shimmer, then a sense of darkness behind the light indicated that in the blackness another listened.

"Repeat!" Speech like ice shivered into Calibe's mind from behind the visible figure of Merktan. Terrified by the presence of Ztavin with the Mergol king, Calibe cowered to the floor as he repeated the tale of Beneban's sudden rise from prisoner to wealth and title.

"What title?" the icy voice demanded.

"Lord of..." Calibe faltered.

"Do not make me wait."

"S-Sartenruhn," the Worf said, barely above a hiss.

A blast of static knocked Calibe sideways. An explosion in the ether turned the room bitter cold, and frost rimed the walls.

"He must never reach Sartenruhn," the icy voice hissed as the cold deepened. The shadow that loomed behind Merktan nearly obscured the Mergol king. "He must not unite the court. Discredit him or kill him. I care not which."

"N-not so easy," Calibe stammered. "His magic is strong for a wizard. How can I, with no resources..."

"Shall I replace you?" Emotionless and disinterested, the words brought protest from Calibe and Merktan both. In mid-protest, they were cut off.

"Do it, then. I believe it is time to release the vardraken." With that, the violet light flickered and both conspirators disappeared.

Calibe curled into a shuddering ball, still cold from Ztavin's appearance. "Not the vardraken," he whimpered to the black floor.

After a moment, still shaken, he drew darkness around himself and vanished through the secret entrance. The room of magic returned to its normal quiet, and slowly, the frost from Ztavin's appearance melted from the windows.

Kati roused with a snarl, released by the end of spell. The evil, which had stirred no one else, shivered through the floor. She hissed in fury.

"Shh, all is well, Kati," Beneban hushed sleepily. "It's," he yawned, "only the night wind. Sleep while you can, my friend." He wrapped his cloak more snuggly around himself and settled once more against the giant kalting.

His thoughts melted into the quiet. His mind slipped deeper into slumber. He left questions for tomorrow, and slept.

Kati did not return to sleep.

CHAPTER 28

Early the following morning, Beneban grimly gathered the few supplies he would need for himself and Kati, mainly food they couldn't hunt for along the way. He added a warm cloak for himself, as they would be heading for high country. *Kati is excited to be leaving*, he thought as he smiled and watched her pounce ahead. He wondered where everyone was. He regretted having sent them away last night. Now it would be good to wish them well, to say goodbye…

"Wizards don't have friends," he muttered. "No one will care."

He rounded the final turn, and stopped. The path before the stables was blocked. His retainers, Worf and Othering, stood stolidly before the exit. They wore makeshift armor, and carried various tools and weapons. Kati wound around them, sniffing each individual.

Sel had returned. He wore a cook pot on his head and strutted proudly in front of the group. He waved a carving knife nearly as long as his torso.

Touched by this show of support, Beneban knelt before them.

"You can't come with me," he tried to explain. "It is a hard march even for experienced troops. There will be many dangers."

They—*his* people, he realized in shock—refused to move. Finally he stood and stepped into the group. He patted a shoulder here and straightened a weapon there.

"I depend on you good folk, good *friends*, to stay and care for this, my new home, until I return. Please," he urged them. "It will comfort me to know that when I return I will find my home has been in good hands."

Finally, they nodded, and a few murmured acceptance. As they turned away, some patted his arm, his leg, whatever they could reach. But Sel disappeared without a farewell. Beneban assumed he was in a corner pouting.

As he turned to the gate, Kati nearly knocked him down to go through first.

"Silly kalting," he muttered as he stepped through then stopped in shock. Me'ekalar and the first troop of the Kaltingcorps were drawn up at rest.

Me'ekalar strode forward and saluted. "You must have overslept," he said with a grin. Then, at the astonishment on his friend's face, he sobered. "What? Did you think we'd let you go alone?"

"How... How did you even *know?*" Bene looked over the gathered men. There were Borno and Lodar and Hundak; others he recognized from the battle for Mergol Ford; and Trog towered behind the small troop.

"We are your friends, Beneban," Me'ekalar growled.

"But wizards don't... have friends," Beneban whispered.

Me'ekalar laughed aloud and clapped him on the shoulder. "Then you must not be a wizard, because you obviously do have friends!" He turned to the troop. "Kaltingcorps, move out!" he bellowed. As one, they turned sharply and started off. There was nothing else for it. Beneban, on Kati, quickly caught up.

BENEBAN AND HIS troop made an easy trek from Larlingarde. After a week of marching north, as they neared the border of Oreling Estate, someone hailed them.

"Hold up. Wait." Several men galloped toward them.

Stunned, Beneban recognized the red and gold banner of Ariling, and in the lead, he saw the distinctive form of Lar Ari.

"Not leaving you to find Tor alone," Ari grumped as he pounded on the wizard's shoulder. "Did you expect me to stay behind? You have friends, Beneban."

Before Beneban could answer, before he could even repeat his mantra about wizards and friends, Ari ordered his men into the troop.

"Well... We won't find that fool Tor here," he grumbled, leaving Beneban wordless as the troop moved off.

THE SCENE IN the valley of Oreling was grim. The ground was stripped and torn from what had been a fierce battle. No word of armed conflict had reached Larlingarde, and it seemed unlikely that Tor would be fighting the very lars he hoped to convince to join him. Something other than human forces seemed to have been at work there. The destruction left little but bare shrubs and trampled greenery. Ore Keep was barred and silent. There were guards on the wall, but no one answered a repeated hail.

Beneban's force had hoped for supplies, but there was no choice but to travel on. It was evening when, with minimal water and short rations, the troop stumbled wearily up the last brush-covered boulders to the thin high forest above. This, the border of Ameling and Boriling Estates, was far north of Larlingarde.

Beneban and his companions had barely reached the plateau when a shadow froze the air above and vanished past the trees with a shriek.

"Find water and set up camp," the wizard began. He was interrupted by a shrill whistle that twisted the air.

"We'll camp here," Beneban ordered more quietly. "No fires. Be ready to move." He slipped toward the edge of the stunted forest as they heard a scream.

"That," Lar Ari hissed, close at Beneban's heels, "was human."

Beneban nodded and pushed quietly through tangled brush toward what appeared to be open sky. Abruptly he dropped to his knees as he waved the old lar back and slid forward on his elbows. Ari followed stubbornly in the same way. They emerged from the cover of the thin trees onto the edge of a high cliff as Kati slithered between them.

Close above them a vardraken soared. The whistle came again, its hunting call. Kati hissed as its shadow chilled them. Then the vardraken roared.

The ice dragon's silken wings cast rainbows of
across the cliff where they lay. As she roared, i
formed on the grasses and the edge of the rocks. She
ignored or possibly didn't see them. Her prey was on
the plains below.

Legend said the sheer beauty of a vardraken could
hold a man spellbound until a blast of her icy breath
turned him to frozen, brittle crystal.

Legend told that the Varkinde, the devotees of the
vardraken, worshipped the mystical beast and that they
offered sacrifice of young men and women to pacify
them.

Legend failed to warn that three of the beasts,
ridden by warriors, would lead the Varkinde into
battle. It did not mention that each vardraken could
paralyze a dozen or more troopers with one blast of
freezing breath.

There, above the North Plains, flew a legend that
paralyzed watchers and prey alike. The great vardraken
soared on icy pinions and dealt death with every
glistening wing beat. Beneban and his comrades were
transfixed by the sight and by the threat the legendary
beasts posed to the very real rebel troops who were
massed below.

Somewhere among them was Tor, but his friends
could do nothing but watch as the peril out of
storybooks soared and spat out icy death.

THE END

**Thank you for reading *Wizard Stone*. If you enjoyed
Beneban's adventures, please consider leaving
a review, or chatting about it with your
book-loving friends.**

The Adventure continues in
WIZARD WIND, The Magic of Larlion, Book 2.

Wizards aren't supposed to have hearts, but Beneban's heart is in two places at once. Commanded to the far north to capture his friend, the rebel Lar Tor, he longs instead to be in Larlingarde. There, Laraynia has become heir to the Grand Lar and is in constant peril from the evil forces that strive to take over the realm. Can Beneban find the power he needs to defeat the black wizard Ztavin and avoid betraying Rayni without losing his freedom?

Laraynia is torn between her beloved Forest and Larlingarde. She will need all her powers to heal her uncle and save the kingdom. In Rayni's moment of greatest peril, will the mysterious vardraken queen aid her, or set her winged, ice-breathing dragons loose on everyone Laraynia holds dear?

And does Sartenruhn, the legendary school of wizardry, hold the key to their salvation or their downfall?

Visit deemaltbyauthor.com for a sneak preview of
WIZARD WIND The Magic of Larlion Book 2,
and sign up for Dee's Newsletter
for news about more exciting upcoming releases!

BOOKS BY DEE MALTBY

The Magic of Larlion Series
Wizard Stone
Wizard Wind
Wizard Storm
Wizard Search
Wayward Wizard
Wild Wizard

ACKNOWLEDGEMENTS

This author gives heartfelt thanks to the following people, all of whom have facilitated and helped to make this book possible:

Angie Ramey, a super editor and first-rate encourager,

Mary Pat McCarthy of McCarthy Arts and Letters for great cover design, and patience with my quibbles,

Jonathan Moeller, author of the *Cloak Mage* and *The Ghosts* series, and Meara Platt, author of the *Dark Gardens* fantasy series, for reading and encouraging my first book,

Seamus McCarthy, the latest, but not the only, cat who has been my inspiration,

Hollis McCarthy, for patient and enthusiastic editing and reading, for building my web page, for frequent suggestions and contributions of ideas and scenes. She is also a specialist on cats and kaltings, and her enthusiasm for my work has buoyed me up when my imagination failed.

Finally, but always first in my heart, my husband Bob, who with determination has supported my writing, facilitated my publication, and gone beyond the limits. He has tolerated cold meals, dug for information, and been my support system for hours and days of a frequently absent-minded wife.

ABOUT THE AUTHOR

Dee Maltby, author of *Wizard Stone, Wizard Wind* and *Wizard Storm*, has raised five kids while giving birth to a slew of wizards, sorceresses, ice dragons, giant kalting cats and of course, a magical sword. A lifelong writer, artist, baseball fan, advocate for differently abled education, and sometime freelancer for local publications, Dee lives in Ohio and speaks several languages. She's traveled the world with her not-so-mad scientist inventor husband, Bob Maltby, while inventing the world of her fantasy series, *The Magic of Larlion*.

Made in the USA
Coppell, TX
28 January 2022